"THESE *TALES OF THE SOUTH PACIFIC* ARE MAGNIFICENTLY ENTERTAINING. BUT THEY ARE MORE THAN THAT. MR. MICHENER IS AN ACUTE OBSERVER OF HUMAN CHARACTER, AN ADROIT LITERARY ARTIST, A MAN WITH A PHILOSOPHY OF LIFE WHICH MAKES HIM TOLERANT OF MANY HUMAN WEAKNESSES, BUT NOT OF ALL. HE IS CERTAINLY ONE OF THE ABLEST AND ONE OF THE MOST ORIGINAL WRITERS ON THE AMERICAN LITERARY SCENE."

—*Yale Review*

About the Author

James A. Michener was born in New York City. Brought up in Bucks-County, Pennsylvania, he was graduated from Swarthmore. In 1948, while an editor in a New York publishing house, he won the Pulitzer Prize in Fiction for his *TALES OF THE SOUTH PACIFIC*. Today he is internationally known as the author of such world-famous bestsellers as *HAWAII, THE SOURCE,* and *IBERIA.*

James A. Michener

Tales of
the South Pacific

FAWCETT CREST • NEW YORK

TALES OF THE SOUTH PACIFIC

THIS BOOK CONTAINS THE COMPLETE TEXT OF
THE ORIGINAL HARDCOVER EDITION.

Published by Fawcett Crest Books, CBS Educational and Professional Publishing, a division of CBS Inc., by arrangement with The Macmillan Company.

ISBN: 0-449-23852-0

Printed in the United States of America

First Fawcett Crest printing: February 1973

31   30   29   28   27   26   25   24   23   22

Contents

Tales of
the South Pacific

The South Pacific

I wish I could tell you about the South Pacific. The way it actually was. The endless ocean. The infinite specks of coral we called islands. Coconut palms nodding gracefully toward the ocean. Reefs upon which waves broke into spray, and inner lagoons, lovely beyond description. I wish I could tell you about the sweating jungle, the full moon rising behind the volcanoes, and the waiting. The waiting. The timeless, repetitive waiting.

But whenever I start to talk about the South Pacific, people intervene. I try to tell somebody what the steaming Hebrides were like, and first thing you know I'm telling about the old Tonkinese woman who used to sell human heads. As souvenirs. For fifty dollars!

Or somebody asks me, "What was Guadalcanal actually like?" And before I can describe that godforsaken backwash of the world, I'm rambling on about the Remittance Man, who lived among the Japs and sent us radio news of their movements. That is, he sent the news until one day.

The people intervene. The old savage who wanted more than anything else in the world to jump from an airplane and float down to earth in a parachute. "Alla same big fella bird!" he used to shout, ecstatically, until one day we took him up and shoved him out. Ever afterward he walked in silence among the black men, a soul apart, like one who had discovered things best hidden from humanity.

Or I get started on the mad commander who used to get up at two o'clock in the morning and scuff barefooted over the floors of his new hut. "Carpenter! Carpenter!" he would shout into the jungle night. "There's a rough spot over here!" And some drowsy enlisted man would shuffle from his sweating bunk and appear with sanding blocks. "See if you can get those splinters out, son," the commander would say softly.

Take the other night up in Detroit. Some of us were waiting for a train. The air in the saloon was heavy. For more than an hour a major told us about his experiences with Patton in Africa, in Sicily, and in France. He used great phrases such as "vast deployment to the east," "four crushing days into Palermo," "a sweeping thrust toward the open land south of Paris," "a gigantic pincers movement toward the heart of Von Rundstedst's position."

When he had won the war, he turned to me and asked, "What was it like in the Pacific?" I started to reply as honestly as I could. But somehow or other I got mixed up with that kid I knew on a rock out there. Twenty-seven months on one rock. Heat itch all the time. Half a dozen trees. Got involved in the bootlegging scandal. Helped repair a ship bound for the landing at Kuralei. And then he got a cablegram from home.

"Why, hell!" the major snorted. "Seems all he did was sit on his ass and wait."

"That's exactly it!" I cried, happy to find at last someone who knew what I was talking about.

"That's a hell of a way to fight a war!" he grunted in disgust, and within the moment we had crossed the Rhine and were coursing the golden tanks down the autobahnen.

But our war was waiting. You rotted on New Caledonia waiting for Guadalcanal. Then you sweated twenty pounds away in Guadal waiting for Bougainville. There were battles, of course. But they were flaming things of the bitter moment. A blinding flash at Tulagi. A day of horror at Tarawa. An evening of terror on Kuralei. Then you relaxed and waited. And pretty soon you hated the man next to you, and you dreaded the look of a coconut tree.

I served in the South Pacific during the bitter days of '41

through '43. I was only a paper-work sailor, traveling from island to island, but I did get to know some of the men who actually directed the battles. There was Old Bull Halsey who had the guts to grunt out, when we were taking a pasting, "We'll be in Tokyo by Christmas!" None of us believed him, but we felt better that we were led by men like him.

I also knew Admiral McCain in a very minor way. He was an ugly old aviator. One day he flew over Santo and pointed down at that island wilderness and said, "That's where we'll build our base." And the base was built there, and millions of dollars were spent there, and everyone agrees that Santo was the best base the Navy ever built in the region. I was always mighty proud of McCain, for he was in aviation, too.

Then there was little Aubrey Fitch who fought his planes in all the battles and banged away until the Japs just had to stop coming. I knew him later. I saw Vandegrift, of the Marines, who made the landing at Guadal, and bulldog General Patch who cleaned up that island and then went on to take Southern France.

Seeing these men in their dirty clothes after long hours of work knocked out any ideas I had of heroes. None of them was ever a hero to me. It was somewhat like my introduction to Admiral Millard Kester, who led the great strike at Kuralei. I was in the head at Efate, a sort of French *pissoir*, when I heard a great swearing in one of the improvised booths. Out came a rear admiral with the zipper of his pants caught in his underwear. "Goddamned things. I never wanted to buy them anyway. Sold me a bill of goods."

I laughed at his predicament. "Don't stand there gawking. Get someone who can fix these zippers," he snapped, only he had a lot of adjectives before the infuriating *zippers*. I went into the bar.

"Anybody in here fix a zipper?" I asked, and a chief machinist said he thought he could, but he was drunk and all he did was to rip the admiral's underwear, which made me laugh again. And finally my laughing made Admiral Kester so mad that he tore off both his pants and his underwear and ripped the cloth out of the offending zipper and threw it away. Even then the zipper wouldn't work.

So there he was in just a khaki shirt, swearing. But finally we got a machinist who wasn't drunk, and the zipper was fixed. Then Admiral Kester put his pants back on and went into the bar. Fortunately for me, he didn't know my name then.

There were the men from the lesser ranks. Luther Billis, with doves tattooed on his breasts. And good Dr. Benoway, a worried, friendly man. Tony Fry, of course, was known by everybody in the area after his brush with Admiral Kester. The old man saw Fry's TBF with twelve beer bottles painted on the side.

"What in hell are those beer bottles for, Fry?" the admiral asked.

"Well, sir. This is an old job. I use it to ferry beer in," Tony replied without batting an eyelash. "Been on twelve missions, sir!"

"Take those goddam beer bottles off," the admiral ordered. Tony kept the old TBF, of course, and continued to haul beer in it. He was a really lovely guy.

They will live a long time, these men of the South Pacific. They had an American quality. They, like their victories, will be remembered as long as our generation lives. After that, like the men of the Confederacy, they will become strangers. Longer and longer shadows will obscure them, until their Guadalcanal sounds distant on the ear like Shiloh and Valley Forge.

Coral Sea

I am always astonished when an American says, "The Coral Sea? Where is that? I never heard of the Coral Sea." Believe me, Australians and New Zealanders know all about it. The battle we fought there will be in their history books for some time. Perhaps I can explain why.

In mid-April of 1942 I was one of a small group of officers who went ashore on the extreme eastern tip of Vanicoro Island, in the New Hebrides. We carried with us a broadcasting station, enough food for two months, and twelve enlisted men who knew how to repair PBY's. It was our intention to make daily reports on the weather and whatever other information we obtained. The airplane repair men were to service any flying boats forced down in our large bay.

Admiral Kester personally saw us off in the tiny tramp steamer which took us north from Noumea. "We can't go back any farther," he told us. "Take along plenty of small arms and ammunition. If the worst should come, destroy everything and head for the high hills of Vanicoro. I don't think they can track you down there. And you can depend on it, men. You can absolutely depend on it. If you can stay alive, we'll be back to get you. No matter what happens!"

Ensign Aberforce, our radio expert, hurried out from the meeting with Admiral Kester and somehow or other stole an emergency pint-sized radio transmitter. "If we go up into the hills, we'll be of some use. We'll broadcast from up there." Each of us strapped a revolver to his belt. We were a rather grim crew that boarded the rough little ship.

At Vanicoro we were thrown out upon a desolate, jungle-ridden bay where mosquitoes filled the air like incense. Of those who landed that day, all contracted malaria. No one died from it, but eleven men ultimately had to be evacuated. The rest of us shivered and burned with the racking fever. Not till later did we hear about atabrine.

We built lean-to's of bamboo and coconut fronds. A few venturesome natives came down from the hills to watch us. In silence they studied our rude efforts and then departed. Centuries ago they had learned that no one could live among the fevers of that bay. Nevertheless, our shacks went up, and on the evening of our arrival Aberforce broadcast weather reports to the fleet.

Six times a day thereafter he would repair to the steaming shack, where jungle heat was already eating away at the radio's vitals, and send out his reports. On the eighth day he informed Noumea that we had withstood our initial Jap bombing. A Betty came over at seven thousand feet, encountered no antiaircraft fire, dropped to two thousand feet, and made four runs at us. Radio and personnel escaped damage. Two shacks were blown up. At least the Japs knew where we were. After that we were bombed several more times, and still no lives were lost. By now we had dug a considerable cave into the side of a hill. There we kept our precious radio. We felt secure. Only a landing party could wipe out the station now. The second, smaller set we buried in ten feet of earth. A direct hit might destroy it. Nothing less would.

As men do when they have been frequently bombed, we became suspicious of every plane. So we ducked for foxholes that afternoon when our lookout cried, "Betty at four thousand feet." We huddled in the sweating earth and waited for the "garummmph" of the bombs. Instead, none fell, and the Betty slowly descended toward the bay.

Then a fine shout went up! It wasn't a Betty at all. It was a PBY! It was coming in for a water landing! It was a PBY!

The lookout who had mistaken this grand old American plane for a Betty was roundly booed. He said it was better to be safe than sorry, but none of us could believe that anyone in the American Navy had failed to recognize the ugly, wonderful PBY. Slowly the plane taxied into the lagoon formed by coral reefs. Since none of us had experience with the lagoon, we could not advise the pilot where to anchor. Soon however, he had decided for himself, and ropes went swirling into the placid waters.

Our eager men had a rubber boat already launched and went out to pick up the crew. To our surprise, a New Zealand flying officer stepped out. We watched in silence as he was rowed ashore. He jumped from the rubber boat, walked stiffly up the beach and presented himself. "Flight Leftenant Grant," he said. Our men laughed at the way he said *leftenant*, but he took no notice of the fact.

His crew was an amazing improvisation. One Australian, three New Zealanders, four Americans. The Allies were using what was available in those days. Our officers showed the crew to their mud-floored quarters.

"I'm reporting for patrol," Grant said briefly when he had deposited his gear. "The Jap fleet's on the move."

"We heard something about that," I said. "Are they really out?"

"We think the entire southern fleet is on the way."

"Where?" we asked in silence that was deep even for a jungle.

"Here," Grant said briefly. "Here, and New Zealand. They have eighty transports, we think."

We all breathed rather deeply. Grant betrayed no emotion, and we decided to follow his example. "I should like to speak to all of my crew and all of your ground crew, if you please." We assembled the men in a clearing by the shore.

"Men," Grant said, "I can't add anything which will explain the gravity of our situation. That PBY must be kept in the air. Every one of you take thought now. How will you repair any possible damage to that plane? Find your answers now. Have the materials ready." He returned to his quarters.

We did not see much of Grant for several days. His PBY was in the air nine and ten hours at a stretch. He searched the water constantly between the New Hebrides and Guadalcanal. One night he took off at 0200 and searched until noon the next day. He and his men came back tired, red-eyed, and stiff. They had done nothing but fly endlessly above the great waters. They had seen no Japs.

In the last few days of April, however, action started. We were heavily bombed one night, and some fragments punctured the PBY. Early the next morning men were swarming over the flying boat as she rode at anchor in the lagoon. That afternoon she went up on patrol. As luck would have it, she ran into three Jap planes. The starboard rear gunner, a fresh kid from Alabama, claimed a hit on the after Jap plane. The Japs shot up the PBY pretty badly. The radio man, a youngster from Auckland, died that night of his wounds.

Grant came to our quarters. "The Japs are out. Something big is stirring. I must go out again tomorrow. Mr. Aberforce, will you ride along as radio man?"

"Sure," our expert laughed. "I think I can figure out the system."

"I'll help you," Grant said stiffly. There was no mention of the radio man's death, but in the early morning the leftenant read the Church of England service over a dismal mound on the edge of the jungle. Some native boys who now lived near us were directed to cover the grave with flowers. There the radio man from New Zealand, a little blond fellow with bad teeth, there he rests.

That afternoon there was further action. Grant sighted a collection of Jap ships. They were about 150 miles northwest of the Canal and were coming our way. All transports and destroyers. The heavy stuff must be somewhere in The Slot, waiting for the propitious moment.

Aberforce blurted the news into his microphone. He added that Jap fighters were rising from a field on some near-by island to attack the PBY. We heard no more. There was anxiety about the bay until we heard a distant drone of motors. The PBY limped in. It had received no additional bullets, but it was a tired old lady.

Grant called the ground force to attention as soon as he landed. "It is imperative," he said in the clipped accents which annoyed our men, "that this plane be ready to fly tomorrow. And you must show no lights tonight. The Nips will be gunning for us. Hop to it, lads!" He turned and left. The men mimicked his pronunciation, his walk, his manner. All that night our men urged one another, "Hop to it, lad! Come, now, there! Hop to it!"

It was difficult to like Grant. He was the type of New Zealander who repels rather than attracts. He was a short man, about five feet eight. He was spare, wore a bushy mustache, and had rather reddish features. He affected an air of austere superiority, and among a group of excitable Americans he alone never raised his voice, never displayed emotions.

Unpleasant as he sometimes was, we had to respect him. That evening Aberforce, for example, told us three times of how Grant had insisted upon going closer, closer to the Jap vessels. "The man's an iceberg!" Aberforce insisted. "But it's grand to ride with him. You have a feeling he'll get you back." Grant, in the meantime, sat apart and studied the map. With a thin forefinger he charted the course of the gathering Jap fleet. Inevitably the lines converged on the New Hebrides . . . and on New Zealand. Saying nothing, the flight leftenant went out along the beach.

"Throw a line, there!" he called. "I'll have a look at how you're doing." It was after midnight before he returned.

Early next morning there was a droning sound in the sky, and this time our watch spotted the plane correctly as another PBY. It circled the bay and landed down wind, splashing heavily into the sea. We were accustomed to Grant's impeccable landings, in which the plane actually felt for the waves then slowly, easily let itself into the trough. We smiled at the newcomer's sloppy landing.

The plane taxied about and pulled into the lagoon. "Tell them to watch where they anchor!" Grant shouted to the men on his plane. "Not there! Not there!" He looked away in disgust and went into his quarters. A moment later, however, he was out in the early morning sunrise once more. A youthful voice was hailing him from the beach.

"I say! Grant!" A young flight officer, a New Zealander, had come ashore.

"Well, Colbourne! How are you?" The friends shook hands. We were glad to see that Colbourne was at least young and excitable. He was quite agitated as he took a drink of coffee in our mess hut.

"We won't come ashore," he said. "We must both go out at once. There is wretched news. The entire Jap southern fleet is bearing down upon us. You and I must go out for the last minute look-see. This may be the day, Grant. We've got to find where the carriers are. I have orders here. They didn't send them by wireless. But fellows! There's a chance! There really is! I understand Fitch and Kester are on the move. I don't know with what, but we're going to fight!" The young fellow's eyes sparkled. After the long wait, we would fight. After Pearl Harbor and Manila and Macassar and the Java Sea, we would go after them. After one string of crushing defeats upon another, the American fleet, such as it was, would have a crack at the Japs!

"What is happening at home?" Grant asked, apparently not moved by the news.

Colbourne swallowed once or twice. "They are waiting," he said grimly. "It has been pretty well worked out. The old men—well, your wife's father and mine, for example. They are stationed at the beaches. They know they dare not retreat. They have taken their positions now." He paused a moment and took a drink of our warm water. We waited.

"The home guard is next. They've been digging in furiously. They occupy prepared positions near the cities and the best beaches. The regular army will be thrown in as the fighting develops. Everyone has decided to fight until the end. The cities and villages will be destroyed." He paused and tapped his fingers nervously against his cup.

"Many families have already gone to the hills. Cars are waiting to take others at the first sign of the Jap fleet. My wife and the kiddies have gone. Your wife, Grant, said to tell you that she would stay until the last." Grant nodded his head slowly and said nothing. Colbourne continued, his voice sounding strange and excited in the hot, shadowy hut. We leaned forward, thinking of Seattle, and San Diego, and Woonsocket.

"The spirit of the people is very determined," Colbourne reported. "A frightful Japanese broadcast has steeled us for the worst. It came through two nights before I left. A Japanese professor was describing New Zealand and how it would be developed by the Japs. North Island will be a commercial center where Japanese ships will call regularly. South Island will be agricultural. Wool and mutton will be sent to Japan. Maoris, as true members of the Greater East Asia Coprosperity Sphere, will be allowed special privileges. White men will be used on the farms. The professor closed with a frenzied peroration. He said that the lush fields, the wealth, the cities were in their grasp at last. The day of reckoning with insolent New Zealanders was at hand. Immortal Japanese troops would know what to do!"

No one said anything. Grant looked at his wrist watch. "It's 0630," he said. "We'll be off." He started from the hut but stopped. "Aberforce," he asked, "will you handle the radio again?"

Aberforce, somewhat subdued, left the hut. Colbourne and Grant went down to the rubber rafts and were rowed to their planes. The newcomer was first to take off. He headed directly for the Canal. Then Grant taxied into free water. His propellers roared. Slowly the plane started along the smooth water. Then it raised to the step, like a duck scudding across a still pond. It poised on the step for a moment and became airborne. It did not circle the bay, but set out directly for the vast Coral Sea.

All day we waited for news. I helped to code and transmit the weather reports Aberforce should have been sending. About noon a cryptic message came through the radio. It was apparently Grant, using a new code. Later a plain-word message came from the south. It was true. The Jap fleet was heading for our islands!

I issued the last rounds of ammunition. We dug up the tiny transmitter and drew rough maps of the region we would head for. Reluctantly we decided that there would be no defense of the beach. Each of us studied the native boys suspiciously. What would they do when the Japs came? Would they help track us down?

At about four o'clock in the afternoon Colbourne's PBY came back. His radio was gone, so he rushed to our set and relayed a plain-code message to the fleet: "The Jap fleet has apparently formed. What looked like BB's steamed from Guadalcanal. Going westward. No carriers sighted. Little air cover over the BB's. But the fleet is forming!" He then continued with a coded description of exactly what he had seen. Before he finished, Grant's plane came in. It was smoking badly. The entire rear section seemed to be aflame. At first it seemed that Grant might make his landing all right. But at the last minute the crippled plane crashed into the sea. It stayed afloat for several minutes, at the mouth of the lagoon. In that time Grant, Aberforce, and four of the men escaped. The co-pilot was already dead from Jap fire. Two men drowned in the after compartments.

We pulled the survivors from the sea. Aberforce was pale with cold and fear, cold even in the tropics. Grant was silent and walked directly in to consult with Colbourne, who stopped broadcasting. They consulted their notes, compared probabilities and started all over again. It was now dusk.

When the message was finished, Grant went down to the seaside with his crew and read once more the burial service. Aberforce stood beside him, terribly white.

That night we had a wretched scene at dinner. We didn't serve the meal until late, and as soon as we sat at table, Grant announced that tomorrow he would fly Colbourne's plane. To this Colbourne would not agree. Grant insisted primly that it was his right and duty, as senior officer. In the end Colbourne told him to go to hell. Grant had crashed his damned plane and wrecked it and now, by God, he wouldn't get the other one. The younger man stamped from the room. Grant started to appeal to us for a decision but thought better of it.

In the morning Colbourne and his crew set out. We never saw them again. They submitted only one report. "Entire Jap fleet heading south."

All day we sat by the radio. There was news, but we could make nothing of it. That some kind of action was taking place, we were sure. We posted extra lookouts in the trees. In midafternoon an American plane, an SBD, lost from its carrier, went wildly past our island. It crashed into the sea and sank immediately.

Two torpedo planes, also American, flashed past. Night came on. We did not eat a regular meal. The cook brought in sandwiches and we munched them. No one was hungry, but we were terribly nervous. As night wore on, we gave up trying to work the radio. We had long since surrendered it to Grant, who sat hunched by it, his hands covering his face, listening to whatever station he could get.

Finally, he found a strong New Zealand government transmitter. We stood by silently waiting for the news period. A musical program was interrupted. "It can now be stated that a great fleet action is in progress in the Coral Sea, between forces of the American Navy and the Japanese fleet. Elements of the Royal Australian Navy are also participating. It is too early to foretell what the outcome will be. Fantastic Japanese claims must be discounted. Word of the impending action came this morning when monitors picked up a message from a New Zealand Catalina which had sighted the enemy fleet." The broadcast droned on. "The nation has been placed on full alert. Men have taken their places. In this fateful hour New Zealanders pray for victory."

At this last Grant impatiently snapped off the radio and

left the hut. Soon, however, he was back, hunched up as before. He stayed there all night and most of the next day. By this time we had fabricated another receiver. A wonderfully skilled enlisted man and I sat by it throughout the day. Heat was intense, and a heavy stickiness assailed us every time we moved. Once I looked up and saw Grant down by the shore, watching the empty sky. He walked back and forth. I stopped watching him when I heard the first real news we had so far received. American fleet headquarters officially announced that the full weight of the Jap fleet had been intercepted. A battle was in progress. Our chances appeared to be satisfactory.

A wild shout from the other radio indicated that they had heard the broadcast, too. Immediately fantastic conjecture started through the camp. At the noise Grant walked calmly into my hut. "What is the news?" he asked. I told him, and he left. But in a few minutes he was back and elbowed me away from the set. For the rest of that day and night he was there. Once or twice he drowsed off, but no one else touched the radio for sixteen hours.

At about 1900, after the sun had set, we heard two pilots talking back and forth. They were over the Coral Sea. They had lost their ship. Or their ship had been sunk. They encouraged one another for many minutes, and then we heard them no more.

At 0500 the next morning a coded message came through calling on all aircraft to be on the alert for Jap ships. This message goaded Grant furiously. He stomped from the hut and walked along the beach, looking at the spot where his PBY had gone down.

By now no one could talk or think. We had been three days in this state of oppressive excitement. Three of our men lay dead in the bay; an entire plane crew was lost. And we were perched on the end of an island, in the dark. We were not even doing our minimum duty, for our planes were gone. All we could do was sit and wonder. There was much discussion as to what the cryptic message about Jap ships meant. Could it be that the Japanese fleet had broken through? In anxiety we waited, and all about the silent jungle bore down upon us with heat, flies, sickness, and ominous silence.

At 1500 we intercepted a flash from Tokyo announcing our loss of the *Lexington,* two battleships, and numerous destroyers. So frantic were we for news that we believed. After all, we *had* heard those pilots. Their carrier *could* have been sunk. The news flashed through our camp and disheartened us further.

It was at 1735 that Grant finally picked up a strong New Zealand station. An organ was playing. But something in the air, some desperation of thought, kept everyone at Grant's elbow, crowding in upon him. Then came the fateful news: "Profound relief has been felt throughout New Zealand. Admiral Nimitz has announced that the Jap fleet has been met, extensively engaged, and routed." A fiery shout filled the hut. Men jumped and clapped their hands. The radio droned on: ". . . losses not authenticated. Our own losses were not negligible. Carrier aircraft played a dominant role. At a late hour today the Prime Minister announced that for the moment invasion of New Zealand has been prevented." Three Americans cheered wildly at this. The New Zealand men stood fast and listened. ". . . so we have taken the privilege of asking a chaplain of the Royal New Zealand Air Force to express our gratitude . . ." Grant was drumming on the radio with his fingers. He rose as the chaplain began to intone his prayer. Others who were seated followed his example. There, in the silence of the jungle, with heat dripping from the walls of the improvised hut, we stood at attention. ". . . and for these divine blessings our Nation and its free people . . ." One by one men left the hut. Then it began to dawn upon them that the waiting was over. Someone began to shout to a sentry up in the tree.

In disbelief he shouted back. Soon the land about the bay was echoing with wild shouts. One young officer whipped out his revolver and fired six salutes in violent order. Natives ran up, and the cook grabbed one by the shoulders. He danced up and down, and the native looked at him in wonderment. In similar bewilderment, two New Zealand enlisted men—beardless boys—who had escaped from Grant's wrecked plane, looked over the waters and wept.

Grant himself disappeared right after the broadcast. Others hung about the radio and picked up further wonderful news. Commentators were already naming it the Battle of the Coral Sea. From Australia one man threw caution far aside and claimed, "For us it will be one of the decisive battles of the world. It proves that Japan can be stopped. It proves that we shall be saved."

Grant was late coming in to chow. When he appeared, he was neatly washed and shaved. His hair was combed. In his right hand he held, half hidden behind his leg, a bottle. "Gentlemen," he said courteously, "I have been saving this for such an occasion. Will you do me the honor?" With courtly grace he presented the bottle to me and took his seat.

I looked at the label and whistled. "It's Scotch, fellows!" I reported. "It's a fine thing for a night like tonight!" I opened the bottle and passed it to the man on my right.

"After you, sir," that officer said, so I poured myself a drink. Then the bottle passed and ended up before Grant. He poured himself a stiff portion.

"I believe a toast is in order," an American officer said. We stood and he proposed, "To an allied victory." Americans and New Zealanders congratulated him on the felicity of his thought. Another American jumped to his feet immediately.

"To the men who won the victory!" he said in a voice filled with emotion. No one could censure his extremely bad taste. We knew it was unseemly to be drinking when Colbourne, Grant's fellow pilot, and so many men were missing, but we had to excuse the speaker. It was Ensign Aberforce. After that display no more toasts were given.

Instead we sat around the hut and talked about what we thought had happened, and what would happen next. It might be months before we were taken off Vanicoro. Through all our discussions Grant sat silent. He was, however, drinking vigorously. From time to time someone would report upon late radio news, but since it was favorable news, and since one doesn't get whiskey very often on Vanicoro, we stayed about the table.

At about 2300 the radio operator got a Jap broadcast which he turned up loud. "The American fleet is in utter flight. The American Navy has now been reduced to a fifth-rate naval power. Our forces are regrouping." At that last admission everyone in the room cheered.

It was then that Grant rose to his feet. He started to speak. Surprised, we stopped to listen. We knew he was drunk, but not how drunk. "Today," he began in a thick voice. "Today will undoubtedly be remembered for years to come. As the gentleman from Australia so properly observed, this was one of the decis—— . . ." He stumbled badly over the word and dropped his sentence there.

"If you have not been to New Zealand," he began, and

then lost that sentence, too. "If you were a New Zealander," he started over with a rush, "you would know what this means." He took a deep breath and began speaking very slowly, emphasizing each word. "We were ready to protect the land with all our energy . . ." His voice trailed off. We looked at one another uneasily. "From the oldest man to the youngest boy we would have fought. It was my humble duty to assist in preparing the defenses of Auckland. I issued several thousand picks, crowbars, and axes. There were no other weapons." He reached for his whiskey and took a long, slow drink.

"My own wife," he resumed, "was given the job of mobilizing the women. I urged her to go to the hills . . ." He fumbled with his glass. "In fact, I ordered her to go, but she said that our two children . . ." He paused. It seemed as if his voice might break. A fellow New Zealander interrupted.

"I say, Grant!"

Leftenant Grant stared at his subaltern coldly and continued: "There are some of us in New Zealand who know the Japs. We know their cold and cunning ways. We know their thirst for what they call revenge." His voice grew louder, and he beat the table. "I tell you, we know what we have escaped. A heel of tyranny worse than any English nation has known!" He shouted this and upset his glass. Two officers tried to make him sit down, but he refused. He upset another glass defending himself from his friends. We wanted to look aside but were fascinated by the scene. Grant continued his speech.

"Gentlemen!" he said with a gravity one might use in addressing Parliament. "Especially you gentlemen from our wonderful ally. I pray to God that never in your history will you have an enemy . . . will you have an enemy so near your shores!" He paused and his voice took on a solemn ring as if he were in church. His drunkenness made the combined effect ridiculous. "I pray you may never have to rely upon a shield like this." He surveyed the tiny shack and our inadequate materials. We followed his eyes about the wretched place. The radio that was pieced together. The improvised table. The thin pile of ammunition. Grant's voice raised to a shout. "A shield like this!" he cried. He exploded the word *this* and swept his right arm about to indicate all of Vanicoro.

As he did so, he lost his balance. He grabbed at a fellow officer. Missing that support, he fell upon the table and slipped off onto the floor. He was unconscious. Dead drunk.

Mutiny

WHEN I returned to Noumea from the island of Vanicoro, Admiral Kester called me into his office. He had one of the rooms near the gingerbread balcony on Rue General Gallieni. He said, "We were lucky at Coral Sea. It's the next battle that counts." He waved his hand over the islands. His finger came to rest, I remember, on a large island shaped like a kidney, Guadalcanal.

"Some day we'll go into one of those islands. When we do, we've got to have a steady flow of planes from New Zealand and Australia. Now look!" Spreading his fingers wide he dragged them down the map from Bougainville, New Georgia, and Guadal. He brought them together at Santo. "We have Santo. We'll keep it. It's the key. And we can supply Santo from Noumea. But if we ever need planes in an emergency, we must be able to fly them up to Noumea from New Zealand and Australia." He slashed his thumb boldly from Guadalcanal to Auckland. "That's the life line.

"Now if you'll look at the air route from Noumea to Auckland you'll see a speck in the ocean not far from the route from Australia to Noumea. That speck's an island. It's vital.

Absolutely vital!" His chin jutted out. His stubby forefinger stabbed at the map. The vital speck was Norfolk Island.

There is no other island in the South Pacific like Norfolk. Lonely and lost, it is the only island in the entire ocean where no men lived before the white man came. Surrounded by gaunt cliffs, beat upon endlessly by the vast ocean, it is a speck under the forefinger of God, or Admiral Kester.

"You'll find some Americans down there," the admiral continued. "Building an airstrip. They're bogged down. Look." He handed me a dispatch from Norfolk: "TWO SITES CHOSEN X OPPOSITION TO BETTER SITE TERRIFIC X CAN WE IGNORE LOCAL WISHES X ADVISE X TONY FRY X."

"This man Fry," the admiral remarked, "is a queer duck. One of the best reserves I've seen. He wouldn't bother me with details unless something important had developed. Obviously, we can ignore local opinion if we have to. The Australian government has placed responsibility for the protection of Norfolk squarely on us. We can do what we damned well want to. But it's always wisest to exercise your power with judgment. Either you do what the local people want to do, or you jolly them into wanting to do what you've got to do anyway."

He studied the map again. "They're the life lines." His broad thumb hit Guadal again. "We've got to have an airstrip on Norfolk. And a big one." He turned away from the map. "Now you run on down to Norfolk. Take the old PBY. And you tell Fry you have my full authority to settle the problem. Don't make anyone mad, if you can help it. But remember the first job: Win the war!"

The old PBY flew down from Noumea on a day of rare beauty. We did not fly high. Below us the waves of the great ocean formed and fled in golden sunlight. There was a fair breeze from Australia, as if that mighty island were restless, and from the Tasman Sea gaunt waves, riding clear from the polar ice cap, came north and made the sea choppy. The winter sun was low, for it was now July. It hurried across the sky before us.

After six hours I saw a speck on the horizon. It grew rapidly into an island, and then into an island with jagged cliffs. Norfolk was below us. I remember clearly every detail of that first view. Not much more than ten square miles.

Forbidding cliffs along all shores. A prominent mountain to the north. Fine plateau land elsewhere.

"Oughtn't to be much trouble building an airstrip there," I mused aloft. "Run it right down the plateau. Throw a cross strip about like that, and you have an all-wind landing area. Looks simple. This guy Tony Fry must have things screwed up."

"We'll land in that little bay," the pilot said.

"I don't see any," I replied.

"Between the cliffs," he said.

I looked, and where he pointed there was a small bay. Not protected from the sea, and terribly small. But a bay. "The waves look mighty high to me," I said.

"They are," he laughed. "Damned high."

He went far out to sea and came in for his landing. But he had too much speed and zoomed over the island, climbing rapidly for another attempt. We came roaring in from the tiny bay, sped over a winding hill road leading up to the plateau and then right down the imaginary line I had drawn as the logical location for the airstrip. It was then that I saw the pines of Norfolk.

For on each side of that line, like the pillars of a vast and glorious cathedral, ran the pine trees, a stately double column stretching for two miles toward the mountain. "My God," I whispered to myself. "That's it. That's the problem."

We flew to sea once more, leveled off and again tried the tricky landing. Again we had too much speed. Again we gunned the old PBY over the hill road, up to the plateau and down the pines of Norfolk. We were so low we could see along the dusty road running between the columns. An old woman in a wagon was heading down to the sea. She looked up sharply as we roared overhead. And that was my first view of Teta Christian.

We landed on the third try, bouncing our teeth out, almost. A tall, thin, somewhat stooped naval officer waved to us from the crumbling stone pier. It was Lt. (jg) Tony Fry, dressed in a sloppy shirt and a pair of shorts. He greeted us when we climbed ashore and said, "Glad to have you aboard, sir. Damned glad to have you aboard." He had twinkling eyes and a merry manner. "Now if you'll step over here to our shed, I'll make the welcome more sincere."

He led us through the crowd of silent islanders to a small stone cow shed not far from the pier. "But this cow shed is built of dressed stone," I said. "It's better than you see back home."

"I know," Tony said. "The convicts had to be kept busy. If there was nothing else to do, they built cow sheds."

"What convicts?" I asked.

"Gentlemen, a real welcome!" Tony produced a bottle of Scotch. I learned later that no one ever asked Tony where or how he got his whiskey. He always had it.

"This island," he said to me as we drank, "is the old convict island. Everything you see along the shore was built by the convicts."

"From where?"

"From Australia. England sent her worst convicts to Australia. And those who were too tough for Australia to handle were sent over here. This isn't a pretty island," Fry said. "Or wouldn't be, if it could talk."

"Well!" I said, looking at Tony. "About this airstrip?"

He smiled at me quizzically, "Admiral Kester?" he asked.

"Yes."

He smiled again. "You came down here to see about the airstrip?" I nodded. He grinned, an infectious, lovely grin showing his white and somewhat irregular teeth. "Commander," he said. "Let's have one more drink!"

"I have a terrible premonition that the trouble is that row of pine trees," I said as he poured.

Fry didn't bat an eye. He simply grinned warmly at me and raised his glass. "To the airstrip!" he said. "Thank God it's your decision, not mine."

At this moment there was a commotion outside the shed. "It's Teta!" voices cried. A horse, panting from his gallop, drew to a halt and wagon wheels crunched in the red dust. A high voice cried out, "Where is he? Where's Tony?"

"In there! In with the new American."

"Let me in!" the high voice cried.

And into our shed burst Teta Christian, something over ninety. She had four gaunt teeth in her upper jaw and two in her lower. Her hair was thin and wispy. But her frail body was erect. She went immediately to Tony. He took her by the hand and patted her on the shoulder. "Take it easy, now, Teta," he said.

She pushed him away and stood before me. "Why do you come here to cut down the pine trees?" she asked, her high voice rising to a wail.

"I . . ."

But Tony interrupted. "Be careful what you say, commander. It's the only adequate site on the island."

"You shut up!" old Teta blurted out. "You shut up, Tony."

"I merely came down to see what should be done," I said.

"Well, go back!" Teta cried, pushing me with her bony hand. "Get in the airplane. Go back. Leave us alone."

"We'd better get out of here," I said. "Where do I bunk?"

"That's a problem," Fry said, whimsically. "It's a damned tough problem."

"Anywhere will do me," I assured him. "Why not put up with you? I'll only be here one night."

Tony raised his eyebrows as if to say, "Want to bet on that?" He laughed again. "That's what the problem is, commander. I sort of don't think you should live with me." He fingered his jay-gee bar on his collar flap. "I . . . I . . ."

"Hm!" I said to myself. "Woman trouble. These damned — Yanks. Let them get anywhere near a dame. I suppose Fry has something lined up. Officers are worse than the men."

"Very well," I said aloud. "Anywhere will do."

I reached for my single piece of luggage, a parachute bag battered from the jungle life on Vanicoro. As I did so a chubby young girl of fifteen or sixteen came into the shed and ran up to Tony in that strange way you can spot every time. She was desperately in love with him. To my utter disgust, I noticed that she was vacant-eyed and that her lower jaw was permanently hung open.

"This is Lucy," Fry said, patting the young girl affectionately on the shoulder. Lucy looked at me and grinned. "Hello," she said.

"We could find quarters for you in the old convict houses," Tony suggested. "Down here along the shore."

I felt a bit sick at my stomach: American officers and native women. "If the convict houses are as well built as this shed, I'll be in luck," I said.

"Oh, they're much finer construction," he assured me.

"Why don't you get in the plane and fly back?" old Teta whined.

"I can drive you over in the jeep," Fry suggested.

"I'm much more interested, really, in surveying the island," I said. "Let's just drop the bag and get going."

"You tell him, Tony," Teta wailed. "You tell him the truth!"

Fry wiped his forehead. I found out later that he perspired more than any man in the Pacific. He was always looking for a cool spot or someone else to do his work. "Now look, Teta. You run along. Get us some orangeade fixed up. Get us a nice dinner for tonight." He reached in his pocket and pulled out what change he had. Mostly pennies. "Have you a buck?" he asked me. I gave him one. "You take this, Teta, and scram!" He slapped her gently on the bottom and pushed her out of the shed. We followed and climbed into his jeep. Lucy was already sitting in front.

"No, Lucy!" Fry said. "You'll have to get in back." As the girl climbed over the seats, Tony returned to the shed to speak to a group of sullen native men. In this instant a young Army lieutenant hurried up to the jeep.

"Boy, are we glad to see you?" he blurted out. "It's about time somebody came down here to straighten things up. We were all ready to start building the strip when Fry called the whole thing off. You got to be firm, commander," he whispered. "Stop all this damned nonsense. That old Teta is the worst of the lot."

I looked over my shoulder at Lucy. She was sitting there quietly, saying nothing, hearing nothing. "Don't bother about her, commander," the lieutenant said. "She's crazier than a bedbug." Fry left the shed and the Army man hurried off.

"That was the big prison," Tony said as we drove up the red road from the pier. "And that's Gallows Gate. They used to hang prisoners there for everyone to see. Had a special noose that never tightened up. Just slowly strangled them. They didn't tie their feet, either. Some of them kicked for fifteen minutes. Kept guards standing about with clubs and guns. Sometime I'll tell you about what happened one day at a hanging here."

I studied the superb gate. The lava rock from which it was built was cleaner and fresher, more beautifully cut and matched than in 1847, when the magnificent structure was built. Proportioned like the body of a god, this gate was merely one of hundreds of superb pieces of construction. There were walls as beautiful as a palace at Versailles, old houses straight from the drawing boards of England, towers, blockhouses, salt works, chimneys, barns, a chapel, granaries, and lime pits, all built of gray lava rock, all superb and perfect. They clustered along the foreshore of Norfolk Island in grim memory of the worst convict camp England ever fostered. They moaned beneath the Norfolk pines when winds whipped in at night, for they were empty. They were dead and empty ruins. They were not rotting by the sea, for they were stronger than when they were built. But they were dead and desolate.

"I can never go past this one without stopping," Fry said. "It seems to cry out with human misery." We climbed out of the jeep beside an exquisite piece of building. "If you want to," Fry said to Lucy. "Come along." The girl scrambled out and stood close to Fry as we studied the officers' bath house.

"They were afraid to swim in the sea," he said. "Sharks. And too many officers were drowned there by the prisoners. They'd hide behind rocks and drag the officers under the waves. So this was built." The bath house was a small building beside the road. Twenty steps or more, perfectly carved out of rock, descended to a flagstone bath possibly twenty-four feet square. The western end of the bath dipped slightly so that water would run free to the ocean.

The bath was a superb thing, walled with matched rock, patiently built in the perfection of men who had endless time. But it was not the bath which captivated Tony's imagination and my horror. It was the conduit by which the water of a little stream was diverted into the bath. This tunnel was six feet high. It was dug completely through the base of a small hill about three hundred feet long. It was paved with beautiful stone. It was arched like the most graceful portico ever built. Down the roof of the three-hundred-foot conduit were keystones of perfect design. And all this was buried under a hill of dirt where no man would ever see.

I studied it in horror. I thought of the endless hours and pain that went into its building, the needless perfectionism, the human misery, when a pipe would have done as well. Tony and Lucy stood beside me in the dank place as I studied the exquisite masonry. Fry spoke in the grim silence: "And when any of the stone dressers or skilled masons died, the governor sent word back to England. And the word was passed along. Then judges kept a sharp lookout for stone masons. Some were sent here for life because they stole a rabbit."

When Tony dropped me off at my quarters he coughed once or twice. "I'm terribly sorry to leave you down here," he said. "But I think this is best." Lucy was crawling over the seats to the front of the jeep.

"This will do me," I said.

"I'd have you up to my diggings," he continued. "But it would be embarrassing. It would be terribly embarrassing to you. That's the mistake I made. You see, I board with old Teta Christian. She'd love to have you stay with her. The soul of hospitality. But if you did, she'd capture you the way she has me."

"The pine trees?" I asked.

"Yes," he replied. "The only good site on the island."

"Then why don't you cut them down and build the strip?"

Fry looked at me for more than a minute. His eyes were clear and joking. He had a sharp nose and chin. He was about thirty years old and didn't give a damn about anything or anybody. He was taking my measure, and although I was his superior officer I stood at attention and tried to pass muster. Apparently I did. He punched me softly on the arm. "You see, commander," he said. "Old Teta Christian is the granddaughter of Fletcher Christian, the mutineer. All those people at the pier were *Bounty* people. They don't push around easy." He winked at me and left. Lucy leaned over and blew the horn as he backed the jeep into a tight circle.

"*Bounty* people!" I said to myself. "So this is where they wound up when they left Pitcairn Island? This paradise!"

And it was a paradise! Oh, it was one of the loveliest paradises in the vast ocean. Untouched by man for eons, it grew its noble pine trees hundreds of feet high and always straight. It developed a plateau full of glens and valleys to warm the heart of any man. It grew all manner of food and protected its secrets by forbidding cliffs. I came to Norfolk for a day. I stayed a week, and then another. And I lived in a paradise, cool, fresh, clean, and restful after the mists of Vanicoro.

Late that afternoon Tony drove down for me. I said, "We'll look the two sites over and I can fly back in the morning."

"Now don't rush things, commander," Tony replied. "We can study the island tomorrow. Old Teta asked a few of the *Bounty* people in for dinner. They want to meet you. Purely social."

"Fry, I don't want to be brusque about this, but the reason I'm down here is that Admiral Kester is pretty well browned off at the shilly-shallying. There's a war on!"

"That I'm aware of," Tony replied. "I'm in it."

"So if you don't mind, I'd like to see the two sites right

now. Then, if we have time, we'll stop by the old woman's."

"Very well," Fry said. I was glad to see that Lucy was not waiting for us in the jeep. The fat little moron was becoming somewhat unnerving. But as we drove past the deserted ruins of the prison, she ran out into the road. "We better take her along," Tony said. "She never says much." So he stopped the jeep and Lucy climbed in back.

"The first site," Tony said, "is at the northwestern tip of the island. Up by the cable station." We drove along the shore road to reach the place. Inland I could see one sweeping valley after another, each with its quota of pine trees tall against the late afternoon sky.

The location we had come to visit was disappointing indeed. To the east and south the mountain encroached on the potential field. Landings would be difficult. Cliffs prohibited much more than a four thousand foot runway. Any cross runway for alternate winds was out of the question. "Not much of a location for an airstrip," I said.

"Not too good," Tony agreed. "Want to see the other?"

"I'd like to," I answered. He drove south from the cable station until he came to a sight which made me blink my eyes. There, on this lonely island, was a chapel, a rustic gem of architecture. It was built of wood and brown stone among a grove of pines. It was so different in spirit from the precise, brutal buildings on the water front that I must have shown my surprise.

"The old Melanesian Mission," he said. "From this spot all the Hebrides and Solomons were Christianized. This is where the saints lived."

"The saints?" I asked.

"Yes. Lucy's great-uncle was one. He went north from here. To an island called Vanicoro. The natives roasted him alive. And during his torment he kept shouting, 'God is love. Jesus saves.' The old men of the village decided there must be something to his religion after all. They set out in canoes to a near-by island and brought another missionary back. A whole village was converted. There were lots of saints around here."

"Was he . . ." I inclined my head toward the rear seat.

"Sure. They all are, more or less. Listen to names at the party tonight. Christian, Young, Quintal, Adams. Do they mean anything to you?"

"The mutineers from the *Bounty?*" I asked. Old Matthew

Quintal was a favorite of mine. I could not believe that his descendants lived and remembered that unregenerate scoundrel.

"That's right. And Nobbs and Buffet, the missionaries that followed. The mutineers have been intermarrying for more than a hundred years. I guess they're all a little nuts." The frankness of Fry's comment startled me. I turned to look at Lucy, expecting to find her in tears. She grinned at me, with her mouth open.

"This is the other site," Fry said. We were on a little hill. Before us spread the heart of the plateau, with the pines of Norfolk laid out along an ideal runway.

"I saw this from the air," I said. "Ideal. We can even run a six thousand foot auxiliary strip for alternate landings."

"That's right," Tony agreed.

"Let's get going tomorrow," I suggested.

"Good idea. Let's eat now." Tony threw the jeep into low and started slowly down the hill. When he reached the bottom, Lucy cried out, "Blow the horn! Blow the horn!" Fry did not obey, so Lucy leaned over the seat and pushed the button for about a minute. From a ramshackle house a host of children ran into the dusty road beside the crawling jeep. "It's Lucy! It's Lucy!" they screamed. "It's Lucy in the jeep!" Our chubby moron grinned at them, threw them kisses, and twisted the horn button. Then she sat back in her seat quietly and said no more.

When we were past the half-ruined house, Tony threw the jeep into high and we hurried toward old Teta's farm. In doing so, we had to enter the avenue of pine trees down which I had seen Teta hurrying that morning. As we passed under their vast canopy noise from the jeep was muffled. Eighty feet above us, on either side, tree after tree, the pines of Norfolk raised their majestic heads. There was a wind from the south, that wind which sweeps up from the Antarctic day after day. It made a singing sound among the pines. Nobody said anything, not Tony nor I nor Lucy.

I was not unhappy when we turned off the road of the pines and into a little lane. It led past some ruins that, in the midst of the South Pacific, were breath-taking. Above me rose what seemed to be a large portion of an aqueduct that might have graced the Appian Way.

"What's that?" I cried.

"Part of a series of stables," Tony replied. "The convicts

were building it for the governor's horses when the lid blew off the island." I looked at the fantastic stables. Graceful curved archways, ten or a dozen in number, had been erected in the 1850's. Now they stood immaculately clean, the stone finished with exquisite care, and arches proportioned like the temples of ancient Rome.

"For his horses?" I asked.

"That's right," Tony said. "He had to think of something to keep all the stone masons busy."

I studied this grotesque folly. Imperial ruins in Carthage and Syracuse I could understand. But this massive grandeur lost in the heart of a tiny island ages of time from anywhere . . .

Two hundred yards from the end of the stables we entered a garden filled with all kinds of flowers, shrubs, and fruit trees. This was Teta Christian's home. "When the *Bounty* folk first came here, commander," she said in her high thin voice, "my father, Fletcher Christian, chose this place for his farm. He liked the view down that valley." She drew the curtain aside and showed me her prospect, a valley of lovely pine trees, a thin stream, and curves lost in the vales that swept down to the sea. "My father, Fletcher Christian, planted all this land. But I put in the orange trees." It was uncanny, oranges growing so luxuriantly beside the pines. It was like having a citrus grove in Minnesota, difficult to comprehend.

"When my father, Fletcher Christian, came to this island," she said, "he and Adams Quintal looked over the land. Am I boring you, commander?"

"Oh, no! Please, go ahead. I'm very interested."

"He and Adams Quintal looked over the land. Nobbs Buffet and Thomas Young were along. They decided that they would not live along the shore. That was prison land."

"Were there no prisoners there?" I asked.

"Oh, no! After the great mutiny all the prisoners were taken away. Two years later they gave the empty island to us. I am the last person living who came here from Pitcairn," she moaned on. "I was five years old when we sailed. I remember Pitcairn well, although some people say you can't remember that far back." She lapsed into the strange Pitcairn dialect, composed of sea-faring English from the *Bounty* modified by Tahitian brought in by girls the mutineers had stolen. Her friends argued with her for a moment or two in the impossible jargon. They were Quintals and Nobbs and Buffets and endless Christians.

"They still don't believe me," Teta laughed. "But I remember one day standing on the cliffs at Pitcairn. It was right beside the statue of the old god my father found when he came to Pitcairn . . ." Her mind wandered. I never knew whether the original Christian, that terrible-souled mutineer, was her grandfather or her great-grandfather, or someone even farther back.

"So my father, Fletcher Christian, and Adams Quintal decided that they would have nothing whatever to do with the prison lands. Let them die and bury their dead down there. Let those awful places go away. My father, Mr. Fletcher Christian, was a very good man and he helped to build the Mission which you saw today. He would not take any money for his work. My father said, 'If the Lord has given me this land and this valley, I shall give the Lord my work.' Am I boring you with this talk, commander?"

I assured her again and again that night that I was not bored by the memories of Norfolk Island. I made my point so secure that she promised to visit me in the morning and to show me the records of the first settlement of the mutineers. Accordingly, at 0900 the jeep drove up to my quarters. Tony and Lucy were in front. Old Teta sat in the back. "We'll just go down the road a little way," she said. She led us to the largest of the remaining prison buildings. It was hidden behind a wall of superb construction. This wall was more securely built, more thoroughly protected with corner blockhouses and ramparts, than the jail itself.

"What did they keep in here?" I asked. "The murderers?"

"Oh, no!" she said in a high voice of protest. "The jail keepers lived in here."

"But that twenty-foot wall? The broken glass?"

"To keep the prisoners out. In case they mutinied. They did, too. All the time. This was an island of horror," she said.

Up past the postoffice old Teta led us, up two flights of stairs and into a large, almost empty room. It was the upper council chamber, and upon its walls rested faded photographs of long-dead Christians, Buffets, Quintals, and members of the other families. Lucy stood on one foot and studied their grim faces.

Teta, however, went to an old cupboard built into the wall. From it she took a series of boxes, each thick with dust and tied with red string. She peered into several boxes and finally selected one. Banging it on the table until her white hair was lost in a cloud, she said, "This is the one." From it she took several papers and let them fall through her idle hands onto the table. I picked up one. A petition from Fletcher Christian to the governor. "And I therefore humbly beg your permission to let my white bull Jonas run wild upon the common lands. If he can get to plenty of cows, he will not have a bad temper, and since he is the best bull on the island, everybody will be better off." It was signed in an uncertain writing much different from the petition.

"This is the one," Teta said. It was another petition signed by Fletcher Christian, Adams Quintal, Nobbs Buffet and Thomas Young: "Because God has been kind in his wisdom to bring us here, it is proposed that an avenue of pine trees that grow upon this island and nowhere else in the world be planted and if we do not live to see them tall our children will." The petition was granted.

"I ought to go out to survey the field," I said.

"Well, you needn't go till afternoon," Tony replied. "Tell the PBY to lay over another day. Some of the villagers are having a picnic lunch for us."

I attended. The more I heard of Teta's stories the more interested I became. After we had eaten and I had consumed half a dozen oranges she said, "Would you like to see the old headstones? In the cemetery?"

I was indeed interested. She led me to the cemetery, this old, old woman who would soon be there herself. It lay upon a gently rising hillside near the ocean. "In this section are the *Bounty* people," she said. There were the white headstones, always with the same names: Quintal, Young, Adams, Christian. "I am a Quintal," she said. "I married this man." She pointed to the gravestone of Christian Nobbs Quintal. Beside it were the inevitable tiny stones: "Mary Nobbs Quintal, Aged 3 Mos." "Adams Buffet Quintal, Aged 1 Yr." "Nobbs Young Christian Quintal, Aged 8 Mos."

"My father, Fletcher Christian, is buried over there," she said. "He's not really buried there, either. He was lost at sea. And down here are the convict graves. This corner is for those that were hung." I studied the dismal relics. "Thomas Burke, Hung 18 July 1838. He struck a guard and God struck him." "Timothy O'Shea, Hung 18 July 1838. He killed a guard. May God have Mercy on his Soul." The tragic

story of hatred, sudden death, breaks, and terrible revenge
was perpetuated in the weathering stones. "Thomas Bates,
Worcester, America, 18 Yrs. Old." The rest was lost.

"They buried the mutineers over here," old Teta whined.

I looked at the close cluster of graves. English peasant
names, Irish peasants. "What did they do?" I asked.

"These are the men who killed the guards and buried their
bodies in the bridge. There where we had our picnic. Bloody
Bridge."

"They hung them all?"

"All of them. They hung them with the slow knot. The
last man fainted, so they waited till he came back. A prisoner
cried out against this, and they beat him till he died." She
looked over the graves to the restless sea. "My father, Fletcher
Christian, said he wanted none of their bloody buildings. So
the *Bounty* people tore down the houses we were given along
the shore. When my father said that."

It was now too late for me to inspect the airstrip that day,
so I told the PBY pilot to take off early next morning and
return to Noumea without me. I would send a dispatch when
I got my work done. That night I sat in Teta's house by the
ruined stables and listened as she told us about the days on
Pitcairn. "My father, Fletcher Christian," she said, "was
known as the leader of the mutineers. But Captain Bligh was
a very evil man. My father told me that Mr. Christian had
to do what he did. There are some who say it is a shame
Tahitian girls went to Pitcairn, too, but my father, Fletcher
Christian, said that if Tahitian girls didn't go, who would?
And that is a question you cannot answer. I am half Tahitian
myself. Nobody in our fmily has ever married outside the
mutiny people. That is, the Pitcairn people. A lot of people
think this is bad." She spoke to her island friends in Pitcairn,
and they laughed.

"Teta!" a Mr. Quintal said. "You're drinking too much of
the lieutenant's rum. You're getting drunk."

Teta leaned over and patted Fry on the arm. "Drinking a
little rum isn't getting drunk," she said. Fry poured her some
whiskey. To Teta everything from a bottle was rum, a relic
of the old sea-faring days.

"What we are laughing about, commander, is a funny old
man came here some time ago. Measured all our heads. He
was a German. He made pictures of who everybody married
and then proved we were all crazy people. His book had

pictures, too. I was one of the people that wasn't crazy, but Nobbs over there," and she pointed to an islander, "his picture was in the front of the book. He was very crazy!"

"You might as well stay here the night," Fry said, but I disagreed. I preferred to sleep in my own quarters. "As you wish." We got into the jeep and Lucy climbed in back.

"Blow the horn! Blow the horn!" she cried as we crept past the ramshackle house. This time Tony blew the horn for her. Into the darkness tumbled a dozen childish forms. They screamed in the night, "It's Lucy! It's Lucy! In the American jeep!" In the darkness I could almost hear dumb Lucy grinning and laughing behind me.

I went up to the proposed airstrip next morning and surveyed the job that lay ahead. Tony was not visible, but the energetic young Army lieutenant was wheeling his tractors into position with help supplied by the Australian government. "Well," he said. "I guess we're ready to go now."

I was about to nod when I looked over toward the Norfolk pines and there was old Teta. She was in her wagon, the reins tied to the whip. Just watching. "You can start clearing away the brush," I said.

"But the trees, commander!"

"We'll wait a few days on that," I said.

"But damn it all, commander! It will take us a long time to get those trees down. We can't do anything till that's done."

"I want to look over that other site, first. We can get that land cheaper."

"But my God!" the lieutenant cried. "We been through all that before."

"We'll go through it again!" I shouted.

"Yes, sir," he replied.

I walked over to study one of the trees. It was six feet through the base, had scaly bark. Its branches grew out absolutely parallel to the ground. Its leaves were like spatulas, broad and flat, yet pulpy like a water-holding cactus. In perfect symmetry it rose high into the air. I thought, "It was a tree like this that Captain Cook saw when he inspected Norfolk. He was the first man, white or black, ever known to visit the island. It was a tree like this that made him say, 'And the hospitable island will be a fruitful source of spars for our ships.' "

"I'm going down to the Mission," old Teta said as she drove up. "Would you like to ride along?" I climbed into her wagon. When we drove past Lucy's corner, that grinning girl saw us. Quick as an animal she ran to her own horse and vaulted into the saddle. Whipping him up with her heels, she soon caught up to us.

"Going to the Mission?" she asked.

"Come along," the frail old woman said. "Lucy's a good girl," Teta said. "She's not too bright."

At the Mission we tied the horse and Lucy let hers roam free. The chapel was even lovelier than I had thought from the road. Inside, it was made of colored marble, rare shells from the northern islands, wood from the Solomons, and carvings from the Hebrides. Not ornate, it was rich beyond imagination. Gold and silver flourished. Each pew end was set in mother-of-pearl patiently carved by some island craftsman. Scenes from Christ's life predominated in the intaglios, but occasionally a free Christian motif had been worked out. The translucent shell spoke of the love that had been lavished upon it.

The windows perplexed me. They reminded me of something I had seen elsewhere, but the comparison I made was so silly that I did not even admit it to myself.

"The windows," Teta said, "were made by a famous man in England and sent out here on a boat."

"Good heavens!" I said, "it is Burne-Jones." How wildly weird his ascetic figures looked in that chapel.

"Bishop Patteson built this chapel," old Teta whined on. But her memories were vague. She got the famous Melanesian missionaries all confused. She had known each of them, well. Selwyn and Patteson and Paton.

"My brother, Fletcher Christian, went up north with good Bishop Selwyn," she said. "They went to Vanicoro where my uncle, Fletcher Christian, was burned alive. He converted a whole village by that. He was a very saintly man. My brother was also named Fletcher Christian. That tablet up there is to him, not to my uncle. My brother came home one day and knelt down. It was right after my father died at sea. He said, that is my brother Fletcher Christian said, 'I am going to follow God! I am going with Bishop . . .'" She faltered. "'I am going with Bishop Patteson.' He went up north to an island right near Vanicoro. Bali-ha'i. He was a very good missionary. Bishop Paton said of him, 'Fletcher Christian rests with God!'" He rests with God because the natives shot at him with a poisoned arrow. They shot him through the right arm. He got well, at first, but blood poisoning set in, and Bishop Patteson knew he was going to die. They prayed for my brother for three days, and all that time he twisted on the ground and cried out, 'I am saved! I am washed in the blood of the Lord.' And for three days he cried like that, and his jaws locked tight shut and he cried through his teeth, 'God is my salvation!' And on the fourth day he died." Teta sat in the now-empty Mission, deserted because its function was fulfilled. Its word had been carried north to all the islands.

"I remember in Pitcairn," she said. "We were all sick and had no medicine. The medicine of Tahiti had been forgotten, because we had no herbs. We had no food either. My father, Fletcher Christian, went to a meeting. They decided that we must leave Pitcairn. Everybody. Not only those that wanted to go, but everybody. When we got here we were happy for a while. Enough food, at least. But in two years many of us wanted to go home. Back to Pitcairn. Some of the families did go back." Teta thought of the far-away people. "I always wanted to go back. My mother, she was a Quintal, she wanted to go home very much. But my father, Fletcher Christian, wouldn't hear of it. He said, 'God in His wisdom brought us to these flowering shores. God meant us to stay here.' We never went with the others."

Back at my quarters that afternoon I was in a confusion of thoughts. No one could tell how urgently we might need the airstrip on Norfolk, nor how soon. Suppose the Japs defeated us in some great battle in the Hebrides! In such an event the airstrip on Norfolk might be essential to our life itself. Thought of this steeled me to the inescapable conclusion. The pines of Norfolk must go. An end to this silly nonsense!

I walked slowly down to the old stone cow shed where the Army had its headquarters. "We'll start in the morning," I told them. "Get the trees out of there."

"It's only three now, sir," the eager young lieutenant said. "We could get a couple down this afternoon!"

"Time enough in the morning," I said. "Get your gear ready."

"It's been ready for two weeks," he said coldly.

I felt honor-bound to tell the islanders that the irrevocable decision had been made. I planned to do so that evening, at Teta's. I climbed the dusty road from the prison camp to the free lands and the pine-filled valleys. Fry must have been sleeping that afternoon, as he frequently did, for Lucy clattered past me on her horse, riding like a centaur, raising a fine hullabaloo. She would tear past going in one direction, then stop, wheel her big horse, and rush by me the other way. She kept this up for eight or ten sallies, never saying a word.

When I reached the avenue of pines my resolution wavered. I said, "I can't permit this thing! The loveliest monument in the South Pacific completely destroyed. No, by God! I'll do everything I can. Up to the hilt. I've got to!" And I hurried back to the prison lands, the compressed, pain-saddened shore, and sent an urgent dispatch to Admiral Kester. It was a long one. Gave the dimensions of the two fields. Told him that the north field could have no cross runway and would be hampered by the small mountain. I said there was great opposition to the central field. I closed the dispatch as follows: "REQUEST PERMISSION PROCEED NORTH FIELD."

I did not go to Teta's for dinner. I missed dinner, and was not aware of that fact. About ten o'clock that night I got my answer. It was brief, and in it I could hear many oaths from the admiral such as: "What are those damned fools doing down there?" and "By God, why can't they look at the goddam facts and make up their minds?" His dispatch had its mind made up: "RE UR 140522 X NEGATIVE X REPEAT NEGATIVE X KESTER."

But the dispatch relieved me. I clutched it in my hand and walked up the hill to the plateau where the *Bounty* people lived. I walked down the long avenue of trees and thought, "You are not dying by my hand." At the side road I turned toward Teta's house, and to my left were the grim yet lovely stables. "The stone masons had been sentenced for life. They were already out here," Tony had said. "They had to be kept busy doing something." Against the rising moon the stables of Norfolk stood silent in solemn grandeur, each stone delicately finished, each mortised joint perfect.

Teta and Tony were alone, drinking rum. Lucy, of course, sat in a corner and watched Tony all night. "My father, Fletcher Christian, was a very good sailor," Teta said. "It was a great pity for this island when he was killed at sea. It was at the Cascade Landing. There are only two places where boats can possibly land on Norfolk. It reminds me of Pitcairn in that respect. My grandfather, Fletcher Christian, said that if a man could sail in and out of Pitcairn Island, he was indeed a sailor. I have been told my father was the best sailor on either island, but he was killed at sea. At Cascade Landing, which is very rough and brutal. A very bad place to land in any weather. The waves crushed his boat and threw him on the rocks. Right at the landing. Then pulled him back out to sea and we never got the body. I think we could have found the body, but there were no other sailors as brave as my father, and no one searched for him until the storm was over."

"Bad news," I said. Tony poured old Teta another drink. Lucy came to the table and asked for some rum. "No, Lucy!" Tony said. "You go back and sit down."

"From Noumea?" Tony asked.

"Yes. I wired the admiral."

"I know," Tony said. "I did the same thing."

"He made the decision," I said.

"I know," Tony replied. "I passed the buck to you. And you passed it to the admiral."

"Teta," I said quietly. "We start to take the trees down tomorrow."

The old mutineer looked at me and started to speak. No words came. She licked her six gaunt teeth and took a big drink of rum. "I remember when my father, Fletcher Christian, planted those trees," she said. "I ran along beside the men. They laid out two lines. There was no road there, then. Four men stood with poles and my father said to Adams Quintal—it was his son Christian Nobbs Quintal that I married. We were married by a missionary from the mission. Bishop Patteson married us, and then he took my brother, Fletcher Christian, up to the islands, where the young man died of blood poisoning. Tony, my brother, died with his jaws tied shut with bands of iron. He could only speak through his teeth." The old woman dropped her head on her hands. The lamp threw an eerie glow upon her white hair.

"She's drunk again," Lucy said. "Too much rum."

"Lucy!" Fry said. "I told you to sit over there and not talk."

"We'll have to start tomorrow. In the morning," I said. I waved the dispatch at him.

"You don't have to prove it to me, commander," Fry chuckled. "I know what you feel, exactly. It's the islanders you've got to prove it to. Save the dispatch for them."

I don't know who spread the word. I can't believe it was

Teta, and Lucy was sitting tight-lipped in the corner when I left. Perhaps the islanders heard it from the Army. At any rate, early next morning a crowd of people gathered at the pine trees. As I approached with the Army engineers, Nobbs Quintal, whose photograph had served as the frontispiece to the book which proved that all Norfolk *Bounty* people were degenerate, tipped his hat and asked me if he could speak. I clenched my hands and thought, "Here it comes!"

"Commander," Nobbs Quintal said. "We know the trees have to go. We know there's war. My son is at war. In Egypt. Old Teta has five grandsons in the Army. We know you've tried to change the airport. We heard about your message yesterday. But won't you wait one more day? We want to take some pictures of the trees."

They had an old box camera and some film. An American soldier had a pretty good miniature camera, and an Australian had a very good French job. All morning they took pictures of the trees. The Quintals and the Christians and Nobbses and all the others stood beneath the trees, drove wagons along the dusty road, and made family groups. About noon Nobbs Quintal went over by the stables and hitched up Teta's wagon. The old woman appeared between the trees and looked sadly into space as she was photographed with various families and alone. The reins were wrapped about the whip post. Saliva ran into the corners of her mouth from the six teeth. Her white hair reflected the dim sunlight that pierced the green canopy. She was the last of the Pitcairn people.

All film was used up by two o'clock. The last shots were taken of Teta Christian, Tony, and me. On the very last shot Lucy ran from the crowd to stand beside Tony. In that picture her head almost covers Teta's, but the old woman leaned sideways in the wagon and peeked from behind my shoulder.

The engineers moved in. With rotary saws they cut part way through the first tree. Then two bulldozers shoved against the trunk. The great pine broke loose and almost imperceptibly started to fall. As it did so, it caught for a moment, twisted in the air like a soldier shot as he runs forward. The tree twirled, mortally wounded, and fell into a cloud of dust. Three more were destroyed in that manner.

The island people said nothing as their living cathedral was desecrated. The old *Bounty* people watched the felling of the trees as simply one more tragedy in the long series their clans had had to tolerate.

"You'll have to move back," the Army engineers said. "We've got to blast the stumps."

We moved to a safe distance and watched the engineers place sticks of dynamite among the roots of each fallen tree. Then a detonator was attached and the wires gathered together at a plunger box. The charge was exploded, but nothing much happened. Just some dirt and dust in the air, with a few fragments of wood. It was not until the bulldozers came back and nudged the stumps that we saw what had happened. The roots had been destroyed. Like old hulks of men who can be pushed and bullied about the slums of a large city, the stumps of Norfolk were pushed and harried into a dump.

I could not go back to Teta's that night. I was lonely, and miserable in my loneliness. I stayed with some Australians who had built their camp near the line of trees. "It's a bloody shime," one of them said in barbarous Anzac cockney. "One bloody line of trees on the bloody island, and we put the bloody airport there!"

Our thoughts were broken by a crashing explosion outside. We rushed to the door of our tent and saw in the moonlight a cloud of dust rising by the trees.

"Fat's in the fire!" an Australian cried.

We hurried across the field to where the explosion had taken place. We found one of the smaller bulldozers blown to bits. Dynamite. "Those dirty bastards!" an Army engineer said. Then, in true military fashion, he got busy proving that it wasn't his fault. He shouted, "These things were supposed to be guarded. Sergeant! Didn't I tell you to have these guarded?" He ran toward some lights shouting, "Sergeant! Sergeant!"

I left the Australians and headed for the stone stables. As I did so, I caught a glimpse of a woman running ahead of me. I hurried as fast as I could and overtook fat Lucy. I grabbed her by the shoulders and started to shake her, but she burst into a heavy flow of tears and blubbered so that I could make nothing of her answers. I turned, therefore, toward old Teta's house and did so in time to see her door open and close. "Come along, Lucy!" I said. She scuffed her bare feet in the dust behind me.

In Teta's house Fry and the old woman were drinking rum. Teta was not puffing, but she seemed out of breath. Fry had obviously not moved for some time. "My father,

Fletcher Christian," Teta said, "always told us that it did not matter whether you lived on Norfolk Island or Pitcairn Island so long as you lived in the love of God. My mother did not believe this. She said that this island was very good for people who had never lived on Pitcairn. But she could not see how a little more food and steamers from Australia could make up for the life we had on Pitcairn. She said that she would rather live there, on the cliff by the ocean, than anywhere else in the world. But when my father died at sea, she had a chance to go back to her home on Pitcairn. A boat was going there. I begged her to go on the boat, and take us all. But she said, 'No. Fletcher is buried out there at sea. My place is here.' It was shortly after this that my brother, Fletcher Christian, was killed up north. Like my father he was a very saintly man. But the religion in the family was all in the men. Not the women. Although I did know Bishop Paton. He was a fine man."

The old woman droned on and on until it was obvious to me that she was drunk again from too much of Tony's rum. Toward morning she left us and went into her bedroom. I sat drumming my fingers on the table and Tony said, "Come on! We'll drive Lucy home."

"I don't want to go home!" she cried.

"Get in the jeep!" Tony commanded, adding in a low voice, "You've done enough for one night."

The crazy girl climbed in behind us. At the hill Tony drove very slowly and pushed on the horn. The reaction was delayed, but when it came it was more explosive than before. Kids from everywhere piled out of the old house and came screaming in the night. "It's Lucy!" they shouted. "Lucy comin' home in the American jeep!"

"So she blew up the bulldozer?" I asked.

"That's right," Tony said sleepily. "She and Teta."

"Fry," I said coldly. "Those two women could never in a million years figure out how to explode dynamite." A guard stopped us.

"Good evening, commander," he said. "Saboteurs about. Blew up a half-track."

"They couldn't figure it in a million years, Tony."

"It was an old bulldozer anyway," Fry said as we drove back to Teta's. "Something somebody in the States didn't want. Commander, I can just see him, rubbing his hands and saying, 'Look! I can sell it to the guv'mint. Make money on the deal, too. And it's patriotic! You can't beat a deal like that!' Well, his tractor did a lot of good."

"We need that bulldozer for the airstrip."

"I don't think you do," Tony replied. "As a matter of fact, I'm damned sure you don't. Because that's the one that broke down this afternoon and the Army man said it couldn't be fixed." He brought the jeep to a stop by Teta's fence.

"Fry," I said. "You could be court-martialed for this."

Tony turned to face me. "Who would believe you?" he asked.

"By God, man," I said grimly. "If I had the facts I'd press this case."

"With whom?" he asked. "With Ghormley? With Admiral Kester? You tell your story. Then I'll tell mine. Can you imagine the look on Kester's face? There was an old, useless bulldozer. A couple of women blew it up as a last gesture of defiance. A woman ninety and a crazy girl. That story wouldn't stand up. Especially if I said how you came here to do a job and just couldn't make up your mind to knock down a few trees. It's too fantastic, commander. Kester would never believe that."

"I could understand your helping them, in peacetime," I said. "But this is war."

"That's when people need help, commander!" Fry said quietly. "Not when everything is going smoothly."

"It's all so damned futile," I said, looking away toward the stone stables. "Blowing up one bulldozer."

"Commander," Fry said with quiet passion. "Right now I can see it. Some sawed-off runt of a Jew in Dachau prison. Plotting his escape. Plotting to kill the guards. Working against the Nazis. One little Hebrew. You probably wouldn't invite him to your house for dinner. He smells. So futile. One little Jew. But by God, I'm for him. I'm on his side, commander." Fry punched me lightly on the shoulder. I hate being mauled.

"These people on Norfolk can't be dismissed lightly," he continued. "They're like the little Jew. Some smart scientists can come down here and prove they're all nuts. But do you believe it? We took down a map the other day, Teta and I. We figured where her grandsons are fighting. She can't remember whether they're grandsons or great-grandsons. All the same names. They're in Africa, Malaya, India, New Guinea, England. One was at Narvik. Crete. They may be stupid, but they know what they want. They knew what they wanted when they knocked that Nazi Bligh off his ship. They knew what they wanted when they turned their backs on the prison lands. Refused convict homes all ready waiting for them. The saints knew what they wanted when they went north as missionaries. I'm on their side. If blowing up a broken bulldozer helps keep the spirit alive, that's OK with me."

Tony submitted a vague report on the bulldozer. I endorsed it and sent it on to my own files in Noumea. I don't know where it is now. When Fry handed it to me he said, "Doesn't it seem horrible? The trees all down. We don't destroy one single memento of the prison days. Not one building do we touch. The airstrip runs twenty yards from the stone stables, but they're as safe as the Gallows Gate. We won't touch a rock of Bloody Bridge, where they buried the murdered guards, nor that obscene officers' bath. But the cathedral of the spirit, that we knock to hell."

"Fry," I said. "The Melanesian Mission's safe."

"That lousy thing!" Fry shouted. "A rustic English mission built on a savage island. A rotten, sentimental chapel with Burne-Jones' emaciated angels on an island like this. If you wanted to build an airstrip, why couldn't you have built it over there? Let the real chapel stand?"

"My father, Fletcher Christian," Teta said on my last night, when graders were working by flares to speed the airstrip. "He told us that God meant to build Norfolk this way. A man has to love the island to get here, because there are no harbors and no landings. My father said, 'A man has to fight his way ashore on this island!' That's what he was doing when the boat crashed on the rocks. Am I boring you with this, commander?"

An Officer and a Gentleman

IT was too bad that Ensign Bill Harbison joined the Navy. He was tall and slim. He wore his uniform superbly, had a small black mustache, a slow deep voice, and a fine manner. He had a sharp mind. In almost any group he was out-standing.

But in the Navy he was merely another ensign. And no matter how good he was, he would stay an ensign for about a year. Then he, and every other ensign, would be promoted. The ill-kempt, stupid, lazy officers would be promoted, just like him. It was too bad. In the Army Bill would surely have been a lieutenant-colonel. In the Air Corps he might even have become a full colonel.

Of course, Bill would never remotely consider shifting to the Army; that would be little better than being an enlisted man. He might bitch about the fact that he could progress no faster than farm boys from Iowa and plodding clerks from East St. Louis. But he loved the Navy.

Inwardly, Bill admitted that he was good. He had ample reason to think so. In college he had been a master athlete. Had played basketball in the Mountain States, where the game is rough and fast. His height and grace made him a star. In the six times he appeared in Madison Square Garden he outshone the competition. He was a crack tennis player, a bit of a golfer, a wizard at table tennis, and a good first baseman. In his studies he was also quite a man. Not an honor student, but he got far more A's than C's. He was a member of the best fraternity, a welcomed guest at the sororities, and a popular man among the younger set in Denver, Salt Lake, and Albuquerque. He was, in short, the kind of man the Navy sought. He was an officer and a gentleman.

In Albuquerque Harbison married the daughter of a wealthy family. She was a Vassar graduate and found Bill a fine combination of dashing Western manhood and modest cultural attainment. He at least knew what the *Atlantic Monthly* was. That was more than could be said for the rest of her suitors. And he could write the sweetest letters.

Bill was working for her father when the war started. Two evenings a week he ran a boys' club, where the roughest kids in Albuquerque met and worshipped the lithe athlete who taught them how to play basketball and keep out of trouble. When he volunteered for a commission, these tough kids collected more than $35 and bought Bill a watch.

Lenore was pleased when Bill got his commission. She thought he deserved to be more than an ensign. But she liked being able to say to her friends, "My husband, who is in the Navy . . ." or "Bill finds Navy life . . ." She had to admit that even though her brother did get a higher rank in the Army, it was rather nice to be a Navy wife.

Lenore followed Bill to Dartmouth, where he took his indoctrination in freezing weather, and then on to Princeton, where she knew dozens of other young Vassar graduates. Her father gave her money for rooms at the Princeton Inn. There she kept open house for hundreds of young married women whose husbands were taking the Princeton course in small boats and Diesel engines.

Lenore Harbison graced Princeton in the way that Bill had graced Denver and Albuquerque. She was doubly sorry to find Bill's stay at Princeton drawing to an end. It meant that her man was on his way to sea. It meant their wonderful days were over. Sadly she packed her things and waited in her sunny rooms for Bill to come back after the end-of-term review.

Bill hurried across the campus to take her to the train.

He was solemn, but he was handsome in his blue uniform and white-covered cap. The gold on his sleeve, the brilliant buttons, and the carefully tied black tie graced his thin, sharp body. Lenore doubted if ever again he would appear so handsome.

Bill was quiet when he kissed her. He liked her flattering comments on his appearance. He had his orders! They took him to the South Pacific! Together they traced out the long Navy sentences. "To whatever port ComSoPac may be located in."

"The sentence dangles!" Lenore said, half crying.

"I wonder what it means?" Bill said half aloud. "I wonder what kind of small boats they have out there?"

And so, like millions of others, Bill and Lenore trekked across continent to San Francisco, waited there in the steam and flurry of the grand old city, and went their separate ways. Lenore returned to an empty Albuquerque. Bill reported in at Noumea.

All the way across the Pacific he hoped that ComSoPac "had something good for him." He thought of what he might do in a staff job. Travel about and check up on units that were slacking off. Might be flag secretary to an admiral. Might get on some pretty important committee. Might help to draft orders and sit on flag courts-martial. There was practically nothing available to an ensign that Bill overlooked, and to play safe, he also considered jobs usually assigned to full lieutenants and even commanders.

He was not, therefore, prepared when he was assigned as recreation officer to a small unit in Efate! In fact, he was astonished and asked frankly if some mistake had not been made. "No, there's no mistake." He heard the words in complete disbelief. It was not until he went aboard an ugly Dutch freighter heading north from Noumea that he accepted his temporary fate.

The freighter was slow and dirty. It had a roll that kept him seasick. Harbison hated every minute of his trip to Efate. He was even more disgusted when he found that he was stationed, not at Vila, the capital town of the New Hebrides, but miles away. He was stuck off in a remote corner of a remote island with a useless job to do. Ensign Bill Harbison, USNR, had found his Navy niche. And he did not like it.

He could do his work with one hand tied behind his back. He had some enlisted men to keep happy. He had two assistants to help him. In addition he did some censoring and once a month he had to audit the accounts of the Wine Mess. After he got his job organized, he found that he had to work about half an hour a day and censor letters for about twenty minutes. The rest of the time was his own.

Landbased Aircraft Repair Unit Eight, his unit was called. In Navy style it was LARU-8. Enlisted men knew it as URIN-8. It had no clearcut duties, no job. It was waiting. One of Bill's friends ran a crash boat, in case an airplane should go down at sea. Another sat for hours each day in a tower, in case an airplane should need to establish radio communication. Another officer with eighty men waited in case certain types of planes should land and need overhaul. A friend waited with another eighty men to service another kind of plane, in case it should land. A doctor was present in case sickness should break out. A skipper and his exec kept things on an even keel and filled out reports that everything was in readiness, in case . . .

At the end of three weeks Harbison applied for transfer. "To what?" his skipper, a fat, bald, easy-going duck hunter from Louisiana asked.

"Some activity that needs a man like me," Harbison said frankly.

"What can you do?" the skipper asked.

"Small boats. Landing craft. Anything."

The skipper looked at the handsome young man before him. "Better relax, son!" he said. "You're doing a fine job here. Boys all like you. Better relax!"

"But I came out here to fight a war, sir!" Bill insisted. He wasn't afraid to press a point with the Old Man. The skipper was mighty easygoing.

"You'll never get anywhere in the Navy that way, son," the Old Man said quietly. "Most young men find you get along much better taking things as they come. If they want you to pilot a battleship into Truk, they'll come and get you!" The Old Man chuckled to himself. "They'll know right where you are! As a matter of fact, Bill, you'll be right here on Efate! Taking care of LARU-8."

Such manner of doing business appalled Harbison. Again in five weeks he applied for transfer, and again he was advised to take it easy. "You can write out the letter if you wish," the Old Man suggested. "But I'll tell you frankly what I'll do. I'll write at the bottom, 'First Endorsement: Forwarded but not approved.' Don't you see that we can't have every young feller deciding what he can do and can't do? You're needed where you are. You're a good influence in LARU-8. Everything's going along smoothly. Now don't upset the apple cart. By the way, you ought to come hunting with me one of these days. We're going up to Vanicoro!"

But Bill had no taste for hunting. And especially he had no taste for the Old Man. As a matter of fact in all the complement of his unit, officers and enlisted men alike, he found no one with whom he could be truly congenial. Day after day he read the stupid letters of his men and listened to the stupid conversations of his fellow officers. He got so that he dreaded the pile of letters that appeared on his desk each morning:

Dear Bessie,
Just like you said your getting fat but I dont mind because if your fat there will be more of you to love. Goodness nos somebody must be getting the food god nos we aint.

He could shuffle through a dozen of them and not find one intelligent letter. Of course, when he did find one, he ignored it and refused to think, "Here is a human being like me. He thinks and feels and hates to be here. He reacts the way I do. Strange, he must be a lot like me."

Bill never saw human dignity in the letters he read. They all fell into the slightly ridiculous, largely naïve classification:

Dear Mom,
You tell Joe that if he wants to go through with it and join the Navy he had better get used to handling his temper cause the first time he lets go at a chief or an officer hes going to learn what for and it aint going to be like flying off the handle at me because in this mans Navy they play for keeps. You tell Joe that and it will save him a lot of trouble.

The officers were no better. The crash boat skipper was a moron. Thank heavens no pilot lost at sea had to depend on him! The operations officer came from some hick town in Kentucky, and the engineering officer was an apple-knocker from upstate New York. Only Dr. Benoway was of any interest, and he was largely ineffectual. Harbison thought of Benoway as a mild-mannered, unsuccessful small town doctor who had joined the Navy as the easy way out of financial difficulties. "Probably makes more now than he ever did before!" Bill reasoned.

If it were not for sports Bill might have lost his sanity. But on the diamond or basketball court he was superb. Enlisted men loved to watch him play or to play with him. They put two men on him in basketball, and still he scored almost at will. They played on an open concrete court which Bill helped them to build. Even on its rough surface Bill could dribble and pivot so easily that he got away for one basket after another. In a way, it pleased the men to see him score against their own team mates. "Boy," they would write home. "Have we got a smoothie on our staff? He was All-American and set Long Island U on its ear last year in the Garden!"

Unlike most naval officers in the South Pacific, Bill kept in fine condition. There was no fat on his stomach muscles. He kicked a football half an hour a day, played an hour of basketball, went swimming for two hours in the morning, and usually found time for some badminton in the afternoon. But it was volleyball that captured his enthusiasm!

At first Harbison ridiculed the game. Wouldn't play it. But that was before he was inveigled into a match against the old hands. He played on a green team. Against him were the Old Man and Benoway plus four other officers. Bill smashed the round ball furiously, but he found to his surprise that the fat Old Man usually popped it into the air right where Dr. Benoway could tap it out of reach. This went on all afternoon, and Bill said to himself, "Say, there's something to this game!"

From then on he studied it in earnest. He found a place on the Old Man's team. He played on one side of the skipper and Benoway played on the other. Patiently and with great skill the Old Man would push the ball high and near the net. Bill would smash it for a point. He thought he was getting pretty good until one day the Old Man couldn't play. A stranger took his place, and that afternoon Bill missed most of his shots. He thought at first he was off his game. Then he realized with astonishment that the Old Man was unbelievably good as a "setter-upper." From then on he, Benoway, and the Old Man formed an invincible team. "Have we got a fine volleyball team?" the men wrote home. "Usually we play the officers, and mostly they win. But when we get a game with some other team, we have a mixed team. We haven't lost yet!"

Shortly after Bill learned to play volleyball, he made junior grade lieutenant, automatically. He was chagrined at the promotion, especially when he read in a letter from home that Lenore's brother Eddie, who had joined the Army, was already a captain! The news made Bill restless. He wanted to be doing something. There was great activity in the air. Things were happening in the world, and he was sitting on Efate, sunning himself, becoming a volleyball champion.

Tormented by the inchoate drives of a healthy young man who has left a beautiful wife at home, Bill went impatiently to the Old Man. "Won't you reconsider now?" he asked. "I'd like to get farther north."

"But Bill, we need you here," the skipper replied. "If you went, we'd only have to find somebody else. Our unit specifies a recreation officer. We'd have to have a replacement, and where would we find one as good? Don't you see, Bill? You want to break up a smooth team. And what better job would you get? We leave you to yourself. You're your own boss. And you have everybody's respect. I can't let you go. It would only mess us up!"

From then on Bill Harbison started to relax in earnest. He missed breakfast because he wanted to stay slim. Appearing at his recreation shack about nine o'clock he would eat a papaya with a bit of lime juice. His admiring assistants supplied them from the near-by jungle. By ten he was through with censoring and ordinary routine. He would then have a catch with any men who might be around. At ten-thirty he would head for the beach four miles away, and there he would lie in the sun, perhaps swim a while, perhaps dive with the deep-sea mask his men had made him. At eleven-thirty he would return to his hut, shower, rub his feet with talcum, and lie on his sack until twelve-thirty. After lunch he would sleep until two, when he might play some badminton or read. At four sharp he would appear at the volleyball court and warm up for the afternoon game. In the evenings he would attend the movies and after that have a beer in the Officers' Club. He usually went to bed at ten o'clock.

Each week he read *Time, Life,* the *Denver Post,* and at least two good books. He listened to news broadcasts four times a day from Australia on a radio set his men had built for him, and once or twice a week he tried to get Tokyo Rose, whom he found most amusing. He wrote a long letter to his wife every other day, and received one from her every day.

Bill's main contributions to LARU-8 were his splendid personal appearance, which everyone envied and some tried to copy, his neatness and bearing as an officer, and the fact that he found a French plantation owner who would butcher steers at regular intervals. Thanks to Bill, his fellow officers ate some of the finest food in the South Pacific. They had fresh papaya, those excellent pepsin melons, fresh limes and lemons, fresh oranges, fresh pineapple, fresh corn on the cob, and steak at least once a week. As a matter of principle Bill insisted that the Officers' Mess must never have steak more than twice before the enlisted men had it once. They got the tougher cuts, it was true, but a steer gave only so many filets.

In nine more months Bill would be a full lieutenant. In ten more months he would be eligible to return to the States. Everything would have turned out all right for Bill if a slight accident hadn't intervened. Nurses came to Efate!

They came late one afternoon, on the other side of the island. They were Navy nurses and were attached to a hospital that was temporarily established on Efate. They arrived with inadequate provisions and among the would-be gallants on the island a great rush developed as to who would help them first and most. An Army unit provided cots and blankets. One of the airfields found a refrigerator. Eight electric fans, valuable as rubies, were given the nurses outright as a gift. But Bill Harbison topped them all. He got a small truck, butchered a steer, got twelve bushels of fresh vegetables and set out for the hospital!

He drove up to the locked gate of the nurses' quarters and started to shout. "Here's the butcher boy! Come and get it!" From their windows the nurses looked down at the strange sight below. "Isn't he cute?" several of them whispered to one another.

"Here it is, girls!" Bill shouted, and soon his truck was surrounded by the nurses. They were hungry. Their stores had not yet been unpacked. They had been living on meager rations.

"Where's the kitchen?" he cried. Suddenly, after all the indifferent months on Efate, he felt good. He was smiling and almost excited. The girls led him off to a big, empty wooden structure that would one day be the mess hall.

"Light up the stoves!" he cried merrily. "We'll have a steak fry right here. See if you have any salt." The nurses made a quick survey and provided salt, a few onions, some bread, some potatoes and a surly mess attendant.

"You can't fool around in here," he whined.

"The lieutenant brought us some food!" one of the older nurses said.

"He ain't got no right in here," the attendant replied.

"Look, Oscar!" Harbison said. Some girls giggled. "How do you suppose I could start that fire? 'Cause listen, Oscar. If I get it started, you get a steak!"

The attendant snarled something. He was a thin, small man and disliked everybody." Mess hall won't be opened for two more days," he said. "And you better quit fooling around here, too." He stood defiantly by the stoves as he spoke.

"All right, Oscar!" Harbison cried. "You keep the stoves! We'll keep the steaks. Grab some of this stuff, girls!" With that he started throwing pots and pans to nurses who caught them. "We'll have a barbecue outside!" he announced.

"You'll get into trouble for this," the attendant said dolefully.

"It's our funeral!" Harbison replied. All his lethargy was gone. Here was something to do, and it was fun! He led the nurses out of the forbidden mess hall and into the edge of the jungle beneath some large trees. Acting as general manager, he directed them to build a fire and cut long sticks. Then, with some rocks, he built several grills, and before long steaks and onions and dehydrated potatoes were cooking. Bill showed the girls where to find papayas and how to select the ripe ones. Soon the smell of sizzling steaks, expertly cut by Harbison, filled the air. A fat doctor, catching a whiff of the delectable odor, waddled out to see what was going on. Pretty soon another followed, and before long a collection of doctors and nurses stood around the four fires.

Harbison acted as toastmaster, chef, and fireman. He was a delightful man for such an affair, and he bore himself with distinction. The steaks were good. One doctor had three. Bill ate sparingly of one choice filet. A young nurse prepared it for him, and he thanked her graciously.

There were, among the nurses, several attractive girls. They looked lovelier, perhaps, than they were, for Bill had seen no white women for some time. They were witty and neat, two wonderful attributes for any girl; and they were exotic, standing as they did at the very edge of the jungle. Bill watched them as they ate. Some wore slacks becomingly; others wore seersucker dresses, and one or two wore mixed clothes. Three were in white uniform, for they had official duties. Bill particularly liked the manner in which many of the girls wore bandanas to control their hair. They looked doubly colorful against the dull green of the jungle.

It is probable that several of the young nurses would have enjoyed knowing Bill Harbison. But Bill was already married and had no wish to set up illicit amours of any kind on the side. He smiled at the girls, showed courtesies to the women, and was the very spirit of a naval officer to all. When the party was over, he helped pack the remaining steaks in the ice box. As he drove off, the nurses clustered about his truck and thanked him again. Bill smiled at everyone, waved his hand out the side and started back over the hill to his camp. "He was nice," one of the nurses said to another. "Not like those Army men. They bring you a fan or something and think it's an introduction to spend the night."

When the hospital was established Bill became a frequent visitor. He would bring the nurses things, take them swimming in large groups, show them how to build equipment they needed, and introduce them to his circle of acquaintances. He became a familiar sight on the hospital grounds, but never in the manner of other officers who came, gaped at the pretty nurses, and started a flirtation immediately. Harbison, it might be said, flirted with the entire hospital staff. He never told any of the girls that he was married, but he conducted himself as if he were. That made him doubly intriguing.

In time Bill naturally gravitated toward two or three nurses in particular, and after the first month of mass gallantry he had selected for himself one nurse to whom he paid special attention. It was she who first ate at Bill's mess; it was she who accompanied him on the boat trip to Vanicoro.

She was, it might have seemed, the least likely of all candidates for the honor. Her name was Dinah Culbert, a woman about 42 years old, from some nondescript place in Indiana. She was taller than the average nurse, quiet, not good looking. She had minor intellectual pretensions, and she worshipped Bill. Thus, in one deft maneuver, Bill accomplished what would have eluded many a lesser man. He had a feminine cheering section without danger of emotional complications.

No one can say what the precise arrangement was between Bill Harbison and Dinah Culbert. Two good looking young nurses who would have enjoyed going places with Bill were sure it meant he was a pansy. Three shrewd gals on Wing Three got half the diagnosis correct: He's got a mother-complex and will probably never get married. One little fluff who was soon sent back to the States said, "I don't care what's wrong with him. I think he's cute!"

There was much for an officer and a nurse to do on Efate. There were boat trips to near-by islands, trips inland toward the volcanoes of Vanicoro, pig roasts, fishing for tuna and barracuda, visits to native villages, work in carpentry shops, and swimming. Sometimes in the evening there were informal dances, and every night there was some officers' club to visit for light conversation and cokes, or beer, or whiskey. But most of all, over your entire life there hung the great Pacific tropics. At night you would be aimlessly driving home and suddenly, around a bend you would come upon a vista of the ocean, framed in palm trees, under a moon so large and brilliant that the night seemèd day! Or again, driving along the shore your jeep would reach a point where ocean spray spumed across the road and engulfed you in a million rainbows. Or hiking into the jungles for ivory nuts you might meet a naked native with his naked wives and children, walking somewhere, going to do some unimportant thing. The tropics never left you, and in time you accustomed yourself to them. They were a vast relaxation, nature growing free and wild. An officer and a nurse in such surroundings usually fell in love.

There was one nurse, for example, who was escorted everywhere by a weak-chinned naval ensign. She did not like him, but he was a kindly young man. One night driving home from a dance he unexpectedly turned a bend in the road and there before them, across the ocean, the volcanoes on Vanicoro were in eruption! Great lights played from the jagged cones, and pillars of ashen cloud spiraled into the darkness. The nurse had never seen anything so magnificent, and on the impulse of the moment put her head on the ensign's shoulder. He kissed her. "It was strange," she said afterward.

"No chin. That's a funny kiss." She never went with the young ensign again.

It is not certain whether Bill and Dinah ever saw the volcanoes in eruption. It is not even certain that they ever kissed. There was some speculation on this point, but no one knew anything definitely. Had not Lenore Harbison's brother Eddie been promoted to a major in the Army, Bill and Dinah might have gone on for many more months in their fine aimless manner.

But when Bill heard that Eddie, who was his own age, had been jumped to a major, he could not restrain himself. "Why is it," he asked himself over and over again, "that a guy can go up so fast in one service and not in another? Eddie's a good boy, but he hasn't half my stuff. This is a damned raw deal!" He brooded over the situation for several days and called Dinah to tell her he wouldn't be able to take her to the beach. He stayed in his sack for the better part of two days, reading *War and Peace*. He didn't even get up for his meals. Just ambled down to the shack and ate some papayas and canned soup his men provided. He played no volleyball and did not go swimming. He was disgusted with everything. He wrote to his wife every day for six days and tried to get the poison out of his system. But when he was done two facts remained: He was getting nowhere, and he had given up a good life in Albuquerque to do so.

The thought of Dinah Culbert infuriated him. He had been playing a game, that was all. He closed *War and Peace,* which he could not follow anyway, and thought of good old Aunt Dinah. He was ashamed of himself, a young man of twenty-three escorting a woman of forty. From that moment in his own mind he never referred to Dinah as anything but Grandmom. He even used the word aloud once or twice, and soon it was common gossip at the hospital that Bill Harbison, the fine naval lieutenant, had joked about Aunt Dinah as his Grandmom.

Otherwise Bill let Dinah down easily. He took her to lunch at the restaurant in Vila once more, took her to dinner at his own mess, had drinks with her at the hospital club, and that was all. Dinah was not dismayed. When rumor first reached her that he had called her his grandmother, there was a sharp pang of unbelief. Then she laughed, right heartily. She was a nurse and no dumb cluck. She thought she knew pretty well what Bill's trouble was. "I pity the next girl he goes with," she said to herself.

The next girl was Nellie Forbush. She was a slender, pretty nurse of twenty-two. She came from a small town in Arkansas and loved being in the Navy. Never in a hundred years would Bill Harbison have noticed her in the States. She wouldn't have moved in his crowd at all. In Denver she would have lived somewhere in the indiscriminate northern part of the city, by the viaduct. In Albuquerque she would have lived near the Mexican quarter. But on the island of Efate where white women were the exception and pretty white women rarities, Nellie Forbush was a queen. She suffered no social distinctions.

Military custom regarding nurses is most irrational. They are made officers and therefore not permitted to associate with enlisted men. This means that they must find their social life among other officers. But most male officers are married, especially in the medical corps. And most unmarried officers are from social levels into which nurses from small towns do not normally marry. As a result of this involved social system, military nurses frequently have unhappy emotional experiences. Cut off by law from fraternizing with those men who would like to marry them and who would have married them in civilian life, they find their friendships restricted to men who are surprisingly often married or who are social snobs.

Bill Harbison did not stop to formulate the above syllogism when he started going with Nellie Forbush. Yet in his mind he had the conclusion well formulated. Put into words it began, "What the hell! If I'm going to waste three years of my life . . ." It went on from there to a logical end. Nellie Forbush just happened to be around when the decision was reached.

Bill was lovely to her. He took her swimming and gasped when he saw her for the first time in a swimming suit. She wore a gingham halter and a pair of tight trunks with only a suggestion of a flared ballet skirt. She did not bathe. She dived into the ocean and swam with long easy strokes to the raft. Perched upon the boards, she shook her bobbed hair free of water and laughed. "Some difference," Bill thought. "Not much like Grandmom!"

Nor was she much like Grandmóm driving home along the narrow road through the coconut plantation. It was still daylight, but shadows were so thick it seemed like evening. Bill pulled the jeep to the side of the road and kissed his beautiful nurse. It was no chivalrous kiss. It was a kiss born of seeing her the most lovely person on the beach. It was a long, helpless kiss, and both officers found it thrilling and delicious.

After that there were many more swims and even more kisses. Bill wasn't around LARU-8 much after that. If Nellie had any free time, he was sure to be somewhere with her. Since he ate no breakfast he might be absent from meals several days in a row. His men found no difficulty in doing the work he was supposed to do. Late at night he would censor his mail, so that fellow officers came to expect a thin light from his bunk at two or three in the morning. He rarely rose from his sack before ten. He was still slim, browner than before, and fastidious in dress. He played no basketball, and volleyball only occasionally. Long hours at the beach kept him in shape.

Twice after he started going with Nellie he went to his skipper and asked for a transfer to some unit farther north. The first time the Old Man simply said no! On Bill's second visit, however, the skipper asked him to sit down. "I know how you feel, Bill," the chubby, jovial Old Man said. "You want to get out and win the war. We all do, and maybe we'll get a chance . . . later. There's some talk that LARU-8 may be in on the next big strike. But the point is this, Bill. Even if LARU-8 sits right here for the duration, that's not your problem. You're in the Navy now. You'll be called to action when you're needed." The Old Man looked hard at Bill. "If you don't mind my butting in, young feller, don't mix your Navy life and your private life. Don't expect to use LARU-8 to help you settle personal problems!" He half smiled at Bill and returned to fixing his fishing rod.

It was after this second refusal that Bill scared Nurse Forbush. They were driving home from a wienie roast on the beach and he took a back road through the coconuts. Nellie was not unhappy about this, for she had grown to love the handsome lieutenant. She was surprised, however, when he insisted that she leave the jeep. He had a blanket with him, and before Nellie knew what had happened, she found herself wrestling with him on the ground. She succeeded in pushing him away, but his renewed attempt was more successful. He ripped her dress and brassiere.

"Bill!" she cried softly. "Bill! Stop! What's the matter?"

He paid no attention to her entreaties but kept clawing at her underwear. In desperation she grabbed a coconut and swung it with all her strength against his head. She did not knock him out, but she did stun him. He staggered around for a minute and then realized what had happened. He came back to where Nellie was mending her clothing with ill-tied knots.

She was neither crying nor nervously hysterical. She was merely shocked beyond words. Bill stood silently by until she was ready to leave. Then he helped her to her feet and picked up the blanket.

"We'd better go," she said.

They drove home in silence. Bill tried to say something once or twice but couldn't. Besides, his head ached where the coconut had crashed. At the armed gate to the nurses' quarters Bill said a stiff goodnight. "I'm sorry," he added. Nellie said nothing, and disappeared between the guns of the two guards.

Nellie tried to go to sleep in the long corridor used as a dormitory by the younger nurses. She couldn't. While she lay there wondering what she ought to do, she saw a light coming from Dinah Culbert's room. Instinctively, and without much forethought, Nellie went in to see Dinah.

"Hello!" the latter said pleasantly. "Been up late?"

"Yes," Nellie answered. "I see you are, too."

"It is rather late for me," Dinah replied. "I'm trying to plough through War and Peace."

"Lots of people read that book out here," Nellie said naïvely.

"Yes," Dinah said sweetly. "At least they start it. I'm going to be the one that finishes it."

"Dinah," Nellie said hesitatingly. "May I bother you for a minute?"

"Of course, my dear. What is it?"

"It's about Bill," Nellie said. "Bill Harbison."

"What about Bill?" Dinah asked, pulling her long lounging gown about her knees.

"I'm in love with him, Dinah. Very much."

"That's nothing to worry about, Nellie. Bill's a fine young man."

"I wondered if you could help me, Dinah?"

The older woman instinctively went on the defensive. "I

wonder what's happened," she thought. Aloud she said, "Of course, my dear. What's up?"

"Is Bill married?"

Dinah thought, "It is serious, isn't it?" She answered, "I don't know, Nellie."

"I thought you might," the lovely girl in the soft night-gown replied.

"No, Nellie," the older woman explained. "You see, when I went with Bill, whether or not he was married was of no consequence. How could it possibly have interested me? I never deluded myself with even the faintest suspicion that we might fall in love." She paused and then added, "Of course, if you really want to know all you have to do is call his commanding officer."

"Oh, I couldn't do that!" Nellie gasped.

Dinah smiled and thought, "You couldn't do that! No! But you could take a chance on your whole life. That's all right! Girls, girls! No wonder I never got married. I guess God made a mistake and gave me a brain!"

Nellie persisted. "Dinah?" she asked. "What do you think?"

"Darling, I told you. I don't think anything. But I will tell you something that I thought a couple of months ago. You might not like it, but here it is. When Bill stopped taking me places he was in a foul mood. I said to myself, 'God help the next girl he goes with.' If I'm not mistaken, you're that next girl."

"What did you mean?" Nellie asked, half shuddering at Dinah's cold statements.

"I don't know, Nellie. I think it was something like this. Bill Harbison went with me only to fill a need in himself. It was unnatural, and I knew it. But it was fun. I now go with several older men whom I met through Bill. I bear him no grudges at all. But I never deceived myself for a moment that Bill was the handsome, winsome, gallant boy he played at being. He's just like you and me, Nellie, a huge bundle of neurosis which this climate makes worse."

"I know that, Dinah," Nellie said. "I feel it in myself, sometimes. But what did you mean about God helping me? That's what I've got to know."

"I meant that it was just as unnatural for Bill to go with you as it was for him to go with me. Bill is a snob. Nellie, you may not like this, but it would be as impossible for Bill to marry you as it would be for him to marry me. That's why it doesn't make any difference whether or not he's married. But if you want to know, I can make some discreet inquiries among my friends. Although, of course, it wouldn't be exactly easy for me to do so." She smiled.

"I know what you mean, Dinah. I think I know all of what you mean. Thanks for talking." The handsomely built young girl folded her nightgown about her thin waist and left. Dinah watched her go.

"She thinks I'm jealous of her," the older woman mused. "I wonder what happened tonight? Probably tried to rape her." She sighed, from what cause she did not know, and returned to *War and Peace*.

Next morning Bill was at the hospital. Before she went to sleep Nellie had decided not to see him if he called, but when she looked down from her window and saw him standing penitently by his jeep, she hurried down. They went for a drive and Bill apologized. "Seeing you so beautiful on the beach made me lose my head," he said.

She was on the point of asking him if he were married. But she didn't. All over the world at that moment men torn from their homes were meeting strange girls and falling in love with them. On every girl's tongue was the question she almost never asked: "Are you married?" At first she reasoned, "Well, we're not in love, so it doesn't matter." Later she reasoned, "We love one another, so it doesn't really matter." In strange ways they discovered that their lovers were married men, or in jubilation they found they were not. But rarely did they ask the simple question: "Are you married?" For they knew that most men would tell them the truth, and they did not wish to know the truth.

So Nellie did not ask. Instead, she did a very foolish thing. She told him about Charlie Benedict back home who worked in a store and wanted to marry her. He was 4-F and miserable about it. He wrote her the funniest letters. Poor Charlie! Instead of the plan's working as she thought it might, Bill said nothing about marriage. Instead he pulled her to him and almost crushed her with kisses. "My darling!" he whispered. Then, in a delirium of love, he calmly proceeded to do what twelve short hours before she had hit him over the head with a coconut for doing. He had her partly undressed when a native unexpectedly came along the unused road.

With great relief and yet with some regrets, Nellie recovered her determination and hastily dressed. She sat in the jeep with her head in her hands. Her short hair, attractive and brown, fell in cascades over her fingers. Her world was in turmoil. Then, suddenly she knew what she should do. The sunlight falling between the interstices of the leaves helped her make up her mind.

"Bill," she said simply. "I love you very much. Desperately. You know that. I want you, and I'm not afraid of you."

Harbison leaned back against his jeep seat, his eyes filled with the lovely girl. He hardly knew what was happening, the blood was pounding in his ears so strongly. His hand reached for her arm, bare knee and rested there a moment. Then she pushed it away. She put her own hand on his cheek.

"Bill," she asked directly. "Do you love me?" In reply he clutched her to him in a long kiss and started fumbling at her clothes again.

"Bill," she insisted. "Tell me. Is there any chance that we might one day get married? When the war's over?"

The words knocked Bill's head back. The damned girl was proposing to him! What was happening here? He swallowed hard and looked at her, a common little girl from some hick town. What did she think was going on? This was a furious turn of events!

Nellie saw that Bill was dumbfounded. "I'm sorry, Bill," she said, keeping her hand against his cheek. In a torment of conflicting passions Bill thought of that cool hand, the soft breasts, the waiting knees. Now the sunlight was on him, too, and he scarcely knew what to do. He knew Nellie was his for the asking, but damn it all she was nothing but a little country girl. Hell, he wouldn't look at her twice in the States.

"And besides," he said to himself with great resolution. "After all I am an officer!" That decided it. He pushed Nellie's hand away from his cheek.

"I'm married," he said. "I thought you knew."

Nellie heard the words like hammers upon her brain. "I'm married!" That was it, but so much was ended with those words. She looked at Bill and in her heart thanked him for telling her the truth. She leaned over and kissed him. "Thanks, Bill," she said. "Now let's go back."

On his way home from the hospital Lt. (jg) Bill Harbison, USNR, who would soon be a full lieutenant if he didn't drop dead, felt pretty pleased with himself. The silly girl was obviously in love with him, and he had turned her down. He could have had her for a whistle. He slapped himself in the stomach. He was disturbed. He could feel a thin line of fat attacking him. "All this party business and nurses," he said as the jeep bounced along. "Soft living. I better get back to kicking that football in the afternoon."

The Cave

IN those fateful days of 1942 when the Navy held on to Guadalcanal by faith rather than by reason, there was a PT Boat detachment stationed on near-by Tulagi. It was my fortune to be attached to this squadron during the weeks when PT Boats were used as destroyers and destroyers were used as battleships. I was merely doing paper work for Admiral Kester, but the urgency of our entire position in the Solomons was so great that I also served as mess officer, complaints officer, and errand boy for Lt. Comdr. Charlesworth, the Annapolis skipper.

The job at Charlesworth's squadron was to intercept anything that came down The Slot. Barges, destroyers, cruisers, or battleships. The PT's went out against them all. The Japs sent something down every night to reinforce their men on Guadal. The PT's fought every night. For several weeks, terrible, crushing weeks of defeat, the defenses of Guadalcanal rested upon the PT's. And upon Guadal rested our entire position in the South Pacific.

I have become damned sick and tired of the eyewash written about PT Boats. I'm not going to add to that foolish legend. They were rotten, tricky little craft for the immense jobs they were supposed to do. They were improvised, often unseaworthy, desperate little boats. They shook the stomachs out of many men who rode them, made physical wrecks of others for other reasons. They had no defensive armor. In many instances they were suicide boats. In others they were like human torpedoes. It was a disgrace, a damned disgrace that a naval nation like America should have had to rely upon them.

Yet I can understand their popularity. It was strictly newspaper stuff. A great nation was being pushed around the Atlantic by German submarines. And mauled in the Pacific by a powerful Jap fleet. Its planes were rust on Hickam Field and Clark Field. Its carriers were on the bottom. Americans were desperate. And then some wizard with words went to work on the PT Boat. Pretty soon everybody who had never seen a real Jap ship spitting fire got the idea our wonderful little PT's were slugging it out with Jap battleships. Always of the Kongo Class.

Well, that crowd I served with on Tulagi in 1942 knew different. So far as I ever heard, none of my gang even sank a Jap destroyer. It was just dirty work, thumping, hammering, kidney-wrecking work. Even for strong tough guys from Montana it was rugged living.

The day I started my duty with the PT Boats we were losing the battle of Guadalcanal. Two American warships were sunk north of Savo that night. Eight of our planes were shot down over Guadal, and at least fifteen Jap barges reached Cape Esperance with fresh troops. Toward morning we were bombed both at Tulagi and at Purvis Bay. A concentration of Bettys. At dawn a grim bunch of men rose to survey the wreckage along the shore.

Lt. Comdr. Charlesworth met me at the pier. A stocky, chunky, rugged fellow from Butte, Montana. Stood about five feet nine. Had been an athlete in his day. I found him terribly prosaic, almost dull. He was unsure of himself around other officers, but he was a devil in a PT Boat. Didn't know what fear was. Would take his tub anywhere, against any odds. He won three medals for bravery beyond the call of duty. Yet he was totally modest. He had only one ambition: to be the best possible naval officer. Annapolis could be proud of Charlesworth. We were.

"We got by again," he said as we studied the wreckage of the night before. "Any damage to the gasoline on Gavutu?"

"None," his exec replied.

"Looks like some bombs might have hit right there beside that buoy."

"No, sir. One of the PT's hit that last night. Tying up."

Charlesworth shook his head. "How do they do it?" he asked. "They can hit anything but a Jap barge."

"Sir!" an enlisted man called out from the path almost directly above us on the hillside. "V.I.P. coming ashore!"

"Where?" Charlesworth cried. As an Annapolis man he was terribly attentive when any V.I.P.'s were about. He had long since learned that half his Navy job was to fight Japs. The other half was to please "very important persons" when they chanced to notice him. Like all Annapolis men, he knew that a smile from a V.I.P. was worth a direct hit on a cruiser.

"In that little craft!" the man above us cried. Probably someone aboard the small craft had blinkered to the signal tower. Charlesworth straightened his collar, hitched his belt and gave orders to the men along the shore. "Stand clear and give a snappy salute."

But we were not prepared for what came ashore. It was Tony Fry! He was wearing shorts, only one collar insigne, and a little go-to-hell cap. He grinned at me as he threw his long legs over the side of the boat. "Hello, there!" he said. Extending a sweaty hand to Charlesworth he puffed, "You must be the skipper. Y'get hit last night?"

"No, sir," Charlesworth said stiffly. "I don't believe I know you, sir."

"Name's Fry. Tony Fry. Lieutenant. Just got promoted. They only had one pair of bars, so I'm a little lopsided." He flicked his empty collar point. It was damp. "Holy cow! It's hot over here!"

"What brings you over?" Charlesworth asked.

"Well, sir. It's secret business for the admiral. Nothin' much, of course. You'll get the word about as soon as I do, commander," Fry said. "I hear you have a cave somewhere up there?"

"Yes, we do," Charlesworth said. "Right over those trees." Above us we could see the entrance to the cave Fry sought. Into the highest hill a retreat, shaped like a U, had been dug. One entrance overlooked the harbor and Purvis Bay, where our big ships were hidden. The other entrance, which we could not see, led to a small plateau with a good view of Guadal and Savo, that tragic island. Beyond Savo lay

The Slot, the island-studded passage leading to Bougainville, Rabaul, Truk, and Kuralei.

"I understand the cave's about ten feet high," Tony mused.

"That's about right," Charlesworth agreed.

"Just what we want," Tony replied. He motioned to some men who were carrying gear in black boxes. "Let's go, gang!" he called.

Charlesworth led the way. With stocky steps he guided us along a winding path that climbed steeply from the PT anchorage where Fry had landed. Hibiscus, planted by the wife of some British official years ago, bloomed and made the land as lovely as the bay below.

"Let's rest a minute!" Fry panted, the sweat pouring from his face.

"It's a bit of a climb," Charlesworth replied, not even breathing hard.

"Splendid place, this," Fry said as he surveyed the waters leading to Purvis Bay. "Always depend upon the British to cook up fine quarters. We could learn something from them. Must have been great here in the old days."

As we recovered our breath Charlesworth pointed to several small islands in the bay. "That's where the Marines came ashore. A rotten fight. Those ruins used to be a girl's school. Native children from all over the islands came here." I noticed that he spoke in rather stilted sentences, like a Montana farmer not quite certain of his new-found culture.

"It'll be a nice view from the cave," Fry said. "Well, I'm ready again."

We found the cave a cool, moist, dark retreat. In such a gothic place the medieval Japs naturally located their headquarters. With greater humor we Americans had our headquarters along the shore. We reserved the cave for Tony Fry.

For once he saw the quiet interior with its grand view over the waters he said, "This is for me." He turned to Charlesworth and remarked, "Now, commander, I want to be left alone in this cave. If I want any of you PT heroes in here I'll let you know."

Charlesworth, who was already irritated at having a mere lieutenant, a nobody and a reserve at that, listed as a V.I.P., snapped to attention. "Lieut. Fry," he began, "I'm the officer-in-charge . . ."

"All right, commander. All right," Fry said rapidly. "I'm going to give you all the deference due your rank. I know what the score is. But let's not have any of that Annapolis fol-de-rol. There's a war on."

Charlesworth nearly exploded. He was about to grab Fry by the arm and swing him around when Tony turned and grinned that delightfully silly smirk of his. Sunlight from the plateau leaped across his wet face. He grinned at Charlesworth and extended a long hand. "I'm new at this business, commander," he said. "You tell me what to do, and I'm gonna do it. I just don't want any of your eager beavers messing around. They tell me over at Guadal that you guys'd take on the whole fleet if Halsey would let you."

Charlesworth was astounded. He extended his hand in something of a daze. Tony grabbed it warmly. In doing so he engineered Charlesworth and me right out of the cave. "Men bringin' in the stuff," he explained.

This Fry was beyond description, a completely new type of naval officer. He didn't give a damn for anything or anybody. He was about thirty, unmarried. He had some money and although he loved the Navy and its fuddy ways, he ridiculed everything and everybody. He was completely oblivious to rank. Even admirals loved him for it. Nobody was ever quite certain what he was supposed to be doing. In time no one cared. The important thing was that he had unlimited resources for getting whiskey, which he consumed in great quantities. I've been told the Army wouldn't tolerate Fry a week.

We were several days finding out what he was doing on Tulagi. Late that afternoon, for example, we heard a clattering and banging in the cave. We looked up, and Tony had two enlisted men building him a flower box. That evening he was down in the garden of the old British residency digging up some flowers for his new home. A pair of Jap marauders came winging in to shoot the island up. Tony dived for a trench and raised a great howl.

"What's the matter with the air raid system?" he demanded that night at chow. "That's why I like the cave. It's safe! They'd have to lay a bomb in there with a spoon!"

It soon became apparent that Charlesworth and Fry would not get along. Tony delighted in making sly cracks at the "trade-school boys." Charlesworth, who worshipped the stones of Annapolis, had not the ready wit to retaliate. He took no pains to mask his feelings, however.

It was also apparent that Fry was rapidly becoming the

unofficial commanding officer of the PT base. Even Charlesworth noticed that wherever Tony propped his field boots, that spot was headquarters. That was the officers' club.

Settled back, Tony would pass his whiskey bottle and urge other men to talk. But if there was anything pompous, or heroic, or ultra-Annapolis in the conversation, Fry would mercilessly ridicule it and puncture the balloons. The PT captains delighted to invite him on their midnight missions.

"Me ride in those death traps? Ha, ha! Not me! I get paid to sit right here and think. That's all I'm in this man's Navy for. You don't get medals for what I do. But you do get back home!" Unashamedly he would voice the fears and cowardice that came close to the surface of all our lives. Men about to throw their wooden PT's at superior targets loved to hear Fry express their doubts. "Those sieves? Those kidney-wreckers? Holy cow! I'd sooner go to sea in a native canoe!"

But when the frail little craft warmed up, and you could hear Packard motors roaring through Tulagi, Tony would pull himself out of his chair in the cave, unkink a drunken knee, and amble off toward the water front. "Better see what the heroes are doing," he would say. Then, borrowing a revolver or picking up a carbine as he went, he would somehow or other get to where Charlesworth's PT was shoving off.

"Room for a passenger?" he would inquire.

"Come aboard, sir," Charlesworth would say primly, as if he were back at San Diego.

Enlisted men were especially glad to see Tony climb aboard. "He's lucky!" they whispered to one another. "Guys like him never get killed."

Tony, or God, brought the PT's luck one night. That was when Charlesworth got his second medal. His prowling squadron ran smack into some Jap AKA's south of Savo. Charlesworth was a little ahead of the other PT's when the Japs were sighted. Without waiting a moment he literally rushed into the formation, sank one and hung onto another, dodging shells, until his mates could close in for the kill.

Tony was on the bridge during the action. "You handle this tub right well, skipper," he said.

"It's a good boat," Charlesworth said. "This is a mighty good boat. A man ought to be willing to take this boat almost anywhere."

"You did!" Fry laughed.

In the bright morning, when Charlesworth led his PT's

roaring home through the risky channel between Tulagi and Florida, Tony lay sprawled out forward, watching the spray and the flying fish. "What a tub!" he grunted as he climbed ashore. "There must be an easier way to earn a living!"

And if one of the enlisted men from Charlesworth's PT sneaked up to the cave later in the day, Fry would shout at him, "Stay to hell out of here! If you want a shot of whiskey that bad, go down to my shack. But for God's sake don't let the commander see you. He'd eat my neck out." Whether you were an enlisted man or an officer, you could drink Fry's whiskey. Just as long as he had any.

We had almost given up guessing what Fry was doing when he woke Charlesworth and me one morning about five. "This is it!" he whispered.

He led us up to the cave but made us stand outside. In a moment an enlisted radio man, Lazars, appeared. "Any further word?" Fry asked.

"None, sir," Lazars said.

"Something big's up," Tony said in a low voice. We moved toward the cave. "No," Fry interrupted. "We had the boys rig a radio for you over in that quonset," he said. Dawn was breaking as he led us to a half-size quonset at the other side of the plateau. When we stepped inside the barren place Lazars started to tune a radio. He got only a faint whine. He kept twirling the dials. It was cool in the hut. The sun wasn't up yet.

"It may be some time," Fry said. The sun rose. The hut became humid. We began to sweat. We could hear the metal expanding in little crackles. New men always thought it was rain, but it was the sun. Then you knew it was going to be a hot day.

Lazars worked his dials back and forth with patient skill. "No signal yet," he reported. Fry walked up and down nervously. The sweat ran from his eyes and dropped upon his thin, bare knees. Finally he stopped and wiped the moisture from his face.

"I think this is it, Charlesworth," he said.

"What?" the commander asked.

"We sneaked a man ashore behind the Jap lines. Somewhere up north. He's going to try to contact us today. Imagine what we can do if he sends us the weather up there. News about the Jap ships! How'd you like to go out some night when you knew the Japs were coming down? Just where they were and how many. How would that be, eh?" Tony was excited.

Then there came a crackle, a faint crackling sound. It was different from the expansion of the burning roof. It was a radio signal! Fry put his finger to his lips.

From far away, from deep in the jungles near Jap sentries, came a human voice. It was clear, quiet, somewhat high-pitched. But it never rose to excitement. I was to hear that voice often, almost every day for two months. Like hundreds of Americans who went forth to fight aided by that voice, I can hear it now. It fills the room about me as it filled that sweating hut. It was always the same. Even on the last day it was free from nervousness. On this morning it said: "Good morning, Americans! This is your Remittance Man. I am speaking from the Upper Solomons. First the weather. There are rain clouds over Bougainville, the Treasuries, Choiseul, and New Georgia. I believe it will rain in this region from about 0900 to 1400. The afternoons will be clear. It is now 94 degrees. There are no indications of violent weather."

The lonely voice paused. In the radio shack we looked at one another. No one spoke. Lazars did not touch the dials. Then the voice resumed, still high, still precise and slow:

"Surface craft have been in considerable motion for the last two days. I think you may expect important attempts at reinforcement tonight. One battleship, four cruisers, a carrier, eight destroyers and four oilers have been seen in this region. They are heading, I presume, toward Kolombangara rendezvous. In addition not less than nineteen and possibly twenty-seven troop barges are definitely on their way south. When I saw them they were making approximately eleven knots and were headed right down The Slot. I judge they will pass Banika at 2000 tonight. Landing attempts could be made near Esperance any time after 0200 tomorrow morning. You will be glad to know that the barges appear to be escorted by heavy warships this time. The hunting should be good."

The speaker paused again. Charlesworth rubbed his chin and studied a map pasted on wallboard and hung from the sloping tin. No one spoke.

"And for you birdmen," the voice continued. "Four flights have set out for your territory. They are in rendezvous at present. North of Munda. I cannot see the types of planes at present. I judge them to be about forty bombers. Twenty fighters. If that proportion makes any sense. I'm not very good on aircraft. Ah, yes! This looks like a flight down from Kieta right above me. Perhaps you can hear the motors! Thirty or more fighter planes. Altitude ten thousand feet, but my distances are not too accurate. I'm rather new at this sort of thing, you know."

The Remittance Man paused and then for the first time gave his closing comment which later became a famous rallying cry in the South Pacific: "Cheerio, Americans. Good hunting, lads!"

As soon as the broadcast ended Charlesworth dashed from the quonset and started laying plans for that night's foray. At every subsequent broadcast it was the same way. No sooner would the Remittance Man finish speaking than Charlesworth would bound into action and move imaginary PT's all through the waters between Guadal and the Russells. For him the Remittance Man was an abstract, impersonal command to action.

But to Tony Fry the enigmatic voice from the jungle became an immense intellectual mystery. It began on this first morning. After Charlesworth had dashed down to the PT's Fry asked me, "What do you make of it?"

"Very clever intelligence," I replied.

"Holy cow!" he snorted. "I don't mean that! I mean this chap. This fellow up there in the jungles. Japs all around him. How can he do it?"

"He probably volunteered for it," I replied.

"Of course he did!" Fry agreed with some irritation. "But what I mean is, how does a guy get courage like that? I should think his imagination alone would drive him frantic."

"He's probably some old duffer's been out in the islands all his life."

"I know who he is," Fry said, kicking at pebbles as we walked over to the cave. "Chap named Anderson. Trader from Malaita. An Englishman. But why did he, of all the men out here, volunteer? How can he face that?" Tony gripped my arm. "A single man goes out against an island of Japs? Why?"

We didn't see Tony that day. He ate canned soup and beer in the cave. That night the PT's went out without him. They did all right, thanks to the Remittance Man. The Japs came down exactly as he said. Charlesworth slipped in and chopped them up. The black year of 1942, the terrible year was dying.

But as it died, hope was being born on Guadalcanal and Tulagi.

Next morning at 0700 all those who were not in sickbay getting wounds and burns from the night before patched up were in the steaming quonset. Promptly on time the Remittance Man spoke. Fry stood close to the radio listening to the high-pitched voice extend its cheery greeting: "Good morning, Americans! I have good news for you today. But first the weather." He told us about conditions over Bougainville, Choiseul, and New Georgia. Flying weather was excellent.

"In fact," he said, "flying looks so good that you shall probably have visitors. Very heavy concentrations of bombers overhead at 1100 this morning. If I can judge aircraft, not less than ninety bombers and fighters are getting ready for a strike this morning. Some are in the air ready to leave. They appear to be at 12,000 feet. Don't bet on that, though. I can't say I've learned to use the estimating devices too well yet. Let's say not less than 10,000. Some fighters have moved in from Bougainville. Look at them! Rolling about, doing loops and all sorts of crazy things. There they go! It's quite a circus. This will be a fine day. Cheerio, Americans! Good hunting!" The radio clicked. There was silence.

Immediately, Charlesworth called his men together. "They'll want some PT's for rescue work!" he snapped. "If that man is right, this may be a big day. A very big day. We'll put B Squadron out. Shove. And don't come home till you comb every shore about here. Pick them all up! Get them all!" He hurried his men down to the shore.

A phone jangled. It was headquarters. "Admiral Kester wants the PT's out for rescue," intelligence said.

"They've already left," I reported.

"This Remittance Man," Tony said when the others had gone. "Commander, where do you suppose he is?"

"I thought Bougainville," I said.

"No. I was studying a map. He's on some peak from which he can see Munda."

"Maybe you're right," I said. "He confuses his broadcasts nicely."

"Don't be surprised if he was on Sant' Ysabel all the time," Fry said.

But not then, nor at any other time, did he or any of us say what was in our minds: *How desperately the Japs must*

*be searching for that man! How fitful his sleep must be! How
he must peer into every black face he sees in the jungle,
wondering, "Is this my Judas?"*

Tony and I went out into the brilliant sunlight to watch
the miracle below us. From the unbroken shoreline of Tulagi
bits of green shrubbery pulled into the channel. Then camou-
flage was discarded. The PT's roared around the north end
of the island. Off toward Savo. The PT's were out again.

"I've been trying to find out something about the man,"
Tony continued. "Just a man named Anderson. Nobody
knows much about him. He came out here from England.
Does a little trading for Burns Philp. Went into hiding when
the Japs took Tulagi. Came over to Guadal and volunteered
for whatever duty was available. Medium-sized chap. You've
heard his voice."

At 1100 the first Jap plane came into view. It was a Zero
spinning wildly somewhere near the Russells. It flamed and
lurched into the sea. The battle was on!

For an hour and ten minutes the sky above Guadal and
Tulagi was a beautiful misery of streaming fire, retching
planes, and pyres flaming out of the sea. The Japanese broke
through. Nothing could stop them. We heard loud thunder
from Purvis Bay. Saw high fires on Guadal. Eight times Jap
fighters roared low over Tulagi. Killed two mechanics at the
garage. But still we watched the breathless spectacle overhead.

Yes, the Japs broke through that day. Some of them broke
through, that is. And if they had unlimited planes and
courage, they could break through whenever they wished.
But we grinned! God, we even laughed out loud. Because we
didn't think the Japs had planes to waste! Or pilots either.
And mark this! When Jap pilots plunged into the sea, The
Slot captured them and they were seen no more. But when
ours went down, PT Boats sped here and there to pick
them up.

So, we were happy that night. Not silly happy, you understand, because we lost a PT Boat to strafers. And we could
count. We knew how many Yank planes crashed and blew
up and dove into the sea. But nevertheless we were happy.
Even when Tony Fry came in slightly drunk and said, "That
guy up there in the jungles. How long can he keep going?
You radio men. How long would it take American equipment
to track down a broadcasting station?"

There was no reply. "How long?" Fry demanded.

"Two days. At the most."

"That's what I thought," he said.

Next morning at seven the Remittance Man was happy, too. "The Japanese Armada limped home," he reported in subdued exultation as if he knew that he had shared in the victory. "I myself saw seven planes go into the sea near here. I honestly believe that not more than forty got back. And now good news for one squadron. My little book tells me the plane with that funny nose is the P-40. One P-40 followed two crippled Jap bombers right into New Georgia waters. They were flying very low. He destroyed each one. Then the Nips jumped him and he went into the water himself. But I believe I saw him climb out of his plane and swim to an island. I think he made it safely."

The distant speaker cleared his throat and apparently took a drink of water. "Thank you, Basil," he said. "There will be something in The Slot tonight, I think. Four destroyers have been steaming about near Vella Lavella. Something's on! You can expect another landing attempt tonight. If you chappies only had more bombers you could do some pretty work up here today. Cheerio, Americans! Good hunting!"

Charlesworth was more excited than I had ever seen him before. Jap DD's on the move! His eyes flashed as he spread maps about the baking quonset. At 1500 Fry came down the winding path, dragging a carbine and a raincoat along the trail. "Might as well see if you trade-school boys can run this thing," he said as he climbed aboard.

At 2300 that night they made contact. But it was disappointing. The big stuff was missing. Only some Jap barges and picket boats. There was a long confused fight. Most of the Japs got through to Guadal. The PT's stayed out two more nights. On the last night they got in among some empty barges heading back to Munda. Got five of them. Fry shot up one with a Thompson when the torpedoes were used up. But the kill, the crushing blow from which the Japs would shudder back, that eluded them.

On the dreary trip home Fry asked Charlesworth if he thought the Remittance Man moved from one island to another in a canoe. "Oh, damn it all," Charlesworth said. "Stop talking about the man. He's just a fellow doing a job."

Tony started to reply but thought better of it. He went forward to watch the spray and the flying fish. As the boats straggled into Tulagi he noticed great activity along the shore.

A PT blinkered to Charlesworth: "The coastwatcher says tonight's the night. Big stuff coming down!"

"What's he say?" Fry asked.

"We're going right out again," Charlesworth said, his nostrils quivering.

Tony barely had time to rush up to the cave. He dragged me in after him. It was my first trip inside since he had taken charge. I was surprised. It looked much better than any of the quonsets. Spring mattresses, too. "I told the men to fix it up," Fry said, waving a tired hand about the place. "Commander," he asked quietly. "What did the . . ." He nodded his head toward Bougainville.

"He was off the air yesterday," I said. "This morning just a sentence. 'Destroyers definitely heading south.' That was all."

Tony leaned forward. He was sleepy. The phone rang. "Holy cow!" Fry protested. "You been out three nights runnin', skipper. You're takin' this war too hard." There was a long pause. Then Fry added, "Well, if you think you can't run it without me, OK. But those Jap destroyers have guns, damn it. Holy cow, those guy's shoot at you in a minute!"

They left in mid-morning sunlight, with great shafts of gold dancing across the waters of Tulagi bay. They slipped north of Savo in the night. They found nothing. The Japs had slipped through again. Halsey would be splitting a gut. But shortly after dawn there was violent firing over the horizon toward the Russells. Charlesworth raced over. He was too late. His exec had sighted a Jap destroyer! Full morning light. Didn't wait a second. Threw the PT around and blazed right at the DD. On the second salvo the Jap blew him to pieces. Little pieces all over The Slot. The exec was a dumb guy, as naval officers go. A big Slav from Montana.

Charlesworth was a madman. Wanted to sail right into Banika channel and slug it out. He turned back finally. Kept his teeth clenched all the way home. When Fry monkeyed with the radio, trying to intercept the Remittance Man, Charlesworth wanted to scream at him. He kept his teeth clenched. A big thing was in his heart. His lips moved over his very white teeth. "Some day," he muttered to himself, "we'll get us a DD. That big Slav. He was all right. He was a good exec. My God, the fools can't handle these boats.

They haven't had the training. Damn it, if that fool would only stop monkeying with that radio!"

Tony couldn't make contact. That was not his fault, because the Remittance Man didn't broadcast. Fry clicked the radio off and went forward to lie in the sun. When the PT hove to at its mooring he started to speak to Charlesworth, but the skipper suddenly was overwhelmed with that burning, impotent rage that sneaks upon the living when the dead were loved. "By God, Fry. Strike me dead on this spot, but I'll get those Japs. You wait!"

Fry grinned. "I ain't gonna be around, skipper. Not for stuff like that. No need for me to wait!" The tension snapped. Charlesworth blinked his eyes. The sun was high overhead. The day was glorious, and hot, and bright against the jungle. But against the shore another PT was missing.

Back in the quonset Tony studied his maps, half sleeping, half drunk. In the morning the cool voice of the Remittance Man reported the weather and the diminishing number of Jap aircraft visible these days. Fry strained for any hint that would tell him what the man was doing, where he was, what his own estimates of success were. Charlesworth sat morosely silent. There was no news of surface movements. It was a dull day for him, and he gruffly left to catch some extra sleep.

Tony, of course, stayed behind in the hot quonset, talking about the Remittance Man. "This Basil he mentioned the other day? Who is he?" We leaned forward. For by this time Tony's preoccupation with the Englishman affected all of us. We saw in that lonely watcher something of the complexity of man, something of the contradictory character of ourselves. We had followed Tony's inquiries with interest. We were convinced that Anderson was an ordinary nobody. Like ourselves. We became utterly convinced that under similar circumstances we ordinary people would have to act in the same way.

Fry might ask, "What makes him do that?" but we knew there was a deeper question haunting each of us. And we would look at one another. At Charlesworth, for example, who went out night after night in the PT's and never raised his voice or showed fear. We would ask ourselves: "What makes him do it? We know all about him. Married a society girl. Has two kids. Very stuffy, but one of the best men ever to come from Annapolis. We know that. But what we don't know is how he can go out night after night."

Tony might ask, in the morning, "Where do you suppose he is now?" And we would ponder, not that question, but another: "Last night. We knew Jap DD's were on the loose. But young Clipperton broke out of infirmary so he could take his PT against them. Why?" And Clipperton, whose torpedo-man was killed, would think, not of the Remittance Man, but of Fry himself: "Why does a character like that come down to the pier each night, dragging that fool carbine in the coral?"

And so, arguing about the Remittance Man we studied ourselves and found no answers. The coastwatcher did nothing to help us, either. Each morning, in a high-pitched, cheerful voice he gave us the weather, told us what the Japs were going to do, and ended, "Cheerio, Americans! Good hunting!"

I noticed that Charlesworth was becoming irritated at Fry's constant speculation about the coastwatcher. Even Anderson's high voice began to grate upon the skipper's ears. We were all sick at the time. Malaria. Running sores from heavy sweating. Arm pits gouged with little blisters that broke and left small holes. Some had open sores on their wrists. The jungle rot. Most of us scratched all the time. It was no wonder that Charlesworth was becoming touchy.

"Damn it all, Fry," he snapped one day. "Knock off this chatter about the Remittance Man. You're getting the whole gang agitated."

"Is that an order?" Fry said very quietly, his feet on the table.

"Yes, it is. You're bad for morale."

"You don't know what morale is," Fry grunted, reaching for the whiskey bottle and getting to his feet. Charlesworth pushed a chair aside and rushed up to Tony, who ignored him and slumped lazily toward the door of the quonset.

"You're under quarters arrest, Fry! You think you can get away with murder around here. Well, you're in the Navy now." The skipper didn't shout. His voice quivered. Sweat was on his forehead.

Fry turned and laughed at him. "If I didn't know I was in the Navy, you'd remind me." He chuckled and shuffled off toward the cave. We didn't see him in the quonset ever again.

But it was strange. As the tenseness on Tulagi grew, as word seeped down the line that the Japs were going to have one last mighty effort at driving us out of the Solomons, more and more of the PT skippers started to slip quietly into the cave. They went to talk with Tony. Behind Charlesworth's back. They would sit with their feet on an old soap box. And they would talk and talk.

"Tony," one of them said, "that damn fool Charlesworth is going to kill us all. Eight PT's blown up since he took over."

"He's a good man," Tony said.

"The enlisted men wish you'd come along tonight, Tony. They say you're good luck."

"OK. Wait for me at the Chinaman's wharf." And at dusk Fry would slip out of the cave, grab a revolver, and shuffle off as if he were going to war. Next morning the gang would quietly meet in the cave. As an officer accredited directly to Charlesworth I felt it my duty to remain loyal to him, but even I found solace of rare quality in slipping away for a chat with Tony. He was the only man I knew in the Pacific who spoke always as if the destiny of the human soul were a matter of great moment. We were all deeply concerned with why we voyagers ended our travels in a cave on Tulagi. Only Fry had the courage to explore that question.

As the great year ended he said, "The Remittance Man is right. The Japs have got to make one more effort. You heard what he said this morning. Ships and aircraft massing."

"What you think's gonna happen, Tony?" a young ensign asked.

"They'll throw everything they have at us one of these days."

"How you bettin'?"

"Five nights later they'll withdraw from Guadal!"

The men in the cave whistled. "You mean . . ."

"It's in the bag, fellows. In the bag."

You know what happened! The Remittance Man tipped us off one boiling morning. "Planes seem to be massing for some kind of action. It seems incredible, but I count more than two hundred."

It was incredible. It was sickening. Warned in advance, our fighters were aloft and swept into the Jap formation like sharks among a school of lazy fish. Our Negro cook alone counted forty Zeros taking the big drink. I remember one glance up The Slot. Three planes plunging in the sea. Two Japs exploding madly over Guadal.

This was the high tide! This was to be the knockout blow at Purvis Bay and Guadal. This was to be the Jap revenge against Tulagi. But from Guadal wave after wave of American fighters tore and slashed and crucified the Japs. From Purvis our heavy ships threw up a wall of steel into which the heavy bombers stumbled and beat their brains out in the bay.

In the waters around Savo our PT's picked up twenty American pilots. Charlesworth would have saved a couple of Japs, too, but they fired at him from their sinking bomber. So he blasted it and them to pieces.

He came in at dusk that night. His face was lined with dirt, as if the ocean had been dusty. I met him at the wharf. "Was it what it seemed like?" he asked. "Out there it looked as if we . . ."

"Skipper," I began. But one of the airmen Charlesworth had picked up had broken both legs in landing. The fact that he had been rescued at all was a miracle. Charlesworth had given him some morphine. The silly galoot was so happy to see land he kept singing the Marine song:

> Oh we asked for the Army at Guadalcanal
> But Douglas MacArthur said, "No!"
> He gave as his reason,
> "It's now the hot season,
> Besides there is no USO."

"Take him to sickbay," Charlesworth said, wiping his face.

The injured pilot grinned at us. "That's a mighty nice little rowboat you got there, skipper!" he shouted. He sang all the way to sickbay.

At dinner Charlesworth was as jumpy as an embezzler about to take a vacation during the check-up season. He tried to piece together what had happened, how many Japs had gone down. We got a secret dispatch that said a hundred and twelve. "Pilots always lie," he said gruffly. "They're worse than young PT men." He walked up and down his hut for a few minutes and then motioned me to follow him.

We walked out into the warm night. Lights were flashing over Guadal. "The Japs have got to pull out of that island," Charlesworth insisted as we walked up the hill behind his hut. When we were on the plateau he stopped to study the grim and silent Slot. "They'll be coming down some night." To my surprise he led me to the cave. At the entrance we could hear excited voices of young PT skippers. They were telling Tony of the air battles they had watched.

We stepped into the cave. The PT men were embarrassed and stood at attention. Tony didn't move, but with his foot he shoved a whiskey bottle our way. "It's cool in here," Charlesworth said. "Carry on, fellows." The men sat down uneasily. "Fry," the commander blurted out, "I heard the most astonishing thing this morning."

"What was it?" Tony asked.

"This Remittance Man," Charlesworth said. "I met an old English trader down along the water front. He told me Anderson was married to a native girl. The girl broke her leg and Anderson fixed it for her. Then he married her, priest and all. A real marriage. And the girl is as black . . . as black as that wall."

"Well, I'll be damned!" Fry said, bending forward. "Where'd you meet this fellow? What was he like? Holy cow! We ought to look him up!"

"He said a funny thing. I asked him what Anderson was like and he said, 'Oh, Andy? He was born to marry the land-lady's daughter!' I asked him what this meant and he said, 'Some fellows are born just to slip into things. When it comes time to take a wife, they marry the landlady's daughter. She happens to be there. That's all.' "

The cave grew silent. We did not think of Jap planes crashing into The Slot, but of the Remittance Man, married to a savage, slipping at night from island to island, from village to hillside to treetop.

At 0700 next morning all of us but Fry were in the steam-ing quonset listening to the Remittance Man. We heard his quavering voice sending us good cheer. "Good morning, Americans!" he began. "I don't have to tell you the news. Where did they go? So many went south and so few came back! During the last hour I have tried and tried to avoid optimism. But I can't hide the news. I sincerely believe the Nips are planning to pull out! Yes. I have watched a con-siderable piling up of surface craft. And observe this. I don't think they have troops up here to fill those craft. It can mean only one thing. I can't tell if there will be moves tonight. My guess, for what it is worth, is this: Numerous surface craft will attempt to evacuate troops from Guadalcanal to-night. Some time after 0200." There was a pause. Our men looked at one another. By means of various facial expressions they telegraphed a combined: "Oh boy!" Then the voice continued:

"You may not hear from me for several days. I find a little trip is necessary. Planes are overhead. Not the hundreds that used to fly your way. Two only. They are looking for me, I think."

From that time on the Remittance Man never again broadcast at 0700. He did, however, broadcast to us once more. One very hot afternoon. But by then he had nothing of importance to tell us. The Japanese on Guadal were knocked out by then. They were licking their wounds in Munda. They didn't know it at the time, but they were getting ready to be knocked out of Munda, too.

The Remittance Man guessed wrong as to when the Japs would evacuate Guadal. It came much later than he thought. When the attempt was made, we were waiting for them with everything we had. This time the PT boats were fortified by airplanes and heavy ships. We weren't fighting on a shoestring this time.

I suppose you know it was a pretty bloody affair. Great lights flashed through the dark waters. Japs and their ships were destroyed without mercy. Our men did not lust after the killing. But when you've been through the mud of Guadal and been shelled by the Japs night after night until your teeth ached; when you've seen the dead from your cruisers piled upon Savo, and your planes shot down, and your men dying from foes they've never seen; when you see good men wracked with malaria but still slugging it out in the jungle . . .

A young PT skipper told me about the fight. He said, "Lots of them got away. Don't be surprised if Admiral Halsey gives everybody hell. Too many got away. But we'll get them sometime later. Let me tell you. It was pitch black. We knew there were Japs about. My squadron was waiting. We were all set. Then a destroyer flashed by. From the wrong way! 'Holy God!' I cried 'Did they slip through us after all?' But the destroyer flashed on its searchlights. Oh, man! It was one of ours! If I live to be a million I'll never see another sight like that. You know what I thought? I thought, 'Oh, baby! What a difference! Just a couple of weeks ago, if you saw a destroyer, you knew it was a Jap!' " The ensign looked at us and tried to say something else. His throat choked up. He opened his mouth a couple of times, but no words came out. He was grinning and laughing and twisting a glass around on the table.

Of course, one Jap destroyer did get through. As luck would have it, the DD came right at Charlesworth. That was when he got his third ribbon. It happened this way. We got a false scent and had our PT's out on patrol two days early. All of them. On the day the little boats ripped out of Hutchinson Creek and Tulagi Harbor Charlesworth stopped by the cave. "The boys say you're good luck, Tony. Want to go hunting?"

"Not me!" Fry shuddered. "There's going to be shooting tonight. Somebody's going to get killed."

"We're shoving off at 1630."

"Well, best of luck, skipper."

Tony was there, of course, lugging that silly carbine. They say he and Charlesworth spent most of the first day arguing. Fry wanted to close Annapolis as an undergraduate school. Keep it open only as a professional school for training regular college graduates. You can imagine the reception this got from the skipper. The second day was hot and dull. On the third afternoon word passed that the Nips were coming down. Fourteen or more big transports.

"Those big transports have guns, don't they?" Tony asked at chow.

"Big ones."

"Then what the hell are we doin' out here?"

"We'll stick around to show the others where the Japs are. Then we'll hightail it for home," Charlesworth laughed.

"Skipper, that's the first sensible thing you've said in three days."

That night the PT's were in the thick of the scramble. It was their last pitched battle in the Solomons. After that night their work was finished. There were forays, sure. And isolated actions. But the grand job, that hellish job of climbing into a ply-wood tug, waving your arms and shouting, "Hey fellows! Look at me! I'm a destroyer!" That job was over. We had steel destroyers, now.

You know how Charlesworth got two transports that night. Laid them wide open. He had one torpedo left at 0340. Just cruising back and forth over toward Esperance. With that nose which true Navy men seem to have he said to Fry and his crew, "I think there's something over there toward Savo."

"What are we waiting for?" his ensign asked. The PT

heeled over and headed cautiously toward Savo. At 0355 the lookout sighted this Jap destroyer. You know that one we fished up from the rocks of Iron Bottom Bay for the boys to study? The one that's on the beach of that little cove near Tulagi? Well, the DD they sighted that night was the same class.

Tensely Charlesworth said, "There she is, Tony."

"Holy cow!" Fry grunted. "That thing's got cannons!"

This remark was what the skipper needed. Something in the way Tony drew back as if mortally afraid, or the quaver in his voice, or the look of mock horror on his thin face was the encouragement Charlesworth wanted.

"Pull in those guts!" he cried. The PT jumped forward, heading directly at the destroyer.

At 2000 yards the first salvo landed to port. "Holy cow!" Fry screamed. "They're shooting at us!"

At 1800 yards three shells splashed directly ahead of the PT. One ricocheted off the water and went moaning madly overhead. At 1500 yards the PT lay over on its side in a hard turn to starboard. Jap shells landed in the wake. The PT resumed course. The final 500 yards was a grim race. Jap searchlights were on the PT all the time, but at about 950 Charlesworth nosed straight at the port side of the destroyer and let fly with his last torpedo.

I wish that torpedo had smacked the Jap in the engine-room. Then we might have some truth to support all the nonsense they write about the PT's sinking capital ships. A little truth, at any rate. But the damned torpedo didn't run true. You'd think after all this time BuOrd could rig up a torpedo that would run true. This one porpoised. The Jap skipper heeled his tug way over, and the torpedo merely grazed it. There was an explosion, of course, and a couple of the enlisted men were certain the Jap ship went down. But Charlesworth knew different. "Minor damage," he reported. "Send bombing planes in search immediately." So far as we knew, our planes never found the Jap. We think it hid in some cove in the Russells and then beat it on up to Truk.

Back at Tulagi our officers and men tried to hide their feelings but couldn't. Nobody wanted to come right out and say, "Well, we've licked the yellow bastards." But we were all thinking it. Tulagi was exactly like a very nice Sunday School about to go on a picnic. Everybody behaved properly, but if you looked at a friend too long he was likely to break out into a tremendous grin. Fellows played pranks on one another. They sang! Oh, Lord! How they sang. Men who a few days before were petty enemies now flopped their arms around each other's necks and made the night air hideous. Even the cooks celebrated and turned out a couple of almost decent meals. Of course, we starved for the next week, but who cared? The closest anyone came to argument was when Charlesworth's ensign ribbed a pilot we had fished from The Slot. "If you boys had been on the job, you could have knocked over a Jap DD." A week earlier this would have started a fight. But this time the aviator looked at the red-cheeked ensign and started laughing. He rumpled the ensign's hair and cooed, "I love you! I love you! You ugly little son-of-a-bitch!"

But there was a grim guest at all of our celebrations. Fry saw to that. He would come out of the cave at mealtime, or when we were drinking. And he would bring the Remittance Man with him. He dragged that ghostly figure into every bottle of beer. The coastwatcher ate every meal with us. Officers would laugh, and Fry would trail the ghost of that lonely voice across the table. The aviator would tell a joke, and Tony would have the silent broadcaster laughing at his side. He never mentioned the man, his name, or his duties. Yet by the look on Fry's face, we all knew that he was constantly wondering why the morning broadcasts had not been resumed.

One night Charlesworth and I followed Tony to the cave. "Fry, goddam it," the skipper began. "You've got me doing it, too!"

"What?"

"This coastwatcher. Damn it all, Fry. I wish we knew what had happened to that chap." The men sat on boxes in the end of the cave toward the bay.

"I don't know," Tony said. "But the courage of the man fascinates me. Up there. Alone. Hunted. Japs getting closer every day. God, Charlesworth, it gets under my skin."

"Same way with me," the skipper said. "His name comes up at the damnedest times. Take yesterday. I was down at the waterfront showing some of the bushboys how to store empty gas drums. One of them was from Malaita. I got to talking with him. Found out who this Basil is that Anderson referred to one morning."

"You did?" Fry asked eagerly.

"Yes, he's a murderer of some sort. There was a German trader over on his island. Fellow named Kesperson. Apparently quite a character. Used to beat the boys up a good deal. This chap Basil killed him one day. Then hid in the bush. Well, you know how natives are. Always know things first. When word got around that Anderson was to be a coastwatcher this Basil appears out of the jungle and wants to go along. Anderson took him."

"That's what I don't understand, skipper," Fry commented. "The things Anderson does don't add up to an ordinary man. Why would a good man like that come out here in the first place? How does he have the courage?"

Fry's insidious questions haunted me that night. Why do good men do anything? How does any man have the courage to go to war? I thought of the dead Japs bobbing upon the shorelines of The Slot. Even some of them had been good men. And might be again, if they could be left alone on their farms. And there was bloody Savo with its good men. All the men rotting in Iron Bottom Bay were good men, too. The young men from the *Vincennes,* the lean Australians from the *Canberra,* the cooks from the *Astoria,* and those four pilots I knew so well . . . they were good men. How did they have the courage to prowl off strange islands at night and die without cursing and whimpers? How did they have the courage?

And I hated Tony Fry for having raised such questions. I wanted to shout at him, "Damn it all! Why don't you get out of the cave? Why don't you take your whiskey bottles and your lazy ways and go back to Noumea?"

But as these words sprang to my lips I looked across the cave at Tony and Charlesworth. Only a small light was burning. It threw shadows about the faces of the two men. They leaned toward one another in the semi-darkness. They were talking of the coastwatcher. Tony was speaking: "I think of him up there pursued by Japs. And us safe in the cave."

And then I understood. Each man I knew had a cave somewhere, a hidden refuge from war. For some it was love for wives and kids back home. That was the unassailable retreat. When bad food and Jap shells and the awful tropic diseases attacked, there was the cave of love. There a man found refuge. For others the cave consisted of jobs waiting, a farm to run, a business to establish, a tavern on the corner of Eighth and Vine. For still others the cave was whiskey, or wild nights in the Pink House at Noumea, or heroism beyond the call of valor. When war became too terrible or too lonely or too bitter, men fled into their caves, sweated it out, and came back ready for another day or another battle.

For Tony and Charlesworth their cave was the contemplation of another man's courage. They dared not look at one another and say, "Hell! Our luck isn't going to hold out much longer." They couldn't say, "Even PT Boats get it sooner or later." They dared not acknowledge, "I don't think I could handle another trip like that one, fellow."

No, they couldn't talk like that. Instead they sat in the cave and wondered about the Remittance Man. Why was he silent? Had the Japs got him? And every word they said was directed inward at themselves. The Englishman's great courage in those critical days of The Slot buoyed their equal courage. Like all of us on Tulagi, Tony and Charlesworth knew that if the coastwatcher could keep going on Bougainville, they could keep going in the PT's.

Then one morning, while Tony sat in the cave twisting the silent dials, orders came transferring him to Noumea. He packed one parachute bag. "An old sea captain once told me," he said at lunch, "to travel light. Never more than twenty-five pieces of luggage. A clean shirt and twenty-four bottles of whiskey!"

At this moment there was a peremptory interruption. It was Lazars. "Come right away!" he shouted. "The Remittance Man."

The coastwatcher was already speaking when we reached the cave. ". . . and I judge it has been a great victory because only a few ships straggled back. Congratulations, Americans. I am sorry I failed you during the critical days. I trust you know why. The Nips are upon us. This time they have us trapped. My wife is here. A few faithful boys have stayed with us. I wish to record the names of these brave friends. Basil and Lenato from Malaita. Jerome from Choiseul. Morris and his wife Ngana from Bougainville. I could not wish for a stancher crew. I do not think I could have had a better . . ."

There was a shattering sound. It could have been a rifle. Then another and another. The Remittance Man spoke no more. In his place came the hissing voice of one horrible in frustration: "American peoper! You die!"

For a moment it was quiet in the cave. Then Fry leaped to his feet and looked distractedly at Charlesworth. "No!

No!" he cried. He returned to the silent radio. "No!" he insisted, hammering it with his fist. He swung around and grabbed Charlesworth by the arm. "I'm going over to see Kester," he said in mumbling words.

"Fry! There's nothing you can do," the skipper assured him.

"Do? We can get that man out of Bougainville!"

"Don't be carried away by this thing, Fry," Charlesworth reasoned quietly. "The man's dead and that's that."

"Dead?" Tony shouted. "Don't you believe it!" He ran out of the cave and started down the hill.

"Fry!" Charlesworth cried. "You can't go over to Guadal. You have no orders for that." Tony stopped amid the flowers of the old English garden. He looked back at Charlesworth in disgust and then ran on down the hill.

We were unprepared for what happened next. Months later Admiral Kester explained about the submarine. He said, "When Fry broke into my shack I didn't know what to think. He was like a madman. But as I listened to him I said, 'This boy's talking my language.' A brave man was in trouble. Up in the jungle. Some damn fools wanted to try to help him. I thought, 'That's what keeps the Navy young. What's it matter if this fool gets himself killed. He's got the right idea.' So there was a sub headed north on routine relief. The skipper would try anything. I told him to take Fry and the Fiji volunteer along." The admiral knocked the ashes out of his pipe as he told me about it. "It's that go-to-hell spirit you like about Tony Fry. He has it."

The sub rolled into Tulagi Bay that afternoon. The giant Fiji scout stayed close to Tony as they came ashore. Whenever we asked the Fiji questions about the trip into the jungle he would pat his kinky hair and say in Oxford accents, "Ah, yes! Ah, yes!" He was shy and afraid of us, even though he stood six-feet-seven.

I dragged my gear down to the shore and saw the submariners, the way they stood aloof and silent, watching their pigboat with loving eyes. They are alone in the Navy. I admired the PT boys. And I often wondered how the aviators had the courage to go out day after day, and I forgave their boasting. But the submariners! In the entire fleet they stand apart.

Charlesworth joined us, too. About dusk he and Fry went to the PT line and hauled out a few carbines. They gave me

one. We boarded the sub and headed north. In the pigboat
Tony was like the mainspring of a watch when the release is
jammed. Tense, tight-packed, he sweated. Salt perspiration
dripped from his eyebrows. He was lost in his own perplexing
thoughts.

We submerged before dawn. This was my first trip down
into the compressed, clicking, bee-hive world of the submariners. I never got used to the strange noises. A head of
steam pounding through the pipes above my face would make
me shudder and gasp for air. Even Charlesworth had trouble
with his collar, which wasn't buttoned.

At midnight we put into a twisting cove south of Kieta on
the north shore of Bougainville. I expected a grim silence,
ominous with overhanging trees along the dark shore. Instead
men clanked about the pigboat, dropped a small rubber boat
overboard, and swore at one another. "Ah, yes!" the Fiji
mused. "This is the place. We were here four weeks ago. No
danger here." He went ashore in the first boatload.

While we waited for the rubber boat to return, the submariners argued as to who would go along with us as riflemen.
This critical question had not been discussed on the way
north. Inured to greater dangers than any jungle could hold,
the submariners gathered in the blue light of a passageway
and matched coins. Three groups of three played old-man-
out. Losers couldn't go.

"Good hunting," one of the unlucky submariners called as
we climbed into the boat. "Sounds like a damned fool business to me. The guy's dead, ain't he?" He went below.

Ashore the Fiji had found his path. We went inland half
a mile and waited for the dawn. It came quietly, like a pur-
poseful cat stealing home after a night's adventure. Great
trees with vine-ropes woven between them fought the sun
to keep it out of the jungle. Stray birds, distant and lonely,
shot through the trees, darting from one ray of light to
another. In time a dim haze seeped through the vast canopy
above us. The gloomy twilight of daytime filled the jungle.

As we struggled toward the hills we could see no more
than a few feet into the dense growth. No man who has not
seen the twisting lianas, the drooping parasites, the orchids,
and the dim passages can know what the jungle is like, how
oppressive and foreboding. A submariner dropped back to
help me with my pack. "How do guys from Kansas and
Iowa fight in this crap?" he asked. He went eight steps ahead

of me, and I could not see him, nor hear him, nor find any trace that a human had ever stood where I then stood. The men from Kansas and Iowa, I don't know how they cleaned up one jungle after another.

The path became steeper. I grew more tired, but Tony hurried on. We were dripping. Sweat ran down the bones at the base of my wrist and trickled off my fingers. My face was wet with small rivulets rising from the springs of sweat in my hair. No breath of air moved in the sweltering jungle, and I kept saying to myself, "For a man already dead!"

The Fiji leaned his great shoulders forward and listened. "We are almost there," he said softly, like an English actor in a murder mystery. The pigboat boys grinned and fingered their carbines. The jungle path became a trail. The lianas were cut away. Some coconut husks lay by the side of a charred fire. We knew we were near a village of pretensions.

Fry pushed ahead of the Fiji. He relaxed his grip upon the carbine and dragged it along by the strap. He hurried forward.

"There it is!" he cried in a hoarse whisper. He started to run. The Fiji reached forward and grabbed him, like a mother saving an eager child. The giant Negro crept ahead to study the low huts. Inch by inch we edged into the village square. We could see no one. Only the hot sun was there. A submariner, nineteen years old, started to laugh.

"Gosh!" he cried. "Nobody here!" We all began to laugh.

And then I saw it! The line of skulls! I could not speak. I raised my arm to point, but my hand froze in half-raised position. One by one the laughing men saw the grim palisades, each pole with a human head on top. I was first to turn away and saw that Fry was poking his carbine into an empty hut.

"Hey!" he shouted. "Here's where he was. This was his hut!"

"Tony!" I cried. My voice burst from me as if it had a will of its own.

"What do you know?" Tony called out from the hut. "Here's the guy's stuff! I wouldn't be surprised if he . . ."

Fry rejoined us, carrying part of a radio set. The bright sun blinded him for a moment. Then he saw my face, and the row of skulls. He dropped his carbine and the rheostat. "No!" he roared. "God! No!" He rushed across the sun-drenched square. He rushed to the fifteen poles and clutched each one in turn. The middle, thickest and most prominent, bore the sign: "Amerrican Marine You Die."

Charlesworth and I crossed to the skull-crowned palisades. I remember two things. Fry's face was composed, even relaxed. He studied the middle pole with complete detachment. Then I saw why! Up the pole, across the Jap sign, and on up to the withering head streamed a line of jungle ants. They were giving the Remittance Man their ancient jungle burial.

Charlesworth's jaw grew tense. I knew he was thinking, "When I get a Jap . . ." I can't remember what I thought, something about, "This is the end of war . . ." At any rate, my soliloquy was blasted by an astonished cry from a submariner.

The skulls had shocked us. What we now saw left us horrified and shaken. For moving from the jungle was a native with elephantiasis. He was so crippled that he, of all the natives, could not flee at our approach.

I say he moved. It would be more proper to say that he crawled, pushing a rude wheelbarrow before him. In the barrow rested his scrotum, a monstrous growth that otherwise would drag along the ground. His glands were diseased. In a few years his scrotum had grown until it weighed more than seventy pounds and tied him a prisoner to his barrow.

We stepped back in horror as he approached. For not only did he have this monstrous affliction, but over the rest of his body growths the size of golf balls protruded. There must have been fifty of them. He, knowing of old our apprehensions, smiled. Tony Fry, alone among us, went forward to greet him and help him into the shade. The man dropped his barrow handles and shook hands with Tony. Fry felt the knobs and inwardly winced. To the man he made no sign. "You talk-talk 'long me?" Tony asked. The man spoke a few words of Pidgin.

Fry gave the man cigarettes and candy. He broke out some cloth, too, and threw it across the wheelbarrow. Without thinking, he placed his right foot on the barrow, too, and talked earnestly with the crippled native.

All that steaming midday, with the sun blazing overhead, Tony asked questions, questions, and got back fragments of answers in Pidgin. "Japoni come many time. Take Maries. Take banan'. Take young girls. Kiss missi. One day white man come. Two bockis. Black string. There! There! There! Chief want to kill white man like Japoni say. Now chief he pinis. That one. That he skull.

"White man got 'long one Mary. Black allasame me. She

say, 'No killim.' White man live in hut 'long me." We were revolted at the thought of the Remittance Man and his wife living with the scrofulous man and his wheelbarrow. The dismal account droned on. "One day Japoni come. Fin' white man. Break bockis. Tear down string. Shoot white man. White man he not die."

Tony reached out and grabbed the man by his bumpy arm. The man recoiled. Fry turned to us and called in triumph, "He isn't dead! They didn't kill him, did they?"

"Not killim," the diseased man replied. "Jus' here!" The man indicated his shoulder and tried to simulate blood running from a wound.

"Where did they take him?" Tony pressed, his voice low and quick.

"Bringim out here. Tie him to stick. Big fella b'long sword cut him many time." With his cigarette the native made lunging motions. Finally he swished it across his own neck. "Cut 'im head off."

Tony wiped his long hand across his sweating forehead. He looked about him. The sun was slanting westward and shone in his eyes. He turned his back on the barrow and studied the ants at their work. "We'll bury the guy," he said.

Immediately the native started to wail. "Japoni say he killim all fella b'long village we stop 'im 'long ground. All fella b'long here run away you come, like Japoni say." It was apparent the Japs had terrified the jungle villages. "No takem skull. Please!"

We looked up at the whitening remnants. The ants, impervious to our wonder, hurried on. Fry raised his right hand to his waist and flicked a salute at the middle skull. He shook hands with the thankful native and gave him four packages of cigarettes. He gave him his knife, a penknife, his handkerchief, the last of his candy and two ends of cloth. Again he shook the knobby hand. "Listen, Joe," he said sharply, his eyes afire. "We'll be back to get you one of these days. Won't be long. We fix you up. American doctors. They can cut that away. No pain. Good job. All those bumps. All gone. Joe! I've seen it done in Santo. We'll fix you up, good. All you got to do, Joe. Watch that one. Don't let it get lost. We'll be back. Not long now."

In a kind of ecstasy Fry motioned us into the jungle. When we were halfway back to the submarine he stopped suddenly. He was excited. "You heard what I told that guy. If any of you are around when we take Bougainville, come up here and get him. Haul him down to a hospital. A good doctor can fix that guy up in one afternoon. Remember. And when you're up here bury that skull."

We plunged into the deepest part of the jungle and waited for the submarine to take us to whatever caves of refuge we had fashioned for ourselves. Fry hid in his atop Tulagi for the better part of a week, drunk and unapproachable. On the seventh day he appeared unshaven, gaunt, and surly.

"I'm gettin' to hell out of here," he said. He went down to the bay and caught a small boat for Guadal.

I can't say he left us, though, for his fixation on the Remittance Man remained. We used to say, "Who do you suppose that guy actually was?" We never found out. We found no shred of evidence that pointed to anything but a thoroughly prosaic Englishman. As I recall, we added only one fact that Fry himself hadn't previously uncovered. On the day that Charlesworth received notice of his third medal he rushed into the mess all excited. "What do you know?" he cried. "That fellow up in the jungle. At least I found out where he came from! A little town near London."

The Milk Run

IT must make somebody feel good. I guess that's why they do it.—The speaker was Lieut. Bus Adams, SBD pilot. He was nursing a bottle of whiskey in the Hotel De Gink on Guadal. He was sitting on an improvised chair and had his feet cocked up on a coconut stump the pilots used for a foot rest. He was handsome, blond, cocky. He came from nowhere in particular and wasn't sure where he would settle when the war was over. He was just another hot pilot shooting off between missions.

But why they do it—Bus went on—I don't rightfully know. I once figured it out this way: Say tomorrow we start to work over a new island, well, like Kuralei. Some day we will. On the first mission long-range bombers go over. Sixty-seven Japs come up to meet you. You lose four, maybe five bombers. Everybody is damn gloomy, I can tell you. But you also knock down some Nips.

Four days later you send over your next bombers. Again you take a pasting. "The suicide run!" the pilots call it. It's sure death! But you keep on knocking down Nips. Down they go, burning like the Fourth of July. And all this time you're pocking up their strips, plenty.

Finally the day comes when you send over twenty-seven bombers and they all come back. Four Zekes rise to get at you, but they are shot to hell. You bomb the strip and the installations until you are dizzy from flying in circles over the place. The next eight missions are without incident. You just plow in, drop your stuff, and sail on home.

Right then somebody names that mission, "The Milk Run!" And everybody feels pretty good about it. They even tell you about your assignments in an offhand manner: "Eighteen or twenty of you go over tomorrow and pepper Kuralei." They don't even brief you on it, and before long there's a gang around take-off time wanting to know if they can sort of hitch-hike a ride. They'd like to see Kuralei get it. So first thing you know, it's a real milk run, and you're in the tourist business!

Of course, I don't know who ever thought up that name for such missions. The Milk Run? Well, maybe it is like a milk run. For example, you fill up a milk truck with TNT and some special detonating caps that go off if anybody sneezes real loud. You tank up the truck with 120 octane gasoline that burns Pouf! Then instead of a steering wheel, you have three wheels, one for going sideways and one for up and down. You carry eight tons of your special milk when you know you should carry only five. At intersections other milk trucks like yours barge out at you, and you've got to watch them every minute. When you try to deliver this precious milk, little kids are all around you with .22's, popping at you. If one of the slugs gets you, bang! There you go, milk and all! And if you add to that the fact that you aren't really driving over land at all, but over the ocean, where if the slightest thing goes wrong, you take a drink . . . Well, maybe that's a milk run, but if it is, cows are sure raising hell these days!

Now get this right, I'm not bitching. Not at all. I'm damned glad to be the guy that draws the milk runs. Because in comparison with a real mission, jaunts like that really *are* milk runs. But if you get bumped off on one of them, why you're just as dead as if you were over Tokyo in a kite. It wasn't no milk run for you. Not that day.

You take my trip up to Munda two days ago. Now there was a real milk run. Our boys had worked that strip over until it looked like a guy with chicken pox, beriberi and the galloping jumps. Sixteen SBD's went up to hammer it again.

Guess we must be about to land somewhere near there. Four of us stopped off to work over the Jap guns at Segi Point. We strafed them plenty. Then we went on to Munda.

Brother, it was a far cry from the old days. This wasn't The Slot any more. Remember when you used to bomb Kieta or Kahili or Vella or Munda? Opposition all the way. Japs coming at you from every angle. Three hundred miles of hell, with ugly islands on every side and Japs on every island. When I first went up there it was the toughest water fighting in the world, bar none. You were lucky to limp home.

Two days ago it was like a pleasure trip. I never saw the water so beautiful. Santa Ysabel looked like a summer resort somewhere off Maine. In the distance you could see Choiseul and right ahead was New Georgia. Everything was blue and green, and there weren't too many white ack-ack puffs. I tell you, I could make that trip every day with pleasure.

Segi Point was something to see. The Nips had a few anti-aircraft there, but we came in low, zoomed up over the hills, peppered the devil out of them. Do you know Segi Passage? It's something to remember. A narrow passage with maybe four hundred small pinpoint islands in it. It's the only place out here I know that looks like the South Pacific. Watch! When we take Segi, I'm putting in for duty there. It's going to be cool there, and it looks like they got fruit around, too.

Well, after we dusted Segi off we flew low across New Georgia. Natives, and I guess some Jap spotters, watched her roar by. We were about fifty feet off the trees, and we rose and fell with the contours of the land. We broke radio silence, because the Japs knew we were coming. The other twelve were already over target. One buddy called out to me and showed me the waterfall on the north side of the island. It looked cool in the early morning sunlight. Soon we were over Munda. The milk run was half over.

I guess you heard what happened next. I was the unlucky guy. One lousy Jap hit all day, on that whole strike, and it had to be me that got it. It ripped through the rear gunner's seat and killed Louie on the spot. Never knew what hit him. I had only eighty feet elevation at the time, but kept her nose straight on. Glided into the water between Wanawana and Munda. The plane sank, of course, in about fifteen seconds. All shot to hell. Never even got a life raft out.

So there I was, at seven-thirty in the morning, with no raft, no nothing but a life belt, down in the middle of a

Japanese channel with shore installations all around me. A couple of guys later on figured that eight thousand Japs must have been within ten miles of me, and I guess that not less than three thousand of them could see me. I was sure a dead duck.

My buddies saw me go in, and they set up a traffic circle around me. One Jap barge tried to come out for me, but you know Eddie Callstrom? My God! He shot that barge up until it splintered so high that even I could see it bust into pieces. My gang was over me for an hour and a half. By this time a radio message had gone back and about twenty New Zealanders in P-40's took over. I could see them coming a long way off. At first I thought they might be Jap planes. I never was too good at recognition.

Well, these New Zealanders are wild men. Holy hell! What they did! They would weave back and forth over me for a little while, then somebody would see something on Rendova or Kolombangara. Zoom! Off he would go like a madman, and pretty soon you'd see smoke going up. And if they didn't see anything that looked like a good target, they would leave the circle every few minutes anyway and raise hell among the coconut trees near Munda, just on chance there might be some Japs there. One group of Japs managed to swing a shore battery around to where they could pepper me. They sent out about seven fragmentation shells, and scared me half to death. I had to stay there in the water and take it.

That was the Japs' mistake. They undoubtedly planned to get my range and put me down, but on the first shot the New Zealanders went crazy. You would have thought I was a ninety million dollar battleship they were out to protect. They peeled off and dove that installation until even the trees around it fell down. They must have made the coral hot. Salt water had almost blinded me, but I saw one P-40 burst into flame and plunge deeply into the water off Rendova. No more Jap shore batteries opened up on me that morning.

Even so, I was having a pretty tough time. Currents kept shoving me on toward Munda. Japs were hidden there with rifles, and kept popping at me. I did my damnedest, but slowly I kept getting closer. I don't know, but I guess I swam twenty miles that day, all in the same place. Sometimes I would be so tired I'd just have to stop, but whenever I did, bingo! There I was, heading for the shore and the Japs. I must say, though, that Jap rifles are a damned fine spur to a man's ambitions.

When the New Zealanders saw my plight, they dove for that shore line like the hounds of hell. They chopped it up plenty. Jap shots kept coming after they left, but lots fewer than before.

I understand that it was about this time that the New Zealanders' radio message reached Admiral Kester. He is supposed to have studied the map a minute and then said, "Get that pilot out there. Use anything you need. We'll send a destroyer in, if necessary. But get him out. Our pilots are not expendable."

Of course, I didn't know about it then, but that was mighty fine doctrine. So far as I was concerned. And you know? When I watched those Marine F4U's coming in to take over the circle, I kind of thought maybe something like that was in the wind at headquarters. The New Zealanders pulled out. Before they went, each one in turn buzzed me. Scared me half to death! Then they zoomed Munda once more, shot it up some, and shoved off home.

The first thing the F4U's did was drop me a life raft. The first attempt was too far to leeward, and it drafted toward the shore. An energetic Jap tried to retrieve it, but one of our planes cut him to pieces. The next raft landed above me, and drifted toward me. Gosh, they're remarkable things. I pulled it out of the bag, pumped the handle of the CO_2 container, and the lovely yellow devil puffed right out.

But my troubles were only starting. The wind and currents shoved that raft toward the shore, but fast. I did everything I could to hold it back, and paddled until I could hardly raise my right arm. Then some F4U pilot with an IQ of about 420—boy, how I would like to meet that guy—dropped me his parachute. It was his only parachute and from then on he was upstairs on his own. But it made me a swell sea anchor. Drifting far behind in the water, it slowed me down. That Marine was a plenty smart cookie.

It was now about noon, and even though I was plenty scared, I was hungry. I broke out some emergency rations from the raft and had a pretty fine meal. The Jap snipers were falling short, but a long-range mortar started to get close. It fired about twenty shots. I didn't care. I had a full belly and a bunch of F4U's upstairs. Oh, those lovely planes! They went after that mortar like a bunch of bumblebees after a tramp. There was a couple of loud garummmphs, and we had no more trouble with that mortar. It must have been infuriating to the Japs to see me out there.

I judge it was about 1400 when thirty new F4U's took over. I wondered why they sent so many. This gang made even the New Zealanders look cautious. They just shot up everything that moved or looked as if it might once have wanted to move. Then I saw why.

A huge PBY, painted black, came gracefully up The Slot. I learned later that it was Squadron Leader Grant of the RNZAF detachment at Halavo. He had told headquarters that he'd land the Cat anywhere there was water. By damn, he did, too. He reconnoitered the bay twice, saw he would have to make his run right over Munda airfield, relayed that information to the F4U's and started down. His course took him over the heart of the Jap installations. He was low and big and a sure target. But he kept coming in. Before him, above him, and behind him a merciless swarm of thirty F4U's blazed away. Like tiny, cruel insects protecting a lumbering butterfly, the F4U's scoured the earth.

Beautifully the PBY landed. The F4U's probed the shoreline. Grant taxied his huge plane toward my small raft. The F4U's zoomed overhead at impossibly low altitudes. The PBY came alongside. The F4U's protected us. I climbed aboard and set the raft loose. Quickly the turret top was closed. The New Zealand gunner swung his agile gun about. There were quiet congratulations.

The next moment hell broke loose! From the shore one canny Jap let go with the gun he had been saving all day for such a moment. There was a ripping sound, and the port wing of the PBY was gone! The Jap had time to fire three more shells before the F4U's reduced him and his gun to rubble. The first two Jap shells missed, but the last one blew off the tail assembly. We were sinking.

Rapidly we threw out the rafts and as much gear as we could. I thought to save six parachutes, and soon nine of us were in Munda harbor, setting our sea anchors and looking mighty damned glum. Squadron leader Grant was particularly doused by the affair. "Second PBY I've lost since I've been out here," he said mournfully.

Now a circle of Navy F6F's took over. I thought they were more conservative than the New Zealanders and the last Marine gang. That was until a Jap battery threw a couple of close ones. I had never seen an F6F in action before. Five of them hit that battery like Jack Dempsey hitting Willard. The New Zealanders, who had not seen the F6F's either, were amazed. It looked more like a medium bomber than a fighter. Extreme though our predicament was, I remember that we carefully appraised the new F6F.

"The Japs won't be able to stop that one!" an officer said. "It's got too much."

"You mean they can fly that big fighter off a ship?" another inquired.

"They sure don't let the yellow bastards get many shots in, do they?"

We were glad of that. Unless the Jap hit us on first shot, he was done. He didn't get a second chance. We were therefore dismayed when half of the F6F's pulled away toward Rendova. We didn't see them any more. An hour later, however, we saw thirty new F4U's lolly-gagging through the sky Rendova way. Four sped on ahead to relieve the fine, battle-proven F6F's who headed down The Slot. We wondered what was up.

And then we saw! From some secret nest in Rendova, the F4U's were bringing out two PT Boats! They were going to come right in Munda harbor, and to hell with the Japs! Above them the lazy Marines darted and bobbed, like dolphins in an aerial ocean.

You know the rest. It was Lt. Comdr. Charlesworth and his PT's. Used to be on Tulagi. They hang out somewhere in the Russells now. Something big was on, and they had sneaked up to Rendova, specially for an attack somewheres. But Kester shouted, "To hell with the attack. We've gone this far. Get that pilot out of there." He said they'd have to figure out some other move for the big attack they had cooking. Maybe use destroyers instead of PT's.

I can't tell you much more. A couple of savvy Japs were waiting with field pieces, just like the earlier one. But they didn't get hits. My God, did the Marines in their F4U's crucify those Japs? That was the last thing I saw before the PT's pulled me aboard. Twelve F4U's diving at one hillside.

Pass me that bottle, Tony. Well, as you know, we figured it all out last night. We lost a P-40 and a PBY. We broke up Admiral Kester's plan for the PT Boats. We wasted the flying time of P-40's, F4U's, and F6F's like it was dirt. We figured the entire mission cost not less than $600,000. Just to save one guy in the water off Munda. I wonder what the Japs left to rot on Munda thought of that? $600,000 for one pilot. —Bus Adams took a healthy swig of whiskey. He lolled back in the tail-killing chair of the Hotel De Gink.—But it's sure worth every cent of the money. If you happen to be that pilot.

Alligator

ONE day in November, 1942, a group of admirals met in the Navy Building, in Washington. They discussed the limited victory at Coral Sea. They estimated our chances on Guadalcanal. They progressed to other considerations, and toward the end of the meeting the officer who was serving as improvised chairman said, "We will take Kuralei!"

It was a preposterous decision. Our forces at that moment were more than a thousand enemy-held miles from Kuralei. We barely had enough planes in the Pacific to protect the Marines on Guadalcanal. Our ability to hold what we had grabbed and to digest what we held was uncertain. The outcome in the Pacific was undecided when the men in Washington agreed that next they would take Kuralei.

Equally fantastic men in Russia made equally fantastic decisions. They forgot that Van Paulus was at the gates of Stalingrad. They were saying, "And when we have captured Warsaw, we will sweep on directly to Posnan. If necessary, we will bypass that city and strike for the Oder. That is what we will do."

And in London, Americans and British ignored Rommel at the threshold of Alexandria and reasoned calmly, "When we drive Rommel out of Tunisia, and when you Americans succeed in your African venture, we will land upon Sicily in this manner."

That each of these three grandoise dreams came true is a miracle of our age. I happened to see *why* the Kuralei adventure succeeded. It was because of Alligator. I doubt if anything that I shall ever participate in again will have quite the same meaning to me. Alligator was a triumph of mind, first, and then of muscle. It was a rousing victory of the spirit, consummated in the flesh. It was to me, who saw it imperfectly and in part, a lasting proof that democratic men will ever be the equals of those who deride the system; for it was an average group of hard-working Americans who devised Alligator.

First the admirals in Washington conveyed their decision to their subordinates. "We will take Kuralei!" One of the subordinates told me that his head felt like a basket of lead when the words were spoken. "Take Kuralei!" he laughed in restrospect. "It was as silly as suggesting that we sail right in and take Rabaul, or Truk, or Palau. At that time it was a preposterous imagination."

But he and perhaps sixty other high-ranking officers set out to take Kuralei. Specialists of all branches of the service studied Kuralei day and night, to the exclusion of all else. Map-makers were called in to make complete maps of Kuralei . . . and four other islands so that no one could say for sure, "Kuralei is next." It was soon discovered that there were no maps of the island that could be trusted. Months later, lonely aircraft stole over Kuralei at great speed, and unarmed. They photographed the island . . . and four other islands, and some were never seen again. A submarine one night put six men ashore to reconnoiter a Kuralei beach. They returned. The men who crept ashore on another island did not return, but even in the moments of their darkest torture those men could not imperil the operation, for they knew nothing. In five months the first maps of Kuralei were drawn. They proved to be sixty percent accurate. Hundreds of lives paid for each error in those maps; hundreds more live today because the maps contained so much accurate information.

The admiral in charge of providing the necessary number of destroyers for the operation studied eighteen or twenty contingencies. *If* the submarine menace abates within four months; *if* we could draw twelve destroyers from the Aleutians; *if* we had only eight carriers to protect; *if* we can insist upon using only those transports that make sixteen knots; *if* we can rely upon complete outfitting in Brisbane; *if* Camden and Seattle can finish outfitting the cruisers we need; *if* the job between here and Ascension can be turned over to destroyer escorts; *if* the African experiment needs all the destroyers allocated to it; *if* we could draw heavily upon MacArthur's fleet for the time being; *if* reports from Korea four weeks previous to D-day continue favorable as to the desposition of the Jap fleet; *if* we decide to knock out most of the shore batteries by aerial bombardment; *if* we have a margin of safety at Midway; *if* we have an air cover as powerful as we plan; *if* we can suspend all convoys south of Pearl Harbor, and so on until a truly perplexing number of possibilities had been considered. But when a man whose life has been planned to the sea, whose whole purpose for living is meeting an emergency like this, spends four months on the problem of destroyers at Kuralei, one has a right to expect a judicious decision.

The medical corps attacked their problem somewhat differently. They made a study of all amphibious landings of which there was any history. Landings by a large force, by a small force. Landings with a ground swell and in calm water. Landings with air cover and without. Landings with fierce air opposition and with moderate. Landings with no air opposition. Landings in the tropics, in the arctic, and in temperate climate. Landings with hospital ships available and with hospital ships sunk. In fact, where no experience was available to draw upon, the doctors spent hours imagining what might conceivably happen. Slowly and with much revision, they proceeded to draw up tables. "Against a beach protected by a coral reef, with a landing made at high tide against effective, but harassed enemy opposition, casualties may be expected as follows . . ." Specialists went to work upon the tentative assumption. "Of any 100 casualties suffered in this operation, it is safe to predict that the following distribution by type will be encountered." Next research doctors computed the probable percentages of leg wounds, stomach wounds, head wounds, arms shattered, faces blown away, testicles destroyed, eyes lost forever, and feet shot off. Then the hospital men took over. "It can be seen from the accompanying table that xx hospital ships with xx beds must be provided for this operation. Of the xx beds, no less than *xx* percent must be adjustable beds to care for wounds in categories k through r." Next the number of surgeons required was determined, the number of corpsmen, the number of nurses and their desired distribution according to rank, the number of enterologists, head specialists, eye men, and genito-urinary consultants. The number of operating tables available was determined, as were all items of equipment. A survey was made of every available hospital and medical facility from Pearl Harbor to Perth. "By the time this operation commences, it is reasonable to assume that we shall have naval hospitals on Guadalcanal, the Russells, Munda; that we shall have increased facilities in the New Hebrides and Noumea; and that projects already under way in New Zealand and Australia will be completed. This means that at the minimum, we shall have . . ." Four medical warehouses were completely checked to see that adequate supplies of all medicines, plasma, bandages, instruments, and every conceivable medical device would be available. "If, as is reasonable to suppose, we have by that time secured an effective airstrip, say at some point like Konora, we will have available fourteen hospital planes which should be able to evacuate critically wounded men at the rate of . . ." At this point a senior naval doctor interrupted all proceedings.

"Let us now assume," he said, "that this operation is a fiasco. Let us imagine for the moment that we have twenty-five percent casualties. That our schedule for operations is doubled. That head wounds are increased two hundred percent. What will we do then?" So the doctors revised their tables and studied new shreds of past experience. About this time a doctor who had commanded a medical unit for the Marines on Guadalcanal returned to Washington. Eagerly, his fellow physicians shot questions at him for three days. Then they revised their estimates. A British doctor who was passing through Washington on a medical commission that would shortly go to Russia was queried for two days. He had been on Crete. Slowly, with infinite pains, ever cautiously, but with hope, the doctors built up their tables of expectancy. Long before the first ship set sail for Kuralei, almost before the long-range bombers started softening it up, the medical history of the battle was written. Like all such predictions, it was bloody and cruel and remorseless. Insofar as our casualties fell short of the doctors' fearful expectations, we would achieve a great victory. And if our losses amounted to only one half or one third of the predictions, hundreds upon hundreds of homes in the United States would know less tragedy than now they could expect to know. In such an event Admiral Kester would be able to report on the battle in those magic words: "Our losses were unexpectedly light." It was strange. The men who would make up the difference between the expected dead and the actual dead would never know that they were the lucky ones. But all the world would be richer for their having lived.

About this time it was necessary to take more and more men into the secret of Kuralei. Seven months had passed. An inspiring whisper was sweeping the Navy: "A big strike is on." Everyone heard the whisper. Stewards' mates in Australia, serving aboard some harbor tug, knew "something was up." Little Japanese boys who shined shoes in Pearl Harbor knew it, and so did the French girls who waited store in Noumea. But *where* was the strike directed? *When* was it timed to hit?" More than half a year had passed since the decision had been reached. Evidences of the decision were everywhere, but the ultimate secret was still protected. A manner of referring to the secret without betraying it was now needed.

Alligator was the code word decided upon. It was the Alligator operation. Now the actual printing of schedules could proceed. Wherever possible, names were omitted. Phrases such as this appeared: "Alligator can be depended upon to suck the Japanese fleet . . ." "Alligator will need not less than twenty personnel planes during the period . . ." "Two weeks before Alligator D-day, hospitals in the area south of . . ." The compilation of specific instructions had begun. Mimeograph machines were working, and over certain offices and armed guard watched night and day. Alligator was committed.

The day upon which the Kuralei operation was named, Captain Samuel Kelley, SC, USN, left Washington for the island of Efate, in the New Hebrides. He was instructed to assume full command of all supply facilities in that area and to be prepared to service a major strike. "Nothing," he was told, "must interfere with the effective handling of this job. Our entire position in the Pacific depends upon the operation."

At the same time a captain close to Admiral King was dispatched with verbal instructions to Admiral Kester, to the top-flight officers at Pearl Harbor, and to General MacArthur.

This captain did not know of Captain Kelley's commission, and the two men flew out to the South Pacific in the same plane, each wondering what the other was going to do there.

Meanwhile, in Washington plans had gone as far as they could. In minutely guarded parcels they were flown to Pearl Harbor, where Admiral Nimitz and his staff continued the work and transmuted it into their own.

No commitments had been made as to when D-day should be, but by the time the project was turned over to Admiral Nimitz, it did not look half so foolish as when it was hatched in Washington. By the time I heard of it much later, it seemed like a logical and almost inevitable move. The subtle difference is that when *I* saw how reasonable it was, the plan was already so far progressed that only a major catastrophe could have disrupted it. I think that therein lies the secret of modern amphibious warfare.

In Pearl Harbor the mimeograph machines worked harder and longer than they had in Washington. Day by day new chapters were added to the pre-history of Alligator. Old ones were revised or destroyed, and yet ther was no printed hint as to where Alligator would strike. All that could be told for certain was that a tremendous number of ships was involved. The super-secret opening sections of Alligator had not yet been printed, nor would they be until the last few weeks before the inevitable day.

At this stage of developments I was sent to Pearl Harbor on uncertain orders. I had a suspicion that I might be traveling there in some connection or other with the impending strike. I thought it was going to be against some small island near Bougainville. For a few electric moments I thought it might even be against Kavieng. Kuralei never entered my head.

I landed at the airfield and went directly to Ford Island, where I bunked with an old friend, a Lt. English. Sometime later Tony Fry flew up on business, and the two of us lay in the sun, swapped scuttlebutt, and waited in one dreary office after another. Since I was a qualified messenger and had nothing to do, I was sent out to Midway with some papers connected with Alligator. The island made no impression on me. It was merely a handful of sand and rock in the dreary wastes of the Pacific. I have since thought that millions of Americans now and in the future will look upon Guadalcanal, New Georgia, and Kuralei as I looked upon

Midway that very hot day. The islands which are cut upon my mind will be to others mere stretches of jungle or bits of sand. For those other men cannot be expected to know. They were not there.

Finally Tony Fry left for Segi Point, an infinitesimal spot in the Solomons. English had to go on a trip somewhere, and I was alone in the rooms on Ford Island. Young officers reported in by the hundreds in those exciting days prior to the big strike, and after brief interviews, hurried on to islands they had never heard of, to ships they had never known. I stayed, and stayed, and stayed. I did the usual things one did in Pearl Harbor, but somehow the crowds appalled me, and an evil taste never left my mouth. Other men have had similar experiences, in California, or New York, or Oklahoma. They were home, yet there was an evil taste in their mouths; for not even Chicago or Fort Worth can solace a man who has been in the islands and who knows another great strike is forming. His wife and his mother may tell him that he is home now, and order him to forget the battles, but he knows in his heart that he is not home.

It was in this mood that I reported one day to fleet headquarters. That time the call was not in vain. I was given a medium-sized briefcase, unusually heavy. I was told that if our plane went down at sea, I must throw the case into the water. It was guaranteed to sink in eight seconds. I was given a pistol, and a Marine sergeant as an armed guard. With an armed escort I was taken to a waiting airplane. Seven other officers were in the plane, and I was certain that at least one of them was a guard assigned to watch me, but which officer it was I could not ascertain.

We stopped that night at Funafuti, a speck in the ocean. Two guards were stationed at my quarters, which was shared with no one. In the morning the procedure of the previous day was repeated, and we left Funafuti, a truly dismal island, for sprawling New Caledonia.

When we were about an hour away from Noumea, where Admiral Kester had his headquarters, an unfavorable weather report was received, and we were directed to land at Plaine des Gaiacs, an airstrip some distance from Noumea. We made what I considered a pretty hazardous landing, for we were well shaken up. We had a difficult decision to make. Should we fly to Noumea in a smaller plane? Should we go down by jeep? Or should we lay over until morning? It was decided to wait an hour and to try the first alternative.

A TBF took us down, and it was then that I learned which of my fellow officers was my extra guard. It was a jay-gee who looked exactly like a bank clerk. In the crowded TBF we never acknowledged that either knew why the other was there. At Magenta we made a wretched landing, and both the jay-gee and I were obviously frightened when we left the plane. Bad weather was all about us, and we wondered how the pilot had felt his way through the clouds.

Again an armed car was waiting, and we proceeded directly to Admiral Kester's headquarters. There the admiral was waiting. Three of us, the jay-gee, the Marine, and I, presented the briefcase to him.

Admiral Kester took the case into his room and opened it. It contained a mimeographed book, eight and one half inches by fourteen. The book contained six hundred and twelve pages, plus six mimeographed maps. The most startling thing about the book was the first page. The first sentence designated the forthcoming operation as Alligator. The second sentence was short. It said simply, "You will proceed to Kuralei and invest the island."

Slowly, like one who had acquired a Shakespeare folio after years of dreaming, Admiral Kester leafed idly through the super-secret first pages. The warships of his task force were named. The point of rendezvous indicated. The location of every ship was shown for 1200 and 2400 hours of each of the five days preceding the landings. The barrages, the formation of the landing craft, the composition of aerial bombardment, code words for various hours, radio frequencies, location of spotting points, and every other possible detail which might ensure successful operations against the enemy—all were given in the first few pages. Only the time for D-day was missing.

The admiral passed over the opening pages and dipped at random into the massive volume. Page 291: "At this time of year no hurricanes are to be expected. There is, however, record of one that struck three hundred and eighty miles southwest of Kuralei in 1897. Assuming that a hurricane does strike, it will be certain to travel from . . ."

On page 367 Kester read that "the natives on Kuralei should be presumed to be unfriendly. Long and brutal administration under the Germans was not modified by the Japanese. Instead of finding the natives opposed to Japanese rule, American forces will find them apathetic or even hostile. Under no circumstances should they be used as runners, messengers, or watchers. They should, however, be questioned if captured or if they surrender."

On page 401 the admiral was advised that fruit on Kuralei was much the same as that on islands farther south and that in accordance with the general rule of the South Pacific, "if something looks good, smells good and tastes good, eat it!"

It was on page 492 that the Admiral stopped. "Casualties may be expected to be heavy. The landing on Green Beach will probably develop an enfilading fire which will be aimed high. Chest, head, and face casualties are expected to be above that in any previous operation. If barbed wire has been strung at Green Beach since the reconnoiters of December, casualties will be increased. Every precaution must be made to see that all hospital ships, field hospital units, and base hospitals in the area are adequately staffed to handle an influx of wounds in the head and chest. This is imperative."

On page 534 a clear night was predicted from the hours of 0100 on until about 0515. Depending upon D-day, the moon might or might not be bright enough to completely silhouette the fleet. It was to be noticed, however, that even a crescent moon shed enough light to accomplish that purpose. The brighter planets were sometimes sufficiently strong, in the tropics, to outline a battleship.

Admiral Kester closed the book. Alligator, it said on the brown stiff-paper cover. At that moment similar Alligators were being studied by men responsible for submarine patrols, aircraft operations, battleship dispositions and supply. Each of the men—and it is easy to understand why—said, as he closed the book after his first cursory study of it, "Well, now it's up to me."

D-day would be selected later, and some officer-messenger like me would fly to various islands and move under heavy guard. He would, like me, be some unlikely candidate for the job, and to each copy of Alligator in circulation he would add one page. It would contain the date of D-day. From that moment on, there would be no turning back. A truly immense project would be in motion. Ships that sailed four months before from Algiers, or Bath, or San Diego would be committed to a deathless battle. Goods that had piled up on wharves in San Francisco and Sydney would be used at last. Blood plasma from a town in Arkansas would find its merciful destination. Instruments from London, salt pork from Illinois, Diesel oil from Louisiana, and radio parts from a little town in Pennsylvania converged slowly upon a small island in the remote Pacific.

Men were on the move, too. From Australia, New Zealand, the Aleutians, Pearl Harbor, Port Hueneme, and more than eight hundred other places, men slowly or speedily collected at appointed spots. Marines who were sweating and cursing in Suva would soon find themselves caught in a gasping swirl which would end only upon the beach at Kuralei, or a mile inland, or, with luck, upon the topmost rock of the topmost hill.

Each of the remaining bits of gossip in this book took place after the participants were committed to Kuralei. That is why, looking back upon them now, these men do not seem so foolish in their vanities, quarrels, and pretensions. They didn't know what was about to happen to them, and they were happy in their ignorance.

The intensity, the inevitability, the grindingness of Alligator were too great for any one man to comprehend. It changed lives in every country in the world. It exacted a cost from every family in Japan and America. Babies were born and unborn because of Alligator, and because of Alligator a snub-nosed little girl in Columbia, South Carolina, who never in a hundred years would otherwise have found herself a husband, was proposed to by a Marine corporal she had met only once. He was on the first wave that hit the beach, and the night before, when he thought of the next day, he cast up in his mind all the good things he had known in life. There was Mom and Pop, and an old Ford, and Saturday nights in a little Georgia town, and being a Marine, and being a corporal, and there wasn't a hell of a lot more. But there was that little girl in Columbia, South Carolina. She was plain, but she was nice. She was the kind of a girl that sort of looked up to a fellow. So this Marine borrowed a piece of paper and wrote to that girl: "*Dear Florella, Maybe you dont no who i am i am that marine Joe Blight brot over to see you. You was very sweet to me that night Florella and I want to tell you that if i . . .*"

But he didn't. Some don't. To Florella, though, who would never be married in a hundred years anyway, that letter, plus the one the chaplain sent with it . . . well, it was almost as good as being married.

Our Heroine

TWO weeks after Nurse Nellie Forbush proposed to Lieut. Harbison she received a newspaper clipping from Little Rock, Arkansas. In the section devoted to rural news was a large and pretty picture of her in formal uniform. The caption read: "Our Heroine. Otolousa Girl Arrives in New Hebrides to Help Wounded Americans."

Nellie looked at the photograph smiling at her from the newspaper. She was younger then, and much more sure of herself. She hadn't been seasick for eight days. When that photograph was taken she hadn't lived in mud, on poor food, under a stinking mosquito net. Nor did she have a lonely feeling about her heart, so that days and nights were the same.

No, she was a happy girl when she posed for that picture. She had gone into Little Rock with her mother and Charlie Benedict. They were both proud of her, her mother because she looked so fine and patriotic in her new uniform. Charlie because he hoped to marry her.

Charlie had been unexpectedly glum when the pictures were delivered to Otolousa. You're beautiful!" he said. "You'll never come back to a 4-F."

"I want to see the world, Charlie," she had replied. "I

want to meet other people. I want to see what the world's like. Then, when the war's over, I'll come back." Neither she nor Charlie believed that she would.

In the New Hebrides she was seeing plenty of people. Too many! She was often the only girl among a hundred men. Most of them wanted to make love to her. But that isn't what Nellie Forbush meant when she said she wanted to see the world. She had meant that she wanted to talk with strange people, to find out how they lived, and what they dreamed about, interesting little things that she could treasure as experience.

Hers was the heart-hunger that has sent people of all ages in search of new thoughts and deeper perceptions. Yet at the end of a year in Navy life Nellie had found only one person who shared her longing for ideas and experiences. It was Dinah Culbert. She and Dinah had a lust for sensations, ideas, and the web of experience. She and Dinah were realists, but of that high order which includes symbolism and some things just beyond the reach of pure intelligence.

She was sorry, therefore, when Dinah was ordered north to help set up a new hospital. They were talking together the night before Dinah left. Together they were laughing at poor, handsome Bill Harbison. They heard that he was drinking a good deal. Nellie had already told Dinah of how she had proposed to Bill and been refused. Dinah recalled that one night recently Bill had been slightly drunk at a party and had greeted her affectionately with a lurch and a loud, "Hi, Grandmom!"

The two nurses were talking when they heard a commotion by the guard house. An Army officer was helping a nurse out of a jeep. A doctor was running over. Soon heads popped out of all the windows. They saw another doctor come up and start to attend the officer. Like fire, news spread through the dormitories.

It was that quiet nurse who liked the Army captain. The one stationed in Vila. He was driving her home. They had stopped for a while. Near the air field. No, she didn't neck with him much. They were watching the planes. Three men jumped out of the bushes at them. They had clubs. They knocked the captain down and started to pull the nurse out of the jeep. When she screamed and fought, one of them tried to hit her with a club. He missed her and broke one of the assailants' arms. The wounded man bellowed. Then they got mad and grabbed her by one arm and one leg. She held onto the steering wheel, and the captain started to fight again. They hit him once more, and then . . .

A car came by. The three assailants saw it coming and fled. Two Army enlisted men were in the jeep and gave chase to the culprits. But by that time the would-be rapists were gone. One of the enlisted men drove the captain's jeep to the hospital. The captain was badly beaten around the head. The nurse was shivering from shock, but was not hurt.

All night cars whizzed by. They stopped all vehicles. At 0300 all hands at all stations were mustered in dark, sleepy lines. Officers checked enlisted men and other officers. Finally, toward morning, a man was found with a broken arm. He had slipped on a coconut log. Why hadn't he reported it? Just got in. What was he doing out? Hunting flying foxes. What with? A gun. Where was it? His friend took it. Who was his friend? He didn't know. How could he be a friend if he didn't know his name? He didn't know. Where did the friend live? He didn't know. Did anybody see him go hunting flying foxes? No. Was anyone along whom he did know? Nobody. Just him and his friend? Yes. Was his friend in the Army or Navy? He didn't know.

They locked up the suspect in a hospital ward. He knew nothing and the police were never able to establish that he was a rapist. If he was, his accomplices were not detected.

From then on nurses rarely went out at night unless their dates carried loaded revolvers. In the hot mornings Lieut. Harbison and his friends practiced target shooting so that in the cool nights they could protect their girls from enlisted men. Of course, the Army captain who had defended his nurse so well supplanted Harbison as the local hero. The captain became a greater hero when he proposed to his nurse and was accepted. They used to sit in the corner of the hospital club and talk. She would drink root beer and he usually had a coke. Lieut. Harbison was now going with a scatter-brained floozy. They used to spend a good deal of their time in the bushes. After she was sent home he took up with a divorced nurse who knew he was married. They worked out some kind of arrangement. Nellie used to nod at them whenever she saw them. She noticed that Bill was getting fat.

There were many other attacks or near attacks on nurses in the islands. They were grim, hushed-up affairs. Nobody ever knew exactly what had happened. Just rumor and surmises. But in time every nurse knew she lived in danger. She could see in the baleful looks of enlisted men that they considered her little more than a plaything brought out to amuse the officers. With thousands of men for every white woman, with enlisted men forbidden to date the nurses, it was to be expected that vague and terrible things would occur. In spite of this, Nellie found herself watching men with a deeper interest. The good men seemed better when there was trouble. The armed enlisted man who drove the hospital car when she went riding with officers seemed more willing to protect her. And every man who was apprehended as a rapist was obviously degenerate in some way or other. Back home they would have been evil, too.

"Men seem even nicer now than they did before," she said one day as Dinah was packing. "I thought it would be the other way around."

"Men are always nice," Dinah laughed.

"I was thinking the other night, Dinah. Out here good people seem to get better and bad people get worse."

"That's true back home, too, Fuzzy-brain. Wait till you know some small town really well, Nellie."

"But this is the first time I knew that everybody lives in danger all his life. We do, really. It's just that bit by bit we make arrangements that cancel out the dangers. We have certain girls to take care of certain men. If a man wants to become a crook or a gangster, we have . . . Well, we seem to have certain areas more or less staked out for him. Is that true?"

"I don't know, Nellie," Dinah said as she packed her duffle bags. "All I know for sure is that so far as I have been able to determine, nothing you can possibly imagine is impossible. Somebody's doing it or is going to do it. That goes for the good as well as the bad."

Shortly after Dinah's departure, shocking word was received at the hospital. Bill Harbison and some men from LARU-8 were flying down to Noumea for fresh vegetables. The plane caught fire. Radioed its position east of Noumea. It went into the rough ocean and all hands were lost.

Nellie could not work and had to be excused from her duties. She lay down, and against her will, she cried. It was horrible to think of a man so young and able dying so uselessly. In that moment Nellie found that war itself is understandable. It's the things that go along with it, things that happen to people you know, that are incomprehensible, and have been in all ages. She was physically ill for three days.

Then, in a flash, word came that all but one of the men had been found on a life raft. They were knocked about, but they would be all right. Harbison was saved. Again Nellie stayed in her room. She found that she did not want to see Bill, but that she was very glad he was alive. She realized that Bill carried part of her with him, and she was happy when that part lived again. Yet when the handsome young lieutenant appeared in the hospital with his indefinite nurse trailing along, Nellie felt sorry she had seen him again. He was sunburnt from his exposure, handsomer than ever. Every night for a week he sat at one table or another with his nurse, telling about the days on the raft. They must have been horrible.

Nellie was rescued from her emotional impasse by thoughtful Dinah, who asked for her to be sent north. Gleefully, she packed and waited for the plane. She had never ridden on an airplane before. She watched it come in from Noumea, carefully noted the busy work that accompanies any landing or takeoff, and gasped when she saw how exquisite Efate and Vanicoro were from the air. The pilot purposely flew east a bit so his passengers could see the volcanoes. The landing was perfect, and Nellie stepped out of the plane in much the same manner that Cinderella must have stepped from the pumpkin. This was living!

Dinah met her at the airfield. That night she met Emile De Becque. It was at a dinner given in a French plantation home in honor of the new nurses. Nellie, Dinah, three other nurses and some doctors were seated in an open-air, roofed-in pavilion by the ocean. Candles provided flickering light. Screens kept moths away, and a small Tonkinese boy went around periodically with a mosquito bomb which he delighted to make fizz. Young Tonk men served the food, which was very good.

At another table sat two Frenchmen having their dinner. One was short and fat, the proprietor of the plantation. Nellie had met him earlier in the evening. The other was a remarkable fellow. He was in his middle forties, slim, a bit stoop-shouldered. His eyes were black and deep-set. His eyebrows were bushy. He had long arms and wrists, and although he used his hands constantly in making conversation, they were relaxed and delicate in their movements.

Nellie tried not to stare at the Frenchman, but while waiting for the lobster and rice, she was detected by the proprietor studying his guest. The fat Frenchman rose and approached one of the doctors. "Ah, docteur!" he cried in bonhomie. "May I present my very good friend, Emile De Becque? He is our foremost De Gaullist!" At this recommendation everyone at the table looked up.

De Becque nodded slightly and rose. As he stepped toward the hospital dinner party, the rotund plantation owner continued his introduction: "M. De Becque was our first and bravest De Gaullist. He rounded up much support for the general. And when the Japanese threatened, M. De Becque and a young sea captain went to all the islands and arrested all suspicious persons. If the Japs had landed, he would have been our resistance leader."

M. De Becque nodded again and smiled in turn at each nurse as he was introduced. He had a gold tooth in front, but it did not detract from his strong features. Nellie noticed that he looked particularly French because his hair came so far down on his forehead. He wore it short, and the neatness of his head offset the inevitable sloppiness of tropical clothes.

"M. De Becque arranged the details for our flight to the hills," the plantation owner went on. "Did you know we were going to hide out until you came? M. De Becque arranged for many natives to act as guides. All women were armed."

Nellie was later to discover that in all the New Hebrides, if you could believe what you were told, there was not one Pétainist. And yet, as she looked at the fat proprietor and many others like him, she had a strange feeling that of them all only Emile De Becque acted from conviction. She felt he would have continued to act so had Pétain himself occupied the islands.

She saw a good deal of De Becque in the ensuing weeks. The tall Frenchman was eager for someone to talk to, and although he could not express himself perfectly in English, he could make himself understood. De Becque never called on Nellie. The doctors, always an interested group of men, asked De Becque to their dinners from time to time. After dinner was over, Nellie and Dinah and one or two other nurses usually joined the party and argued politics or when the war in Europe would end. The Frenchman was an able arguer, and not even the handicap of language prevented

him from impressing on all present the fundamental sound-
ness of his reasoning. Soon he was the only Frenchman at-
tending the informal arguments at the hospital; for whereas
any plantation owner was interesting once or twice as the
product of an exotic world, De Becque was of himself interesting. He was as good a man as his interrogators.

"I suppose," he once said, "that men were either De
Gaullists or Pétainists a long time ago. I think they grew up
that way. Of course," he added slyly, "some never grew up,
and it was those we had to play with."

"But why," a doctor asked, "did you elect to follow De
Gaulle, in particular?"

"De Gaulle?" the Frenchman asked contemptuously.
"What's De Gaulle? Who cares what De Gaulle is? He looks
puffed up to me. I don't like him." He snorted and waved
his hands. "Ah!" he added. "But what De Gaulle stands for!
What decent man could do otherwise?"

After De Becque had been a guest at the hospital several
times he proposed that he act as host one night at his plantation. The doctors were delighted. "The nurses, too?" the
Frenchman suggested, lifting his shoulders and stretching the
word *too* into three syllables.

"Why not?" the doctors asked, and a few nights later a
small party of Americans chugged up the hill to De Becque's
plantation. It was situated upon an extensive plateau overlooking islands and the sea. Most Englishmen and Frenchmen in
the islands like their houses abutting on the ocean, but not
De Becque. He favored the grand view! And from his veranda
there was such a view.

His house was built in an octagon with one side twice as
long as the others. In that side he lived, had a few books,
a radio, and an old gramophone. In the other seven sides
he had a dining room, a warehouse, a store, a series of bedrooms, and a completely furnished room for guests. In the
latter one might expect to find a missionary, a Tonkinese
family, a government official, or a trader. On the night of his
dinner the room was empty.

In the center of the octagon was placed the kitchen, a
small, low, sooty building into which only the Tonkinese
cooks went. From it came a series of fine dishes. Around the
one-storied house clustered an odd collection of buildings
whose original purposes were long since lost. Tonkinese and
natives lived in them and followed their mysterious ways.

A Buddhist temple crouched on the edge of the jungle. It gave visiting missionaries much concern, for natives found its tinkling bells and rhythmic drums much more fun than Methodism or provincial Catholicism.

The long room with its deep veranda faced south, and from it one could see four lovely things: the channel where the great ships lay; the volcanoes of Vanicoro; the vast Pacific; and an old Tonk's flower garden.

Nellie thought she had never before seen so florid a garden. There were flowers of all kinds, azaleas, single and double hibiscus, hydrangeas, pale yellow roses, and types she did not know. About the garden were flamboyants and bougainvilleas, red flaming bushes. And everywhere there were capriciously placed frangipani trees. De Becque pulled half a dozen branches for his guests and showed them how native men wear the four-leafed, white and yellow flowers in their hair. The nurses smelled the flowers their host gave them, and were delighted. The frangipani was the odor of jungle. It was sweet, distant, and permeating. In addition it had a slightly aphrodisiac quality, a fact which natives learned long ago.

De Becque's dinner put to shame any the doctors had ever offered him. It started with soup, grilled fresh-water shrimp, lobster and rice, and endive salad. Next came in succession three courses: filet of porterhouse, lamb chop, and a delicious concoction of rice, onions, string beans, and black meat of wild chicken. Then De Becque served the "millionaire's salad" consisting of tender shoot of coconut palm sliced wafer-thin and pressed in olive oil, vinegar, salt and pepper. Cup custard with rum, small cakes, coffee, and a choice of six liqueurs ended the meal. And all this was on the edge of the jungle, 550 miles from Guadalcanal!

To say that the hospital staff was astounded would be an underestimate of their reactions.

"Where did you get lobster?" a doctor inquired.

"We catch them here by various means. Out in the deep water."

"How about the wild chicken?"

"Those black men you saw by the gate when you came in. They shoot them with arrows or with .22's. They are wonderful shots, I think."

"I think so, too," the doctor replied. "But where do you get such big shrimp?"

"Far up the island rivers. You see, my friends, we don't eat this way every day. That's obvious. Not more than once every two weeks. You see for lobster I must tell the men five days in advance. For shrimp a week. For wild chicken, two days."

"How did you train the natives to serve so well?" Dinah asked. "They actually seemed to enjoy it."

"I am patient with them," the Frenchman answered. "They make their mistakes on me, and when they serve you they are prepared to do a good job. Isn't it that way at the hospital?"

"Tell me, M. De Becque," an inquisitive doctor asked, "how long did it take you to organize and build this plantation?"

"Twenty-six years," De Becque said. "I came here as a young man."

"You chop it out of the jungle yourself?"

"With some natives and a family of Javanese workers."

"The yellow people I saw outside. They're not Javanese, are they?"

"No," De Becque replied. "They're Tonkinese. Very fine workers. We bring them over from Tonkin China."

"Twenty-six years!" an older doctor said. "Wonder what I'll have to show for my life at the end of twenty-six years?"

"You were willing to throw all this away in the event that Pétain won?" Dinah inquired. The Frenchman smiled at her.

"I thought this was the war to prove that Pétain could never win," he said graciously. "You Americans worry about De Gaulle and De Gaullists, and yet every one of you acts as if he were a De Gaullist. Your speeches and your actions don't coincide."

After dinner the guests sat in the screened-in veranda. A doctor had brought along two mosquito bombs to keep the pests away. Their host served whiskey, beer, coke, ginger ale, root beer, and rum. As the evening wore on and a fine crescent moon rose into the midnight sky, talk turned to the islands.

"How can a man have stayed so healthy here?" one doctor inquired.

"Hard work and temperate living," the Frenchman replied. "I serve a great deal of alcohol but use it sparingly myself. I have tried to do all things in moderation."

The nurses wondered what "all things" covered. "Do you

think other white people could live in the tropics, too?" one asked. "That is, as well as you have?"

"They do," he said. "I think will power has a lot to do with it. You take the island of Malaita in the Solomons. Oh, what a place! Yet a man I know well, fellow named Anderson. He found life there quite successful."

"Tell me, M. De Becque," a nurse asked. "Is it true that most white men in the tropics are running away from something?"

The Frenchman turned in his chair to face his impertinent questioner. She was a young girl, so he smiled. "Yes," he said. "I believe that is true. Suppose that I was running away from something. Where could I find a lovelier spot than this?" He swept his hand across the front of the veranda and pointed toward the silent peaks of Vanicoro. "As a matter of fact," he said in a quiet voice, "is not each of you running away from something? You were not married yet, your lovers were at war, or your wives were beginning to bore you. I don't think it wise to inquire too closely into reasons why anybody is anywhere!" He smiled at the embarrassed nurse.

"Oh, M. De Becque!" she said. "I didn't mean it that way!"

"I know you didn't, my dear! But that's the way I understand the question. It's no good to think that all the men in Marseilles are normal and happy without secrets and everyone out here is a fugitive! That sort of thinking is foolish in today's world. I wonder how many men and women in Marseilles envy me right now?"

It was after midnight, and the nurses had to return. They were reluctant to leave the plantation. At the gateway where the jeeps were parked M. De Becque detached Nellie from the group. She had stood so that he could if he were so minded. "Ensign Forbush," he said. "You have shown great interest in my home. I would like to have you visit the plantation again."

"I should like to," Nellie replied frankly.

"With your permission I shall stop by for you one afternoon. You would enjoy my cacao grove."

Three days later, in the cacao grove, Nellie admitted that she had never seen anything which so impressed her with its natural, unexploited beauty. Within that grove she was to spend many of the happiest hours she would ever know, and one of the bitterest.

Plantation owners in the tropics usually plant their coconut trees in stately rows along the ocean front and inland for a mile or two. Grass is kept closely cropped beneath the trees so that fallen nuts can be gathered without difficulty. Most coconut groves look very neat. The tall palms appear like thin ballet dancers with fantastic headdresses. But a cacao grove grows haphazardly. It usually forms the boundary between plantation and jungle. Trees spring up helter-skelter from year to year, and around them jungle brush proliferates. At times it is difficult to tell where cacao trees end and violent jungle begins.

At the point where his cacao and coconut met, De Becque had long ago built himself a pavilion big enough for two or three people. Its base was teak wood in eighteen-inch planks, its half-sides of woven coconut palm, and its roof of heavy thatch. Two benches of mahogany and two massive, comfortable chairs of teak were the only pieces of furniture. Four grotesque rootoos, native masks carved of coconut log, decorated the four corners. Two were incredibly long-nosed jungle gods and two were native views of white women, with red lips. The masks gave color to what might otherwise have been a barren pavilion.

It is doubtful, however, if anything could be barren within a cacao grove. As Nellie waited in the pavilion while De Becque talked with his natives, she could hardly believe that what she had thought of as the montononous jungle could be so varied. Above her flew an endless variety of birds. White, green, red, purple, and yellow lorikeets more beautiful than any bird except the quetzal swirled and eddied through the grove. Their harsh cries were modified by the delicate chirping of a graceful swallowlike bird that flew in great profusion among the cacao trees. This gracious bird was sooty black except for a white breast and belly. Gliding and twisting through the shadows it looked like a shadow itself. Then, bursting into the sunlight, its white body shone brilliantly. At times sea birds flew as far inland as the cacao grove, and occasionally a gaunt hawk from the distant hills would settle there for a day and drive the darting swallows away.

But it was the cacao tree that won Nellie's admiration. The cacao is small, hardly more than a bush, reaching at most twenty feet in height. It has a sturdy trunk, thick branches about five feet from the ground, and grows symmetrically. Its leaves are brilliantly glistened like poison ivy, only more shimmering. And they are of myriad color! Some are pale green, others darkest green, some purple, some almost blue, or gray, or bright yellow. And on most trees at least fifty leaves are brilliant vermillion, shading off to scarlet and deep red. Each leaf is iridescent, and dead leaves drop immediately from the tree.

A cacao grove, in rainy weather, is a mournful and lovely place. In bright sunlight it is a hall of mirrors, and at dusk it has a quality of deep jungle quiet and mysteriousness that is equaled nowhere else in the tropics. In large measure these attributes are aided by the beauty of the cacao pods themselves. They grow in fairy-tale manner. In late January and February the cacao puts out buds that will later grow into pods. They appear without reason at the strangest places! Two inches from the ground on a barren, stiff trunk, a pod will suddenly appear. On one branch there may be a dozen pods. On another, none. In the crevice formed where a branch leaves the trunk a cluster of pods may appear and the branch itself may be bare. A mature cacao in full season looks as if someone had stood at a distance and flung a huge handful of random pods upon it.

At first the miniature pods are light purple. Then as they grow to full size, they become a weird greenish purple, like the paintings of Georges Bracque. Next they are all green, and from then on they become the chameleons of the jungle. On one tree mature pods, which now look like elongated cantaloupes seven and eight inches long, will be bright green, golden yellow, reddish yellow, red, purple, and greenish purple. And on each tree a few will be dead, charred, black, ugly, with small holes where rats have eaten out the sweet seeds, which, when toasted and ground, become cocoa.

While Nellie waited for De Becque to finish the work he was doing, she studied the grove and mused upon the perverseness of people whereby *cacao* in French becomes *cocoa* in English. The multicolored lorikeets, the iridescent leaves, and the flaming cacao pods formed a superb picture for a hot afternoon. Later, when her host appeared, tall, stooped, and breathing hard, she asked him to sit by her.

"Why did you build this pavilion?" she asked.

"I like to be near the jungle," he said, remaining in the doorway.

"Do you come here on rainy days? Is it nice then, too?"

"It's best on rainy days," he said. "But it's strange. The place serves no purpose. It's too far from the kitchen to eat here. There's no bed, and it isn't screened in. Yet I think I like it better than any place on my plantation."

"I was looking at the cacaos," Nellie said in a sing-song kind of voice. To herself she was saying, "I shall marry this man. This shall be my life from now on. On this hillside shall be my home. And in the afternoons he and I will sit here." Aloud she continued, "They are beautiful, aren't they?"

"A rugged tree," he said. "Not like coconuts. But they don't pay as well."

"Mr. De Becque," she began. "That sounds silly, doesn't it. I meant M. De Becque."

"Why don't you call me Emile?"

"I should like to," she said half laughing in self-consciousness.

To himself De Becque said, "This is what I have been waiting for. All the long years. Who ever thought a fresh, smiling girl like this would climb up my hill? It was worth waiting for. I wonder . . ."

"Emile?" Nellie began. "May I ask you a question?"

"Of course you may," he replied smiling.

"Why did you leave France?"

There was a long pause. Nellie and Emile studied one another across the little distance of the pavilion. Outside swallows darted through the cacao trees and lorikeets screamed at them for trespass. It was a jungle day, warm, heavy, thick with sunlight.

"It was not to my discredit," the Frenchman replied.

"I know that," Nellie assured him.

"I killed a man," Emile went on, dreamily, his voice blending into the heavy silence of the cacao grove.

"Why?" Nellie asked, not the least disturbed. It seemed as natural a mode of behavior for Emile De Becque as writing a letter. He had said, "I killed a man," and she was relieved that it was not something serious.

"A town bully. A town cheat. It was in a little place near Marseilles. Everyone was glad to see him die, and the fault was his. But they thought I should leave. The police investigated for three days, giving me time to get away. I could not make up my mind and an old man who had been a sailor told me, 'I was on an island once. The men wore pig's teeth and the women wore nothing. Anything you planted would grow on that island. With a little money a daring man could make a fine living there and become rich.' I listened to him,

my mind in revolt. Then he said something that decided me:
'And opposite the island is another island with two volcanoes.
You can see them all the time.' That did it. My mother had
always wanted to see Naples. She read a book about Pompeii
and wanted to see Naples. She never did. Lived all her life
right near Marseilles. I clapped the old sailor on the back
and shouted, 'You have a good idea, old man! I'll see *two*
volcanoes!' I left that night, and the next day the police
came to my home. 'Where is Emile De Becque?' they demanded. 'He is wanted for murder.' The old people in the
house said, 'He ran away!' 'The scoundrel!' said the police.
'If he comes back, we'll arrest him. Mark our words, we'll
get him!' They were furious, and all the time I was sitting
in a café in Marseilles, waiting four days for a ship. They
knew it and were afraid to send news to Marseilles, because
they knew that sometimes ships lay over three or four days.
Finally they sent a young fellow in to spy me out. He found
that I was gone, and posters soon appeared in Marseilles.
But I have never gone back."

"How did you kill him?" Nellie asked, surprised at her
courage.

"With a knife," Emile said, showing some satisfaction,
even at that distance.

"You've never regretted being out here, have you?" she
asked.

"Never!" he said emphatically and simply. Then he added
a peculiar comment. "This plantation is worth more than a
hundred thousand dollars."

In the cacao pavilion the two strangers looked at one
another. Each had a half smile. De Becque's gold tooth
showed. Nellie's infectious grin fought for possession of her
full lips. She thought that he was not an old man, and yet
not a young man, either. He was a respected man, wealthy,
a man with deep ideas. He was one who killed with a knife,
came out for De Gaulle, and was to have led resistance
against the Japs.

"Nellie," he said quietly, scarcely audible above the lorikeets. "In the hottest months you could go to Australia."
Nellie made no reply. She merely watched De Becque as he
rose, crossed the silent pavilion, and bent over her. She
raised her lips. Although he merely brushed her lips with his,
she had the distinct impression that she had been kissed by
a man, a whole man, a man worthy to be loved.

He sat upon the arm of her teakwood chair for several minutes. "I must go soon," she said quietly. As she rose, standing beside him, she noticed that her nose came to his shoulder. Standing there, with it pressed against his moist shirt, she asked, "Are you married, Emile?"

"No," he replied.

"I'm so glad," she murmured, pressing her funny nose deep into his shoulder. He patted her on the head and led the way down the long path that wound among the coconuts.

"You have dinner?" the Tonkinese cook asked.

"Just for me," De Becque replied. "I'll be back soon."

"Emile," Nellie said as he stopped his Australian car by the guarded wire gate. "Let me think for a few days. I'll tell you then."

"All right," he said.

That evening Nellie confided the news to Dinah. "I think I'll marry him," she said.

"It's hot on this island," Dinah replied.

"It's hot in Arkansas, too," Nellie said, laughingly.

"But you can get out of Arkansas."

"And I can go to Australia, too. Many women do in these islands. During the hot season.

"I don't suppose it's up to me to tell you that you hardly know the man," Dinah said, looking at the pretty young nurse.

"I don't want you to say that, Dinah," Nellie said. "But when I was in love with Bill Harbison you said that you knew I was heading for trouble. Do you feel that way now? Do you, Dinah?"

The older woman thought a moment. "No," she said. "As a matter of fact, I envy you. That is, if you have the courage to do it. This isn't an easy life."

"But it's a life, Dinah! We can get books here, too. Emile reads a lot in French. We can talk about things."

"Nellie," Dinah said seriously, "why don't you write a long letter to your mother?"

When the airmail answer arrived from Mrs. Forbush it was filled with pocket knowledge accumulated from a long life. It read in part; "Marriages of older men and young girls work for a while. But you must think of the future. Will you be happy there if he dies before you do? . . . The women of the place, if they are mostly French, will not like it having you there. Have you thought of that . . . Love can make almost any marriage work, and if he has money, as you say, that is all so much the better . . . What do you really know about him? Why did he leave France . . . He is probably a Catholic, too . . . Nellie, I always thought you might marry Charlie Benedict. He has a good job now . . . If your Pop was alive, he would probably say, 'Go ahead. Three square meals a day is as good there as here!' But life ought to have more than three square meals a day. You ought to have friends and old places to help you along . . ."

Mrs. Forbush rattled on, casting merits against demerits and came to the tentative conclusion that it was Nellie's life and she would have to lie in it. Mrs. Forbush had her metaphors mixed, but her conclusions were sound. Nellie showed the letter to Dinah. "Your mother has good sense," the older nurse said.

"She'd have to have to raise four of us," Nellie laughed. "But I want something more in life than she had. Mom didn't have much."

"She had enough to raise four pretty good kids," Dinah laughed. "And she didn't learn good sense out of a book."

"I think I'll marry him," Nellie said. Dinah had no comment. She wondered to herself what she would have done, and like Mrs. Forbush could come to no conclusion.

When De Becque called for Nellie next day she suggested they spend the afternoon in the pavilion. When they reached it, they were warm and breathing hard. Again the sun was hot upon the cacaos, and the lorikeets were wild in protest over some imagined slight. Suddenly they grew quiet.

"Look!" Nellie cried. "Look!"

A great hawk of the islands was sweeping overhead in long circles. It had come down from the mountains. No swallows were to be seen. With a delicacy foreign to his intent, the hawk sailed quietly by, moving a wing slightly now and then. Soon he was gone, and the brave lorikeets were out once more with furious chatter.

"I've thought as best I can, Emile," the young nurse said. "I want to marry you!"

"Fine!" Emile said with much restraint. They kissed twice. Then they sat in massive chairs and watched the life and beauty of the cacao grove.

"It will be a good life, Nellie," the Frenchman said. "You will like it. There is a good hospital on the other island. And if you like, you can go to Australia to have your children. The boat comes once every three months, and there are many people here. I have my own small boat, and two plantation owners have a large power launch. I shall teach you to read French, too. I have many books. And we can get English books, too. I have not told you, but I have a lot of money saved."

At the thought of having saved things over the years Emile grew pensive. Outside the birds called to one another and the golden cacaos reflected sunlight from their myriad facets. "I will die before you, Nellie, since I am older," he said in a reflective manner. "But if you like the islands, then, you will have no need to fear hunger or poverty. And if you have children, they will be growing up. By that time there will be an American base here. Your little girls will have fine American young men to choose as husbands. And if you don't like the islands, you can then return to America. You will have enough to live on."

Nellie could say nothing at this comment on eventual death. The hawk was idling in the dark sky and the lorikeets, like Nellie, were silent. They, too, were thinking of death.

Before De Becque left Nellie at the wire gate of the nurses' quarters, he told her that he would be gone for a few days. He had to deliver some beef to the island on which the French government had sequestered all young girls and unmarried women. It was a small island some sixteen miles distant, and there white, yellow, and black girls lived protected from the inroads of American troops far from home and inhibitions. De Becque and other planters kept the island supplied with food. For the first time, Nellie kissed him goodbye at the gate. She winked at the guard. "We're getting married!" she said.

While De Becque was gone, she visited the Navy captain who commanded her hospital. She told him that she intended to marry De Becque and asked what arrangements could be made.

"It's a long process," the captain warned her. "I don't understand it myself. The Army has charge of details in this area. But I'll take you to see the general, Ensign Forbush."

He did, and Nellie found the general a kindly old man who had daughters about her age. "I don't approve," he said half severely, "but I know how it is when girls make up their minds. One thing, Ensign Forbush: Have you or your friends made inquiries into M. De Becque's past? You have. Then we'll start the papers through the mill. But he'll have to appear in person. Bring him in when he gets back."

Nellie sighed and smiled at her commanding officer. The step was taken! She was surprised at the interest a captain and a general took in her affairs. She felt happy and important.

At dinner that night Dinah Culbert asked Nellie if, seeing that De Becque was away, she might like to sit at a table where an entertaining naval aviator was a guest. He was back from a tour of the islands and had some witty stories. At dinner Nellie sat next to the guest, a Lieut. Bus Adams. As the meal progressed he told one fascinating story after another. He made himself the butt of most of the humor, but as the evening wore on he finally asked for another drink and said, "I've never told this story before to a mixed group. It's really a man's story, but women might enjoy it, too. It's the only story I've run upon that fulfills the promise of these islands. I call it *The Frenchman's Daughter!* It took place on Luana Pori, and I know it's true. I know the Frenchman's daughter. She's a magnificent woman, about twenty-three. Half French, half Javanese!" Adams continued with a rambling narrative that captivated his listeners.

Doctors and nurses alike were following him with intense interest as he finished. "There!" he said. "Didn't I tell you it was a tropical story?"

"That is!" one of the doctors agreed. "You ought to write that down, lieutenant."

"No, no!" Bus said, wagging his finger. "I've found that these stories don't sound half so good when told in daylight. It's the wine, and the night, and the moon out there. That's what turns the trick."

"I suppose all these islands are loaded with unbelievable happenings," a doctor suggested. "As strangers, we don't hear about them!"

"That's interesting!" Adams said. "Because if I understand correctly, the Frenchman in this story lives on your island. Quite a character, I'm told. Raised hell when they wanted to go Pétain some years ago."

Before anyone could stop him, Adams had blurted out the news. The Frenchman's notorious daughter was De Becque's daughter. Her mother was a Javanese. The Frenchman's three other daughters who lived on Luana Pori were half-Javanese, too, but by a different mother. And somewhere near Vanicoro, on a small island, he had four other daughters, more beautiful than their sisters. The mothers of these girls were Polynesian and Tonkinese.

"He never married," Adams concluded. "Women were crazy about him, and he treated them fine."

Nellie Forbush sat very straight and smiled at the aviator as he spoke. Later on he refused to believe what the doctors whispered to him. "Jesus!" he said.

Nellie smiled at the doctors and the other nurses. Taking Dinah's hand, she excused herself. The two nurses went out the long corridor leading to their own quarters.

It was strange, but Nellie found no cause to cry. De Becque was a man of the islands. He had lived here for twenty-six years. He was a powerful man, and women were plentiful. Through him they saw a chance of rearing fine daughters, half white, and they eagerly took that chance. To judge from Bus Adams' story, the De Becque girls were fine and beautiful. Latouche, the eldest, was apparently wild, but she was smart and lovely.

"I'll not make up my mind about anything," Nellie said to Dinah when they were alone.

"What's past is past, Nellie," Dinah reasoned. "I told you less than a week ago that I wasn't worried about De Becque. I'm not now. This is a rough life out here. He's lived it. And kept everyone's respect. Only fighters do that, Nellie!"

"I'm not going to make up my mind," Nellie repeated. "Mom had a funny idea about that. Once she wanted a hat very much and had saved enough money to buy one. She went in to Little Rock with all the money in her hand. 'I won't make up my mind,' she kept saying to herself. Finally she was in front of the department store. There was exactly the hat she wanted. She looked at it for a moment and then started crying. Because that ornery store had put new baby carriages in the next window. She had to have a baby carriage. It was for me. Mom always said it was best to live right and make up your mind on the spot."

The two women talked late into the night. Other nurses, catching the story by grapevine, spent the night telling one another what a rotten break it was that Nellie . . . They were somewhat disappointed when she appeared at breakfast bright and chipper. She hadn't yet made up her mind to be heartbroken.

Two days passed, and finally De Becque called her on the

hospital telephone. Mustering up her courage, she smiled at the girls on her hall and hurried down to meet him. She noticed with apprehension that he was morose, too! In strained silence the two lovers drove along the coral roads and up the hill to his plantation. They parked his car by the gate and walked slowly between the coconut palms. De Becque was silent, as if worried. Nellie's heart was pounding harder than her lungs. As they neared the end of the coconuts and the beginning of the cacaos, De Becque stopped impulsively and kissed his bride-to-be tenderly. "You are my hope," he whispered.

Nellie consciously placed her hand in his and walked with him toward the pavilion. She felt him trembling, and thought it was she. They paused a moment to watch the dipping black and white swallows. Then they stepped into the cool pavilion.

"Aloo! Nellie!" cried four young voices.

Nellie looked in astonishment at four little girls who stood behind one of the teakwood chairs. "Aloo, Nellie!" they cried again. Then they came forth, in gingham frocks, pigtails, and curtseys.

Two were Tonkinese, that is, they were half Tonkinese, and they were beautiful as only Eurasian girls can be. They were seven and nine. Their almond eyes were black. Their foreheads were clean and high. They had very white teeth and golden complexions.

The two other girls were half Polynesian, daughters of that strange and proud race. They were round of face and darker than their sisters. Their eyes were black as pools at night, their hair the same, long and straight even in pigtails. They had rich mouths and splendidly proportioned bodies. They were ten and eleven.

At the end of their curtsey they said once more, "Aloo, Nellie!"

"They're my daughters," De Becque said proudly. "I have four others. They live in Luana Pori with their married sister. I have their pictures here." From an envelope he produced a well-thumbed photograph of four tall, thin, sharp-eyed girls. The first and third were exquisite beauties, lovelier than Bus Adams had painted them in his story. The second and fourth were handsome girls, and only their sisters' storybook charm made them seem plain. It was noticeable that each had a quizzical smile on her lips.

"My family!" De Becque said. He put his hand on Nellie's shoulder. "I had to tell you first," he said.

Nellie Forbush, of Otolousa, Arkansas, could not speak. She was glad that her mother had taught her never to make up her mind beforehand. Besides her was a strong, tough man. It was someone like him she had in mind when she said long ago, "I want to get out and meet people." It was not old ladies in white lace sitting by the fireside that Nellie wanted to meet. It was men and women who had courage. She looked at the picture of Latouche, De Becque's eldest daughter, and saw in her Emile's fire and determination. Yes, Latouche could kill a man and fight the entire American Army. The aviator's story was believable. Nellie thought that she would like Latouche.

But before her were other indisputable facts! Two of them! Emile De Becque, not satisfied with Javanese and Tonkinese women, had also lived with a Polynesian. A nigger! To Nellie's tutored mind any person living or dead who was not white or yellow was a nigger. And beyond that no words could go! Her entire Arkansas upbringing made it impossible for her to deny the teachings of her youth. Emile De Becque had lived with the nigger. He had nigger children. If she married him, they would be her step-daughters.

She suffered a revulsion which her lover could never understand. Watching her shiver, he motioned to the little girls and they left the pavilion. "Nellie," he said, pulling her into a chair and standing over it, "I have no apologies. I came out here as a young man. There were no white women in this area. I lived as I could. No woman ever hated me or tried to hurt me. You must believe me, Nellie. I loved those women and was kind to them. But I never married because I knew that some day you would come to this island."

He stood before her in considerable dignity. He was not crawling, and yet by every word and gesture he was fighting to have her believe in him.

"Oh! Look at that big one!" the little girls cried in French. Their soft voices drifted through the pavilion like the sound of distant music. Nellie looked at them running among the cacaos. The little Polynesians were dark, she thought. Almost black.

She swallowed hard. The pounding in her chest was still strong. "Where are their mothers?" she asked.

De Becque clasped his hands and looked away. "The

Javanese are back in Java. They went a long time ago. I don't know where the Tonkinese is. She was no good. The Polynesian girl is dead."

Nellie was ashamed of herself, but a surge of joy ran through her entire body when she heard the nigger was dead. Yet even as she entertained that thought the oldest Polynesian girl looked in at the window and cried in softest tones, "Papa! Voilà une petite souris dans ce cacao!" Nellie's hands went toward the window. The child had in her eager face and soft voice the qualities that made De Becque a man to love.

"Va-t-en jouer!" Emile said quietly.

"Oui, papa," the golden little girl replied.

"I don't know what to say, Emile," Nellie mumbled. "You don't understand."

"I know it's a surprise, Nellie. And a rude one. I know that."

"No!" Nellie cried in real anguish, stamping her foot. "It isn't that! It's something you don't know."

De Becque, defeated by tears, stood aside. Why Nellie thought he was incapable of understanding, it would be difficult to say. He had read of America. He knew something of its *mores* and shibboleths. And yet Nellie was correct in assuming that no Frenchman could understand why, to an Arkansas girl, a man who had openly lived with a nigger was beyond the pale. Utterly beyond the bounds of decency!

"I can't . . ." She stopped in her explanation. It was no use. The inescapable fact remained. She buried her head in her hands, and in the torment of conflicting thoughts and ideals started to cry.

"Please take me home," she said.

At the foot of the hill the Tonkinese cook expressed his astonishment that she was leaving. He held up his hands in horror. "Dinner all fine. He cooked. He good!" the cook protested. Moved by his appeal, Nellie agreed to have dinner and then go immediately. At a separate table the four little girls, obviously great favorites of the cook, had their dinners. They babbled quietly in French, displayed exquisite manners, and excused themselves when they went to bed. They, too, like the nigger wife, were indisputable facts. Nellie caught herself whispering, "I would be happy if my children were like that!"

Emile drove down the hill in silence, but at the turn onto the coral road four thugs were waiting for the car. They had been planning this assault for some time, four crazy young Americans, their minds addled by wild emotions. As they leaped at the car, Emile sped the motor and whipped out a brass pipe on the end of a knotted chain. It cut across the face on one assailant and hit another on the head. The swerving car wiped the remaining two loose against a tree. De Becque drove furiously until he met some enlisted men coming the other way in a truck. Wheeling around in a spire of dust, he led them back to where the assault had taken place. One rapist had been unable to run away, his leg bashed in by the car. The enlisted men jumped on him and started beating the bushes for the others. They found one, dazed, his face and head bleeding. The others were gone.

"Take them to the police, if you please," De Becque said quietly.

"You bet we will, mister!" an Army man said.

The truck pulled away. De Becque slumped over the wheel for a moment. Then he carefully rewound his lethal weapon and stowed it where it could be most easily grabbed in a hurry. Nellie was afraid to talk. She rested her head on his shoulder. De Becque drove very slowly.

"The world is not pretty," he said. "It's only the hard work of some people that makes it so. Remember that, Nellie. This could be your island. Your home. You'd make it that!"

"You don't understand," she whispered. At the barred gate she made up her mind.

"What is it, Nellie?"

"I can't marry you," she said. "I could never marry you!"

De Becque kissed her goodbye. The guards smiled. They knew she was going to be married soon. She was a damned nice girl, too. If they were all like her. One guard made a circle with his forefinger and thumb. He winked at De Becque.

"Hey!" he whispered to his pal when Nellie had gone. "The guy had tears in his eyes! What the hell goes on here?"

In her room Nellie undressed and lay upon the bed. She was excited and nervous. She could still see the ugly, hungry looks of the men who had tried to pull her out of the car. She thought, "Maybe they're the men who have to drive cars while officers and nurses neck in the back seat." She flung her arms over her head. "This whole thing is so rotten. Oh, I never should have come out here at all. It's all wrong!"

She thought of Emile De Becque and the little brown girls in the cacao grove. Her thoughts were as chaotic and tormented as those of the men who had attacked the car. "This place does something to you," she groaned. "I just can't think!"

And then she knew what she wanted. Her mind was made up. She rose, pulled a dressing gown from a nail over her head, and started to write a feverish letter. It was to Charlie Benedict in Otolousa, Arkansas. She told him something he had been waiting years to hear. She would marry him. She wanted more than anything in the world to marry Charlie Benedict. Right away. Now! She yearned for the safety and security of knowing what was happening and what had happened. She wanted Otolousa and its familiar streets. She didn't give a damn if she never saw another strange place the rest of her life.

At that moment Dinah Culbert entered the room. "Made up your mind?"

"Yep! I'm going to get married!"

"Good! Nellie, that's a fine decision!" Dinah's enthusiasm upset Nellie a bit.

"But to Charlie Benedict back home!" She bit her lip and laid the pen down. "Oh, Dinah!" she cried. "I couldn't marry a man who had lived with a nigger!"

"Of course not," Dinah said dryly. She didn't live in Arkansas and wouldn't understand. "Hello! What's this?" She picked up from Nellie's desk a picture from an Arkansas newspaper. "Why, Nellie!" she cried. "This is you!" Dinah looked at the picture approvingly. Then she read the caption, "Our heroine!" She repeated the words, "Our heroine!" Then she looked at Nellie, tears in her eyes, nose red, mouth drooping. "Our heroine!" she shouted, waving the picture in Nellie's wet face.

Nurse Forbush caught a fleeting glimpse of herself in the clipping. She thought of the afternoon the picture arrived in Otolousa. *"I want to see the world, Charlie. I want to live with people!"* The ridiculousness of her situation amused her. She started laughing at Dinah. Then she laughed at herself. The two nurses caught one another by the arms and started dancing.

"Our little heroine!" Dinah repeated over and over again until her chuckling became uncontrolled. Then she sat in Nellie's chair. In doing so, she knocked the letter to Charlie Benedict on the floor. With a grand sweep Nellie picked it up and crumpled it into a little ball.

"So long Charlie!" she cried, tossing the ball into a corner.

"Nellie!" Dinah cried. "Where did you get this?"

"What?" the now half-hysterical Nellie answered.

"This picture. It was on the floor by your jacket." It was the picture of the four De Becque girls.

"Oh!" Nellie cried in astonishment. "Emile must have . . ."

"What lovely girls!" Dinah said.

Nellie stopped laughing. She looked over Dinah's shoulder. They were lovely girls. Look at Latouche! Winsome and confident. Her three sisters, too. Calm, happy, cocky young girls. They seemed to be afraid of nothing. They seemed like their father.

"They *are* like De Becque!" Nellie said in a whisper.

"What did you say?" Dinah asked.

"Look, Dinah! Look at them! How much fun they seem to have!"

"You'd never have a bored moment around them," Dinah replied sagaciously.

"And the four little girls! Dinah, they're sweet. And so well behaved. Oh damn it all!" Nurse Forbush walked up and down. She saw her letter to Charlie in the corner. "Damn it all!" she cried again, kicking at the letter.

"Very reasonable behavior!" Dinah laughed. "For a little heroine!"

"What's the use of bluffing, Dinah?" Nellie confessed. She ran over to the older nurse. "Now I *have* made up my mind. I want to marry him . . . so very much!" She started crying and sank her head on Dinah's shoulder. Dinah thereupon consoled her by crying, too. In mutual happiness they blubbered for a while.

"I think your mind is made up the right way this time," Dinah whispered.

"Quick!" Nellie cried. "See if you can get a jeep! We've got to get one right away! I've got to tell him, tonight!" She hurried about the room getting her clothes together. "Oh, Dinah!" she chortled. "Think what it will be like! A big family in a big house! Eight daughters, and they're darlings. I don't care who he's lived with. I got me a man! My mind's made up. Mom was right. Wait till the last minute!"

In great joy she dressed and hurried downstairs with Dinah. While they waited for the jeep the guard asked, "Changed your mind, ensign?"

"Yep!" she laughed. "I did!" He made a circle with his

thumb and finger and winked at her. "Good hunting!" he said.

Dinah urged their driver to hurry. "Can't do but 25," he growled.

"But it's an emergency!" Dinah protested.

"It's always an emergency," the driver replied. "This is an awful island!"

"But this is a real emergency!" Dinah insisted.

"Oh! Well! Why didn't you say so?" the driver asked in a most cooperative spirit. "In a real emergency I always do 26."

Nellie winced as they passed the place where four men had jumped on the car earlier that night. As they reached the plantation, she directed Dinah and the driver to wait. Hurrying across the garden she went to the veranda. It was empty. The dining room was empty, too. Then she heard sounds from one of the bedrooms.

She hurried along the walk and found the source of the sounds. There it was. The little girls' bedroom. She opened the door. The four girls were in nightgowns, standing about a bed on which De Becque sat. They were singing "Au clair de la lune" in childish voices. Emile rose, smiled at Nellie, and hummed along with his daughters. Nellie added her uncertain treble to the chorus, and before long they were singing the old song so loudly that Dinah and the driver could join in from the jeep.

Dry Rot

"**I** won't let it get me down," Joe used to say. He would mumble the sentence over and over to himself. "I ain't gonna let it get me down! It ain't gonna get me down."

What *it* was, Joe never stopped to say. It was the heebie-jeebies or the screaming meemies. It was rock-jolly, or island-happy, or G.I. fever, or the purple moo-moo.

It was hellish stuff to get, and you got it when you had been on one island for a year or more. Joe had been on his rock for twenty-seven months, and he swore by God that it would never get him.

Not like it got some of the other guys! There was the soldier that stole a truck. On an island that had only three miles of roads he stole a truck. Then there was the other soldier that stowed away on a ship. Just a ship going anywhere. One fellow hit an officer. Six others ran the still under the cliffs and were sent up for terms at Mare Island. And then there was Louie, who sneaked into the nurse's room that night the transport crashed. But that's another story.

Joe watched these things happen, and hundreds of others. When something rough took place, there would be a court-martial. Everybody would say, "What the hell? You ain't gonna send the guy up, are you? He was rock-jolly!" But they sent him up, all the same. A steady stream of guys, just as good as Joe, went back to the States, under guard.

"Not for me!" Joe promised himself. "When I leave here for good old Uncle Sugar, I'm goin' on me own two feet, and they ain't gonna be no guard taggin' along! It ain't gonna get me!"

But it got some of the officers. Just like enlisted men. They weren't exempt. Not by a long shot. There was the fine lieutenant who was always smiling. He stood the rock for about thirteen months. Day after day, doing nothing. Then one day he hitch-hiked a plane ride to New Zealand. He was so rock-jolly he went on to Australia and they finally picked him up in Karachi, India.

Just because you were an officer didn't mean you stayed out of trouble. There was the old-timer, a drygoods man from Philadelphia. Took to drinking, and one day they found him breaking into the officers' club. Had to have some whiskey, and it was two o'clock in the afternoon. Couldn't wait the extra two hours. They didn't court-martial him. Just shipped him home, quiet like. Tried to keep the enlisted men from hearing about it. But they heard. And nine-tenths of them felt sorry for the old man.

It seemed as if old men didn't stand the rock as well as young men did. There was that chief petty officer who started screaming one night. At first nobody knew what had hit him. Anyway, he yelled his head off, and they had to put him in a strait jacket. It took them two days to quiet him down. Found out he'd been drinking torpedo juice. They sent him home, too.

Now nobody on the rock liked a good drink of liquor better than Joe. Not a drunkard, mind you. But a damned good judge of liquor. Before he joined the Navy he had a little shoemaker shop in Columbus, Ohio. He worked pretty hard, saved his money, and drank with the boys every Saturday night. He liked beer, gin, and whiskey. Wine and sweet drinks were for women. Rum tasted funny. Once or twice Joe had just about as much as he could handle. Went home singing till you thought his heart would break. Lullabys, mostly. Songs his mother sang to him a long time ago. She was dead, and he lived with a bricklayer north of the University. When he came home singing the bricklayer's wife

would tease him next morning. Joe would blush, feel tough
in the head, and swear he'd never get drunk again.

Joe wasn't able to keep that promise to himself, but that
was different from getting rock-happy. He could do something about not drinking. That was up to him. But there was
nothing he could do about the rock.

He and eight hundred other guys were put on the rock.
Somebody had to be there. If it wasn't Joe, it would be
somebody else. There he stayed! He was on the rock when
the Marines went into Guadalcanal. He was there when a
new general named Eisenhower landed in Africa. Half the
men on the rock thought he was a Nazi big shot. But later
on they learned. He was on the rock when Mussolini hauled
tail, and on the rock Joe heard the news about Normandy.
Some Marines flown out of Tarawa landed there, and then
flew on. Eddie Rickenbacker was there for a few days. And
so was Mrs. Roosevelt. They went on, but he stayed. For Joe
the war was the rock.

It was a coral atoll west of the date line. From it you
could see absolutely nothing but the Pacific Ocean. Only the
flaming sun, almost directly overhead, told you where east
and west were. At night half the stars were upside down
and the other half you had never seen before.

The island within the atoll was a mile and a quarter long
and a quarter of a mile wide. The airstrip for land planes
used up practically the entire island. The seaplane base used
up the rest. It was, everybody on the rock stoutly believed,
the finest seaplane base in the Pacific. No one told them
that there were at least a dozen better.

Trees had once covered the rock, but now only a fringe
remained, like hair on the head of a bald man. Living quarters
clung to the sides of the island or clustered at the southwest
end.

The rock had one great blessing and one great curse.
There was inadequate drinking water, and each night about
seven a breeze blew off the ocean. Joe, in particular, used
to say, "The only thing keeps me goin' is that breeze. No
matter how tough the day is, you can always look forward
to the breeze."

In a way, the water problem was not an unmixed curse. It
gave the men something to think about and something to
work on. What they said about the water could not be repeated, but what they did about it was amazing. Every spare

piece of tin on the island, every chunk of canvas, every oil drum was put to use. First of all, men built a watershed. For this they used a large, flat, sloping surface. Most were of tin, some of wood, and a few of canvas. Then they built gutters around the sides, and sloped the principal gutter into a spout, which ran into a barrel. Ingenious men, like Joe, somehow procured lengths of rubber hose, which they fitted over the spouts. In this way they could fill three or four drums without shifting them. All they did was shift the hose. Joe was unusual, too, in that he invented the ready-made shower. He built his watershed out from a tree and placed his four drums on stilts. For a bath, he stood under one of the drums and let her go! The water was always warm. He never had a cold shower, but at least he got clean. That was more than he had been able to do for the first five months he was on the rock!

But no matter how much Joe washed, he still got skin diseases. Everybody in the South Pacific got the same disease, but it was somehow worse when you got them over and over again, always on the same rock. Joe first noticed that something was wrong when he began to feel dizzy at two o'clock in the afternoon. He found out later he was short of salt. Sweating, sweating all day long for thirty days a month and thirty-one some months seeps the salt right out. Before Joe got wise, he had a case of prickly heat. One morning he woke up just as usual, but soon after he put on his shirt he felt somebody stick a handful of pins in his back. Right between his shoulder blades. He jumped and looked around.

"Whassa matter, Joe?" one of his friends asked.

"Somethin' hit me!" he claimed.

"Where?" they asked.

"Right here!" He started to point to his shoulder blades, when he was hit again, in back of his left knee. He started to scratch.

"Uh-uh!" the men shouted. "He's got the itch!"

Boy, he had it! And he kept it! For three months. Every morning and afternoon he would be attacked by spells in which he could have sworn people sank darts into his body. It was no good scratching. That only made it worse. After a while large areas of Joe's body were covered with a red rash. Acid perspiration had eaten away small flakes of skin. When new perspiration hit these spots, Joe would close his eyes and swear. He reported to sickbay finally, and there he joined a long line of other sufferers. A big pharmacist's mate, who felt sorry for each of his patients, would appear with a bucket of white stuff and a paper-hanger's brush. He would spend about twenty seconds on each man. Give him a real paint job. There was menthol in the white stuff, otherwise Joe could not have stood the furious itching that came back day after day.

As with all the other men, the itch finally worked down between his legs. Then his misery started. At night the man who slept above him would shake the bed and yell, "Joe! Stop scratching yourself!" Joe would grunt and roll over. But in the morning, skin would be missing from his crotch.

It was then that his legs and armpits became infected. In the morning lineups Joe had noticed half a dozen men who stayed to one side until the big corpsman was through his paint jobs. He used to wonder what happened to them. Now he found out. When the simpler cases were dismissed, the infected cases were attended. With a small scalpel the patient corpsman scraped away accumulations from each blister. Then, upon the open wound, he placed a salve. The healing process was terribly slow. Sometimes a month. And all that time you had to work, just the same. Twenty minutes after you left sickbay, sweat was running over the salve. In twenty more minutes the sore was bare.

Then Joe noticed a funny thing. Everybody he met on the rock had some special medicine that was a sure cure for the itch. But everybody had the itch! The only thing Joe found that cured him was a preparation somebody sent from the States. The man who owned it tried it out, and it worked. A solution of salicylic acid in merthiolate. Four other men used it between their legs, and in half an hour it had eaten away their skin. They went to the sickbay. But even after that some fellows went right on using the dynamite. On some it worked. Joe was one of them. He would lie down, paint himself liberally, and then bite his knuckles. It hurt like the devil. "I'm lucky," he would say. "It works on me." He continued to have heat itch, every month for twenty-seven months, but he had no more infections. He felt most sorry for those who did. He knew they had a tough time of it.

Joe had only one other serious medical affliction. His feet! Like most men on the rock, he fought an endless battle against fungus of the feet. Unlike the itch, this fungus came and went. And it was never bad, unless you were one of the unlucky guys that got poisoned from it. Then your feet swelled up, and one man even lost three toes. It ate them right away at the roots. His friends, when the disease first started, told him he had leprosy. Later on they got plenty scared and a wild rumor sped through camp that it really was leprosy. The doctors put a stop to that in a hurry. Just a deep infection. But the guy lost three toes, all the same.

For the rest, you just took as many showers as you could, ate lots of salt, and hoped for the best. Once Joe got five big lumps under his left arm, but seven walloping doses of sulfa drove them away. "I drank about nine gallons of water a day," Joe told his friends later, "and didn't go to the head at all! Where did the water go to?"

It was the atabrine that gave Joe his worst trouble. He hated the little yellow pills and wasn't sure they did any good. The American Medical Association said they were a waste of time, and Joe was pretty sure the doctors back home knew more than the sawbones on the rock. Hell, these guys couldn't even cure the itch! But all the same everyone had to take his atabrine tablets daily. That was not so bad until you began to turn yellow. Then you got worried.

Joe started to wonder if maybe those stories weren't true after all. "As I got it straight from a doctor," one of the men confided to him one night, "all this atabrine does is keep malaria down. It don't show on you, see? You're yellow, and it don't show. But all the time malaria is runnin' wild! Down here!" He slapped the fly of his pants. "And when they got all the work they can out of you, they send you on home. A livin' wreck! They stop the atabrine and the disease pops out all over you." Then he lowered his voice mysteriously and slapped his fly again. "But mostly here," he said in doleful tones. "You're nothin' but a burned-out wreck."

The men in Joe's hut wondered if there was any truth in what the man said. It stood to reason you took atabrine only to keep something in check. If they were hopping you up with dope, only so you could work without falling down, that was bad enough. But what if taking atabrine for three months, say, made you lose your power? Did it mean you couldn't ever have any babies? Or did it mean something worse? With wonderful funds of ignorance and superstition Joe and his friends considered the question from all angles. They found no answer to their informer's devastating insinuation: "All right! All right! How do you *know* you ain't losin' your power?"

Joe had no way of knowing. In fact, like hundreds of men on the rock, he had no reason to believe that he had any power. He had been in love once or twice, but he had never married. Nor had he slept with a girl. He had wanted to, once or twice, but morals, lost opportunity and all those strange things that keep men from doing what they otherwise want to, had intervened. He had to guess about his power, but he sure didn't want to lose it. As days passed and he became more yellow, he began to wonder darkly if maybe that guy was right. He wanted to talk to somebody about it, but he had noticed that whenever you got started on something like that, you got into trouble. Bad trouble.

Two months before, Joe was lying in his bunk. It was about eleven-thirty at night. Suddenly he heard a loud shout and sounds of a fight. With the rest of his hut he scrambled from bed in time to see two officers and three enlisted men rounding up a chief petty officer and a young seaman whose nose was bleeding.

A third officer hurried to each of the huts. "All right, men!" he said quietly. "Back to bed. Break it up, men. Break it up!"

Next morning hushed whispers flamed through the camp. No one ever said anything officially, but the C.P.O. and the seaman disappeared. Later Joe got the word. The chief got sixteen years in Portsmouth and the seaman two years in Mare Island. Eight nights later Louie sneaked into the nurse's room. The one whose plane was forced down. Louie went to jail, too. After that Joe just stayed away from everything to do with sex. It was an expensive luxury on the rock. "And," he had sworn, "it ain't gonna get me!"

Fortunately, a smart young doctor got wind of what was troubling the men. He wrote to Washington for an official statement that atabrine did not affect virility. It was signed by a Jew, an Irishman, a Protestant, and a doctor from a little town in Missouri. Eight hundred copies were made, and each man on the rock got one. But the young doctor's second idea was even better. He got a clever photographer who could copy pictures from magazines. Then he found two photographs of prominent movie stars who were attracting great publicity as bedroom athletes. He had the photographer make a poster seven feet by ten feet. The two movie stars were leering at one another. Below in big letters was their confession: WE JUST LOVE ATABRINE! Men came from all over the island to see the sign. It did a lot of good.

Joe had fought it out on the rock for sixteen months when two important events occurred in his life. He got a new skipper, and a liberty ship carrying some SeaBees stopped at the island for engine repairs. Joe's old skipper was sent home under some kind of a cloud. Either he went to pieces mentally or he got into trouble over the accounts of the officers' club. Joe never got the right of it.

The new skipper was a Navy type. He was a commander fifty-two years old. He would never go higher. He was a hard-drinking man who could not be relied upon. Yet he was an excellent fellow, and no one would prefer charges against him. So he dragged on and on, from one unimportant job to another. Many loved him but few respected him. Ambitious young men sought to leave his command at any opportunity, but they buttered him up while he was their superior. Some of them even bit their lips in silence when he made passes at their lovely wives. Before he was on the rock a week even Joe knew that he had been sent there as some kind of punishment. Something he had done in the States. Joe never got the right of it.

The Skipper, as he was known, started innovations at once. By God, he was the boss and things were going to be different. If he had to come to this god-forsaken island, he'd show them a thing or two. His first order was that each man must sleep under mosquito nets at all times. He almost had a mutiny on his hands, and the ringleader was Joe.

The huts in which enlisted men slept were foul things. Quonsets for eight men housed twenty-four. Men slept in double deckers, and even though there was a breeze at night, it could not penetrate the crowded quonsets. On some nights Joe lay in bed and sweated all night long. When the order came for mosquito netting, therefore, he rebelled. He tried it for two nights and found that he had what a doctor would have termed claustrophobia. He struggled with the net and almost strangled. In the hot, sweaty night he swore he'd not use a net again. He tore it off.

Next day he was before the new skipper. "I'm going to make an example of you," that red-faced man said.

When the words were spoken, Joe visibly trembled. For sixteen months he had kept out of trouble, and now he was in, up to his ears. "Get me out of this! Get me out of this!" he prayed. "I don't want no trouble!"

"What the hell do you think you're doing?" the Skipper shouted. "You think you can get away with murder around here?" He looked up at the frightened seaman. Joe licked his lips. The Skipper was about to throw the book at Joe when he remembered why it was he had been sent to the rock. "Got to start over!" he muttered to himself. "This time I'm starting over!" he promised under his breath.

"Young man," he said aloud, "don't you *like* the Navy?"

"Oh, sir!" Joe replied in the seaman's stock reply to the Skipper's stock question, "I *love* the Navy!"

"You'd better show it!" the Skipper said gruffly. "If I catch you in trouble again, I'll bounce you right out of the Navy." Then he added the crusher: "And you'll find yourself in the Army!"

Joe came to attention and left. After that he slept under a mosquito netting. It was strange, but out there in the middle of the Pacific, with an island almost to himself, Joe was cramped and stifled. He would wake up at night gasping for breath. He finally solved the problem by compounding his earlier felony. He stole a dynamotor and rigged up an electric fan. "If they ask me about it," he muttered to himself, "I'll say I got it from one of them wrecked planes." He scuffed the dynamotor up a bit to make it look like salvage. The fan was a wonder and helped him to breathe. Once he stuck his hand in it, and several times mosquito netting got caught in the blades. But it was worth it!

The SeaBees landed late one evening. Joe was on the rude dock when they came ashore. He was surprised to see how happy they were to be on land again, even a place like the rock. He guessed that everybody in the Navy wanted to be where he wasn't. He often thought of that night in later years. It was the time he met Luther Billis!

Joe had never seen anybody quite like Luther Billis. The SeaBee was big, fat, and brown. He wore a gold ring in his left ear and several bracelets. He was beautifully tattooed. Billis was accompanied by a young Jewish boy who trailed along behind him. He accosted Joe in a bright, breezy manner. "Hiya, Joe! Whaddaya know?"

"Hello!" Joe replied.

"Got a ship's store here?" Billis asked.

"Over there!" Joe pointed.

"Well, come along, Joe, and I'll set you up! Won a lot of money on this trip. Teaching the boys a few facts of life!" He whisked out a bundle of banknotes. "Come along, Hyman!" he shouted peremptorily at the Jewish boy.

When Billis had treated half a dozen men whom he had never seen before, he pointed admiringly at his Jewish friend. "I want to tell you," he said. "There's a genius. A college professor!" Billis smiled proudly and his friend grinned. "Professor Hyman Weinstein, but it could just as well be Einstein!" He laughed uproariously at his joke. "The Professor can speak five languages. Toss them a little Yiddish, Hyman." Weinstein, who found in Billis both a champion and a wonderful friend, spoke a few words of the Old Testament in Yiddish.

"He ain't kidding, either!" a boy on the sidelines whispered. "The Psalms."

"German, Hyman!" Billis ordered like a ringmaster displaying the tricks of a prize lion. The Professor rattled off some German words.

"Wouldn't that kill Hitler!" Billis shouted. "Professor, give them some Latin." Hyman obliged with some legal phrases, and Billis thereupon asked for French. When his friend had spoken several phrases in French, Billis demanded quiet. "This one will kill you, guys. Give them some Russian, Hyman."

As Hyman rattled off a long series of Russian words, Billis started singing "Yo, heave ho!" to the tune of the *Volga Boatmen*. His listeners started to laugh. "Knock it off! Knock it off!" he shouted. "Them Bolsheviks ain't doin' so bad! Hitler ain't laughin'!" He threw his big hand around Hyman's shoulder and pulled the little Jew to the bench on which he and Joe were sitting.

The next three hours were the most wonderful Joe had spent on the rock. He didn't know that sailors could be such fine people. Billis wasn't afraid of anything, had been everywhere. And Weinstein could speak five languages. They talked about everything. Billis thought there was a God and that after the war there would be a big boom in aviation. Weinstein thought France would be a great country again. "What do you think, Joe?" Billis inquired. Joe was flabbergasted that a stranger would want to know what he thought. But, encouraged by their inquiry, he blurted out his philosophy.

"I think it's dumb to be on this rock when you guys are

going out to do some fightin'. All I do is sit here day after day. Three times a week planes come in, and I gas them up. The rest of the time I try to keep out of trouble. It's a hell of a way to spend the war. I feel ashamed of myself!"

Billis was appalled at Joe's statement. "Whatsa matter?" he demanded. "You ain't thinkin' right at all, Joe! You make me very surprised! I thought you was a much sounder man than that!"

"What did I say wrong?" Joe inquired.

"About you not bein' of any use? If you wasn't here, who would be?" Billis asked contentiously. "You know damn well who would be here. The Japs! And supposin' the Japs was here when we broke down? Where would we go for repairs? We would be in a hell of a mess, wouldn't we?" He appeared to be furious at Joe for turning the island over to the Japs.

"I never thought of it that way," Joe replied.

"We all can't fight the Japs," Billis added sagely.

"That's right, Luther," Joe agreed. "Are you and Hyman goin' up to the front?"

They didn't know where they were going, but they had a lot of heavy machinery. Probably going to some island. Going to invade some island.

"What you goin' to do when peace comes?" Billis asked.

"Back to my shop in Columbus, Ohio. I'm a shoemaker."

"What you goin' to do if we all start wearin' plastic shoes?" Billis demanded. "Won't have to have them mended?" The thought shocked Joe. He had never thought of such a thing before. He had no answer. People would always have to have their shoes fixed. But Luther Billis' agile mind was on to new problems. "You got a girl?" he asked.

"No," Joe replied. "I ain't."

"You ain't got a girl?" Billis shouted. "What the hell kind of a sailor are you?"

"I never went with girls very much," Joe explained.

"I tell you what I do," Billis said with his hand about Joe's shoulder. "I'm gonna get you a girl. I like you. "You're a real Joe, ain't he, Hyman?" Hyman agreed.

"Look at the moon over the water!" Weinstein said. Billis turned to study the rare sight of moonlight upon tropic waters with palm trees along the shore and a ship at the dock.

"God, that's beautiful!" he said. "You ought to come down here lots, Joe. You ought to look at that. Like Hyman just done."

The three men sat there in silence and watched the moon-light wax and wane along the waves. Never before in sixteen months had Joe seen that strange and lovely thing. He suddenly wanted to go with Billis and the Professor. He wanted to be with men that talked happily and saw new things. He wanted . . .

But at midnight the boat pulled out. The SeaBees were gone. Joe followed the ship as long as it rode in the moon-light. He had never before felt so strange. Great inchoate thoughts welled up within him. He could not sleep, and so he walked along the edge of the island. The airstrip shone in the moonlight. "It's beautiful," he said. "And look at the water bouncin' on them cliffs. It's beautiful."

The world was beautiful that night. It was beautiful as only a tropic night on some distant island can be beautiful. A million men in the South Seas would deny it to one another, would ridicule it in their letters home. But it was beautiful. Perhaps some of the million would deny the beauty because, like Joe, they had never seen it.

Something like this was going through Joe's mind when he became aware that men were behind him. He started to walk along the edge of the cliff when a light flashed in his eyes. "No you don't!" a voice shouted. Quickly two men ran up and grabbed him.

"Here's another of them," the voice with the light cried. Joe was hauled off to a jeep.

"Bunch of damned bootleggers!" a gruff voice said as he was thrust into a small truck. He looked at the other prisoners. He knew none of them.

"He ain't one of us!" the apparent leader of the gang said.

"Keep your mouth shut!" the gruff voice ordered.

"But he ain't one of us!"

"Shut up!"

"On your way, big time!" the leader of the gang grunted in surly tones.

That night Joe slept in the brig. He found himself among a group of six enlisted men who had been running a still in a cave along the cliffs. They had finally been caught. They were making pure alcohol from canned corn and sugar. They had a market for all they could make. Each man had been clearing two hundred dollars a month.

Joe studied them. They were guys just like him. He wondered why they got mixed up in such a racket. He wondered if Luther Billis was like them. Luther had lots of money. But somehow he felt that Luther was different. These men were in trouble.

"I'm gonna spill the whole story!" a little machinist's mate said. He had built the still. "If they try to pin a rap on me, I'll spill the whole story!"

"You do," the leader whispered hoarsely, "and I'll kill you. That's a promise!"

But next morning the little machinist's mate did spill the whole story. Joe was shocked. The revelation came shortly after the Skipper had ordered Joe to stand aside. Obviously Joe wasn't implicated. So there he stood, by the window, while the machinist's mate told how a lieutenant had sold them canned corn by the case and sugar by the barrel. He had taken one-fourth of the profits. Made four hundred bucks a month.

That was one time the Skipper didn't bellow. "Get him right away," he said in a very low voice. No one spoke until the lieutenant appeared. He was a young man. He took one look at the six culprits, grew faint, and sat down. "Have you anything to say?" the Skipper asked.

"No, sir!" the lieutenant replied.

"You are confined to your quarters!" the Skipper said briefly. "Take the rest of these men to the brig." Joe felt all funny inside. He knew his turn was next.

"Well," the skipper said. "So it's you again! Always in trouble!"

"Oh, no, sir!"

"How did you happen to be down at the cliffs? One of their watchers?"

"Oh, no, sir! I never had anything to do with these men. Never."

"What were you doing at the cliff?"

Joe swallowed hard. At first the words wouldn't come. "I was watching the ship go, sir!"

In a flash, the Skipper saw himself, once on Haiti. A ship was leaving the bay. He was an ensign then, and sure that he would be an admiral one day. He could understand why young men look at ships. "You better stay out of trouble, young feller," he said. That was all.

It would not be fair to say that Joe had forgotten Billis. But he had ceased thinking constantly about the strange fellow when a letter came to the rock. It was for Joe and came from Miss Essie Schultz, Perkasie, Pennsylvania. Joe read the letter avidly:

Dear Joe,

Please excuse me for writing when we haven't been introduced, but my good friend Mr. Luther Billis told me that you didn't have any girl to write to. I write letters to seventeen sailors and one soldier. I think you boys are the bravest men in America. I would never be brave enough to fight against the Japs. I am glad we have boys like you to fight for us. I wish I had a good looking photograph to send you, but you know how it is these days. One or two prints is all you can get. So I am sending you this one. The one in the middle is me. Skinny, eh? I work in a pants factory. At present we are making sailors pants, so if yours don't fit, blame me. (Ha!) I like to dance and like Benny Goodman and Louie Prima the best. I listen to the radio a good deal and read some books every year. Mr. Billis said you were a very swell guy and that I would like you. I believe I would. Won't you please write and tell me all about yourself? I promise to answer right away.

Yours (?)
Essie Schultz.

P.S. Send me a picture.

The letter simply bowled Joe over! It passed his comprehension that Luther Billis would have taken the trouble to do such a thing. But that Essie should have written to him . . . That was a true miracle! He read the letter eight or ten times. It was so nicely written, in straight lines. And it smelled good. And there was Essie in front of a building. And there was snow on the ground! He looked and looked. Essie wasn't the worst looking, either. Not by a long shot!

He got seven more letters from Essie, sweet, cheerful letters. He showed her picture to several of his friends. You couldn't see much of her face, but what there was looked mighty neat and clean. Joe felt fine. Then one day he got a brief letter. "I am going to marry the soldier," Essie said. "He thinks I ought to stop writing to the rest of you boys. I tell him he's jealous of the Navy. (Ha!)"

Joe was glum for several days. He tore up Essie's picture. "Don't want no picture of no married woman," he said to himself. "I wanta stay out of trouble."

But he was miserable. Essie's letters had been . . . Well, he couldn't say it in words. All he knew was that weeks were a lot longer now. What if she had been writing to seventeen other fellows? She had also written to him, and that was what mattered. Joe tried four times to send her congratulations, but couldn't find the words. Then one day he was at the airstrip when some enlisted men flew in from Noumea. One of them had a grass skirt, a lovely thing of yellow and red.

"How much you want for that, buddy?" Joe asked.

."Fifteen dollars," the seaman replied.

"That's a lot of money," Joe answered.

"That's right," the seaman replied. "You can get 'em cheaper in Noumea, but you ain't in Noumea."

Still, the skirt seemed such a wonderful present for a girl that Joe bought it. He wrapped it carefully, addressed the package to Essie Schultz, Perkasie, Pennsylvania, and had it censored. After the officer had finished looking at the skirt, Joe slipped in the little piece of paper: "All happiness, Joe."

It wasn't that he didn't see girls on the rock. Every three or four months some plane would come in with a USO vaudeville troupe aboard. If they had time, the girls always danced or sang in the Red Cross hut. But that wasn't like having a girl . . . Well, a special girl.

Some time later Joe received a letter direct from Billis. It was brief. "A girl named Alice Baker from Corvallis is going to write to you pretty soon. I know her big sister and her brother. He is a dogface. (Ha!) She is a fine girl. Her sister thinks I am an officer don't tell her different. Your best buddy, L. Billis."

Joe was delighted with news from Luther. He wondered if Luther had worn an officer's uniform when he was in Corvallis. That was dangerous stuff. They really threw the book at you if they caught you.

While Joe waited for news from Alice Baker, a strange thing happened. One night at eleven-thirty he was routed out of bed by the guard. "You're wanted at the Skipper's shack!" he was told. In the darkness he went along coral paths to where the Skipper had had a mansion built for himself. It cost, men figured, about $9,000. The Skipper said that by God, if he was going to live on this rock, he'd live like a gentleman. He had quarters that many an admiral would envy.

"Joe!" he said, "when I was walking across the floor tonight, I felt a splinter over there. There's a sander in the closet. Rub the thing down, will you?"

Joe broke out the sander and went to work. As he did so, the Skipper slid his bare feet from one board to another. "Give this a touch, will you?" "Sand that joint down a little." Joe worked till one-thirty. "Better take the day off tomorrow," the Skipper said.

Joe told nobody of what had happened. A few nights later he was called out again. This time the linoleum in the bathroom was loose. Joe fixed it. In the middle of his work the Skipper interrupted. "Joe," he said, "in that cabinet there's a bottle of very fine whiskey. I'm going to walk along the beach for twenty minutes. If I catch you drinking it when I get back, I'll raise hell with you. What time have you?" The two men synchronized their watches at exactly 0119. "Mind you," the Skipper said, "I'll be back in twenty minutes."

Joe worked on, keeping his mind off the cabinet. He liked whiskey, but he didn't want no trouble with nobody. At 0139 the Skipper returned singing gently. He went archly to the cabinet and peeked in. Then he snorted and pulled out the whiskey bottle.

"I didn't touch it, sir!" Joe protested.

"Goddamned squarehead!" the Skipper shouted. "I told you I was going to be gone twenty minutes."

"I didn't touch it!" Joe insisted.

"I know you didn't, Joe," the Skipper said in a tired voice. "But I meant you to. You're a good boy. You work hard. I'll go out again. If you want a nip, help yourself. But if I ever see you doing it, I'll throw you in the clink!" He went out again, singing. After that Joe spent a good deal of his time fixing up the Skipper's shack. But he never told a soul.

At mail call one day Joe got a letter from Corvallis. It was from Alice Baker. She was eighteen and a senior in Corvallis High School. She had no boy friend, and her brother was a soldier in England. Ensign Billis had told her sister about Joe and her sister had asked her to write. She felt silly, but she guessed it was all right. She concluded, "Ensign Billis said you were slow, but I like slow boys. Some of the boys in Corvallis are so fast they think if they look at a girl, why she falls in love with them. This picture of me is pretty much the way I look. Sincerely, Alice Baker."

Joe could not believe that any girl as lovely as Alice Baker's picture would write to him. He looked at the picture eight or ten times a day, but would show it to no one. He was afraid they wouldn't believe him. After two days he decided that he must reply to her sweet letter. He labored over his answer a long time. It came out like this:

Dear Alice,

I nearly fell out of my chair when they gave me that letter from you. It was the nicest letter I have ever got from anyone. I have read it twenty four times so far and I will keep right on reading till another comes. I don't believe you when you say you have no boy friends. A girl as pretty as you could have a hundred. I am afraid to show your picture to the men in my hut. They would all want to write to you. It is your picture, isn't it, Alice? I suppose Ensign Billis told you all about me. I am a shoemaker in Columbus Ohio and right now I am riding nineteen months on this rock. I am not good looking and I like whiskey but I never get drunk. I hope you will write to me. I would like to send you a picture, Alice, but we can't get none made on this rock. It is no good trying. My uncle has a picture of me took a long time ago. I will ask him to send it to you. I am fatter now. Please anser this letter, Alice, as I think you are one fine girl.

Yours truly,
Joe.

The correspondence went on from there. Finally Alice was writing to Joe three times a week. And finally Joe got up nerve enough to show her picture. In Navy fashion they went mad about her. Half of them called her "that bag" and the other half wanted to know who the movie star was. Joe stood by in rapt pleasure. They kidded him a lot, and that evening an older man who knew a thing or two about sailors came by and asked if he could see the picture again. Joe practically fell over himself to think that anyone had remembered her. They sat on the quonset steps and studied Alice Baker's picture. "A fine girl," the older man said.

One day a letter from Alice arrived soaked with salt water. Joe could barely read the writing. He took it down to the postoffice to find what had happened. "A plane went into the drink somewhere up the line."

"Anybody hurt?" Joe inquired.

"Ten dead. They got the mail bags, though. A diver went down for them."

Joe handled the letter gingerly. It was a terrible thing. A letter from the girl you loved, passed on by the hands of dead men. Joe had seen little of death, but it frightened him vastly. It was like getting into trouble. It ruined everything. One of the officers had said, when the lieutenant's court-martial was read for selling government property to the boot-leggers, "I'd commit suicide!" But the lieutenant, who was sentenced to jail for three years, didn't commit suicide. He lived on, and so did the bootleggers. They went to jail and lived. Joe was also one of the men who live on, no matter what happens.

He assured himself of that the night they found the yeoman hanging in the palm grove. Nobody ever understood exactly why he did it just then. His wife had a baby after he was overseas sixteen months, but he agreed to the divorce and she married the other man. The yeoman took it OK. Joe knew him well, and then seven months after it was all over he strung himself up.

Two other incidents reminded Joe of death on his hot lonely, barren, sticky rock. One was a letter from Luther Billis. It made Joe shudder with apprehension for his buddy. "The Navy took this pitcher of me," he wrote. "Youd a thought it would of busted the camera. You see I aint got the ring in my ear. They made me take it out but now I got it back in. The pitcher is for the Navy when they give me my medal. What I did they should of had a hero do. Anyway I got two Jap swords out of it and they are beauties. I am sending one to my mom and the other I give to my skipper, Commander Hoag, who was the best guy that ever lived, even if he was an officer. I hope you have heard from Alice Baker. She is a fine girl I tried to kiss her once and she slapped my face. Your best buddy, L. Billis."

The second incident occurred on June 7. They had a ball game that afternoon, and as they came in from the game they heard a lot of shouting. "We invaded France!" everybody was yelling. There was some shooting to celebrate, and the Skipper ordered a whistle to blow. "Any goddamned whistle, but blow it!" They used the fire truck's, and it sounded fine. Then the chaplain suggested they have a prayer meeting. The Skipper stood beside him on the platform. "Our prayers go out tonight," the chaplain intoned, "for all the brave men who are fighting the enemy. Wherever brave men are fighting and dying, O Lord, protect them." They sang two hymns and the Skipper asked if anyone could sing the Marseillaise. A former schoolteacher could, and the rest hummed.

These events deepened Joe's perceptions. If a fine man like Luther Billis could risk his life, why was he, Joe, sitting the war out on this rock? If Alice Baker's brother could land in France what was Joe doing on a coral reef? Up to this time Joe had never thought about the men back home. But on the evening of June 7, 1944, he thought about them a great deal. Some men died in France. Some men like Luther Billis fought against the Japs. Some men like the yeoman lost everything they had and committed suicide. Some men like the bootleggers got heebie-jeebies on the rock. Some men worked in airplane factories or helped keep the country running. And some men did nothing.

But before his thoughts ran away with him, Joe stopped. "It's the same on this rock," he mused. "Look how little some guys have! And look what I got! Alice Baker, an electric fan, a shot of the Skipper's whiskey now and then, and a best buddy who is already a hero!"

Thoughts of death, however, persisted. One night he sat bolt upright in bed. He was sweating all over. Phantasms of horror assailed him! Luther Billis was dead! On an island teeming with Japs Luther lay beside a coconut log. Joe wiped the sweat from his face and tried to go back to sleep. But all night, in the hot quonset, he could see Luther Billis and the coconut log. It was not until he received a short letter from Billis that his mind gained rest. The SeaBee was fine and was teaching Professor Weinstein Beche-le-Mer so he would be able to speak six languages!

His worry about Luther decided him upon one thing, however. He wanted Alice and Luther to have pictures of him, just in case. He would have his picture taken after all! That was a solemn decision on the rock. First of all you had to find somebody who had stolen film and photographic paper. Then you had to arrange the sitting surreptitiously. And finally you had to get the photograph through the mail. So Joe, who never wanted any trouble with anybody, set out in search of a bootlegging photographer. He found one on the other end of the island. He was a thin, round-shouldered man. Where he got his equipment no one knew. He had a big deal of some kind on the fire. They all knew that.

"It'll be ten dollars," the photographer growled. "You get two prints and the negative."

Joe whistled. The photographer snapped at him. "You ain't bein' forced into this, buddy. I'm the guy that's takin' the chances. You saw what them bootleggers got. The price is ten bucks."

Joe took out his wallet and gave the man two fives. It was a lot to pay, but if your girl was in Corvallis, had never seen you, had no picture of you but that skinny one your uncle sent, well . . . what better you got to spend ten bucks on?

The photographer made ready with a cheap box camera. "Don't look so stiff!" he told Joe, but Joe was no dummy. If he was paying ten bucks for one photograph, it would be the best. So, like a ramrod, his hair smoothed back, he glanced stonily at the expensive birdie. The photographer shrugged his pale shoulders and went ahead. "Come back in three days. Remember, you get two prints and the negative. I don't want no beefing. I'm the guy that takes the risks."

Three days later Joe got his two pictures. They were pretty good. Mostly you saw his uniform and pronounced jaw. But he looked like a clean, quiet sailor. Just like eight hundred other guys on the rock. Only the others didn't look quite so sure of themselves when they'd been on the rock as long as Joe. He grinned at the pictures and all the way back to camp kept stealing furtive glances at himself.

When he arrived at the camp the chaplain was waiting for him. The padre was a Catholic and Joe a Methodist, but they were friends. The chaplain's business was brief. Alice Baker had been killed. An auto accident. Her sister sent the news.

The padre had never heard of Alice Baker. All he knew was that a human being of greater or less importance to some other human being was dead. No message could transcend that. He cast about for words, which never seemed to be available for such emergencies. The day was hot. Sweat ran down Joe's face until it looked like tears. "Brave people are dying throughout the world," the chaplain said. "And brave people live after them." There was nothing more to say. Joe sat looking at the priest for a few minutes and then left.

He went into the brilliant sunlight. Glare from the airstrip was intense. Even the ocean was hot. Joe looked at the waves whose beauty Luther Billis had discovered. They came rippling toward the rock in overwhelming monotony. Joe counted them. One, two, three! They were the months he had been on the rock. Fourteen, fifteen, sixteen. That was when he met Luther Billis. Seventeen, eighteen. The yeoman had committed suicide. Nineteen, twenty, twenty-one. Alice Baker had become his girl. Twenty-five, twenty-six, twenty-seven. They were all the same, one after the other, like the dreary months.

Joe dropped his head in his hands. A girl he had never seen. A funny town he had never visited. "I want to get out of here," he muttered to himself. "I got to get out of here!"

Fo' Dolla'

ATABRINE Benny had the best job in the islands. Field man for the Malaria Control Unit. He traveled from plantation to plantation with large bottles of atabrine pills. Wherever there might be malaria to infect mosquitoes to infect our men, Benny was on guard. All day long, on one island or another, he gave little yellow pills to little yellow men. His freedom of movement, lack of a boss, and opportunity for spending long hours with plantation owners made his job an enviable one.

Benny was a fat little man with no bottom at all. He went straight down in back and way out in front. He walked with his toes at ten minutes of two and consequently moved with a tireless waddle. He was a druggist from Waco, Texas, a man nearly fifty. He had enlisted in the Navy out of patriotism, boredom, the fact that his two sons were in the Marines, and because his wife was a mean old son-of-a-bitch. "Ornriest goddam woman in Waco, Texas," he confided one day as we climbed a hill to a small French plantation.

"But I should worry about her now!" he added. "What I got to moan about? This job's romantic. I want to see the

South Pacific ever since I am a little guy. Now here I am! Right in the heart of it!"

Benny grinned, adjusting his heavy bottles. As we reached a grubby clearing, with a few coconut trees, bananas, pineapples and cacao bushes, he gave a long, mournful cry, "Yaaaaaooooooo!"

From a hut near the jungle a native Mary shuffled out. She carried a mammoth conch shell, an ancient thing dating back a century or more, encrusted by the lips and hands of numerous villagers. On this shell she blew a long, sad blast. Slowly, from cacao, coconut, and jungle, men and women shuffled. Tonks, natives, and nondescript workers appeared, shy, reticent, nudging one another, and giggling.

Benny and I took our places beneath an open bamboo lean-to. We lined up bottles of atabrine, large tins of candy, and a carton of cigarettes. Little Tonkinese workers approached first, men in the lead, then women. Patiently they leaned their heads back, closed their eyes, and opened their mouths. Deftly Atabrine Benny popped three tablets between each one's jet black betel-stained teeth. Waiting Tonks would laugh and joke while the unfortunate one taking the medicine made a horrible face and gulped a drink from the water jug. Benny and I stood by, our shirts, our pants, our entire bodies dripping with jungle sweat. Benny watched each performer carefully. Usually he would pat the Tonk on the head, give him a couple of cigarettes or a bar of candy, and shove him off.

But occasionally he would become furious. "Goddam pig!" he would shout, cuffing the unfortunate Tonk about a bit. "Open your mouth!" And he would ram a curved index finger into the man's mouth behind the black teeth, twisting the tongue up. With a deft flick he would pop out one or two unswallowed atabrine tablets and catch them in his other hand. "Eat 'em up!" he would shout. And the Tonk would grin sheepishly, lick his beteled teeth, take another drink of water, and swallow the tablets. "Wait a minute!" Benny would bellow. Into the man's mouth once more would go the searching finger. "Good fellow!" Benny would beam, giving the recalcitrant Tonk a pat on the head and a couple of cigarettes.

"You got to watch 'em," he whispered.

"Don't they like the taste?" I inquired, smiling back at a grinning Tonkinese woman who stood waiting.

"Taste ain't nothin' to a guy that chews betel," Benny said. "Everything tastes the same."

"Then why the act with the atabrine?"

"Clever bastards," Benny grinned. "Took 'em about two weeks to discover that them pills is a wonderful yellow dye. They keep 'em back of their tongues and then use 'em to dye grass skirts with."

"Grass skirts?" I inquired.

When the session was ended, Benny grabbed a handful of his precious yellow pills and threw them on the table. "For your skirts!" he shouted, wiggling his hips as if he were wearing one of the grass skirts the Tonks sold to American soldiers.

As Tonkinese women battled for the valuable dyestuff the French plantation owner, a man of forty-eight or more, stopped us. He was a short, sloppy fellow, round-faced, bleary-eyed, stoop-shouldered. His pants hung in a sagging line below his belly. He had a nervous manner and a slight cough as he spoke.

"It's Monsieur Jacques Benoit!" Atabrine Benny cried in a loud pleasant voice. The plantation owner nodded slightly and extended a wet, pudgy hand.

"Mr. Benny," he said forcefully. "Again, once more I asking you. Not give the women pills!" His voice was harsh.

"It don't do any harm!" Benny argued.

"But the gouvernment! Our gouvernment! And yours, too. They say, 'Tonkinese! No more grass skirts!' What I can do?" He shrugged his shoulders apologetically.

"All right!" Benny grumbled. "All right!"

"Remember, Mr. Benny!" the Frenchman said, half pleading, half warning. "Atabrine pills! They drink, OK. They use for grass skirt, no!" Monsieur Benoit shrugged his shoulders and moved away.

"Them damned Frenchies!" Benny snorted as we climbed in our jeep at the foot of the hill.

"What's this about grass skirts, Benny?" I asked.

"The plantation owners is getting scared. That's all," he grumbled. "Why, you wouldn't want a finer bunch of people to work with than them Tonks. You can see that. It's just them damned plantation owners. And the guv'mint."

"You really mean the government has stopped the making of grass skirts?"

"They're tryin' to, sir. But as you can plainly see, I'm

doin' me best to bitch the works, you might say. It's this way. These here Tonks is brought out to the plantations to work the coconuts and coffee. They come from Tonkin China, I been told. A French possession. They come for three or five years. French guv'mint provides passage. Then they're indentured to these plantation owners, just like in the old days settlers was indentured in America, especially Pennsylvania and Georgia. A professor from Harvard explained it all to me a couple of months ago. Said it was the same identical system. Plantation owner promises to feed 'em, clothe 'em, give 'em medical care."

"What does he pay them?"

" 'Bout ninety dollars a year, man or woman, is standard price now. Course, they got good livin' out here. That ninety is almost all profit."

"Do they ever go back to Tonkin?" I asked.

"Sure. Most of 'em do. Go back with maybe four hundred dollars. Wife and husband both work, you see. Rich people in their own country. Very rich people if they save their dough. It's not a bad system."

"But what's this about the government and the grass skirts?" I persisted. We were now in the jeep once more, and Benny, with his stomach hunched up against the steering wheel, was heading for the next plantation.

"Well, that's the economy of the island. It's all worked out. Coconuts worth so much. Cows worth so much. Cloth worth so much. Wages worth so much. Everybody makes a livin'. Not a good one, maybe, but not so bad, either. Then, bang!"

Benny clapped his hands with a mighty wallop, then grabbed for the steering wheel to pull the jeep back onto the road. "Bang!" he repeated, pleased with the effect. "Into this economy comes a couple hundred thousand American soldiers with more money than they can spend. And everybody wants a grass skirt. So a Tonkinese woman, if she works hard, can make eight skirts a week. That's just what a good woman can make, with help from her old man. So in one month she makes more money than she used to in a year. You can't beat it! So pretty soon all of the Tonks wants to quit working for Monsieur Jacques Benoit and start working for themselves. And Tonk men work on plantations all day and then work for their wives all night making grass skirts, and pretty soon everything is in a hell of a mess." Benny jammed on the brakes to avoid hitting a cow.

"It's just like the NRA back in the States. Mr. Roosevelt might be a great man. Mind you, I ain't sayin' he ain't. But you got to admit he certainly screwed up the economy of our country. The economy of a country," Benny said, slapping me on the knee with each syllable, "is a very tricky thing. A very tricky thing."

"So what happened?" I asked.

"Like I told you. The economy out here went to hell. Tonks makin' more than the plantation owners. Their best hands stoppin' work on cows and coconuts. Tonk women who couldn't read makin' five, six hundred dollars a year, clear profit. So the plantation French went to the guv'mint and said, 'See here. We got our rights. These Tonks is indentured to us. They got to work for us.' And the guv'mint said, 'That's right. That's exactly as we see it, too.' And strike me dead if they didn't pass a law that no Tonk could sell grass skirts 'ceptin' only to plantation owners. And only plantation owners could sell them to Americans!"

Benny looked down the road. He said no more. He was obviously disgusted. I knew I was expected to ask him some further question, but I had no idea what. He solved my dilemma by walloping me a hamhanded smack on the knee. "Can you imagine a bunch of American men, just good average American men, letting any guv'mint get away with that? Especially a French guv'mint?"

"No," I said, sensing an incipient Tom Paine. "I can't quite imagine it."

"Neither by God did we!" he grinned. He slowed the car down and leaned over to whisper to me. "Why do you suppose all the grass skirts is yellow these days? Didn't they used to be red and blue? What do you suppose?" And he tapped his big jar of atabrine pills. "And there's nothin' in it for me. Not one goddam grass skirt do I own," he said. "Just for the hell of it!" and he grinned the ancient defiance upon which all freedom, ultimately, rests.

"And I am ashamed to admit," he added in a low voice as he turned into a lane leading toward the water's edge, "that it was the Marines who fought back. Not the Navy! I'm kind of ashamed that the Navy should take such a pushin' around. But not the Marines. Now you watch when we get around this corner. There'll be a bunch of Tonk women and a bunch of Marines. They'll think this is an MP car and they'll all run like hell. Watch!"

Atabrine Benny stepped on the gas and drove like mad, the way the MP's always do when they get out of sight of other MP's. He screeched his jeep around a corner and pulled it up sharp about fifty yards from the water. To one side, under a rude series of kiosks made of bamboo and canvas, sat five or six Tonkinese women surrounded by miscellaneous souvenirs and admiring Marines, fresh from Guadalcanal.

At the sight of Benny's jeep bursting in upon them, Marines dived for the coconut plantation and were soon lost among the trees. The Tonks started to grab everything in sight and waddle like ducks into their incredible little huts. But as they did so, one old woman saw that it was not the malicious MP's but good old Atabrine Benny.

"Haloo, Benny!" she screamed in a hoarse voice. And that was my introduction to Bloody Mary.

She was, I judge, about fifty-five. She was not more than five feet tall, weighed about 110 pounds, had few teeth and those funereally black, was sloppy in dress, and had thin ravines running out from the corners of her mouth. These ravines, about four on each side, were usually filled with betel juice, which made her look as if her mouth had been gashed by a rusty razor. Her name, Bloody Mary, was well given.

Like all Tonkinese women, Mary wore a simple uniform: sandals on her feet, a conical peach-basket hat on her head, black sateen trousers, and white blouse. And like all Tonkinese women, she was graceful, quick in her movements, and alternately grave and merry. Her oval face was yellow. Her eyes were Oriental. Her neck was beautifully proportioned. Around it she wore a G.I. identification chain from which hung a silver Marine emblem.

Because of her ill-fitting sandals, she rolled from side to side as she walked and the Marine emblem moved pendulum-like across her bosom. But her little peach-basket hat remained always steady above her white blouse. She had a sly look as she approached the jeep. Her almond eyes were inscrutable, but jesting. It was clear that she liked Benny.

As soon as she reached the jeep, she darted her strong small hand in, grabbed the atabrine bottle, popped three pills into her mouth, chewed them up, taste and all, and swallowed them without water. She then stole a handful of the precious dye and placed it in a pocket of her sateen pants. In a continuous motion she replaced the bottle, smiled her horrible smile, black teeth now tinged with pale yellow, and walked sedately away. Benny grabbed his bottle and waddled after her. To me, they looked like two old ganders heading for the water.

Bloody Mary, oblivious to everyone, returned to her boot-legger's kiosk and sat cross-legged on the earth beside a weird collection of items. She had some grass skirts, predominantly yellow, some beautiful sea shells, some mother-of-pearl, two bows with arrows, a new peach-basket hat, three toy outrigger war canoes, and two hookahs, the water-filled smoking pipes good either for tobacco or for opium. Mary would probably get not less than eighty dollars for what she had on display.

With rapid motions of her arms she signaled the Marines in the coconuts to come on back. Slowly they emerged, young, battle-old veterans who saw in Bloody Mary a symbol of age-old defiance of unjust laws. I stood to one side and to my surprise the first two men who entered her kiosk were not Marines at all, but terribly embarrassed Seabees. Grinning at me and at the Marines, they unrolled the bundles they had under their arms. Well made grass skirts tumbled out.

So the stories were true! The SeaBees were a bunch of dressmakers! The Tonks were selling grass skirts faster than they could make them or buy them from natives. So the ominpresent SeaBees were in the game, just as they were making Jap flags, Australian bracelets, and New Zealand memorial gods. They were remarkable men, ingenious men, and there just weren't enough airfields to build to keep them busy all the time.

Bloody Mary appraised the skirts of the first SeaBee. She liked them. She held up two fingers. "Two dolla'," she suggested. The SeaBee shook his head. "Two-fifty!" he countered.

"Goddam snovabeech no!!" Bloody Mary screamed at him, hitting him in the stomach and kicking the skirts away.

"Two-fifty!" the SeaBee persisted.

At this Mary went into a paroxysm of rage. Tonkinese profanity ricocheted off the surprised SeaBee's head. When he could stand no more of Mary's cursing and the Marines' laughter, he bundled up his wares and moved away. But Mary kept after him. "Goddam stinker!" she screamed hoarsely, following that with bursting Tonkinese epithets, and ending with the Marine Corps' choicest vilification: "Soandso bastard!"

Then composing her placid face, the old harridan ignored the Marines' applause, smiled sweetly at the next SeaBee, and began fumbling his skirts. When he drew back, she patted him on his shoulder and reassured him in Pidgin English, "Me look, me look, me buy."

On the way home Atabrine Benny told me how Mary had acquired her vocabulary. "After the new laws she sneaked out here. Does a very good business, although I expect they'll close her out one of these days. Well, after she had been here a little while, this bunch of Marines from Guadal moved in. Rest cure. They came to like the old devil." Then Benny went on to tell of how the Marines, with nothing better to do, would hang around the betel-stained old Tonk and teach her their roughest language.

'Stand up like a man, and tell them to go to hell, Mary," the old, tough Marines would tell the old, tough Tonk. Mary would grin, not understanding a word of what they were saying, but after they came to see her for many days in a row the old miracle of the subdued races took place again. The yellow woman learned dozens of white words but the white men learned not one yellow word. When she had mastered their vilest obscenities, they made her an honorary Marine, emblem and all.

The words Mary learned were hardly ones she could have used, say as a salesgirl in Macy's or Jordan Marsh. For example, if a sailor just off a boat asked her the price of a grass skirt, she would smile sweetly and say, "Fo' dolla'."

" 'At's too much for a grass skirt, baby."

Then Mary would scream at him, thrusting her nose into his face, "Bullshit, brother!" She wasn't quite sure what the words meant, but from the way new men would jump back in astonishment as if they had been hit with a board, she knew it was effective. And so she used it for effect, and more men would come back next week and say, "Four bucks for that? Not on your life!" just to hear the weathered old Tonk scream out some phrase they could report to the fellows in the saloon back home, "and then, by God, maybe those guys would know us guys was really seein' somethin' out here!" And for Mary the best part was that after she had cursed and reviled them enough, the astonished soldiers and sailors usually bought what she had to sell, and at her price.

When it became apparent that Bloody Mary was not going to abide by the island order, plantation owners asked the government to intervene with the American military authorities.

"Would the island command place Bloody Mary's kiosk out of bounds?"

"Certainly!" An order went out forthwith, and two military police were detailed to see that no Americans visited the kiosk.

But who was going to keep the kiosk from visiting the Americans? That was a subtle problem, because pretty soon all the military police were guarding was an empty chunk of canvas strung across a pole about five feet off the ground. Mary wasn't there any more.

She was up the island, hidden among the roots of a banyan tree the Marines had found. She was selling her grass skirts to more men than before, because she was the only woman who dared defy both the civil and military governments.

"But commander," the civil representative protested. "Your men are still trading with her. The whole purpose of the law is being evaded."

"What can we do? We put her place under restriction. But she doesn't live there any more. It seems to me that's your problem."

"Please, commander! I beg you. Please see what you can do. The plantation owners are complaining." The civil representative bowed.

The island commander scratched his head. His orders were to keep peace and good will, and that meant with plantation owners, not with Tonkinese or sailors off stray ships. Accordingly he dispatched an underling to seek out this damned Bloody Mary what's her name and see what the score was.

The officer, a naval lieutenant, went. He found Mary under a tree with a half dozen admiring Marines around her. They were teaching her new words. When the lieutenant came up, he bowed and spoke in French. Mary listened attentively, for like most Tonks, she knew French fairly well. The lieutenant was pleased that she followed his words and that she apparently understood that she must stop selling grass skirts not only at the kiosk but everywhere else as well. He smiled courteously and felt very proud of himself. Dashed few officers hereabout could speak French. He was not, however, prepared for Mary's answer.

Standing erect and smiling at her teachers, she thrust her face into that of the young lieutenant and screamed, *"Soandso you, major!"*

The officer jumped back, appalled! The Marines bit their

lips and twisted their stomach muscles into hard knots. Mary just grinned, the reddish betel juice filling the ravines near her mouth. When she saw that the lieutenant was shocked and stunned, she moved closer, until she was touching him. He shrank away from the peach-basket brim, the sateen pantaloons, but he could not writhe away from the hoarse, betel-sprayed shout: "Bullshit, major!"

All he could say was, "Well!" And with that austere comment on Marine-coached Tonkinese women, he walked stiffly away and drove back to the commander, who laughed down in his belly the way the enlisted men had.

The upshot was one of those grand Navy touches! By heavens, Bloody Mary was on Marine property now. She was their problem. She wasn't a Navy problem at all! And the curt, very proper note that went to the Marine Commandant made no bones about it: "Get the Tonkinese woman known as Bloody Mary to hell off your property and keep her off." Only the Navy has a much better way of saying something like that to the Marines. The latter, of course, aren't fooled a bit by the formality.

Next morning First Lieutenant Joe Cable, USMCR, from Philadelphia, was given the job of riding herd on one Bloody Mary. Before he saw her for the first time he wrote home to his girl in Germantown, a lovely fair-haired Bryn Mawr junior, "If you knew my next assignment, you would not believe it. I imagine the fellows at Princeton will vote me their favorite war hero when the news is out. I have been ordered to stop an old Tonkinese woman from selling grass skirts. I understand the entire Navy tried to stop her and failed. I shall send you daily communiqués on my progress." Joe signed the letter and then thought of the disparity between the unknown Tonk and the lovely girl in Germantown. The unreality of the comparison overwhelmed him, and like many fighting men stationed in the South Pacific the terrible question assailed him once more: "What am I, Joe Cable, doing here?"

Cable brushed the gnawing, unanswerable question from his mind, jumped into his jeep, and drove out to where Bloody Mary had set up her new kiosk. It was a strip of canvas, supplied by admirers and tacked by them onto a large banyan tree. In the amazing recesses of the remarkable roots she hid her wares, bringing out only those items which she thought she might sell at any one time.

"Haloo, major!" she said, grinning her best betel juice smile. Lt. Cable winced. What could men see amusing in such an old beast?

He did not return her smile. Instead, he kicked at the grass skirts. "No!" he remonstrated, shaking his forefinger back and forth across her face. "No!"

He spoke so firmly that Bloody Mary withheld her storm of profanity. The men were disappointed.

"You men," Lt. Cable said sharply. "Take down the canvas."

Reluctantly, Mary's tutors stepped forward and grabbed the canvas, gingerly at first. But they had no need to be afraid. Bloody Mary had nothing to say. Slowly, sorrowfully, the Marines pulled down her kiosk, bundled her souvenirs together in a box the lieutenant provided. They just didn't understand. After the way Mary had handled that damned naval lieutenant, too! They would have given a lot to have seen Mary take a fall out of stuck-up Lt. Cable, who claimed he was from Princeton.

But Mary saw something. Just what it was, neither she nor anyone else could ever say. But with her sure instinct, she knew that here was no Atabrine Benny, no pusillanimous French official delegate, no conniving SeaBee, no bored Marine with a few hours and dollars to spend. Here was a man. She smiled at the lieutenant, a real, human, warm smile. Her old face, weathered in Tonkin China and the seas between, hardened in the plantations, beamed. She touched his collar devices with a firm, knotted finger. "You big stuff!" she said. "You no *soandso* G.I."

It would be difficult to say why Lt. Cable kept coming back to check on Bloody Mary after he closed out her kiosk. She was giving no one any trouble. Plantation owners were content with the new arrangement whereby they received their fair cut of the grass-skirt bonanza. The government was pleased. The naval commander was happy that everything was satisfactory, and besides he had a wonderful story about that upstart assistant of his who was such a damned pain in the neck . . . or was it elsewhere?

But Lt. Cable did keep coming back. He rather suspected that Mary was doing a bigger business than ever after dark, and some officers were beginning to wonder exactly where all this bad gin was coming from. Officially, of course, Cable knew nothing and said nothing. He wasn't paid to deal in suspicions.

Perhaps it was Bloody Mary's frank hero worship that attracted him. Whenever Cable appeared, she would jump up, brush her clothes, straighten her ridiculous hat, knock the sand out of her shoes, and smile pleasantly. It was almost as if she were standing at attention.

When Cable tried to make her give up her Marine device, which was sacrilegious around her neck, she refused. "Me no *soandso* G.I." she protested.

"No, no! Mary!" Cable shouted at her, wagging his finger again across her face. "Bad! Bad word!"

Mary knew the Marine word was bad, but she, like the Marines, also knew that it was effective. But Cable spoke with such authority that she willingly forswore the word and its fellows when he was around.

And Cable was around a good deal. He used to drop by in the hot afternoons. Even the flies would be asleep, and cattle would be in the shade. No birds would sing, and from the cacao trees no lorikeets would fly. It was tropic midday, and Bloody Mary with her lieutenant would sit in the cavernous shade of the banyan tree and talk.

"It would be difficult to say what we talk about," Cable wrote to the Bryn Mawr junior. "I can't speak Tonkinese and Old Mary can't speak English. We can both speak a good deal of French, of course, and I've learned some Pidgin English. It is surprising how well we get along. We talk mostly about Tonkin, where Mary lives far inland among the mountains that border China proper. It is very interesting, out here, to talk to human beings."

For myself, I think Lt. Cable hit the nail on the head when he made that observation. It was sometimes terrifying to me to see the mental hunger that men experienced for companionship in the islands. At the laundry on my base, for example, the men had a little banjo-footed dog. They raised him from a pup, and while he was still a pup, a truck ran over him. That afternoon those men could not look at one another. That night none of them wrote letters home. Next morning they stared at the ceiling above their bunks. And I am not fooling when I say that for several days the salt had gone out of life. On the third day one of them bought another pup from an Army outfit. After lunch he hesitatingly presented the scrawny little dog. The laundry workers looked at it. "Goddam skinny little pup," one of them observed, but that dog made a great difference.

So far I have seen men tame pigs, goats, a jackass, a coconut tree cuscus, two chickens, cats, and a bowl of ultramarine tropical fish so beautiful that it was difficult to believe they lived. Pigs were the best pets, after dogs, because you could never look at them without laughing. And when they lived in a hut right along with you, they were surprisingly clean. One man could even housebreak pigs!

Throughout their existence on the edge of a foreign and forbidding jungle, perched right on the edge of the relentless ocean, men lived in highly tense conditions. Throbbing nature was all about them. Life grew apace, like the papaya trees, a generation in five months.

And in all this super-pulsating life there were no women. Only half-scented folded bits of paper called letters.

As a result, sensible men shoved back into unassailable corners of their souls thoughts that otherwise would have surged through and wracked them. They very rarely told dirty jokes. They fought against expressing friendliness or interest in any other man. From time to time horrifying stories would creep around a unit. "Two men down at Noumea. Officers, too. Dishonorable discharge! Couple years at Portsmouth!" And everyone would shudder . . . and wonder.

And so men in the tropics, with life running riot about them, read books, and wrote letters, and learned to love dogs better than good food, and went on long hikes, and went swimming, and wrote letters, and wrote letters, and slept. Of course, sometimes a terrible passion would well up, and there would be a murder, or a suicide. Or like the time a crane fell over and crushed a poor dumb fellow too stupid to operate a crane. All morning a stolid farm boy stood by the body, and no one could move him until the heavy machinery was lifted off the mangled man.

"Come on," the MP's would shout. "Get away from there! Break it up!"

And the stolid fellow would reply, "He was ma' bes' buddy." Then everyone left him alone.

I doubt if Lt. Cable ever thought about himself in just those terms, but he knew very well that he mustn't brood too long over that tousle-headed girl in Germantown. He knew— even though his tour of battle duty on Guadalcanal had been short—that consuming passions are better kept in check. They burn you out too damned quick, otherwise.

And yet there was the need for some kind of continuing interest in something. He'd had a pup, but the damned thing had grown up, as pups will, and it was off somewhere on another island. He'd done a lot of reading, too. Serious stuff, about mechanics, and a little history, too. But after a while reading becomes a bore.

Bloody Mary of course was different. She was old and repulsive, with her parched skin and her jagged teeth. But finer than any dog or any book, she was a sentient being with a mind, a personality, a history, a human memory, and —Lt. Cable winced at the idea—a soul. Unlike the restless tropical sea, she grew tired and slept. Unlike the impenetrable jungle, she could be perceived. Unlike the papayas and the road vines, she lived a generation, grew old, and died. She was subject to human laws, to a human rate of living, to a human world. And by heavens, she was an interesting old woman.

"She has a husband," Lt. Cable wrote his sweetheart. "She says he is on another island where the French have moved all the young girls. She lives here to trade with the Americans. I think if the French knew this they would deport her to the other island, too. But since she stays here and behaves herself, I have no mind to report her. In fact, I find talking French and Pidgin English with her amusing and instructive. I may even arrange to take a few days off and visit the other island with her when she takes money to her husband. She says he will be surprised, for she has not less than nine hundred dollars. That will be a great deal of money in Tonkin. In fact, it would be a lot of money right in Philadelphia."

It was about two weeks after this letter that Atabrine Benny arranged a boat trip to the island upon which Bloody Mary's husband lived. Benny had to see to it that all Tonks had their supply of atabrine, and he visited the outlying islands monthly. This time he agreed to take Bloody Mary along, and at the last minute Lt. Cable decided to join them. He brought with him, a mosquito net, a revolver, a large thermos jug of water, a basket of tinned food, and a bottle of atabrine tablets.

"My God, lieutenant," Benny said. "I got a million of 'em."

Everyone laughed, and the boat shoved off. I was down

in the predawn dark to bid Benny farewell and instruct him
to pick me up a wild boar's tusk, if he could. That was when
I first met Lt. Cable. He was a tall fellow, about six feet one.
He was lean and weighed not more than one hundred and
seventy-five pounds. He had not the graceful motions of a
natural athlete, but he was a powerfully competent man. I
thought then that he would probably give a good account of
himself in a fight. He had a shock of unruly blond hair. His
face, although not handsome, was masculine; and he carried
himself as if he were one of the young men to whom the
world will one day belong. To this quiet assurance he added
a little of the Marine's inevitable cockiness. He was an attractive fellow, and it was clearly to be seen that Bloody
Mary, the embattled Tonk, shared my opinion. Ignoring Atabrine Benny completely, she sat in the bows with Cable and
talked French in barbarous accents.

The island to which Benny was going lay sixteen miles to
the east. It was a large and brooding island, miasmic with
malaria, old fetishes, sickness and deep shadows. It was
called Vanicoro, and in the old times was known as a magic
place. Four peaks lined the center of the island. Two of them
were active volcanoes. Only the bravest natives dared live
on Vanicoro, and they were the last to give up cannibalism.

As the small boat drew near the island Bloody Mary
pointed at Vanicoro and assured Cable, "You like! You like
very much!" The Marine studied the volcanoes. Upon them
the red glow of sunrise rapidly lightened into the gold of early
morning. Mists rose from them like smoke from writhing lava.

"That's right pretty," Benny called back. "Look at them
hills smoke!"

Lt. Cable watched the mists of Vanicoro surrendering to
the early sun. And then, as a child, while playing with an
old familiar toy, sees a new thing from the corner of his eye,
Cable suddenly saw, without looking at it, the island of
Bali-ha'i.

"Benny!" he cried. "There's another island!"

There was another island! Bali-ha'i was an island of the
sea, a jewel of the vast ocean. It was small. Like a jewel, it
could be perceived in one loving glance. It was neat. It had
majestic cliffs facing the open sea. It had a jagged hill to
give it character. It was green like something ever youthful,
and it seemed to curve itself like a woman into the rough
shadows formed by the greater island of Vanicoro.

From two miles distance no seafarer could have guessed that Bali-ha'i existed. Like most lovely things, one had to seek it out and even to know what one was seeking before it could be found.

It was here on Bali-ha'i, within the protecting arm of Vanicoro, that the women of the islands lived. The French, with Gallic foresight and knowledge in these things, had housed on this haven of the seas all young women from the islands. Every girl, no matter how ugly or what her color, who might normally be raped by Americans was hidden on Bali-ha'i.

The little boat swung into the channel. "Look!" Cable gasped. Below him the white coral beach of Bali-ha'i slipped down by slow degrees until twenty fathoms of green water rested over it. But still it could be seen. The entire bay glowed from the whiteness of the sand and the golden sunlight now piercing and probing through the valleys of the volcanoes.

Coconut trees lined the shore of Bali-ha'i. Behind them banyans, giant ferns, and strange tropical trees grew in profusion and smothered the slopes of the hill. Through clearings in the jungle, grass of wondrous green appeared, and through both grass and trees peeped flower gardens of dancing color. Lt. Cable had to close his eyes. The gardens of Bali-ha'i were like the gardens at home. He knew those flowers in the infinite jungle had been planted by women.

His thoughts were jarringly broken when Atabrine Benny tugged at the bell of the small boat and sent loud peals echoing through the narrow channel. Violently he swung the clapper back and forth until the islands fairly sang with music. Even then he continued in sheer exuberance, and melody piled upon melody so that even the peaks of Vanicoro seemed to dance.

From every hut and hovel on Bali-ha'i people poured forth. First the watchful sisters from the hospitals appeared in front of their sickrooms on the hillside. Next a host of screaming children, all boys, all naked, ran down to a rickety pier built by Tonkinese laborers. Then older native boys, perhaps nine and ten years old, piled into their own small outrigger canoes and started paddling furiously across the water. Two old men, in statelier outriggers, sedately plied their paddles and swept with leisurely speed past the frenetic boys.

Then came the girls! There were native girls with conical

breasts, and red sarongs about their hips. There were inquisitive Chinese girls who were pulled back by equally inquisitive Chinese mothers. Tonkinese girls, as yet unmarried,
stood close to their distinctive white and red shacks. And in
the distance, properly aloof, a few French girls demonstrated
their inherited superiority by looking with disdain upon the
entire proceedings. They wore white dresses, and you could
not discern whether their breasts were conical or flabby.

At this moment people on shore were satisfied that Benny
was in the boat! Someone cried, "It's the doctor!" and the
happy call was echoed up and down the beach. The children
shouted it to one another, for it meant that they would have
sweets from the big, green candy tin. Old men laughed for to
them Benny meant cigarettes. Young girls giggled, for they
knew that if they bumped against the jovial fellow and let
him pat them on the bottom, he would give them some more
of the good red cloth. White women were pleased to see him,
for he brought endless and delightful gossip from the home
island. And the sisters in the hospital were ready to welcome
him, for they knew him to be a kindly fellow who could,
by one way or another, get them almost any medicine they
might need.

So everyone on Bali-ha'i laughed and whistled; and someone at the school started ringing a bell, whereupon Benny
rang his louder. But all this time, on Vanicoro across the
channel not a sound was made. Not a leaf rustled. Not a
voice raised welcome. High in the hills at least three hundred
men and women watched the boat come into the channel,
make a ringing of bells, and tie up to the wharf of Bali-ha'i.
In fact, the watchers of Vanicoro had seen the boat when
it was six miles out, and all silently they watched it come . . .
almost to their own island. Silently, they would watch it
while it was there, and in the late afternoon they would watch
it until it was eight or nine miles out to sea.

Atabrine Benny always visited Bali-ha'i with mixed emotions.
On the one hand he enjoyed anything strange and recondite.
He loved seeing brown young girls, black girls with firm
bosoms, trim French girls with white frocks, sedate sisters in
long black. The tragically slim strip of land was part of the
South Pacific, and he reveled in its strangeness. But even
as he did so, he thought of Waco, Texas, and his wife.
Brusquely, he dismissed the thought. In Waco he was a

druggist's helper. On Bali-ha'i he was a doctor. A consulting doctor, and he was happy.

As the boat touched the quivering dock, Benny leaped out. It seemed as if his pudgy stomach would pull him forward onto the wet boards, but he was amazingly agile. "Hello, hello!" he called out to everyone who clustered about the dock. He patted all the Tonks on the head, tried to pat the shy black girls on the bottom, and smiled at the sedate sisters who stood on the stone steps.

"Hello, hello!" he cried, waving his atabrine bottle. "Here comes the doctor!" In his exuberance, in the tireless, sweaty, steaming friendliness and at-homeness of the man everyone could see why Americans were the way they were. Atabrine Benny was all the traveling salesmen of Kansas, Colorado, Utah, Nevada, and California rolled into one. Even the suspicious sisters liked to take atabrine when he dispensed it!

When Benny jumped from the small boat onto the dock, Lt. Cable wondered what he should do. In the excitement of seeing old friends, Benny had completely ignored him. He studied the crowd that had gathered both on the pier and in the water. The little boys were delightful. He wondered how they managed their boats so well. The older boys were adolescently aloof, but there was much shoving amongst them. They professed not to look at the Marine, but subdued whispers sped along the shore.

"Jay-gee! One bar. Silver."

"No! No! Marine! See the little round ball. Marine!"

"Basil is right. Marine. First lieutenant!"

"Jerome is right. Marine. Jerome is right!" The Melanesian boys still refused to look at First Lt. Joe Cable, but every one of them saw that he was armed, that he was sunburnt, that he wore the Guadalcanal patch, that he was not an aviator, and that he didn't quite know what to do. All of the boys liked him on sight, and were prepared to talk with him or trade with him, or show him the trail to the cliffs. But he made no move of friendship, so they scowled all that day along the fringes of the crowd and pushed one another. In the afternoon there was one fairly rough fight.

Of course, Lt. Cable saw the boys. He even wondered what kinds of games they played. But he soon forgot his interest, passing as it was. For this was the first time in his life he had seen so many women . . . in fact, any women . . . walking about with no clothes on above their hips. He was not a prurient felliw, but the natural interests of any young man demand that he know as much about women as he properly can; and since there is not enough time in one man's life to learn all there is to know, one had better study when the opportunity presents. So, purposing each moment to call after Benny, he stood there in the boat bewildered by the scene on the small pier. Above him stood not less than thirty native girls ranging in age from twelve to twenty. They bore melons and pineapples and bananas and mangoes and split coconuts and yams and breadfruit and everything else that grows in such prodigal quantities in the South Pacific.

Cable was truly enraptured. The frieze of women looked like models awaiting the immortalizing brush of Gauguin. Unaware of their forbidding ugliness by American middle class standards, they were equally unaware of their surpassing beauty by the artist's immortal standards.

Cable, being neither exclusively an artist nor an American, had no consistent thoughts as he looked up to the dark faces with their gleaming teeth. Their breasts disturbed him mightily, and when one girl clutched anew at a melon, throwing her gingham sarong awry, he both blushed and found himself unable . . . or unwilling . . . to look away. Like the jungle, like the fruits of the jungle, adolescent girls seemed to abound in unbelievable profusion.

"You like? You like? You like?" they called in musical cadences.

He did like. He liked very much, and before he could stop himself he had bought the stern of the boat full of fruit. When he went to sort out some lengths of red cloth to pay the girls, who were now scrambling over the boat itself, he happened to smell his hands. They were redolent with the gorgeous scent of true tropical pineapples ripened on the ground. Unaware of any change in himself, he discovered that he felt very happy. And from the hills of Vanicoro the watchers looked at the boat and then at one another! It could not be believed that for a few pineapples, for some papayas, and such little papayas, one could get cloth!

It was at this moment that Bloody Mary rescued her lieutenant from more fruit, more breasts, and more thighs. "Psssst!" she exploded at the girls. "You go! You go! Bimeby you come. Bimeby you come. Bring chickens." With masterful gestures and determination she pushed the native girls away, motioned to the men in the outriggers to leave, discouraged the naked boys so that they dropped from the sides of the boat. It was only proper that as a Tonkinese she should exercise her endowed rights over the inferior Melanesians. Like a true *grande dame* she cleared the way for the greater nobility, a white lieutenant, to step ashore.

But as he did so, as he walked down the pier in front of Bloody Mary, he entertained a persistent question that neither he nor any other American fighting man has ever really answered: "What am I doing here? How did I, Joe Cable, of Philadelphia, wind up out here? This is Bali-ha'i, and a year ago I had never heard of it. What am I doing here?" The question pounded upon his ears in exactly the same way it does upon the ears of a commuter from New Rochelle some morning as he stands in Grand Central Station. He has stood in that station daily for nineteen years, and yet on some one unpredictable morning the meaninglessness of it all bursts in upon him, and he asks, "What am I doing here?" It is certain that Herod of Judea asked himself that question, too. Like Herod, like the man from New Rochelle, like Alexander in Afghanistan, Joe Cable could find no logical reason to explain why he was on Bali-ha'i that morning.

But being there, he was disposed to enjoy his experience to the full. He was not, however, prepared for what Bloody Mary had in store for him.

She took the lead as soon as Cable reached the sandy beach. "We go! We go!" she said at every intersection. She took him past the native huts, and the native girls stayed behind. She took him through the wild coconut trees to the climbing path that led through the loveliest tropical gardens he had ever seen. They were the gardens of the Chinese, filled with fruits and flowers. She took him past the small hospital where he heard Benny laughing with the hard-working sisters. Then she beckoned him around a corner, and suddenly he was on a plateau from which he could see the bay, and the boat, and endless blue of water upon coral sand. Between him and the bay stretched the coconut trees, the gardens, the little huts, and the spotless beach. It was impossible to think that a year ago, before the Japs threatened the islands and Americans threatened the girls, Bali-ha'i was a wilderness.

"We go!" insisted Mary, and Lt. Cable stopped his inspection of the bay, but even as he turned his eyes away, they rested upon the peaks of Vanicoro. They, too, were clean and lovely that morning as if the old volcanoes had burned them white.

Cable now followed Mary along a narrow footpath. Up to this moment he had not wondered where she was taking him. Probably to some Tonkinese hut, he concluded, and he had no time to reconsider before the waddling old woman stopped short, stepped aside, and pointed proudly at a clean, whitewashed house beneath a protecting cluster of four large jungle trees. The earth around the house was packed flat. At the door stood an old Tonkinese man, a younger man, and his wife.

Cable stood where he was and watched Mary greet her friends. They talked furiously, but they did not kiss. They grabbed one another's shoulders, but they did not shake hands. Yet when Mary brought them over and jabbered in Tonkinese, each one sedately shook Cable's hand and promptly walked down the path he had just climbed.

At this moment Mary beckoned him to follow her, and he watched her disappear into the open door at which a moment before her three friends had stood. Cable entered behind her, stooping as he did so. When he had blinked once or twice, he saw that he was standing on an earthen floor, miraculously clean. There were few articles of furniture, but against one wall stood a young Tonkinese girl, perhaps seventeen years old. She was a small girl, slender, with very black hair which was smooth about her head. She wore the Tonkinese white blouse and black trousers. She was barefooted, and her face was a lovely oval, yellow, finely modeled. When she smiled, her teeth were as white as the native girls' had been.

As in a trance, Cable sucked in his breath audibly. The girl smiled, and at that moment Cable heard a hissing noise. He turned around, frightened. But it was only Bloody Mary. She had her peach-basket hat in her left hand. Stains of betel juice were drenching the ravines of her mouth, which was grinning, broadly. Her broken teeth showed through, black, black as night. She winked her right eye heavily and asked, "You like?" Then she turned and fled down the path.

Cable stood in complete embarrassment, looking at the little Tonkinese girl. He was pretty sure that Bloody Mary and her kinfolk would not return to the hut for a long time, and that bewildered him. The silent girl, standing straight against the wattled wall, confused him still more. But counteracting all of this uncertainty was a tremendous driving force, deep within him, that resolved all doubts and dispelled faint-heartedness.

"Hello!" he said, stepping toward the quiet, straight girl. She kept her hands pressed to her sides, but she was not afraid. She looked at the tall Marine, and had to raise her head slightly to do so. Standing thus, her fine breasts were outlined by her white smock. Through force of habit, she smiled at the stranger.

As she did so, her oval face looked exquisite against the dark hair and wattled wall. Her teeth shone clearly. Her firm chin looked resolute. She was altogether delectable, and Cable knew it. From that moment there was no uncertainty.

With two long steps he was before the unfrightened girl. He smiled down at her, then enveloped her in his right arm and kissed her feverishly upon her thin, hard lips. She sighed, like a child, and the motion of her sighing thrust her breasts against Cable's hand. Eagerly he sought for them, and in a moment he had drawn the white smock over her head. In rare beauty she stood proudly against the wall, naked to the waist, incredibly feminine. It was then that she spoke to Cable, in French.

"You speak French?" he asked, mumbling as he removed his brown shirt and spread it in the clean, foot-hammered floor. Upon his own shirt he placed hers and then slowly pulled her down to rest upon it. Her bare feet left a reluctant trail along the coral sand, leading from the wall to her nuptial couch.

"So you speak French!" Cable whispered into her tiny, pellucid ear.

"The sisters taught me," she replied, quietly. "They would be angry with me now. They taught me not to do this." She did not smile as she spoke, nor did she turn away in modesty. She was merely informing Cable that in spite if what her mother, Bloody Mary, had advised her in hurried Tonkinese when Cable first entered the hut, she knew that she was doing wrong.

"You speak very good French," Cable whispered hoarsely, his hands seeking her slim, pliant ankles. Slowly he grasped the legs of the black sateen trousers and began to pull them from her frail body. As he did so, he could hear in his mind's recesses the warnings of the sisters, the old preachments of all who had instructed him. But as the sateen trousers pulled free, he clasped the little girl to him with a convulsive motion, and all preachments, old or new, died away.

Later, when the Tonkinese girl was crying softly to herself, Cable found incarnadine proof that he was the first who had loved her. The white smock would have to be washed. "What can you do?" he asked in broken French.

"I'll wash it," she said tearfully.

"Have you another?" he inquired.

"Oh, no!" she responded, as if that were the farthest impossibility in the world. "It will dry." And she proceeded to wash out both her smock and Cable's shirt. Then she placed them side by side on the roof of the red and white hut, on the slope of the roof longest hidden from the path. Cable, who helped her, one hand clasping her breast as he did so, felt the sun pull the water from the cloth.

"You speak well," he said.

"The sisters teach us fine French," she said, demonstrating that her words were not false.

"You will be a beautiful woman," he ventured, but the manner in which he spoke clearly intimated that he was appraising a growth that he himself would never see. The girl sensed this at once, and tears came into her eyes.

"What is your name?" Cable asked, for he did not see the tears.

"Liat," she said. "That is how the French sisters pronounce my name."

"Like you, it's lovely," he replied, truthfully. "We sit under this tree. Then we see the path . . . if anybody comes."

He pulled the half-naked Liat to the earth beside him. Unafraid, and yet vastly unhappy, the girl nestled her black head against his tan bosom. Their skins were almost identical!

"Who is Mary?" he asked.

"Which Mary?" she countered.

"The woman that brought me," he replied.

"My mother," she answered.

"Your mother?" he repeated, his tone betraying his thoughts.

"Yes," the girl explained. "She said that you were very fine. She wanted me to love you."

"Did . . . she want you . . . to . . . ?" Cable pointed nervously at the two shirts.

"I don't know," the girl said. Then she looked up at the

Marine's dark face. "I wanted to, I think," she said simply.

Lt. Joe Cable could say nothing. As he tried to think, words eluded him. He knew that he was very happy. He knew that almost any of the officers of his unit would have envied him that moment on the hillside at Bali-ha'i. The regrets and moral questionings would come later. For the moment, with Liat upon his bare arms, he could defeat any incipient doubts.

Within an hour the shirts were dry. Cable put his on and then helped Liat into hers. Reluctantly he held the bundled smock over her head while she stretched her firm and lovely arms toward the sky. Hers was a motion and a picture he would never forget. At that moment, reaching toward the tall trees and the high peaks of Vanicoro, Liat was the very spirit of Bali-ha'i. In days to come that lovely statuette in brown marble was to be the magnet which would draw him back to the island time after time after time. Liat and the tall peaks of Vanicoro would become great, indefatigable beacons in the jungle night and cool mirrors in the jungle heat. Liat and the peaks were engraved upon his heart. He was aware of this fact as he allowed the smock to slip down her arms and hide her exquisite body. It is not certain that Liat was aware of what had transpired in the Marine's heart and mind and imagery, but she knew that for herself the wonder and the waiting were over.

As they walked down the gently sloping path toward the hospital, they met old Bloody Mary waddling up to meet them. She was perspiring slightly, and her breath was uneven, but as she met them she smiled very broadly, and with great happiness in her wrinkled face. "You like?" she asked, in English. Cable grinned at her, and Liat, seeing him happy, likewise smiled. Together the three conspirators, none knowing exactly what the other thought, but all equally involved, entered the small, barren, white hospital.

There Sister Marie Clément, from Bordeaux, had a small repast awaiting them. Atabrine Benny was there, as were two French ladies and a native medical practitioner who had studied with Dr. Lambert in Fiji. Talk was in French, in English, and occasionally in Pidgin when some native came to the door with his excited problems.

The hospital room was small, like a doctor's reception room in Southern France. It was very white, and had no furniture. Those who wished to sit used built-in benches along the wall, where patients waited for the doctor. A hospital go-cart with a piece of glass for a top was wheeled in with wine, cake, much tropical fruit, and thick cheese sandwiches.

"I am very pleased to see you, lieutenant," Sister Marie Clément said in low, sweet French.

Lt. Cable, vastly ill at ease, bowed low and acknowledged her welcome. Then he spoke to the French ladies, each of which wondered why she had not brought her daughter to the hospital. Benny, sensing nothing, moved toward Liat and grinned at her, saying in his barbarous French, "A fine morning." Liat bowed slightly and agreed.

Bloody Mary was definitely unwelcome in the salon of the hospital, but it was she who had brought the handsome Marine, so she and her daughter had to be tolerated. The old harridan made the most of her visit, ate heartily, beamed at her hosts, showed her funereal teeth to the French women at every opportunity, and felt just wonderful.

After luncheon everyone inspected the other room of the hospital, a barren place with beds for Tonkinese patients, who, in the manner of their country, slept upon bare boards. Upon one such bed, worn shiny from long use, lay an old Tonkinese man with a broken leg. Not understanding a word that was said to him, he smiled and smiled. But when Bloody Mary saw him she loosed a stream of consoling Tonkinese and betel juice, and the old man grinned happily. "Mary," thought Cable, "has a way of making everyone happy. It's a great gift."

At three the entire assembly walked slowly down the path to the white sands. Again the gardens were more lovely than a dream of the imagination. The coconut trees alternately stood straight toward the peaks of Vanicoro or inclined at crazy angles toward the sea. A row of papaya trees, newly planted, lifted their snakelike trunks into the air as if to hand each wayfarer a cluster of their delicious melons. It was midafternoon in the tropics, and everywhere the great heat flooded down, but nowhere more torrentially than in the hearts of Lt. Cable and Liat.

Unable to clasp one another fervently as they stood side by side on the rickety pier, they were also not free to indulge in the orgy of gazing that each had to fight against. Liat held out her hand as Cable stepped into the boat.

"Au revoir," she said quietly.

"I will return," Cable whispered.

Then the same improvisator of the morning began to ring the bell up in the school. Thus inspired, Benny grasped his once more and together the two carillonneurs pealed out their fine, lilting, inspired farewell. Again music swept through the narrow channel. Again little boys and old men pushed their outriggers over white sands. Blue water lapped the prow of the small boat, and suddenly the engine exploded! There was a noisy sputtering. The engine coughed like an old man confused by chattering, then caught its breath and hammered out a steady rhythm.

"Cast her loose!" the coxswain cried, and the boat stood out from the pier. The boat's bell rang clearly, conservatively now, for each sound meant a message. But far up on the hillside the native boy pealed his unrestricted bell as if his heart were breaking. And the sound sped down the hillside, over the waters, even up to the peaks of Vanicoro, until everyone's heart was filled with music.

"Goodbye, goodbye!" shouted Benny to all his friends.

"Au revoir!" cried the French women and their daughters.

"Goo'bye!" cried the native girls, and the native boys threw rocks at the wake left by the disappearing boat.

Liat, on the pier, watched her mother and Lt. Cable sail away. Then she turned slowly and walked back to the beach where her father and his nephew and wife waited, each wondering what had happened that morning, up in the red and white hut.

On Vanicoro the silent watchers followed the boat far out to sea. To do so, they had to look directly toward the setting sun, but since the setting sun was holy, they had no mind to consider their own discomfort. Long before these savages left their posts among the shadows of the great volcanoes, each person on Bali-ha'i had forgotten the frail craft. That is, each person but Liat.

Next morning Lt. Cable rose from his sack and stepped out upon the beach as he had done every morning since he arrived on the island. But this morning he stopped sharply. There on the eastern horizon was Vanicoro in complete outline! Down the beach a friend cried out, "Look at that damned island! I've never seen it so bright before. It's like a mirage!"

From their huts other Marines appeared to study the peaks of the mysterious island. All agreed that never before had

Vanicoro been so clearly defined. It is a miracle of the South
Pacific that islands which are relatively only a few miles away
are rarely seen. Hot air, rising constantly from steaming
jungles, makes omnipresent clouds hover above each island.
So dense are they that usually they obscure and often completely hide the islands they attend. So it is that an island
like Vanicoro, only sixteen miles away, might rarely be seen,
and then only after torrential rains had swept the sky clear
of all but high rain clouds, equalizing temperatures over the
entire vast sea. Then, for a few hours, islands far distant
might be seen. At times land ninety miles away could be
detected by a clear eye. But whenever such distances could
be seen, it was always because there had been a great rain,
and one could look for ninety or a hundred miles beneath
menacing, fast-scudding clouds.

"It must have rained last night," an officer observed. "It
must have. Look at the island." There was further discussion
of when and for how long it rained, but Cable took no part
in this. All that he knew was that Vanicoro, which he had
never before seen from his hut, was strangely visible. It was
so clear upon the waters that one might even . . . No, that
was impossible. Bali-ha'i, at this distance, was merely a part
of Vanicoro.

The thought startled him! Was that, after all, true? Were
Bali-ha'i and all its people merely a part of the grim and
brooding old cannibal island? Were Liat and her unfathomable
mother merely descendants from the elder savages? No! The
idea was preposterous. Tonkinese were in reality Chinese,
sort of the way Canadians were Americans, only a little different. And Chinese were the oldest civilized people on earth.
He thought of Liat. She was clean, immaculately so. Her teeth
were white. Her ankles were delicate, like those of a girl
of family in Philadelphia.

As he said that word, a thousand fears assailed him. That
afternoon he would write to his mother . . . and to the junior
at Bryn Mawr. The letter to his mother was difficult, but not
impossible. He told her of the islands, of the mission, of the
school bell, and of the hospital. He dwelt upon Sister Marie
Clément but made no mention of Bloody Mary . . . nor of
her daughter.

But writing to his sweetheart was another thing! On the
one hand he could not do as he did with his mother, write
in the placid assumption that even if she knew she would

forgive him. And on the other hand he dared not even hint at what had happened. He could make no admissions of any sort. In fact, when he postponed writing to Bryn Mawr at all that day, Lt. Cable acknowledged that he had reached a great impasse in his life. At that time he did not know that never again, as long as he lived, would he write to that girl in Philadelphia. He would try several times thereafter, but false words would not come, and true words he dared not write.

That evening in the officers' club a group of Marines fell to discussing the phenomenon of the morning, when Vanicoro had been so near that you could almost see ravines upon its face. "I'd like to see that island," one officer observed. "It's quite a place, I'm told. One of the tribes up there in the hills preserves heads and sometimes sells them. Cost about twenty bucks apiece. I know a guy sent two home to a museum. Box got sent to his home by mistake, and his old lady fainted."

"Very primitive place," another observed. "I flew over it the other day. Say, those two volcanoes are sure something to see. The west one . . . Well, that is the left one as you're coming in. Well, you can fly right down into it. There's a lake right in it, and it's one damned weird place, I can tell you."

"Do the natives live near the volcanoes?" a young officer inquired.

"One of the traders told me no," the flier replied. "Say, Cable. You know one of the traders. You know, that atabrine guy. Does he know Vanicoro at all?"

"He's never told me about it, if he does," Cable replied.

"Well, I understand the natives there are among the most primitive in all these islands. Filthy, backward, plenty tough guys. They were the last to eat one another, you know."

"What I don't see," the young Marine mused aloud, "is how Hollywood dares to cook up the tripe it does. Boy, oh boy! The reaming they give the American public."

"It's just good, clean malarkey," a newcomer observed. "What harm does it do? Any time Dorothy Lamour wants to wobble them blinkers at me, OK. I ain't kicking."

"What I mean," the young officer insisted, "is that it gives a very wrong impression. I have a girl back in Minneapolis . . ."

"Hell, you'd be lucky if you had a *picture* of a girl!"

"Well, anyway, this is a pretty fine girl, and she writes to me the other day. OK, listen!" And the young fellow, amply blushing, unfolded a letter and began to read: "Dear Eddie, I certainly hope you are not dating one of those luscious South Sea beauties we see so much of in the movies. If you do, I'm afraid you'll never come back to me. After all, Minneapolis is pretty cold, and if we wore what they wear . . . well, you get the idea!"

"Take it from me, Eddie. That bimbo is trying to make you."

"Is that bad?" Eddie cried, throwing his hands up in the air and waving the letter.

"It ain't good, Eddie. Not when you're out here and she's in Minneapolis. Tell me. Did she ever talk like that when you were there? Right with her?"

"Well, as a matter of fact, she didn't. But I think she's beginning to miss me, now that I'm out here."

"Don't fall for that crap, Eddie," his counselor warned. "She's the type of girl can't write too hot a letter, but when you turn up on the spot, she thinks maybe she better not turn off the light! I know a dozen girls like that."

"For your information, this girl isn't like that. Personally, I think she loves me. Anyway, I'm not taking any chances. Look at the picture I'm sending her tonight!" From his shirt pocket Eddie produced a horrendous picture of a Melanesian woman with frizzled hair, sagging breasts, and buttocks like a Colorado mesa. She was wearing a frond of palm leaves.

"Now that's what I call a woman!" one Marine observed. Others whistled. Several wanted copies for their girls.

"Look, Cable!" one officer cried. "The real South Seas!" He passed the repulsive picture to Cable, who looked at it hurriedly and returned it.

"What I don't get," Eddie mused, as he returned the photograph to his pocket, "is how traders out here and planters can marry these women. Or even live with them? My God, I wouldn't even touch that dame with a ten-foot pole."

"But they do!" an older man insisted. "They do. I've heard of not less than eight well authenticated cases in which white men lived with or married native women."

"Yeah," another added, "but just remember that most of those women were Polynesians, and they're supposed to be beautiful. And some were Tonks, too, I'll bet."

"Melanesians, Polynesians, Tonks!" Eddie cried, thinking

of the hot number in cold Minneapolis. "They're all alike."

"The hell they are!" an older officer cried. "They are like so much hell! There's all the difference in the world! I've seen some mighty lovely Polynesians in Samoa. And don't let anybody sell you short on that."

"You can say that again!" a friend added.

"Don't give me that guff!" Eddie cried contentiously. "Maybe they are pretty. But how many of you would . . . well, make love to them? Come on, now put up or shut up. Would you?"

"It all depends . . . If . . ."

"Tell me *yes* or *no*. No hedging."

"You know what the mess cook said. 'They're getting whiter every day.' If I was out here long enough, I can't tell what I'd do."

Eddie was not satisfied with this answer. "We'll poll the club," he announced. Taking the photograph from his pocket he thrust it beneath a fellow officer's nose. "Would you sleep with that?" he cried.

"Hell, no!" the man replied. The older officer ridiculed the test and grabbed a copy of *Life* that was lying on the wine table. He shuffled through the pages until he found the picture of an old, withered Italian woman sitting beside the ruins of her home. He thrust this picture before the earlier judge.

"How about that?" he snorted.

"Hell, no!" the judge replied impartially.

"You're damned right!" the older officer agreed. "You just sit back, Eddie, and let me ask the questions."

"All right," Eddie assented. "But make 'em fair."

Around the room went the questions, in various forms. Roughly, they all added up to the same idea: "Would you, if the opportunity presented itself, sleep with a woman from the islands?"

"No!" answered all the younger officers.

"It depends," said the older men.

"Ask Cable," Eddie shouted. "He's a Princeton man. He's got good sense."

"How you reason!" a friend cried.

"What do you say, Cable?" the inquisitor asked. "Would you sleep with a native girl?"

"No," Cable replied weakly. His voice was not heard above the noise of vigorous side arguments.

"He says *No*," Eddie reported loudly. "And you men are damned right. Very few self-respecting American men would attempt to knock off a piece of jungle julep. And you can take my word for that!"

But next morning rain clouds were low once more, and on the horizon Vanicoro called to Cable like an echo from some distant life.

That afternoon the rain clouds lifted, and fleecy cumulus clouds were piled one upon the other above the volcanoes until, at sunset, there was a pillar of snowy white upon which the infinite colors of the sunset played. As always, the Marines tarried over their evening meal to watch the strange lights come and go upon that mighty and majestic pillar of cloud.

"I've never seen it look so lovely!" the men agreed. From the porch of his Dallas hut Cable watched the subtle procession of lights. As the sun sank lower in the west, colors grew stronger and climbed higher up the great pillar. Finally, only a tip of brilliant red glowed above Vanicoro. It stayed there for a long time, like a marker indicating to Cable where his heart lay that night.

The next afternoon Lt. Cable made his weekly inspection of the camp area. Under the familiar banyan tree he discovered Bloody Mary doing business openly with her band of admirers. The men rose as their lieutenant approached, and sensing displeasure in his manner, quietly drew off, leaving the old Tonk and the officer together. For several moments neither could think of anything appropriate to say. Then, as if she were greeting an equal, Bloody Mary said in English, "Fine day, major."

Lt. Cable looked at her for a long time, and nothing more was said. He kicked at the ground a bit, shuffled through her wares with one hand in a desultory manner, still found no words at his command, and left. The old Tonk watched him until his noisy jeep disappeared around a bend. Then she laughed. The Marines came back, and haggling over prices progressed.

That evening there was a peculiar refraction in the air, and the ocean in front of the mess appeared as it had never done before. Fine sunlight, entering the waves at a peculiar angle, were refracted by the intensely white coral. The waves seemed to be green. No, they were green, a green so light as to be almost yellow, and yet a green so brilliant that it far outshone all the leaves on all the trees.

"Look at that lovely water!" a major cried to the men still eating at table. "It must be because the sun is so low and yet so bright."

His fellow officers piled out of their mess and stood along the beach. They marveled at the mystery and discussed it in all the terms they could command. For a few minutes it was concluded that someone had thrown a life-raft dye-maker into the sea and stained it the way men do when they are lost on the great ocean. Then they can be seen by searching planes.

This theory, however, was discarded when it was pointed out that the location of the green sometimes changed abruptly. Mere currents could not account for the rapid mutations. It must, indeed, be the action of the sun.

Whatever the cause, the ocean was a thing of rare beauty that night. Having nothing else to do, the Marines watched it as long as the sun was up. Slowly the green faded into twilight gray. The sun disappeared and flaming clouds shot up beyond the volcanoes at Vanicoro. There the fine symphony of light played itself out. A bird called. Night insects began to cry. Then, like a Mongol rush, night and darkness bore down through the fragmentary tropic twilight. The ocean, and the sun, and the flaming pillar of cloud, and the island were asleep. Night had fallen, and all things were at rest except Cable's furious mind.

His mind worked on and on. Sometimes he would conclude that he would never see Bali-ha'i again. That he would forget the entire incident. That he would never see Bloody Mary again. That he would erase fat Benny from his mind. That he would ask for an immediate transfer to some other island . . . farther north.

But not one of these resolutions did he have the slightest intention of following. Never did he even mildly deceive himself that any of those courses were open to him. Well he knew that he was tied to Bali-ha'i by chains of his own making.

That evening he went into his hut and determined that he would write letters to his mother and to the girl whom he had intended to marry . . . when the war was over. The first letter was dry and stilted. The old easy comments were gone. The fluency of shared experiences was lost. "He was well. He hoped she was well. The ocean was green tonight." That was it: the ocean was green. It was just *green*. It wasn't a vivid green, or a brilliant green, or a miraculous green, or an iridescent green. It was green, and although half a hundred officers had vocally marveled at the phenomenon, Cable could not share either his or their emotions with his mother.

The letter to his intended wife was not even started. When the paper was on the table before him, Cable knew that he could write nothing upon it. He realized then that what he had experienced in the South Pacific could never be shared with her. He had not told the girl from Bryn Mawr about the Jap charges on Guadalcanal. He hadn't even attempted to tell her about them before he met Liat. He felt that girls in Bryn Mawr wouldn't understand. Or they wouldn't be interested. He had not been able to convey to her his feelings about the islands, nor his long trip into the jungle, nor what he had thought of mysterious Vanicoro even before he had visited Bali-ha'i. Fight against it as he might, Cable had permitted a new world to grow within him. If that world had maintained only a minor importance in his life, all might have been well; but when the hidden world assumed master importance, then all was lost.

Crumpling the untouched piece of letter paper, Cable grabbed his hat and went out into the tropical night. The quiet ocean lapped the white sands. Coconut trees stood out against the crescent moon. Life had no color; all was gray. It had no sound; all was a meaningless, faint buzz. The camp was quiet, for men and officers alike were at the movies. In the mess hall two disgruntled attendants washed the last of the dishes. Cable walked through the darkened camp, and unwittingly made his way toward the banyan tree.

As he approached the tree, he became slowly aware that people were there. He halted and then moved more cautiously. Sure enough, there in the moonlight, aided by a vest-pocket flashlight, Bloody Mary was selling half-pint bottles of gut-rotting homemade whiskey. And in large tins by the tree, Marines and soldiers were bringing her torpedo juice, that murderous high-proof alcohol which in the South Pacific is used indiscriminately to drive torpedoes at Jap ships and men crazy.

"Fo' dolla'," the old Tonk would demand, holding up a beer bottle with half a pint of so-called whiskey sloshing about inside.

"No, Mary! That's too much!" the shadowy buyer would protest.

"*Soandso* you, brother!" Mary would cackle, offering the irresistible delicacy to some other willing buyer. While Cable watched, she sold nine bottles. That meant thirty-six dollars. She was getting sixteen dollars a quart for mere torpedo juice doctored up to taste like whiskey! And she was stealing the torp juice! It was a safe bet some sailor from the torpedo shop was involved in the deal.

In the shadow of his tree, Cable thought for a long time as to what he should do. In the end he went back to his hut and tried to sleep.

He stayed away from Bloody Mary for three days, but each day Vanicoro, or its volcanoes, or its pillar of cloud, did something different, and Cable's entire being was drawn to the island. He was therefore well prepared to see Atabrine Benny when the little man hurried into his quarters one evening and said, "Good news, lieutenant! I'm taking a surprise trip to Bali-ha'i tomorrow at four. Got to take some serum over to the nurses. Want to come along?"

Cable leaped from his chair! "You bet I do!" he cried. The deal was set, and at 0400 next morning, in a fine rain, Cable drove up to the landing, parked his jeep, and hurried into the small boat. Only Benny and the crew were there.

"Ting, ting!" went the bell. The motor hummed for a moment and then burst into irritated profanity, like Bloody Mary when a soldier nettled her. The bow of the craft swung free, ropes were cast off, and the boat headed for the dark, rain-swept sea. Never, since he had left Princeton to play football against Yale, had Joe Cable experienced the almost unbearable excitement which overpowered him at that moment. Only those who have set out before dawn to visit some silent island, or to invade some Jap position, or to sail across the tropic seas to a lover can even imagine the pounding of the human heart at such a moment. Cable stood in the prow of the boat and let the warmish rain play across his heated face. By the time the shrouded sun was up, Vanicoro and the tall peaks were clearly visible.

Then came the anxious peering! Was that Bali-ha'i? There! No, over toward the deepest gully? Was that it? Like all things waited for, in due and natural time the tiny island appeared. As always, it was nestled against the shoreline of the stronger island.

But there was nothing old and familiar about the channel when it appeared around the headland of Bali-ha'i. No! It was as if such a channel had never been seen before. There was a golden quality about it, for now the sun was red. What had been deep blue before was now gray; and the white sand was whiter. And everything looked different . . . that is, everything except the hospital, for it was still very white upon the hillside, and behind it, unseen from the bay, there was a Tonk hut, all white and red with wattled walls! It was there. Of that you could be sure!

Soon bells were ringing their fine antiphonies. People streamed down to the pier, some not yet fully awakened. Little boys popped into little canoes, and native girls appeared, still tucking in the ends of their sarongs. Clear in the red morning sunlight danced their small breasts, and in their arms there were pineapples, and all the air was a censer of delight as tropical fruit spread its abundant aroma. I tell you, I have climbed ashore on many a South Pacific rickety pier in the early morning, and although no Liat ever waited for me behind the second row of coconut trees, I can guess what Joe Cable felt that morning.

At any rate, Atabrine Benny could guess! He stood in the boat and watched his many friends cheering him. Had he been a sentimentalist . . . that is, more than he already was . . . he might have had tears in his eyes. Not being a sentimentalist, he turned to Cable and grinned his foolish face into a fine, toothy smile. "Best goddamned job in the Navy!" he said. Cable winked at him, and nodded.

When the first flood of welcome was exhausted, the Marine studied how he might find Liat. He was certain that she must, by now, know of his coming. So gradually pulling away from the crowd, he started to make his path toward the hospital. Unwilling to let him disappear so easily, boys and girls followed him. He began to feel uneasy and conspicuous, when he was saved by an unforeseen intervention. Upon the path he met birdlike Sister Marie Clément.

"Bon jour, monsieur!" she said in lilting Bordeaux French.

Cable nodded stiffly and acknowledged her friendly greeting. "Today," she continued, "we shall expect you and Monsieur Benny for luncheon at one o'clock. The French people are expecting you." She nodded and bowed and smiled, and Cable had to accept her kind offer. His mother had often instructed him that one of the finest courtesies women can extend . . . one of the few, in fact . . . is an invitation to a dinner prepared by themselves. A gentleman must accept, and graciously.

Cable was more than usually disposed to accept, for the intervention of the sister meant that he was free of the pestering children. Hurriedly he darted up the path, around the hospital, and on toward Bloody Mary's hut. He moved so fast, in fact, that Liat, watching his progress from behind a coconut tree, was barely able to hurry to her hut and herd her relatives away. They left by a back door and did not meet the tall Marine as he approached the front.

"Hello!" he said in dry, agonized voice. Blood was in his head. His breath, from climbing and anticipation, was harsh. His hands were nervous, but as he stood there tall in the doorway, he was, to Liat, the finest man she had ever seen.

"Hello!" she replied. This time she did not wait beside the wall. She advanced to meet him in the middle of the small room. She was still kissing him when his wild hands had finished undressing her, and later she kissed him while he slept on the earthern floor.

About eleven Liat suggested that they walk along a jungle trail to the cliffs. Cable agreed and they set off, barefooted Tonk in the lead, tall Marine swinging a branch he had torn from a small tree. When they reached the cliffs of Bali-ha'i they were about three hundred feet above the pounding surf below. There were two or three delectable places where the cliff was overhanging. There, with no safeguard of any kind, one could look far below his feet to coral piles upon which the surging water boiled and spouted. Liat stood at these places and looked straight down. Her eyes showed no excitement, but her heart pounded faster beneath her white smock. Cable could not force himself to stand near the edge, so Liat described the scene to him in French.

Then, for a while, they sat near the cliff and talked. Strange, but all the things Cable could not write to Bryn Mawr flooded out in half-French, half-English sentences. Liat followed his thoughts with ease, and soon she was telling him of Tonkin China. She lived eighty miles from Hanoi near the Chinese border. Her parents came to the islands when she was nine. They had been here eight years. They had reenlisted, because life was better here, and a pretty girl could learn French, could learn to read and write, might even . . . marry . . . a planter.

"Who told you that?" Cable asked, terribly jealous.

"My mother."

"But it's not true!"

"But it is true," the girl replied in lilting French, in much the same way that Sister Marie Clément spoke. "Two white men in Efate have Tonkinese wives. And a trader wants to marry me, too. Jacques Benoit, who has a plantation, asked my mother." Artlessly . . . or perhaps with great artfulness . . . Liat told of Benoit's wooing. "But now he's going with a nurse. A white nurse! That's because I'm not on the island. Maybe he will marry her!"

Cable hushed her silly chatter with kisses and asked her to lead him to the hospital. "Why?" she cried.

"For dinner," he explained.

"But dinner! It is down there. In my hut. It's all ready!" she insisted with some show of fury. "It's waiting. I made it myself."

"When could you have made dinner?" Cable asked. "When did you have time?"

"Early this morning," she replied, simply. "I saw you coming. I watch here every morning for the boat. I knew you would come back."

Cable followed her small, brown arm as it pointed over the sea toward his island. Clouds covered it, as always, and to him the ocean looked barren and forbidding; but to Liat it was a glorious thing, a carpetway that would bring Cable back to her again and again.

"I can't eat with you," Cable explained. "I promised Sister Marie Clément."

"Sister Clément!" the beautiful girl cried. "No! Not with Sister Clément. With French girls. You wait! All the French people will be there. With their daughters, too! You wait!"

"I don't believe it, Liat!" Cable protested.

"Of course, it's true. You shall see," and she began to cry. The tears were real. They were tears of deep sorrow and perplexity. She clutched his arm. "If I were a French girl, it would be all right, wouldn't it?"

"Liat! Don't say such things!"

"But what will happen? Look! You won't even have dinner with me! And I can't go with you."

"Why not?" Cable asked, snapping his fingers. "Why not? I'll take you with me! Come, we'll go together. You shall be my guest. I am proud of you! I am!"

"But I have no shoes!" Liat sobbed. She was very happy, but she had no shoes.

"You shall go barefoot then! I insist that you go with me!" And so, throwing discretion to hell, ignoring every precept his mother had carefully taught him in the rigorous school of Philadelphia and Main Line Society, Cable half dragged, half carried the girl he loved down the jungle path, away from the gaunt cliffs, away from the pounding sea, and into the very maelstrom of the hospital.

Sister Marie Clément, with the austere grandeur that transcends provincial society, professed to see nothing awry in having the Tonkinese girl attend the soiree. After all, Liat was the finest pupil she had so far had in the islands. The girl was a true gem of the Orient. Would that more of the yellow girls were like her!

But to the French women—and their daughters—the Tonkinese girl was a frightful affront. The meal, an excellent one, was completely spoiled for them. Liat perceived this in a moment. As a woman, she reveled in her triumph; as a good mission Tonkinese who did not chew betelnut and who was a Christian instead of a Buddhist, she was shy, reserved, and deferential. She acted as if she "knew her place," and indeed, she did. Her place was beside Joe Cable, and that is where she was and where she stayed.

The dismal dinner over—only Atabrine Benny enjoyed it— a leisurely procession started for the pier. Liat, secure in her victory, left Cable abruptly at the hospital. He walked with the French ladies and conversed as charmingly as his command of the language would permit. "Perhaps we were wrong! Perhaps we misjudged the dear boy!" the women thought. Sister Marie Clément, walking behind them, mused on the ways of the world. "The Marine is a clever boy!" she thought. In her nun's garb she knew more of the human heart than the stiff French women who had presumably shared several: their husbands' and their children's.

On Vanicoro the watchers perceived all that had happened on the island that day. They saw the boat come—but not before Liat saw it—and now they heard the bells' fine music. One brave soul, of whom there appears to be one or more in every human group, grunted to his friends that now was the time. He would see if there was fine cloth for the asking. He would see!

So, amidst universal prophecy of destruction and failure,

this tested warrior crept toward his hidden outrigger and prepared for the great adventure. He himself was dressed in war clothes: a tightly woven string from which leaves hung behind and to which a penis wrapper was attached in front. He had a hibiscus in his hair. In his canoe he had pineapples and one irreplaceable personal treasure. Cloth looked good to him and, the gods of the volcano willing, by nightfall he would himself be wearing cloth about his loins.

From low hanging trees he pushed his canoe clear and into the channel. The afternoon sun was in his eyes, but with steady stroke he pushed it toward the bells. It was a moment before anyone on Bali-ha'i saw him coming. Then Liat saw him from the coconut where she stood surveying the scene. She could not tell the others, but soon Sister Marie Clément, with her inquisitive French eye, saw him, too, and she called out the news.

Everyone stopped what he was doing and watched the man of Vanicoro draw closer. Native girls looked at him and wondered if they had looked so frightened once. Little boys started yelling at him in island tongues he could not understand, and Cable waited in the boat.

With steady stroke the man approached. The wonder in the eyes and minds of the people who watched him could not approach the alternate hopes and fears that assailed this savage as he brought his frail canoe alongside Benny's boat. Meticulously shipping his paddle, he quietly arranged his single strand of clothing, sought his biggest pineapples, and stood up, thrusting the fruit into Cable's hands.

"It's a gift," Benny whispered. "They always bring a gift!" Cable took the fruit and placed it reverently in the bottom of his boat. Benny nudged him roughly. "You must give him something. You must do so. You gotta give him something."

"Here! Give him this knife." Benny produced a rusty but serviceable knife. Patiently, Cable explained the knife to the savage. At first the man was bewildered, but when Benny rudely grabbed the weapon and sliced a piece of juice-dripping pineapple, the black man understood and grinned. He had never seen a penknife before.

But it was cloth he wanted! Dimly he perceived that with cloth went a certain dignity. Men with penknives, for example, they wore cloth. Grabbing Cable's shirt he endeavored to explain, but the Marine, not understanding, pushed him away. The native was startled, and began to wonder if his mournful advisers on Vanicoro were not right. But having come this far, he was willing to see the thing through. He grabbed at the shirt again. Again Cable was about to rebuff him when Benny caught the significance of the act.

"He wants some cloth!" the druggist shouted. Then rummaging through the duffle bag he always carried on these trips, he produced three long lengths of bright red rayon-silk parachute cloth. Cloth, and red, too! The native stared in complete disbelief. He hoped . . . that is, he wished he dared to hope . . . that one piece of that cloth might be his. He was unprepared, therefore, when Cable caught up the armful and tossed all the pieces into the outrigger!

For a moment the native was unable to do anything but stare at the unbelievable treasure. He fingered it, gently. Then he held one piece out to its magnificent breadth. A tip trailed in the water, and he made a lunge for it. Cable grasped his arm, and at that the bewildered savage broke down completely. From the bottom of his outrigger he dragged forth his greatest prize. Carefully, and with some regret, he handed it up to Cable. Then, without a sound, he grasped his paddle and was off across the bay, his heart pounding faster than when he had first ventured forth upon his expedition.

To Cable his departure went unnoticed, for in his hands he held a dried human head! The features were intact. It was presumably the head of a man, a warrior, no doubt. The eyelids were sewn shut with strands of palm leaf. Pine needles had been stuffed into the nose to preserve its shape. The hair was long, both on the head and face. The gashing wound of the neck was sewn together into a little knot. There were no scars to speak of death and no signs to speak of life. It was nothing but a human head, a small, insignificant round object from which living and thoughts had fled, or been banished.

Cable sat transfixed with his gift. He had seen a Jap's head roll off one morning in bright sunlight. But that was nothing like this. This was a human head, here in his hands. Bewildered, he could not decide what to do with it.

"Chuck it in the boat, lieutenant!" Benny advised. "Somebody always wants something like that." Cable gently laid the grisly object on a tarpaulin. French women on the pier looked away. Little boys laughed. In some of their homes, not so very long ago, such heads had been common gossip, the way gasoline drums, GI cots, and bayonets now were.

But on Vanicoro excitement went beyond all bounds. Of course, only men were allowed to handle the cloth, and only men heard the first telling of the story, but eventually it sifted down even to the women. And as Benny's boat sailed into the sacred sunset, men looked at the cloth, studied the brave fellow who had secured it, and wondered.

Cable, in the boat, wondered too. He wondered if his silly action in taking Liat to the dinner would be reported on his island. It could be embarrassing if it were. He started to ask Benny what he thought, but the druggist was not given to moralizing. He wasn't in Waco, Texas. He was having a damned fine time in the islands, and right now that head was grinning at him from the bottom of the boat. He chuckled and made up all sorts of surmises as to who had owned the head, and when.

A shock equal to the one Cable suffered when the savage gave him the head awaited him when he reached the dock. It was dusk, and as he crawled out of the boat, there was Bloody Mary. "You like?" she asked him, grinning. "You like?" The betel juice was black upon her lips. He could not answer her. Then she saw the head on the tarpaulin. Catlike she jumped into the boat. "How much?" she asked.

"Take it!" Cable cried in disgust.

"Me take?" the old woman asked, uncertain that he was actually giving her this prize.

"Take it and get out!" he cried impatiently. Mary grabbed the head, tucked it under her arm and ran through the crowd of loafers. In a moment she was back, struggling and protesting, in the arms of two Shore Patrol.

"Lieutenant," they demanded roughly. "Did you give her this?"

"Yes. I told her to take it and scram."

"Then get the hell out of here! And don't come back!" They gave the Tonk a shove. She stumbled along for a few steps, clutching madly at the head. Then she righted herself, tucked the head under her arm, turned and heaped profanity on the two Shore Patrol.

"Go on, get out of here!" they threatened.

"*Soandso* you!" she screamed. "*Soandso* Emma Pees."

The loafers laughed at anything which discomfited the Shore Patrol. The latter, seeking to justify themselves, reported to Lt. Cable. "That your jeep over there? Yeah. Well, we found that old biddy perched in it a while ago. Better see if anything's stolen. We tossed her out."

On the way back to his quarters Cable's dancing mind flitted between a vision of Bloody Mary with a head under one arm, screaming at the Emma Pees, and Liat, standing on the cliffs, waving at him. For she had gone there while the native was trading for cloth, and as long as Cable could see Bali-ha'i, he had been able to see the slow, rhythmic waving of the Tonkinese girl.

Cable thought that by now he had seen most of the island mysteries, but he was unprepared for a phenomenon that occurred one strange afternoon. There had been gusts of wind all day, like the beginning of a hurricane. And rain, too! Lots of it. Then clouds began to disperse, and for a moment you could see Vanicoro beneath them. But just at that moment, in the weirdest manner, a heavy raincloud must have passed up the channel beside the volcanoes, for Vanicoro itself was blotted out. Free, wonderful in the dark light, a jewel unmatched, Bali-ha'i stood forth.

"I never knew there was an island there!" one of the Marine officers cried. "Look at that damned thing. Does it show on the charts?"

"Never even saw it before!" another answered. "Look at that damned cloud! Isn't that something to see?" Men called out their neighbors, for where there is so little to do as on a tropical island, every passing fancy of nature is commented on by men who keep their minds active in that way.

"Hey, Cable?" one cried. "Did you ever see this island before? Come here a minute?"

Cable, aroused from a light sleep by the voices, shuffled to the door. Through half-sleepy eyes he viewed the phenomenon. Against his will he cried out, "My God! It's Bali-ha'i!"

"What's that name?" an officer asked who was near him. Months later that officer recalled the scene very clearly. Minutely. He was wont to say, over a whiskey, "Damn it all! I should have known right then! I remarked the incident at the time, but forgot it. He came stumbling out of his hut, took a look at the new island, and cried, 'My God! It's Bali-ha'i!' And I would have suspected something then, but right at that moment another officer gave one hell of a shout down the line. It was Oferthal's roommate. Do you know what Oferthal, that dumb fool, had? You'd never guess!"

No, you'd never guess that a Marine officer would buy a human head, skin on it and all! Everyone left studying Bali-ha'i and surged around Oferthal, who was holding this head up by its long hair. "Ain't it a beauty?" he inquired.

"The son-of-a-bitch paid fifty dollars for it," an admiring friend proclaimed. It was sort of nice to think that your outfit had a guy stupid enough to pay fifty dollars for a human head, with skin on it and all! It gave you something to talk about.

"Yep," Oferthal announced blandly. "I bought it off'n an old Tonk woman. I gave her fifty bucks for it. And to me it's worth every cent."

"Why in hell do you throw your money away like that?"

"What better can I do with it? Shoot craps? Play poker with you sharks? Hell, no! Now I really got me something. Know what I'm going to do with it?"

"Bowl?" an irreverent Marine asked.

"No! I'm gonna take this home and hang it right up in my basement. Right in the rumpus room. Right where we have sandwiches and beer!"

"I hope you have a nurse in attendance, buddy, because one look at that grisly and you can serve my beer all over again to somebody else. It will be right on your floor!"

At that moment Cable, too, felt sick. He felt involved in a net of two colors. One was delicate brown, the other the color of dried betel juice. And no matter which way he twisted, he was not free. About this time he stopped writing to his mother.

The next time he saw Bali-ha'i was when Benny took him there on his regular visit. Four things happened. Six canoes set out from Vanicoro this time, and all the owners were dressed in red loin cloths. He slept with Liat again, more passionately than ever before. She gave him a charm she had carved from the strange ivory nut. And Sister Marie Clément stopped him as he went home past the hospital.

"That is an interesting charm," Sister Clément observed. "Is it from the ivory nut? That is a peculiar nut, is it not? Have you seen one? No? Well, stop by a moment." She disappeared into the hospital and produced a small object about the size of a man's fist. It resembled a small pineapple, brown and with a covering like a pine cone. "If you cut this covering off, there is an interior like the matting of a coconut. Inside that there is a fruit, and if you cut that off—it's like potato—you will find this very hard nut. When it dries, it's like ivory, as you can see. It's one of the strange things of the islands." She paused a long time and then asked, "Did Liat give you the charm?"

"Yes, Sister, she did."

"My son," Sister Clément began. "You know what I have to say. I say it only to reinforce your own conscience, for you must already have said it to yourself. What you are doing is no good. It can only bring hurt to you and disgrace to the girl. If life is so urgent, so compelling now, marry one of the lovely French girls who live on this island. Some of them are beautiful. Some are fairly wealthy. Some are surprisingly well educated. And there are Protestants among them, too. If life is so urgent, it must also be important. Do not waste it, I pray you."

Cable could say nothing for a long time. He stood looking at the channel, this time a greenish blue, lovelier than before. Bali-ha'i was in his heart, and the island fought there against the wisdom of the little birdlike woman from Bordeaux. Finally he asked, "What of Liat?"

"I don't know what has passed between you, lieutenant. That is your affair, and God's. But I think I am doing no harm if I say that Liat can marry almost whom she wishes. Many Tonkinese want to marry her, for she is an industrious girl." Sister Clément bit her lip. She knew she should never have praised the girl. She knew Cable would grasp at those words and remember them long after the rest of her sermon had been dismissed. She continued, more carefully, "There is also a planter who wants to marry her. You have probably heard of him. Jacques Benoit. He could give her a good home. It would be a step up in the world for her. And although Jacques drinks a bit, I think he might make, with Liat's help, a good Christian home. Lieutenant, I beg you to think of this."

Cable studied the channel again. The six canoes from Vanicoro were returning to their own side of the greenish water. He hoped that Benny had accepted no more heads. Dry of mouth he turned his gaze to Sister Marie Clément, who was waiting.

"You see, lieutenant?" she said, weighing each word. "I know you have been on Guadalcanal. You are probably a hero, too. I have been patient, hoping that reason would overtake you. We, here on this island and on all of these islands, know that we owe our homes and perhaps our lives to you men who stopped the Japanese. But you owe yourselves something, too. Remember that. Therefore, I have said nothing, but if you come here again, I shall report it to your commander. I shall have to do that. And not for Bali-ha'i's good, and not to make my own work easier. But to help you to save yourself." Sister Clément smiled frankly at the young man, insisted upon shaking his hand warmly, and returned to the hospital. Cable walked down to the boat in silence. He was dreading the moment when he would have to look in the boat and see a couple of dried heads from Vanicoro.

There were no heads, and this fact so roused his uncertain spirits that when the boat cleared the headland he threw caution away and made frantic gestures to Liat. "There," he pointed. "There. At the bottom of the cliff!" The girl gave no hint that she understood what he meant.

Benny, whom Sister Clément had lectured while Cable slept exhausted upon the earthen floor, studied his fellow passenger in silence. Repeat the lecture he would not, come hell or high water. In Benny's fine philosophy there was "too damned little lovin' in the world, and if a guy is knockin' off a legitimate piece now and then, why, more power to him!" He wondered what had happened? What was happening? He wondered, for example, what Tonkinese women wore under their strange costumes? And he bet that the lieutenant could tell him. In fact, Atabrine Benny rarely had a dull moment in this life, not even when he was with his wife, because his active mind could wonder the damnedest things! In the Renaissance, if a Medici had got hold of him soon enough, he might have made a fair country philosopher, for native inquisitiveness combined with judgment he did have.

At the dock Bloody Mary was waiting. Her persistent question was persistently shot at Cable once more. "You like?" she asked, in a singsong voice. She did not expect an answer, nor did she expect to see any heads in the bottom of the boat. Her disappointment not great, she waddled through the gaping crowd and did not even fight back when some soldiers called after her, "Fo' Dolla'. Hey, Fo' Dolla'."

In the morning Cable's commanding officer demanded to see him. The young Marine reported and saluted stiffly. "Cable," the older man began brusquely, "your work has been going down badly. What's happening? Are you in trouble of any kind?"

"No, sir!" Cable replied promptly. He spoke with considerable assurance, for he did not consider himself to be in trouble.

"Then snap to it, sir. Hold your musters with more snap. Get your reports in on time. Pull yourself together. Set a good example for the men. This sitting around and waiting is tough duty, and you officers must set the example." The colonel spoke sharply and impersonally.

"Yes, sir!" Cable responded. "I'll attend to that, sir." He started to leave.

"And another thing, Cable!" The young officer snapped to attention. "That job I gave you to do some time ago. That Tonkinese woman. I see she's down there by the tree again. I told you to clean her out of there. See that it's done!" The colonel raised his head, then turned to his papers. Cable was dismissed.

In his own quarters he flopped upon his hard bed and stared at the ceiling. He still hadn't written those letters. Damn it all, he'd write them this very afternoon! Right after he saw Bloody Mary and gave her hell. Damn it all, he'd kick her out of there, if necessary. That's what he'd do. Meanwhile, he'd catch a little sleep.

The morning was very hot. No breeze came off the placid ocean, and the white sun beat furiously upon the whiter coral. A thin haze of tropical heat, scented by the sea and strange flowers, hung everywhere, even in Cable's hut. He lay as he had fallen upon his return from his meeting with the colonel. His shoes and trousers were on; his shirt was pulled open.

As he twisted on his hot bed, sweat started forming under his knees, in his arm pits, around his middle. Then, as his body heat rose, perspiration crept upon his forehead, behind his ears, and along his shin bones. His hot clothes resting heavily upon him, his hot bed pushing up from below formed a blanket of sticky, salty sweat that soon enveloped him.

Uncomfortable in his unnecessary sleeping, he tossed and twisted until his clothes began to bind. Sweat ran down the seams in small rivers. Now, as the sun upon the coral grew hotter, his discomfort rose and a kind of half-waking nightmare overtook him, as it attacks all fitful sleepers in the tropics. There were no proportions to his fantasy; like a vision of marihuana his dream consisted merely of geographic shapes propelling themselves into weirder shapes, until his entire mind was filled with whirring and wheeling objects.

At noon some fellow officers endeavored to waken him, but he rolled over soddenly. With a wet forearm, he shooed them away, and continued his sleeping. The same officers, upon returning from chow, decided to have some fun with Cable. One hurried to a near-by shack and returned with an object that caused great merriment among the conspirators. With the aid of string they rigged a suspension over the sleeping man's bed. Then they retired to a corner. When they were hidden, they made a loud noise. What happened next they did not fully anticipate.

Instead of drowsily opening his eyes at the noise Cable, for some unknown reason, sat bolt upright. As he did so, his steaming face hit the object which he was supposed to have seen upon waking. It was the grisly head from Vanicoro! It was hanging by the hair. The force with which his face hit the grim object caused it to swing in a long arc. Before he was fully aware of what was happening, the head swung back and bounced several times against his wet face, spreading the tropic sweat. The moisture felt like blood.

With a scream, the Marine sprang from his hot bed and leaped for the door. Outside, he looked back once at the head, still swinging. The hidden men he never saw.

Cable went to the shower and washed off his face and hands. He was frightened, even when he knew what the object was. He was frightened because he had slept so restlessly, because he had awakened so bizarrely, because he had been reprimanded that morning.

"I must get hold of myself," he repeated, over and over again. "What the devil is happening to me?" He straightened his clothes, wiped the sweat from his arms, washed his face again, and returned for his cap. The head was gone.

"I'll go see Bloody Mary right now," he said with determination. He left his hut, climbed slowly into his jeep and drove down the road toward the banyan trees.

"Hey, sir!" a Marine called. "You got her in second!" He deliberately kept the jeep in that gear so as not to admit that he had been drowsing at the wheel. When the engine heated up, he shifted into high. By then he was near the road leading to the banyan. Again he shifted into second so that any enlisted men near by would hear him coming and have time to hide among the brush. When he reached the banyan, old Mary sat there alone. She grinned as he approached.

"Hello, Mary," he said without enthusiasm.

"You like Liat?" the forthright old Tonk asked.

"Colonel say, 'You go!' This time, you go. And don't come back!" He spoke in English, adding hand movements to enforce his words.

"Me go," Mary said with no disposition to argue. "Goddam colonel." To give effect to her words, she spat into the dust. Cable noticed that she was chewing betel again. She folded her wares as she had often done before, placed them in a small box, and grinned at the lieutenant. "Me go! See!"

Cable, satisfied that she understood and would obey, started to leave, but the old woman grabbed at his arm. Now she spoke in French, her own barbarous version of that lovely language. "You like Liat?" she asked.

Cable blushed deeply. "Yes," he replied. Then he tried to pull his arm loose and climb into his jeep. Mary hauled him back. She sat by her box. Cable was forced to sit upon one of the snakelike roots of the banyan.

"Liat fine girl," Mary observed. "Liat very good girl."

"Yes," the Marine assented, "she is a lovely girl."

"You marry her?" Mary asked directly.

This was the question that Cable had been fearing for a long time. He tried to mask his emotions as he replied, but looking at the repugnant, betel-stained old harridan he could not. There was a slight revulsion in his voice and manner as he answered her. "I can't," he said.

Mary dropped her pretense of pleasantness at this, insulted by the slight and infuriated that her plans might go awry. "Why not?" she demanded.

"I can't marry her," Cable repeated sullenly.

"You don't love her?" Mary asked, using a word that had no exact counterpart in Tonkinese, where men and women marry for almost any reason except love. It was a western extravagance whose meaning had once been explained to her by Benoit, the planter who wanted to marry Liat.

"I love her, Mary," Cable explained. "But I can't marry her."

"Why not?" the hard woman demanded. "Why not? You go over to Bali-ha'i. You make . . ." Here Mary demonstrated a filthy gesture commonly used in the Orient. Cable winced and looked away.

"Yes!" the infuriated woman screamed. "All the time you go there and make . . ."

"Mary! Please!" Cable cried, speaking once more in

English. He looked furtively about him. "At least," he thought to himself, "few enlisted men know French, thank heavens!"

"You afraid? I not afraid!" She put her hand to the side of her face, making a megaphone, and shouted: "*Soandso* lieutenant go to Bali-ha'i! Make . . ."

At this insult Cable could not contain himself. He swung his right hand sharply and slapped Bloody Mary across the face. The effect was startling. The woman perceived that the young man was deeply moved. She had been beaten before by men who were disturbed and unsure of themselves. It was a human thing to do . . . for a man. She understood. Spitting once more into the dust, she tenderly grasped Cable's arm.

"Why you not marry Liat?" she asked in a low voice of great dignity.

Cable, astonished by what he had done and, like Mary, surprised at the depth of his love for Liat, looked dumbly at the old woman and replied, "I can't. I can't take her home with me."

"Look, lieutenant!" she cried with sudden inspiration. "I have much money. I have three thousand dollars, maybe. In Hanoi, my brother, he is rich. Why you not take this money? Live here with Liat? Maybe live in China. Other white men do." She spoke in a persuasive, pleading tone.

"Mary!" he cried in an agony of pain. "I can't. I can't!" Forcing himself free of her grasp, he hurried to his jeep and started it with a roar. Mary pulled herself to her feet and ran over to the side of the car.

"You come back, bimeby?"

He didn't. He stayed away all that day and the next. On the third day, he was awakened from his afternoon nap by Atabrine Benny. "It's none of my business," the fat fellow observed in a confidential whisper, "but I know a boat that's going over to Bali-ha'i tonight. A couple of guys are going fishing. They cleared it with the patrol craft. They could drop you off." He paused archly. "That is, if you wished to go . . ." His voice trailed off in fine southern insinuation.

Cable was perplexed for a moment. If he did this thing, he would be involved with other men, and soon his secret would be shared throughout the island, and on other islands, too. It would be like the secret of the naval officer at Luana Pori who crept into the bed of a lovely De Gaullist when her

Pétainist husband beat it to the hills. Everyone knew it, now.

But Cable's caution was soon drowned in his ardor. "Are you going, too?" he asked. "Good! Then I'll be there. What time?" Arrangements were hurriedly made and Benny, ill at ease in officers' country, slipped away. That night a small craft set out when harbor lights were dimmed. Before midnight it was approaching Bali-ha'i. At quarter past midnight Cable asked if he might use a lantern for a moment. There was some quiet discussion, and one of the men produced a strong flashlight. Slowly, for the space of three minutes or more, Cable waved the light back and forth. Then, climbing into the small yellow rubber boat which the men let down over the side, he started to row for the cliffs.

"Be careful," Atabrine Benny called to him. "We'll be back for you right here at 0400." Each man then set his watch, like a group of aviators about to make a strike and planning their deathly rendezvous. The craft slipped off in search of bonita and barracuda. Silently, the little yellow lifeboat crawled toward the coral at the foot of the cliff. By the time Cable found a satisfactory place to beach the fragile boat, Liat was on the shore calling softly to him.

Like a surge of unconsolable emotion, Cable leaped from the boat, ran to the lovely girl, and enveloped her in his arms. Her own heart was beating as wildly as his, and by the time she lay upon the sand beneath one of the trees, naked in the shimmering moonlight, Cable's torrential passion could restrain itself no longer. He clasped the delicate Tonkinese to him and surrendered all doubts that had made him miserable that week. She was his, she was his, and that single fact outweighed all lesser questions.

Before, in the hut, the love these two had felt for one another had been constrained by the confines of the close walls and by the natural fear that someone would burst in upon them. Now, on the edge of the jungle and the sea, secure in their mutually shared passions, they surrendered themselves throughout that night to the reassurances of immortality that men and women can give to one another.

In their slight talk Cable reported his meeting with Liat's mother. When he came to the part in which he said that he could not marry Liat, the girl did not protest, for indeed, in her heart, she had known from the first that this tall Marine could not marry her if he would. And now, under the jungle tree, with the speckled moonlight falling upon their intermingled brown bodies, Liat was not too concerned about the future.

With that rare indifference bred of thousands of years of life in the Orient, the little girl said quietly, "I knew it could never be. My mother dreamed that something great would happen to me. It has. But not what she dreamed. You love me. You will go away somewhere. I will marry somebody else."

"Oh, Liat, Liat!"

"Oh, yes! I shall. My family is almost rich among the Tonkinese." She stopped speaking and then added, "But I wish that you and I could have a baby. A baby that was yours, too. Then, if you went away . . ."

The little Tonkinese girl grew silent. Perhaps she knew that all over the world women were saying that. For it was war, and the thought and speech were identical in Russia, in New Mexico, in Yokohama, in Dresden, and in Bali-ha'i.

Cable, relaxed, wondered what would happen to a son of his if Liat did become pregnant. It was a happy thought, and he laughed aloud. "What is it, Joe?" she asked, pronouncing the *J* like a *Zh*.

"I was thinking," he said, "that it would be heaven to have children with you. To live somewhere together. Somewhere like Bali-ha'i." Then soberer thought overtook him. He shivered slightly, and Liat pulled herself closer to him. When she asked what was the matter, he replied, "It is almost four o'clock, and I must meet the boat."

They dressed, and Liat helped him to pull the boat into the water. Holding the craft with one foot, he clasped Liat to him again as if he could never let her go. "How did you know I was coming?" he asked.

"I look every night," she said. "I know you cannot stay away." He kissed her passionately and almost roughly shoved her back away from the boat. Then he rowed out slowly to where Atabrine Benny was already flashing a light.

Three more times Cable made that midnight trip. He was now living in a delirium which carried into waking hours the phantasms that assailed him when he slept and sweated at noonday. He and Liat were experiencing a passion that few couples on this earth are privileged to share. Could it have been indefinitely prolonged, it is probable that their love for one another would have sustained them, regardless of their color, through an entire lifetime. This is not certain, however, for Cable and Liat knew of the impossibilities that surrounded them.

Cable, for example, heard from Atabrine Benny that each night when the boat set out for Bali-ha'i, old Bloody Mary knew about it and watched it go. He half suspected that some of his fellow officers knew of what was going on, for they looked at him strangely; but promptly he realized that perhaps it was because he was looking at them strangely. He moved as in a dream. He no longer said, "Tomorrow I will certainly write to my mother. Tomorrow I will get out that paper work." He was beyond deceiving himself. He knew only that one of these days something would break, a terrible scandal, or a new attack on some island further north, or detachment to some other station. Something unforeseen would rescue him from Bloody Mary.

Then everything happened at once! Little Eddie, the Marine with a girl in Minneapolis, came bursting into the Officers' Mess one evening and cried, "It's the McCoy! We move north at once! There's going to be a big push somewhere, and we're in on it! We stage up at Bonita Bay!"

"Where do we hit?"

"When do we leave here?"

"Eddie? Did you see the orders? Or is this just guff?"

"Easy on, there. Easy on," Eddie cried, pleased with his importance. "I saw the orders. The colonel showed them to several of us. Where we strike?" He shrugged his shoulders. "Who knows? Who cares?"

There was furious discussion. Some men felt that it might be Konora, a small island far up. Others suggested Bougainville. One wild theorist proposed Rabaul itself, but like the fool who thought it might even be Kuralei, he was shouted down. It was interesting to note that the wild and general discussion changed not one man's personal opinions as to where the next great strike would be. Even the embryo general who had deduced that Kuralei was the logical place to strike was not deterred by the gibes. He knew he was right.

Next morning the news was made official. Departure from their present base would be immediate. "What does that mean, sir?" "Immediately," the colonel replied, and smiled. Later discussion concluded that it meant six or seven days.

Cable was completely perplexed. On one hand the urgency of the move swept him along like one of the boxes being hastily packed. On the other, his tremendous emotional and spiritual involvement with Liat completely dragged him home to Bali-ha'i. In the confusion thus created in his uncertain mind he drifted, praying that Atabrine Benny might stumble along with some suggestion. Significantly, however, he made no effort to find Benny. He methodically packed and hoped.

Strangely, it was not Benny but Bloody Mary who sensed the problems he would be facing. Fifteen minutes after the colonel had informed his junior officers of the intended move the Tonks knew what was up. It was good news for them, in a way, because for the next few weeks the lid would be off. They could sell whiskey, kill chickens for last-minute barbecues, sell skirts, sell anything that walked or could be carried.

To Bloody Mary, however, the news was intensely drab. She hurriedly put on her peach-basket hat and shuffled down the road to the banyan tree. She waited there for several hours, and finally, like a piece of battered iron drawn to the magnet, Cable drove up. "Mary!" he cried. "We're leaving!"

"Lieutenant," she asked, in deep earnestness, "you marry Liat?"

"I can't," he moaned. "Oh, God! Mary, I love her, but I can't."

The broken-toothed old woman pushed him away. In utmost scorn she cursed him, spitting betel juice blackly as she did so. "*Soandso* fool. Goddam lieutenant. You be *soandso* sorry. You be bullshit sorry! *Soandso* fool!" She turned away from the stunned man and left him sitting bewildered in his jeep.

Spurred by Mary's scorn, he sought out Atabrine Benny. He found the chubby druggist at the Malaria Control headquirters, sitting with his feet higher than his head, drinking beer from a can.

"Come in, lieutenant!" the jovial fellow grunted. "Hear you're going away! Well, I bet I know what you want!"

"You know, Benny?" Cable confessed. "My God, Benny. I've got to get to Bali-ha'i. I've got to!"

"It's all arranged. I thought it all out yesterday evening when I heard about it. We can make an official trip tomorrow. Be ready at about 0400. OK?" He offered Cable a beer, but the Marine, shocked by what was happening to him, was too unsettled to participate.

"You'll enjoy it more than I will," he told Benny.

"You'd be surprised how much beer I drink!" the druggist

said. "I got a special deal where I get it by the case. Not bad, eh?" He laughed to himself as Cable disappeared into the night.

The next morning at 0400 Benny and Cable climbed into the Atabrine Special and set out across the sea. They were well out of the lee of their own island when sunrise started.

There were dark clouds across the entire sky, lying in thick layers upon one another. At five o'clock streaks of an infinitely delicate pastel yellow began to shoot among these clouds. Then, dramatically, a fiery streak of golden yellow pranced clear across the sky and stayed aloft for several minutes. Other pastel shades of blue and gray and lovely purple flickered in the sky, while great shafts of orange and gold radiated from the intense point at which the sun would later rise. These mighty shafts circled the sky, like golden arrows, and wherever they touched, clouds were swept with light. Cable thought it was like a hundred aurora borealises smashed into one.

But even as the orange and gold shafts bored vertically through the sky, the limb of the sun appeared at an opening in the clouds where sky and water met. Suddenly the pastel colors disappeared. The golden barbs were turned aside. Now the flaming red of the sun itself took control, and this sovereign color filled sky and ocean. It was not merely red. It was a vivid, swirling, violent color of blood; and it touched every cloud that hung above the water. It filled the boat, and men's hands looked red for the moment. Hills on distant islands were red, and waves that sped away from the prow of the boat were red, too.

As the sun crept higher into the heavens, the unearthly glow started to subside. Again single shafts of light appeared, piercing the remotest clouds like arrows seeking even the wounded. Then the pastel shades of yellow and gold and red and purple took over, and finally, across the entire seascape, the rare and peaceful blue of steel-gray clouds appeared. It was now day. The majestic sun was risen.

Cable gasped as the violence of the scene subsided. Atabrine Benny whistled to one of the boat crew. "You'd think the world would be worn out after a show like that!"

Onward reaching through calm and lovely blue, the small craft sped toward Bali-ha'i. As it rounded the headland and entered the splendid channel Cable had the sensation of one who comes home after a long voyage. Eagerly his eyes sought out the old familiar landmarks. From the hills of Vanicoro to the red and white hut of the Tonks this was rare and sacred land. Nourishing these thoughts, the young man sat humped in the boat as it crept along the channel to the ringing of bells that Poe would have loved.

At the pier every face seemed like the face of one he loved, and each face smiled at him as if he were an old friend returned from hazards abroad. He was dismayed, therefore, when Sister Clément stopped him at the shoreline.

"I thought you would come!" she said quietly. "We had word of your leaving yesterday."

"How fast bad news travels," he thought. "I suppose even the Japs on Kuralei know it by now." To Sister Clément he said, "Yes. With your permission I came to say goodbye."

"It will be a strange goodbye," Sister Clément replied. "Liat left the island last evening." The good sister was not pleased to convey this news. She took no pleasure in the obvious shock Cable experienced.

"Gone?" he said, not attempting to dissemble his true feelings. "Where could she have gone?" Little boys and girls, black and not knowing what he was suffering, clustered about his knees.

"Go away!" the sister said in Pidgin. Then she turned to Cable. "Liat went home last night. She is going to marry Monsieur Benoit."

"But Sister!" Cable could not speak further. He mumbled something.

"Shall we sit over here?" she suggested. She led him to a rude bench by a coconut tree.

"Going to marry Benoit?" he asked.

"Yes, lieutenant," she replied. "It is strange, is it not, how things work out? Benoit has been a very bad man at times. He has had several children by native women. I understand he tried to marry an American nurse and almost did. Now he returns to his first love, the little Tonkinese girl. You see, nature and God work together in unforeseen ways to accomplish their common purposes."

Cable remained on the little bench. He did not even rise as Sister Clément, with some sorrow in her heart, bade him good day and climbed the hill to her hospital. Now beauty was gone from the channel, and the island of Bali-ha'i was an empty thing. Like the bloom that drops from a thorn and leaves once more the ugly plant, Liat's going had left behind an island that could be seen in its true light. There were the savage hills of Vanicoro. Here was the useless little island with a few coconut trees and a mysterious wartime family of women. The channel was sometimes blue, but no important craft could ever find harbor there, and those little black children, if left alone, would soon revert to savagery. In great discomfort Cable discovered these things about Bali-ha'i, which a few minutes before had been the pearl of the seas, a veritable paradise. Not having the philosophic turn of mind that Atabrine Benny had, he did not speculate upon the multiple manifestations of truth. He was content to be wretched and terribly alone.

As soon as the homeward trip started, Cable began to lay plans with Benny to visit Jacques Benoit the next morning. Benny, who loved intrigue, agreed to change his schedule so as to accommodate his friend. They would leave early in the morning, and if Benoit wasn't there, why that would be just too bad, and no harm done.

That evening at mess Cable overheard a strange conversation among his fellow officers. As a matter of fact, he didn't really hear much of the conversation, merely a bit of heckling directed at little Eddie, who had that warm number in Minneapolis.

"What are you going to tell her now?" one chap asked.

Eddie blushed and replied, "Well, at that price I figured you can't go wrong."

"And the way you talked!" another chided. At this they burst into laughter and broke up.

"What were they talking about?" Cable asked a friend.

"Eddie just changed his mind," the other officer replied.

"What do you mean?"

"You wouldn't be interested," the officer said stiffly. Cable had rebuffed him so frequently in past weeks that he was not disposed to chat with him now.

As they climbed the small hill leading to Benoit's place, Benny asked Cable if he had heard the news? The news about the two sailors who cut one another up after a heavy load of torpedo juice. "There was something else in the story, but I didn't get it straight. It was out by the Tonk village, and I guess they were fooling around too much. You know how it is with that damned torp juice!"

"Benny," Cable interrupted, not interested in the brawling

inevitable at any advanced base, "when we get there, please let me speak to Benoit."

"Sure, sure!" the druggist agreed. "Now look over there. The small lean-to? That's where we hand out the atabrine. The Tonks and natives will line up and you can talk with Benoit." He gave his mournful warning: "Yaaaaaaoooooooo!"

From a dirty shack a native girl let out a scream. It was the pillman! Quickly she brought the heavy memorial conch and tooted a mournful blast upon it. From fields the workers ambled in. Ugh! they were dirty. To Cable the Tonks looked like the endless starving peasantry of China. Natives were sullen-faced and filthy. But to Benny the Tonks looked spirited and friendly. The natives were much cleaner than when he had first visited the plantation months ago.

"Allo, Benny!" a French voice called out. "Pretty early today. What bring you here?" It was Benoit.

"Extra work this week," Benny lied. "You're lookin good."

"And why not?" the gross Frenchman asked in revolting coyness. "I should be lookin' wery good. I going to be married!"

"You?" Benny cried. "Now that's fine. Do I know the girl?"

"No," the plantation owner replied in a sniffling drawl. "She a Tonkinese girl. I want to marry her since a long time. She jus' come back from Bali-ha'i." Benny stopped slapping atabrine pills into yellow mouths and looked at Cable. The Marine's face was impassive. Benoit drooled on: "Be nice if you come to the weddin', Benny. Many American friends will be there. In the church. She is a Catholic, too, fortunately."

Benny shrugged his shoulders and watched Cable indirectly as the blacks lined up for their atabrine. The Marine was studying the Frenchman. Benoit looked like a beachcomber. Once he had been a powerful person. Now he was fat and ugly. His face was marked with tropical diseases. He looked like a man of the islands, tough, sloppy, determined. Cable shivered from the icy fingers of his thoughts. "Let's be going," he whispered to Benny.

"And now!" Benoit cried. "We have one little drink? For the marriage, one little celebration?"

Before Cable could stop him he hurried into his hut, a rude affair. A young native woman snarled at him. He pushed her aside and returned with a bottle and three glasses. "Some fine whiskey," he said. "An American give it to me for the wedding," he explained. He poured three gracious drinks. "To the bride!" he proposed. He winked at Cable, drawing up his pock-marked cheeks. He said, "Only a Tonk! Ah, but such a Tonk!" He made an hourglass of his hands the way Americans had shown him. Then, feeling expansive with white men as his guests, he swept his languid arm about the plantation. "It will be good to have one wife. I get rid of these natives. All of them. We get some Tonks who can really work. Build this all up!" He put his fingers to his bulbous nose. "I got some money. It's wery good to be married!"

On the way down the hill Benny was perplexed as to what he should say. He finally observed, as a feeler, "I'd say that guy was no catch, not even for a Tonk." Cable's shoulders tightened a bit. Benny said no more. The American whiskey, which was good, burned in Cable's throat.

As soon as Benny delivered him to the Marine camp Cable made plans to see Liat somewhere, somehow, that same afternoon. But when he returned to quarters he found that a briefing meeting would be held at 1400. For three stifling hours one dull explanation after another was given. "The unit will move in thus and thus many ships. You will debark at Bonita Bay for one last maneuver. You have got to maintain communications. Any unit failing to maintain communications will be severely disciplined. Fooling has ended. It will be your responsibility to see that each ship is packed for combat. Stow all gear according to battle plan, rigidly." And so on, and so on.

Cable ate no supper. He felt that he had to avoid his fellow officers. As soon as it was dark he drove his jeep to the edge of the Tonk village. If Liat were there he would find her. He stumbled among the little houses and was lost. Like an ever willing guide Bloody Mary's voice came to him through the darkness. "You lost, lieutenant," she called softly. "Here!"

Cable turned. There was the old Tonk waiting, confident that her Marine would come that night. She sat cross-legged on the floor of her small porch. "Allo, lieutenant!" she said. She was chewing betel nuts again.

"What you want, lieutenant?" she asked in French. Then she cackled and pulled herself up. "You come! You come!" she said in English. She motioned for the Marine to enter the small room. As he did so, she disappeared.

"Liat!" he cried.

In unbelievable pleasure the little Tonkinese girl turned from where she sat on an Army cot, and saw that it was truly Cable. Deftly, with the motions of a great dancer, she rose and hurried to his arms. "Zhoe! Zhoe!" she cried.

"What's the matter, Liat?" he asked. The little girl wept for a moment, saying nothing. Then she started to kiss the Marine, but changed her mind and pushed him away.

"You are too late," she said in exquisite French.

"No!" Cable said in a flood of passion for this lovely girl. "I tried to see you yesterday. On Bali-ha'i." Liat's eyes brightened. Impulsively she kissed him three, four times. But as his hands sought her breasts she drew back, frightened.

"No, Zhoe! Please, no! You mus' not! Somebody is coming."

Surprised, Cable left his hand upon her thin stomach. He could feel the tenseness of her body. What had happened? "Who is coming?" he demanded.

There was a long silence. Liat kissed him on the cheek. She started to speak but hesitated. Then she said, "I am going to be married."

"I know," Cable said softly. "They told me. I'm happy for you, Liat." She shuddered. "In a way I am, that is. I hope it will be good for you. The one who's coming? Is it M. Benoit?"

Liat sucked in her breath. "Oh, Zhoe! You know that man?"

"Yes," the Marine said. They looked at one another across the shadow of Benoit, the planter, the gross, ugly man living with his mistresses in the bush. Benoit, so different in spirit and appearance from Lt. Joe Cable. Thin tears trickled from Liat's almond eyes. An old jungle fragrance from Bali-ha'i was in her hair. Cable whispered that most terrible of blackmails: "Tomorrow we are going. I hoped we might . . . again . . . for this last time . . ."

"Oh, Zhoe!" the little girl cried in fright. Outside she could hear Bloody Mary striking a match to light a cigarette. She turned her face away as the impassioned Marine pulled the white smock over her head. "Zhoe?" she whispered. "Tomorrow? You going to fight?" Cable pulled her to the clean floor and tugged at the ankles of the sateen pants. "Zhoe?" she whispered, close to his ear. "You fighting? You won't die?" She heard Cable's wild breathing as he spread his shirt beneath her. "Zhoe!" she wailed in her exquisite misery.

"You're never coming back. Zhoe? Zhoe? How can I live?" Outside Bloody Mary scraped another match across the sole of her sandals.

Cable's goodbyes were brief. "I brought you this watch," he said. "It's a man's watch, but it keeps good time."

Liat pressed her left hand to her lips. "Zhoe!" she cried. "But I have no present for you!"

Cable's exhausted heart allowed him to say nothing. His farewells might have been more tender had not Bloody Mary made a warning sound from the porch. In response, Cable hurried to the door, but Mary blocked the way.

"He's coming!" she warned. Outside a car wormed its way through the coconut trees. Liat pressed her smock out straight. Mary looked at Cable. "This you last chance, lieutenant," she said in soft persuasion. "You like Liat, no? This you last chance. I save her for you till you come back. Benoit? Phhhh! You want her, lieutenant?"

Cable could hear the car coming. He could visualize the driver, gross, ugly Benoit. He was ashamed and distraught. "I can't, Mary. I can't," he cried.

"Get out!" the bitter Tonk shouted. Cable stepped toward the door. "Other way, goddam fool lieutenant!" she hissed like an old rattlesnake. "*Soandso* goddam fool!" The words bit out in horrible accent. The Tonk stood in the doorway with her arms folded. Her black lips were drawn back over still blacker teeth. As she grimaced at Cable betel juice showed in the ravines of her mouth. "You go! You go!" she cried hoarsely. "You one goddam fool, lieutenant. Liat one fine girl for you."

Stunned by the cruelty of Bloody Mary's revilings, bewildered by all that had transpired, Cable climbed out the window. His last sight of that room was of Liat, her hands over her face, her body pressed against the wall as he had first seen her, crying. Behind her stood Bloody Mary, black, black.

He jumped behind a tree. An old French car chugged right up to Bloody Mary's porch. Its lights died in the tropical blackness. From it stepped Benoit, come to court his betrothed. He was dressed in white cotton trousers and a black alpaca coat. He wore a white hat. In his left hand he carried a bunch of flowers. Brushing himself off and checking to see that his fly was buttoned, Benoit stepped up to the porch. Bloody Mary was waiting for him.

"Bon soir, mon ami!" she cried in cackling French.

"Est-ce que Liat est chez elle?" he asked.

"Entrez, entrez, Monsieur Benoit!" The fat planter pulled his tight alpaca coat into position. Liat met him at the door. She turned her face away. He kissed her on the cheek and handed her the flowers. Cable, watching, leaned against a coconut tree for a long time. Finally Bloody Mary appeared on the porch. She took a cigarette from her sateen pants and some matches from her blouse. She struck a match. The light glowed briefly in the jungle dark and showed her weather-beaten face.

In the morning Lt. Joe Cable, fully determined to be the best Marine officer in the coming strike, was up early. He checked his men to see that they were ready for the ship that would take them north. He repacked his battle gear twice to make it ready for a landing. At 0900 he took charge of general muster. When he was finished, the colonel and his staff took over for final instructions. Cable saluted the colonel. "All present, sir!" he reported. He clenched his fist. "It's good to be back in the swing," he said to himself.

Cable and his men climbed into one of the trucks heading for the loading dock. There was a mighty thrill in that moment when the old camp died and its men set out for some distant island where a new camp would be won from the Japs and the jungle. The Marines smiled at one another. Cable sat erect among his men.

But when the trucks reached the Tonk village they became involved in a minor traffic jam. During the interval of waiting old Bloody Mary came down the road with a bundle of grass skirts. From the first truck one of the Marines started teasing her.

"Fo' Dolla', Fo' Dolla'!" he shouted. The black-toothed woman ignored him. The man was disappointed. Bloody Mary stared into one truck after another. She was looking for someone. "Fo' Dolla'!" the men cried. "You lose something?" Mary waddled to the next truck. Her eyes brightened. There sat her friend, Lt. Cable.

" 'Allo, lieutenant!" she cried. Cable did not look at her. She addressed the men in his truck. "Goddam fool lieutenant all time come see my Liat. Bring her things. Lieutenant one bullshit goddam fool!" She raised her right arm and threw a small object forcefully to the ground. Liat's watch, bought for more than a hundred dollars, crashed into the dust. It flew apart. A wheel rolled crazily down the road, hit a truck tire, and stopped.

"That was a watch!" a Marine gasped. "A good watch!" The men looked at their lieutenant.

"Goddam fool Lieutenant Joe!" the old Tonk screamed. "Come all time my girl Liat. Make . . ." Bloody Mary raised her hands high in the air to form the indecent gesture. A dried head which she was carrying by the hair banged against her elbow.

From another truck an enlisted man shouted, "How much for that head, Mary?" The Tonk turned slowly and walked along the dusty road to her questioner.

"You like?" she asked, waving the head before the man.

"Yeah. How much?"

"Fifty dolla'," the Tonk shouted.

"'At's too much, Mary!" the Marine cried. "Give you thirty." Bloody Mary spat and leered at the man.

"*Soandso* you, major!" she cried.

Passion

DR. Paul Benoway of LARU-8 finally recovered from the exposure he suffered during the days and nights he spent on the raft. When he returned to his quarters he tried to write a long letter to his wife. He wanted to tell her about the hours of waiting on the raft, the half-muttered prayers, the mingled thrill and despair of seeing the blood-red sun rise anew each morning.

"On the fourth day, when I saw the sun again," he wrote, "I felt like an Aztec's human sacrifice who waits at the end of the fiftieth year to see whether or not the sun will rise. Like him, I knew that when the sun rises again the world is saved and there is still hope. But like the Aztec I also knew that with the rising of the flaming beacon my individual torture would begin."

Benoway stopped and looked at the words. They sounded phoney. They were not his words. He had never spoken like that to his wife in all of his married life, not even during courtship days. He tore up the offending paragraph.

"Certain men," he mused, "are not able to speak or write that way." And a persistent fear gained utterance, one that had haunted him for several years. "Am I lacking in passion?

227

Is my love on a lower level than that of . . ." The words would not come. In embarrassment he fumbled, even in his own mind. Then, half blushing, he finished the sentence. ". . . lower level than that of the great lovers?"

Reluctantly, Dr. Benoway concluded that he had never known the great passion that seemed to pulsate through the literature and drama of modern America. He had met Nancy, his wife, twelve years before. She was beautiful and engaged to marry his older brother, Robert. But Paul, who had merely finished internship, courted his brother's girl and married her. Sometimes at night Paul writhed because Robert had seemed so hurt and yet had done nothing to prevent the theft.

It would certainly seem that a man who had stolen his brother's girl, and before he had a practice, too, must have known something of passion. But that was not the case. Nancy was simply a lovely and desirable girl who had retained those attributes into womanhood. But the breathless, flaming love that was supposed to precede and follow events like abducting your brother's fiancée was no part of Paul Benoway.

He was reluctant to admit that there was any deficiency in either himself or his wife. He was not given to introspection, but the fears that arose now, when he was trying vainly to write out a passionate avowal of his love, well, those fears made even Paul Benoway consider his sex life. Coldly, he concluded that he was normal. That was all. He halfway apologized to himself for having brought the subject up.

"I don't know what it is," he said to himself. He was in his Dallas hut looking out over the Pacific. It was early evening. He turned out his light. No use trying to work any more tonight. He'd finish the letter tomorrow. Anyway, it was almost done and, if necessary, could be mailed just as it was. He had at least explained that he was safe and with no lasting injuries.

"Nancy is a lovely girl," he mused in the darkness. The waves beat upon the coral in endless symphony. "She's as fine a wife as a man could have. She's beautiful. She loves her children. She's an adornment. And she's not too slow-witted, either! No brainstorm, of course . . ." He banged himself on the knee. "Damn it all," he muttered. "What right have I to analyze my own wife? If this wretched war . . ."

That was it! If this wretched, rotten war had not intervened, millions of people like Paul Benoway could have masked or muffled their uncertainties. They could have postponed admitting to themselves that their loves were bankrupt.

"But my love is not bankrupt!" Paul cried aloud to himself. "It's . . . that . . ." He rose from his chair. "How did I ever get into this mood in the first place? What the hell has passion to do with life on this rock?"

His revery was interrupted by a knock at the door of his hut. "May I come in?" a cheery voice inquired.

Paul peered into the darkness toward the insomniac ocean. "Oh! Come in!" he called. It was Lt. Harbison.

"Thanks, Paul. Lovely night out, isn't it?"

"Yes, a true tropical night. Those palms against the moon make it look like a calendar, don't they?" Harbison was wearing a pilot's flight jacket, a pilot's baseball cap, and an expensive pair of moccasins. He was still very brown from exposure on the life raft.

"I was hoping you hadn't gone to the movies," he said. "Have a request to make of you."

"What can I do for you, Bill?" the doctor asked. He liked to help Harbison out. Everybody liked to work with Harbison.

"Well, Paul, it's this way," the lithe young man said, draping himself into a chair, tapping against the wall with his well oiled moccasin. "I have been approached by the chief censor with a damned tough problem." He tossed a letter on Benoway's table. It had not yet been sealed, nor had it been stamped with the censor's stamp. It was a thick envelope.

"What have I to do with it?" Dr. Benoway asked.

"It's not ordinary censorship, Paul," Harbison replied, somewhat ill at ease. "It's a much tougher problem than that. And," he said in the low confiding voice that made even enlisted men want to work for him twice as hard, "you're about the only fellow who can help us. The only officer."

"That's flattering, I'm sure, Bill. State the case," and the doctor assumed a clinical attitude which he would never lose as long as he lived. He was the consulting physician again.

"There's no case to state, Paul," his visitor said. "It's all right there," and Harbison pointed to the letter.

"Want me to read it?"

"Yes, I do. But I'd rather you'd read it when I'm gone. If you don't mind?" And Bill rose to his feet, coughed in a little embarrassment, and smiled. "Just read it and tell me if we ought to take any action against the boy." Harbison bowed himself out. His cheery voice sounded from the path leading down to the shore: "I'll walk down here and be back in about an hour. Form your own opinion."

Dr. Benoway picked up the envelope. Another was lying beneath it. He ran to the door of his Dallas. "Bill!" he called. "You've left two letters here!"

He heard running footsteps in the darkness. Harbison hurried back into the hut and looked at the second letter. "Of course," he laughed in his clear tones. "That's my own. Brought it over for you to initial and stamp. I'd like to make the early boat with it and get it on the plane." He smiled at the doctor.

"I'll have it for you when you get back," Paul assured his friend. Harbison left once more and Benoway started to read the letter.

The envelope was dirty and addressed in a rough hand. The letter was apparently from Timothy Hewitt, a motor mech third class. He was attached to the doctor's own unit. Funny, he'd never heard of Hewitt. Must be a new man.

The letter appeared to be addressed to Hewitt's wife, or it could be to his mother. "Mrs. Timothy Hewitt, 3127 Boulware Boulevard, El Paso, Texas." It was, like almost all the mail Dr. Benoway ever saw, an airmail letter. V-mail hadn't caught on very well in the South Pacific, and you could say that again.

Dr. Benoway opened the envelope and pulled out the sheets. There were six of them. They were very thin. Hewitt's writing was large and clear. "Dearest, Darling, Gorgeaous, Adorable Bingo!!!" started the letter. Dr. Benoway cleared his throat. "There's passion for you!" he muttered. But there was no ridicule in his voice, nor in his thoughts. "There is passion!" he thought. "That's just what I mean!" He resumed the reading:

My own dearest, darlingest wife how I miss you and how I long that you were here right beside me in this small and dark tent what a time we would have and how I would long to kiss you as you have never been kissed before we would spend all night kissing and other things if you know what I mean and I'll bet you do (ha ha) we would wake up in the morning laughing and everything would be fine wouldn't it my own darling, my adorable wife when I get up in the morning there is only an emptiness about my heart that never goes away all day long even when I am eating the awful chow they serve here and which they call food for a fighting man with me it is like when I first saw you in Louisville that wonderful day four years ago I can see you as plain as if you was right here and thet's just where you are forever and forever throughout all eternity right here in my arms and if I ever thought another day would dawn without you with me forever I would die right now I'm sitting in my tent as usual thinking of you I am in my shorts and as I have had a haircut today there are streaks of my hair all over my shorts which looks very funny I can tell you I know you would laugh it were here but tonight I am there with you my adored darling in who I see everything good and kind that can ever be I'm right there with you and it is almost time for bed You say come on Tim lets go to bed we've got to get up in the morning and I laugh like always and say I know what you want to go to bed for and you laugh and say don't talk like that Tim and I catch you and pull you over to the davenport and start to take off your stockings and you squeal and wiggle and say turn out the lights Tim what will the neighbors think, and I finish undressing you, you turn out the lights and we are all there alone in the darkness, but I can see you very well for a little light comes in from the Abraham's kitchen and there you are . . .

Dr. Benoway was perspiring. Young Hewitt's letter continued with an intimate description of his wife, her attributes, her various reactions, the manner in which she participated in sexual intercourse, and his own emotions throughout the act. Dr. Benoway had never before read a letter quite like it. "The damned thing's absolutely clinical," he said to himself. He looked at the last page again. It ended in an orgy of pictures and words.

"No wonder the censors don't know what to do! I don't know what to do, myself." He carefully folded the many sheets of the letter and returned them to their envelope. He was tapping his left hand with the letter when Harbison reappeared.

"May I come in?" the lieutenant called cheerily from the darkness.

"Glad you're back," laughed the doctor, pouring them both a shot of whiskey.

"Judging from your tone, you've finished the letter," Harbison observed.

"And what a letter, too!" Benoway tossed it over to his guest.

"Don't give it to me, Paul," Harbison laughed. "You're the doctor!"

"I don't know what a letter like that means," Benoway countered, picking it up again. "I'm no psychologist."

"I realize that, Paul," Harbison replied persuasively. "But you see our problem. Is a sailor like that likely to get into trouble with other men? The old phrase, *conduct prejudicial to the welfare of the Navy,* or something like that? Is the boy likely to go off balance some night and wind up with a broken face and some pretty serious charges against him?"

"I can't answer that, Bill. You should know that. Any young man is likely to write a letter like that once in his life. Most girls are good enough to burn the things and never speak to the boy again. Such letters are epi—"

"You don't understand, Paul," Harbison interrupted. "Hewitt writes two or three letters like that every week. Sometimes five in one week. Always the same!"

Dr. Benoway indulged in an unprofessional whistle. "How can he find the energy? God, what kind of man is he?"

"That's what has us worried. Every censor who has hit one of his letters immediately rushes it in the chief censor. He says that he can tell when a new man hits one of Hewitt's letters."

"Who is this man Hewitt? Why didn't I hear of this before?"

"A new man. Came aboard while we were out sunbathing on the raft. The censors waited until I had recovered a bit before they presented me with the poser. I waited until you started seeing patients again. I don't think we'd better wait much longer on this baby. He needs some kind of treatment."

"I'd like to see the fellow, Bill," Dr. Benoway suggested.

"Right now?" Harbison asked.

"Yes! Right now! Will you break him out?" Dr. Benoway did not want to go to bed.

"Shall I bring him over here? Or to the office?"

"Make it here." In civilian life Paul Benoway treated many of his most complex cases in his own home. It gave the patient a feeling right from the start that "the doctor" was taking a personal interest in him. Nancy never objected. Sometimes in women's involved neurotic cases Paul would say, "Wouldn't it be a good idea if my wife joined us for a

few minutes? You know Mrs. Benoway, don't you?" And
nine times out of ten the patient would agree to this most
unprofessional procedure, for everyone knew Mrs. Benoway.

And there stood Timothy Hewitt, motor mech third, and
that was his personal record in the folder on the desk. "Shall
I see you later?" Harbison's pleasant voice inquired, half
suggesting that he would like to stay, half offering to go.

"Yes, Lieut. Harbison," Paul replied in his business voice.
"I'll see you later."

"You may return to your quarters as soon as the doctor
releases you, Hewitt," Harbison said to the perplexed sailor.
"Goodnight!" His cheery smile put the young man at ease.

"Be seated, Hewitt," the doctor said. "Excuse me for a
moment while I study these papers."

The young man breathed deeply and relaxed in his chair.
He was not afraid, but he was on the defensive. As the doctor
started to read he jumped up. "What's all this about, sir?
What I done wrong?"

"Hewitt!"

"Yes, sir!"

"Sit down!"

"Yes, sir!"

"You haven't done anything wrong, yet."

The young man breathed deeply and relaxed in his chair,
obviously and completely bewildered. Dr. Benoway studied
the papers. "Timothy Hewitt. No middle name. Born 1921.
Irish parents. Catholic. Louisville, Kentucky. Baker in civilian
life. Married. No children. Boot camp at Great Lakes. Re-
fused baker's training. First station San Diego A and R shops.
No record of any trouble. Teeth fair. Eyes 18/20 and 20/20.
No scars. Genitals normal. No admission of venereal disease.
Weight 157. Height 5, 7. Intelligence test average. No com-
ments." Dr. Benoway thought a moment. "Average. Average.
Average," he repeated under his breath. "And what is average,
I wonder?"

"Hewitt," he said crisply. The young man rose. "You may
remain seated."

"Thank you, sir."

"So this is the package in which such passion comes!" Dr.
Benoway muttered.

"What, sir?" the sailor asked.

"Nothing, Hewitt. I was just thinking." Lt. Comdr. Benoway studied the man with a military eye. Hewitt was clean

cut, had probably put on a little weight, wore his clothes with a jaunty, Irish air, and looked like a good, average sailor. His eyes were clear and his face gave no evidence of undue self-abuse. If the man was psychopathic, he certainly did not betray it in his bearing.

"It's about this letter," Lt. Comdr. Benoway said suddenly. "All of your letters, as a matter of fact." He tossed the un-sealed, uncensored letter toward the sailor. Hewitt reached for it.

"But that's *my* letter, sir!" he protested.

"I know it is, Hewitt, and that's what I wanted to ask you about."

"What's wrong with it? It's to my wife. I didn't say nothing about no ships or nothing."

"Nobody said you did, Hewitt."

The man breathed more easily and twirled the letter about in his hands. Dr. Benoway searched his papers. Yes, there it was, "Schooling Tenth Grade, Louisville, Kentucky."

"Hewitt," he began. The man leaned forward, a youngish, thin fellow perplexed at what might happen next. "Hewitt," the doctor repeated. "Don't you see anything wrong with that letter?"

Hewitt opened the letter and hastily scanned each page. "No, sir," he said. "There ain't a word about nothing."

Dr. Benoway leaned back in his chair and breathed very deeply. This was beginning to confuse him. "Look at page six, I think it is. The last page, Hewitt." He waited while the sailor shuffled the pages. "Don't you see anything strange about that? I mean is that just an ordinary letter?"

"Oh, no sir!" Hewitt replied briskly. "It's a letter to my wife."

"I realize that, Hewitt. But . . ." Dr. Benoway coughed. The sailor waited. "The language, Hewitt? Is that ordinary?"

Hewitt studied the page. He flushed a little. "Well, sir. It *is* to my wife. That makes it a little different. Special, you might say."

Dr. Benoway looked at the amazing motor mech. Was the boy pulling his leg? Was this a big joke at his expense? Had Harbison staged all this? No, such a thought was preposterous and ungallant. He decided, by heavens, that he'd have this thing out.

"Hewitt," he began again. The obvious perplexity in the young man's face unnerved him, but he went ahead. "You must be aware that the words you use there and the things you talk about, well . . ."

"But this a letter to my wife, sir. That's what we got married for. That's what people get married for. So they can talk about things and things."

"What's your wife say about these letters, Hewitt?" Benoway blurted out.

"Bingo? Why she never says nothing, sir. Nothing that I remember."

"Her letters to you? Are they . . . like . . . that?" Dr. Benoway pointed at the letter which now lay on the table.

Hewitt smiled. "Not exactly like that," he said fondly. "I got one right here," he said suddenly, and before Dr. Benoway could stop him, the sailor whipped out a sweaty wallet and produced a letter written in a fine, Southern hand. It was from Louisville. "You can read it if you wish," the man said with embarrassment. "You're just like a doctor, sort of."

Paul was pleased with the intended compliment. He opened the letter and read a little on the first page. Then he turned abruptly to the last page. He read only a few sentences there —this letter was written in passable English—blushed as if something had happened to him in Independence Square, and returned the letter. Hewitt took it and lovingly replaced it in the disintegrating wallet.

"Do you and your wife always write like that?"

"Well, you might say so, sir."

Benoway gritted his teeth and swore to himself: "Well, son. You asked for it. Here it is . . ." "Hewitt," he said. "I don't know whether you're kidding the pants off me or not." (*Oh, no, sir!*) "But maybe I can tell you a few things that will clear the air. First of all, you could be arrested and put in jail for writing a letter like that." (*Don't interrupt me. Sit down.*) "A letter like that, and especially one like your wife's, is never written by a lady or a gentleman. It just isn't done. I should think you would have more respect for one another. That you might talk that way in your own bedroom is possible. But if you were to show that letter, either of them, around in the Navy, you could be court-martialed. Now don't you know any better, or do you?" Lt. Comdr. Benoway glowered at the sailor.

"But, sir," Hewitt replied. "She's my wife. I'm married to her. That's not just a letter. It's to my wife."

"Damn it all, Hewitt? Is this a game?"

"Oh, no, sir! I don't know what what you're talking about." Hewitt showed no signs of standing on his dignity and playing the role of insulted virtue. He was clearly bewildered by the doctor's blast.

Dr. Benoway shook his head. Maybe the boy was telling the truth. After all, there were the letters. He tried again. "Tell me, Hewitt. Why do you write letters like that?"

"It's just a letter to Bingo, Doctor."

"Have you always written to one another like that?"

"Well, no sir. You see, Bingo. That's my name for her. We were at a Bingo one night and we both yelled 'Bingo' at the same time, and that's how we met. We split a grand prize of twenty-five dollars. Well, at first, sir, Bingo was awful strange. She lived with three sisters. Old women, that is, who brought her up. She wouldn't even let me kiss her. And when we were married . . . Well, you're sort of a doctor, but this is hard to say. Well, Bingo wouldn't sleep with me very much, if you know what I mean and if you'll pardon the expression things was pretty much going to hell. So one night I just up and told her why I got married and what she got married for and from then on things was different I can tell you and we got to love one another all over again and it was like a different world and we used to laugh at her old women. Then when I went away to war it all ended and I didn't know how to write about it, and our letters was pretty much like the old women again, but then one night as I was writing to her I got to thinking about the swell times we used to have, especially on Wednesdays, and this was a Wednesday, too, and I just sort of wrote exactly what I was feeling, and I just didn't give, if you'll excuse the expression, I just didn't give a good goddam, if you'll excuse me, sir."

Dr. Benoway picked the letter from the table, sealed it, wrote his initials on it, and stamped it with his little inked censor's circle.

"I'll tell you what, Hewitt," he said. "You mail all of your letters right here from now on, will you? I'll trust you not to send any military secrets. That is, information of any kind."

"Oh, sir, I'd never do that. No, sir."

"I'll trust you, Hewitt. But I may censor one now and then to make sure." There was a long moment of silence. "You can go, now, Hewitt."

"But, sir?"

"Yes?"

"You said my wife could be arrested . . ."

"Only if you show her letters to anyone else."

"I'd never do that! They're from my wife."

"That's good. Well, goodnight, Hewitt." The doctor extended his hand to the young man. Hewitt grabbed it warmly, shook it, and left.

"Whew!" the doctor whistled to himself as he slumped into his chair. The haunting fear stayed with him that the entire scene had been an obscene joke cooked up by some ghoulish mind. But somehow or other Hewitt acted like a man, and like a man who might write just such a letter.

"Passion!" Benoway said to himself. "By heaven! The Lord certainly dispenses uneven quantities of it to different people."

Ruefully, he picked up his own unfinished letter to his wife. He started to read it. "Dearest Nancy:" it began. The colon looked formidable, but all of Dr. Benoway's letters had a colon in the salutation. He had read somewhere a long time ago: "It is always proper to use a colon in the salutation. It is dignified, universal, and appropriate for all occasions, especially when doubt arises as to the proper greeting." The letter ran:

I would like to be the first to tell you that I have had a somewhat trying experience and that I have safely recovered from it without the slightest harm or injury. The details of this little adventure must remain a military secret until I see you in person. I can only give you the barest outlines at present, and even some of them may be deleted by the censor.

Some time ago I had to make a routine flight over water. You can probably guess the nature of the mission. As sometimes happens, our plane ran into difficulty, and we were forced down into the ocean. We were able to break out a life raft without much difficulty, and before long we were aboard it.

I am sorry to say that we had not too much water or food for the persons aboard. I was not the senior officer—the plane captain was—but I was given the important task of apportioning our rations amongst us. This I did to the best of my ability, and although there was natural complaining about the smallness of the rations, there were no accusations of unfairness.

The Navy has already announced that we were adrift for four days. Some of the passengers suffered from severe sun-

burn. All of us had chills, but I must say that when I think of the poor men who have been lost in the great ocean for twenty and thirty days I consider myself lucky indeed that we were rescued so soon.

On the evening of the fourth day, after twelve hours of blazing sun and no rain, we saw a ship just at dusk, but it could not see us. Our captain made an instant judgment of the course on which we might come closest to the ship, and we started to paddle, swim alongside the raft, and pray. The ship passed us by, and I thought my heart would break, but in the darkness—for it was now pitch black—a little dog saw us, or smelt us, or heard us, and started to bark. Of course, we couldn't hear him bark, for if we could have heard him, the men aboard ship could have heard us, but there he was, barking when we were taken aboard. He was a little mixed dog like the one the Baxters used to have, and I thought him a very lovely dog indeed.

Darling, all during the time I was in that raft and when I was aboard ship, I thought of you. It would have been terrible never to see you again. Once we had a bad time of it when the raft started to ship water, and I prayed pretty furiously, and you were all mixed up in the prayers. I don't want you to worry about anything, Nancy, for I am all right. When I think of what others have gone through, I'm a little bit ashamed, but I must admit that I am somewhat proud to say that I stood up as well as most. Only once was I really beaten down. On the fourth morning, when I saw the great sun again . . .

Then followed the part about the Aztec sacrifice that had seemed so phoney to him that he had torn it up.

Compared with Hewitt's letter, Paul's wasn't much of a job, and he knew it. For example, he hadn't put in the part about getting all mixed up when he prayed, so that he actually prayed to Nancy and not to God at all. Or that time in the third night when all he could see was Nancy. She had even obliterated the ocean then, and one of the gunners had asked, "What you looking at, Doc?" and he had replied, "The ocean." Or the terrible moment when the ship sailed past in the darkness, seen but unseeing, and all that he could think of was not his loneliness in the ocean, but the fact that the silent ship was like Nancy when she left a room: a stately, gracious thing that all eyes followed. Nor could he put on paper the fact that when he saw that blessed little hairy dog aboard the ship, he grinned all over, for it looked just like Nancy's sleepy head tossed in disarray upon a pillow at night.

"No," he said, "I'll tear up that letter and start all over again. It didn't happen the way I have it written at all. It was much deeper than that. By God, it was probably the biggest experience I'll ever have in all my life. And I'll tell Nancy just that . . . and the part she played in it, too."

He took a new piece of paper, but as he did so, he turned over Bill Harbison's unsealed envelope. Usually, like all officers, he merely initialed his friends' mail, relying upon their honesty. But tonight he idly revolved the letter in his fingers.

He opened the envelope and glanced casually at the first page. The salutation caught his eye. *My only Beloved Lenore,* it read. Automatically, in the manner of all censors, he turned to the envelope to see if the letter were to Harbison's wife or to one of the several other girls the man wrote to. It was addressed to *Mrs. Bill Harbison, 188 Loma Point, Albuquerque, New Mexico.* It was to his wife.

Paul Benoway studied the salutation. *My only Beloved Lenore!* That's the way he wished he could write to Nancy, for she was his only girl, and she was his beloved. As beloved, that is, as anything he would ever know. But he never thought of openings like that, and if he had had to say the words aloud, he would have felt undressed. But in Bill Harbison's letter they seemed all right.

Mechanically, Dr. Benoway started to read the first page. Without wishing to do so—and with considerable feeling of guilt—he read the entire pulsating letter:

My only Beloved Lenore,

My darling, I have just returned from a trip which took me almost to the vale of death, and from which I returned loving you more than ever I did before in this life. There is so much to tell you that I hardly know where to begin. I know that all of it will worry you, but I can only say that terrible as it must seem to you, it brought me nearer to you than all the happy days of the past.

We were on a difficult mission toward the Japs. (Dr. Benoway grew a little resentful. The trip was an ordinary, routine one down to Noumea to pick up some fresh vegetables. Harbison had gone along to sleep with one of the

French girls at Luana Pori.) *Our flying boat was only moderately armed, but our skipper was about as resolute a man as I have ever known. I thought when we left that if a flying boat were to tangle with a bunch of Japs, I couldn't think of a better man than Joe to do the dirty work. My reliance in him was proved.*

We were flying at about 3,000 feet near the island of . . . (Here Harbison had cut out a section of his letter to simulate the censor's relentless vigil.) *I must admit that I was half dozing off when I heard our rear gunner cry, "Zeroes at seven o'clock!" And there they were two of them! They had the advantage of the ceiling on us, too. Everyone in the flying boat prepared for the battle, but before I could even get to a gun, the first bullets were smashing at us. They hit one gunner in the leg.*

Fortunately, we had a doctor with us. You remember my remarking about Dr. Benoway. Well, he fixed the lad up in no time. By now the Japs were on their way back, and we were impotent to stop them. Again their slugs tore through the cumbersome plane. They made four more passes at us, and even though our gunners did their best, we never touched the yellow devils.

On their sixth pass, the second Jap knocked out both of our motors and we started to plunge toward the sea. This threw the Japs off us for a few precious minutes.

Down we plunged, and in that terrible time I could think only of you. My heart beat like a mammoth drum, always booming out, "Lenore! Lenore!" It was a horrible fantasy which ended only when our magnificent pilot pulled us up at the last moment and skidded the plane along the tips of the waves and finally into a trough that stopped our flight. ("Heavens," Benoway thought. "We glided in perfectly from 1,500 feet, just the way it's done in a clear bay. There were no waves, thank God, and there wasn't a Jap in sight. Some damned fool mechanic had left two large pieces of sandpaper in the oil tank. Don't ask me why!")

As we perched for a precious half minute on the water, the dastardly Japs came at us again! But after one violent burst of firing which killed the wounded gunner, we saw two American planes on the horizon. The Japs saw them too, and off they went. There was a long dogfight. Three of the planes went into the ocean, all of them in flames. One American fighter limped away into the growing darkness. We don't know whether he reached shore or not, but wherever that boy is tonight, you can pray for him as a great hero who saved a raftful of defenseless men.

There were eight of us on the raft, and I shall not tell you of the misery and the suffering. If it had not been for the iron will of our skipper and the skill of Dr. Benoway, few of us would be alive to write to our loved ones. The days were scorching. The nights were cold. We were fevered, and we had little to eat or drink. The doctor was in charge of the food and . . .

My beloved darling. I'll tell you about those fifteen days when I am once more safe in your cool arms. Suffice it to say that we were rescued. What is important is that all through the terrible days and lonely nights you were with me. I saw your face in the stars, and when the hot sun beat down upon our wretched raft, you were there to shade me. I cried aloud for you, and wherever hope dawned, you were there. A seagull followed us for a day, hoping for scraps that never came, for we, too, were hoping for scraps. All of the men saw in that gull some omen of good, but I saw only you. The soft whiteness was you. The constancy was you. The lovely dip of the wing was your lovely walk, and when the night shadows closed over the white gull, it was the darkness of our love closing over you. ("It was two brown birds," Benoway muttered to himself. "No gulls in sight.")

If I live to be a thousand, my beloved wife, you will never be nearer to me than you were that night. I realized then what I had only half realized before: that you were all the good I know in this world and all the good I shall ever know. My body, my heart, and my immortal soul cried for you, and when we were rescued, it was not the rough arms of the sailors that carried me to safety, but your own dear, cherishing hands.

When I see you again I may be able to tell you all of these things, but sleep tightly tonight, my beloved darling, for my love wings its way across the boundless ocean to you, wherever you are. You are mine tonight, mine forever and forever until my heart is still and time no longer beats for us. I love you, I love you, Oh my darling.

Paul Benoway wiped his forehead and listened to the mighty ocean pounding on the coral reefs. He knew, and every officer in camp knew, that Bill Harbison was having serious girl trouble in the South Pacific. He knew of Bill's escapades at Luana Pori and with the blonde nurse. But he also knew that Harbison had touched a throbbing core of life unknown to many men, unknown particularly to Paul Benoway.

What did it matter how Harbison came to know about this side of life? What did it matter which key the man had used to unlock his heart, so long as it was open, so long as it was a heart to share, a heart that could give freely? What matter were morals and old sayings if they kept you tied up like a burlap bag while other men unfolded their secrets and grew in the way God meant to have men grow?

Dr. Benoway looked at the dulcet words again. They were *his* words! That was the way *he* felt! *What is important is that through all the terrible days and lonely nights you were with me . . . the lovely dip of the wing was your lovely walk . . . my body, my heart, my immortal soul cried for you . . .* That's what he, Paul Benoway, meant to say to his wife. That's what he had been trying to write.

Suddenly, he took up his own unfinished letter to his wife, went with his finger to the part that read, *When I think of what the others have gone through, I'm a little bit ashamed, but I must admit that I am somewhat proud to say that I stood up as well as most. Only once was I really beaten down.* He struck out the last sentence and got a fresh piece of paper What business was it of anyone's that he was beaten down when he thought of an Aztec sacrifice to the sun god? That was a mighty silly thing to say in a letter when you compared it with what Bill Harbison was able to write.

Furtively, he laid Bill's letter on the table before him and began to copy rapidly. *My beloved darling, I'll tell you about it when I am once more safe in your cool arms.* Feverishly, as if this were the ultimate expression of what he had been storing up in his heart, he copied the last two pages of Bill's letter. His pen scrawled on, *I love you, I love you, Oh my darling.*

He dropped his pen and looked at the last line. In his letter it didn't look right. Never in his life had he said anything even remotely like *Oh my darling.* It sounded utterly silly when you said it that way: *Oh my darling, Oh my darling, Oh my darling Clementine! You are lost and gone forever, Dreful sorry, Clementine!*

The words sounded good! He started to sing the whole

song, and as he did so, he began to laugh within himself and to feel very happy. With dancing motions he stuffed Bill Harbison's letter back into its envelope. He sealed the letter and stamped it. Then, with the same mincing, half dancing gestures he neatly tore up the last half of his own letter. Laughing loudly by this time, he signed the part that he had first written. He signed it, *All my love, Paul.*

A Boar's Tooth

LUTHER BILLIS and Tony Fry were a pair! Luther was what we call in the Navy a "big dealer." Ten minutes after he arrived at a station he knew where to buy illicit beer, how to finagle extra desserts, what would be playing at the movies three weeks hence, and how to avoid night duty.

Luther was one of the best. When his unit was staging in the Hebrides before they built the airstrip at Konora he took one fleeting glance at the officers near by and selected Tony Fry. "That's my man!" he said. Big dealers knew that the best way for an enlisted man to get ahead was to leech on to an officer. Do things for him. Butter him up. Kid him along. Because then you had a friend at court. Maybe you could even borrow his jeep!

Tony was aware of what was happening. The trick had been pulled on him before. But he liked Billis. The fat Sea-Bee was energetic and imaginative. He looked like something out of *Treasure Island*. He had a sagging belly that ran over his belt by three flabby inches. He rarely wore a shirt and was tanned a dark brown. His hair was long, and in his left ear he wore a thin golden ring. The custom was prevalent in the South Pacific and was a throwback to pirate days.

He was liberally tattooed. On each breast was a fine dove, flying toward his heart. His left arm contained a python curled around his muscles and biting savagely at his thumb. His right arm had two designs: *Death Rather Than Dishonor* and *Thinking of Home and Mother*. Like the natives, Luther wore a sprig of frangipani in his hair.

It was Luther's jewelry, however, that surprised Tony. On his left arm Billis wore an aluminum watch band, a heavy silver slave bracelet with his name engraved, and a superb wire circlet made of woven airplane wire welded and hammered flat. On his right wrist he had a shining copper bracelet on which his social security and service numbers were engraved. And he wore a fine boar's tusk.

"What's that?" Tony asked him one day.

"A boar's tusk," Billis replied.

"What in the world is a boar's tusk?" Fry asked.

"You got a jeep, Mr. Fry?"

"Yes."

"Then why don't we go see the old chief?" Billis leaned his fat belly forward and sort of hunched up the two doves on his breast.

"Put a shirt on," Tony said. "We'll take a spin."

In the jeep Billis sat back, his right foot on the dash, and gave directions. "Out past the farm, down the hill, past 105 Hospital—say, Mr. Fry, have you seen them new nurses out there—down to Tonk village, and I'll take over from there."

Tony followed the instructions. When he reached the two *séchoirs* where copra and cacao were drying, Billis said, "Drive down that grass road." Tony did so, and soon he was at the seaside. Before him, around the edges of a little bay, a host of native canoes and small trading vessels lay beached. Beside the prows of the ships colored men from all the Hebridean islands had pitched their tents. This was the native market of Espiritu Santo.

Most of the natives knew Billis. " 'Allo, Billis!" they cried.

"Got any cigarettes, Mr. Fry?"

"No, I don't."

"Shouldn't ever come down here without cigarettes." Billis spoke to the men in Beche-le-Mer. Explained to them that this time he had no smokes.

"That's OK, Billis!" an old man said.

"Got any boar's tusks?" Billis inquired.

"We got some," the old trader replied.

"Let's see."

"In ship."

"Well, go get from ship!" Billis cried, slapping the old man on the back. The natives laughed. The old fellow went to the shore, waded in and started swimming toward a ship anchored in the bay. Tony surveyed the market. Chickens were selling at two dollars each. Eggs were a dollar a dozen, and plentiful. Grass skirts were two dollars, shells were a dollar a handful. Watermelons, grown from American seed, were abundant. Eight kinds of bananas were on sale, war clubs, lava-lavas, toy canoes, papayas, and the fragrant pine-apples which grew on Vanicoro.

Soldiers and sailors moved about among the native tents. From time to time thin native men and boys would stagger into camp under mammoth loads of junk. By an island order natives were permitted to strip any junk pile before it was set afire. So they came to Santo from miles around in every kind of canoe. They took home with them old tables, rusty knives, bits of tin, ends of copper wire, and all the refuse of a modern army.

"Looks like he's got a pretty good one, Mr. Fry," Billis said as the old man swam back to shore, holding in his teeth a boar's tusk. The trader came ashore, shook himself like a dog and sat on his haunches before a small fire on the beach.

"All same too good!" he said, offering Billis the tusk.

Luther handed it to Fry, who twirled the ugly thing in his hands. "Grim looking thing, isn't it?" he asked. The tusk was rude, ugly, just as it had been ripped from the under-jaw of a sacrificial wild pig. It was dirty white in color and formed an almost perfect circle about five inches across. At its widest the tusk itself was about a quarter of an inch thick, so that it formed a natural bracelet. Tony slipped it over his right hand. It hung dull and heavy from his wrist.

"You got one cleaned up?" Billis asked the old man.

"He got," the trader replied, pointing to a native friend.

"Let's see," Billis suggested.

"You buy? You look? You look?" the doubtful Melanesian asked.

"I look, I look, I knock your block off," Billis shouted.

This delighted the Negro, who produced a tusk slightly smaller that the first and beautifully polished. Whereas the first was dirty and crude, this one was a pale golden ivory, soft to the eye and lustrous. It curled in a circle and seemed one of the finest bracelets Tony had ever seen. It was solid ivory.

"This comes from this?" Tony asked, indicating the two tusks.

"That's right. The dirty one has the enamel on yet. The ivory is all hidden on that one. Them natives has a secret way of getting the enamel off. I figured out a way of knocking it off with an emery wheel. I do it for them at a buck a tusk. They finish up the polishing."

Tony surveyed the tusks. They were like something from Greek legend. The shimmering, golden jewel and the rude barbaric thing from which it sprang. "What's a tusk like this one worth?" Tony asked, indicating the polished bracelet.

Billis spoke in Beche-le-Mer to the natives. "He says fifteen dollars."

"Whew! Is that a good buy, Billis?" Luther took the tusk and studied it. Like the tusks of all pigs, it was composed of three triangular pieces of ivory welded together by nature. Light played delicately upon the irregular faces. Fry was entranced at the jungle jewel as Billis twirled it around his thumb.

"It's worth fifteen dollars, Mr. Fry," he said. But then a happy thought struck him. "Of course, I know where you can get a better one."

"Where?"

"On Vanicoro."

"Where's that?"

"That island over there."

"Way over there?"

"It's not so far."

"No, Billis. You just want the ride. I know you big dealers. Besides, I get seasick."

"You don't have to go, Mr. Fry. You send me. I'll go."

"What do you have cooking over there, Billis? You have a big deal on?"

"The sacred ceremonial, sir. I've been invited. You know the damned Navy. Can't see its way clear to letting me go."

"What's all this about, Billis? A sacred ceremonial?"

"He'll tell you," Billis said, indicating a young native.

By this time Fry knew he was hooked. When an officer gets in the clutches of a big dealer it's one thing after another. Tony knew he ought to stop right where he was. "I'll take this one," he said. He gave the second trader fifteen dollars and put the tusk in his pocket.

But the young native, dressed in brief shorts, was beside him. "Fine ceremonial," he said in good English. "My uncle kill all his pigs. He got more pigs than any other man on Vanicoro. You like to come, my uncle be very proud. He maybe kill one pig for you. He gonna kill one pig for Billis."

"What's this killing pigs, Billis?" Fry asked.

"Well, they're holy pigs, sir."

"Holy?"

"Yes," Billis replied. The young native shook his head in agreement. "But you see, sir, they aren't really holy till they're dead."

"Wait a minute, Billis! You're getting me all mixed up."

Luther smiled. That's what he was trying to do. He'd been wanting to go to Vanicoro for a long time. This looked like his chance. If he could get his officer sufficiently mixed up and interested, well . . .

"It's simple, sir," he said with mock honesty. "Pigs is their religion. They keep pigs the way we keep churches. The rounder the pig's tusks is, the better the church. Sort of the way it is back home. The Baptists got to have a higher steeple than the Methodists."

"Are you kidding me, Billis?"

"Oh, no! Lenato here will tell you, won't you, Lenato?" The young native smiled and nodded his head. "Billis, he see pigs. He go back jungle one day 'long me."

"So that's where you were? Don't you ever work, Billis?"

"Well, when you're just sitting around waiting . . ."

"What's this about a chief killing a pig for you?"

"Billis one fine man," Lenato said. "He give many presents."

"Oh!" Fry said knowingly. He looked at Billis, who glared at Lenato. "I suppose you'd be happy if I didn't ask what presents."

"That would be very good of you," Billis replied.

"Much stuff!" Lenato said eagerly. "Sheets. Calico. One hammer. Some wire. One carbine." Billis blew air up his fat nostrils and looked out to sea.

"Much stuff?" Fry repeated. "For that you get a pig." Tony looked at the fat SeaBee. "Billis," he said, "I think we ought to go over to Vanicoro. I'd like to see that chief's hut. I'll bet it's wired with Mazda lamps and has an electric ice box!"

On the way back to camp Billis explained more about the

usks to Tony. "When them pigs is young," he said, "they're taked out to a tree on a short length of jungle rope. All heir lives they live in that little circle, tied to the tree. The old Maries of the village feed the pigs. Chew the food up first and spit it out. So the pig won't hurt his tusks nuzzlin' hard food."

"That's a lot of trouble for a pig," Tony observed.

"But the pigs is sacred. I'm tellin' you, the whole religion is pigs. Nothin' more."

"Billis? Where do you find these things out?"

"Oh," the SeaBee replied, "I'm sort of like you. I like to know things."

Fry looked at him sideways. He wondered if the fat fellow were pulling his leg. Billis continued, "For example, if you was to look under my shirt now you'd see a little extra tattoo. They done that up in the jungle. I joined the tribe. They like me pretty much up there. I helped them to kill the last ceremonial pigs."

"Why did you join the tribe?" Fry asked.

"Oh, some fellows out here read and some carve boats, and some go nuts. Me? I sort of like to fool around with people."

"What did you do in civilian life?"

"Sold cars."

"Pretty successful, I guess."

"Made a very good livin'. Say, Mr. Fry, would you like to see the two tusks I got when I joined the tribe?"

"Yes, I would," Tony said.

"Let's pull in up the road a bit."

Billis led Tony to a small shack which had been fitted up by the SeaBees as a recreation hut. It had every known kind of machine or gadget that could be stolen, borrowed, or ripped off a crashed plane. "Where'd you get all this junk?" Tony asked.

"One place and another," Billis replied truthfully. Fry laughed. The room was a monument to the spirit that made America great. "I wouldn't change a splinter of it," Tony said to himself.

From a corner Billis produced a grisly object. It was the lower jawbone of a wild boar. Jungle ants had eaten away the flesh, leaving only the whitened bones, teeth, and the two curving, circular tusks. They protruded upward from where the lower eyeteeth would naturally have been. But they were not teeth. No, cased in enamel they were pure ivory, like the tusks of elephants.

Fry looked at the jawbone for several minutes. Then he asked a cautious question. "Billis? If this is the lower jawbone, as you say. Look at those tusks. They grow right back into the jawbone. That one over there makes a complete circle and grows back through its own root."

"That's the most valuable kind. Of the one-circle tusks, that is."

"But how does it do that?"

"Grows back through the pig's face," Billis said nonchalantly.

"That's barbarous!"

"Very difficult to do. Most pigs die when the tusk starts growing back into their face. Most of those that live die when it starts to grow back into the jawbone. The natives have eight or nine different prayers to a pig to beg him to keep living until the tusk makes a perfect circle. Would you like to hear one?"

Billis grabbed the jawbone and started a weird incantation to the dead pig. "Put it down," Fry said. "The damned pig must live in agony."

"Oh, the pig!" Billis said. "I was thinkin' of the Maries. You see, men don't raise the pig. The Mary raises the pig. If she lets it die, she gets a beating. Yes, the pig. It must hurt him pretty bad. The last four years must be real painful."

"Four years?"

"Yeah, it takes about seven years to grow a good tusk. It begins to enter the face about the fourth year. This here pig lived about five years after the tusks started through the bone."

"How horrible!" Fry said.

"Seems funny to me," Billis said. "But everyone I show this to always thinks about the pig. What about the people? They was mighty proud of this porker. It was the best pig in the area. It was sacred. Men came from all the villages around to see it and worship it. Two tusks right through the face. One of them right through the root of the tusk itself. That's mighty sacred as pigs go!"

"You have an interesting time out here, don't you?" Fry asked, somewhat sick at his stomach.

"Yeah, I do. Uncle Sam says I got to stay out here. But he don't say I got to be bored!"

"I'll tell you, Billis. You see about that trip to Vanicoro. I'd like to check into this."

"Maybe we can get a boat somewhere."

"If you can't, nobody can."

"I may have to use your name. That OK?"

"Get the boat. You know how it's done." Fry smiled at his fat friend.

"Mind if I ride down to the mess hall with you, sir?"

"Come ahead, big dealer."

Tony was unprepared for what happened that night at dinner. He showed the polished tusk to his fellow officers at mess and Dr. Benoway gasped. "Oh! I'd like to buy that from you, Fry!" he cried.

"It cost fifteen bucks," Tony replied.

"I don't care. Will you sell it?"

"What do you want it for?"

"I'd like to send it to my wife," Benoway replied.

"Good idea. Sold!"

"What would a woman want with a thing like that?" an acidulous, sallow-faced officer asked.

"I don't know," Benoway replied. "She might like to see it. See what things are like out here."

"What are you doing? Dressing her up like a savage?" the officer persisted.

"I'm not doing anything. I'm sending her a present."

"It's a hell of a present, if you ask me."

"Nobody asked you," Fry broke in. "These tusks are strange things," he continued. "Have you heard how they grow them?" He repeated what Billis had told him.

"That's absolutely grotesque!" the same officer persisted. He was an unhappy, indifferent fellow.

"Perhaps so," Fry agreed. "A friend tells me they're the center of all native religion."

"They would be!" the sallow officer said grudgingly. "This godforsaken place."

"If it's their religion, it's their religion," Fry said, not wanting to be drawn into an argument, yet not wanting to miss a good fight if one were available. "Sort of like Episcopalians and Buddhists. You can't throw out the whole religion because it's not logical."

"But this filthy stuff! The pain! The misery!"

"Now look, friend. I'm not defending the damned pigs," Fry said. "But for heaven's sake, be consistent. I suppose you're a religious man. You probably believe in something. No, don't tell me what it is. But if it's Christianity, the central fact of your religion is that a living man endured hours of untold agony so that you might be saved." The argumentative officer gasped. "So that you might be ennobled."

"Fry," the officer said, "I always thought there was something wrong with you!"

"Wait a minute! I'm not in this. Leave me out. But you made some statements that needed challenging!"

"All that misery. Yes, even torture!"

"I know," Fry said patiently. "Pain is at the center of all religions. Almost all beauty, too. Fine things, like human beings, for example, are born of pain. Of great suffering. Of intense, in-driving horror. Fine things never come cheaply. Suppose the hog had run wild, ground down his tusks? Done what he damned please? Who would have been richer, or wiser, or better? Only the hog and the guy that finally ate him. But as it was! Well, that boar ennobled the life of an entire village."

"And the boar himself?" the sallow officer asked.

"Friend," Tony said. "I'm going to say a pretty harsh thing. Now please don't get mad at me. But here goes. You seem like a funny man to ask such a question. Really you do. No one in this room ought to ask a question like that. Because you are the wild boar. You are staked out unwillingly to your own little troubles. Your tusks are growing in upon you. From the way you look I think you are feeling the misery." Tony looked at the officer and grinned that silly grin of his.

"Just what do you mean?" the officer asked, leaning forward.

"Oh, damn it all," Tony said. "Who started this anyway?"

"You did," the officer replied.

"Well, what I mean is this. I'm arguing from analogy. Here you are, staked out on a jungle island. God knows you didn't elect to come here. Most of you fellows are naval officers because the draft was hot on your necks, and you know it. Each month you are here you grow older and most of you grow poorer. Take Doc Benoway. If he was back home he could be making a thousand dollars a month, or twice that. Yet he's out here. His wife is growing older. He begins to worry about things. The next push. He may be the one that doesn't make it. What holds you fellows here? A three-foot chain to the stake of custom? An idea of patriotism? I don't know why I act the way I do. But if you're interested . . ."

"Go ahead."

"I think there must be something ennobling in this vast and timeless waste. Not to me, but to somebody who follows me. Look, the boar that raised that tusk is dead. He may have been dead fifty years. Yet here we sit admiring it. Well, fifty years from now somewhere . . . Let's say in Des Moines, Iowa—some high school girl will suddenly catch a faint intimation of what we accomplished out here." Tony lifted a glass of water and held it against his face. It was cool.

"Filthy!" the sallow officer cried. "It's rotten, the whole business! You're nothing but a dirty bunch of communists. That's what you are, communists!" Saying this he banged out of the door and disappeared in the black night.

"Holy cow!" Fry cried. "Who in the world is that guy?"

"He's having wife trouble. Back home. Poor guy is almost going nuts."

"Why in the world didn't somebody tell me?" Tony asked.

"His performance tonight was merely routine. Last night he wanted to fight a man who said Los Angeles was bigger than Philadelphia."

"I sure pick the dillies to argue with," Fry laughed. "What happens to a guy like that?"

"We send them home, mostly. Sometimes they snap out of it when real trouble begins on a beachhead. A couple of them have shot themselves. It all works out all right. But if there was ever a wild boar staked out to a three-foot circle, that's the guy."

"I should follow the advice of my uncle," Fry mused. "He says a gentleman never argues except on one question: 'Who picks up the check?' Then it's perfectly legitimate for you to argue that it's the other fellow's turn. Sage advice, that."

On the following Thursday Billis appeared at Pallikulo landing with a crash boat. Naked to the waist, a frangipani in his hair, the doves flying in stately formation toward his heart, and his bracelets jangling, he was a proper figure of a tropical sailor. He was giving the coxswain orders at the rate of six a minute.

Fry and Benoway met him at the pier. "All aboard!" Billis cried. "Anybody else coming?"

"No," Fry replied. He had invited the sallow officer, but

that sick man had replied, "No! You and your damned wild pigs." "OK," Fry had said. He could never stay angry at anyone. "Would you like us to bring you back some pineapples?" The officer had looked up warmly, clutching at even the straws of friendship. "Would you?" he asked eagerly. "I don't want to take the ride. I get seasick." "Boy," Tony laughed. "You should see me get seasick!"

Aboard the crash boat Tony and Benoway met the officers and crew and a ruddy little man who wore the cross of the Chaplains' Corps. "This is Chappy Jones," Billis said. "From our outfit. I was tellin' him about the new religion I found. Even promised him I'd get him tattooed if he wished!" Billis laughed and the little chaplain beamed.

"Ah, yes!" he said. "And I presume you are the doctor?"

"Yes," Benoway nodded.

"Do you think there might really be an epidemic?" the chaplain asked.

"What?"

"That epidemic you have to go over to investigate," Billis interrupted.

"Merely normal precautions," Fry interposed, glaring at Luther.

"What's this . . ." Benoway began.

"It's a rare opportunity for me!" the chaplain said. "You know, I teach comparative religion at the seminary. Vanicoro is the tabu island in these parts. It's also the leper's island. Interesting, almost a parallel to our medieval belief that the very sick were special wards of God."

The crash boat was gathering speed through the blue waters of Pallikulo Bay. Overhead the early morning planes set out for Guadal and Noumea. Far up the bay the great floating drydock was being assembled, and to the west the daily halo of cloud was gathering upon the gaunt mountains of Espiritu Santo.

"Lovely day for a trip to a sacred island," Benoway said.

"Wonderful opportunity for all of us," the chaplain said. "I don't know of anything in the world quite like this pig worship. It gives us a unique opportunity to see the mind of primitive man at work calling forth his gods."

"What do you mean, chaplain?"

"Here we see a religion spring full blown from the mind of man. We see it flower in answer to man's expressed needs."

"Then Billis was telling the truth when he said the pigs were the religion?"

"Ab-s-o-lute-ly," the ruddy chaplain replied. "The religion is well known in sociological circles. Well known. Well documented. As I said, it's unique in this small circle of islands. From an airplane you can see with a glance the entire region in which it flourishes."

"What's the religion like?" Benoway asked.

"Primarily it's a monument to man's perversity. There is no place on earth where living is so easy as on these islands. They are rich, laden with food, and before the white man came, inordinately healthy. No one had to work, for the world was full of fruit and vegetables, and in the woods there was enough wild boar for everyone. You would have to call it a paradise, even though most of you may never want to see it again.

"But there was one flaw. Amid all this luxury there was no reason for living. That may sound like a silly statement, but it is literally true. There was no reason for living. Men fought bravely, but they didn't collect heads to prove it. They ate one another, but when the meal was done, it was done. They traveled nowhere. They built nothing. But most of all they worshipped no gods. There was nothing in life bigger than they were. Like all people, they had some vague idea of life after death, but their conceptions were not what we call codified. All they had were some rough rules of behavior. Don't kill women. Truce in battle. Things like that. But up here," the chaplain said, tapping his temple, "there was a void. There was no reason for doing anything."

"Are you making this up?" Fry asked in a whimsical manner.

"Oh, no!" the chaplain assured him. "All a matter of record. What do you suppose these people living in their earthly paradise did? Believe it or not, they decided to make life more difficult for themselves. They created, at one swoop, something to live for. Now believe me when I tell you that they took one of the commonest things in their acquaintance, one of the dirtiest: a jungle pig. And they made that pig the center of their aspirations. In one shot they built themselves a god. And the important thing about it is this: When the pig was dead and had some eating value, it was no longer of any merit. Then it wasn't a god any more. Only when the pig lived in his filthy misery, and grew tusks back into his own face, and ate your crops, and took your time, and frightened you when he got sick, only then was the pig a god! In other words, the most carefree people on earth consciously made their lives more difficult, more unhappy, and much more complex." The chaplain stopped and stared eastward at Vanicoro. The sacred island was dim and symmetrical in the morning light. Clouds hung over the topmost volcano where the sacred lake was hidden.

"Are you getting seasick?" the chaplain asked.

"I feel pretty good so far," Benoway replied.

"That's quite a story, chaplain," Tony said.

"This interesting part is still to come," the slightly green chaplain said. "I think I'd better stand over here by the rail. Not only did the natives say that their god had spiritual value only so long as he was a burden. They also say that no pig has social value until it is given away to a friend. If you eat your own pig, you are a glutton and a miser. If you give your pig to somebody else to eat, you're a great man."

"Somewhat like the old Christian religions," Tony mused.

"Very similar," the chaplain agreed. "True spirituality has usually seen that man is happier giving than getting."

"What changed that in our civilization?" Fry asked.

"Some sort of compromise with progress. If you give away all the time, you lose the incentive to gain more, and the incentive to gain is the incentive to create. American civilization has grown too far toward the creating and too far away from the giving. It'll adjust later on. It'll have to. Men will go mad from too much getting. They always have in the past."

"On the other hand," Fry argued, "you'll have to admit that the Melanesian ideal of all giving hasn't produced much."

The chaplain nodded and swept his hand about the horizon. "In these islands you have the lowest ebb of civilization in the world. I don't think mankind can sink much lower than these people. Of course, *sink* is an unfair word. They never reached a point any higher than they are now. Even the Solomon Islanders are ahead of these people."

The crash boat rolled in the swelling sea. Spray came over the prow. The chaplain's face had completely lost its ruddy appearance. "Keep talkin', Chappy!" Billis called encouragingly from his vantage point on the bridge.

"Interesting man, Billis," the chaplain said wanly. "He took me into the jungle a few weeks ago to see a ceremonial. We may see one today. They're unbelievable. A family raises a

pig for nine or ten years. It has value only in the fraction
of a minute when you stand over it with the sacred club,
ready to kill it. Then everybody says, 'Look at the wonderful
pig he is going to kill! He must be a very fine man to kill
such a pig!' After the pig is dead and the meat given to
friends they say, 'The owner of this pig is a wonderful man.
Look at all the meat he gave to his friends.' " The chaplain
laughed as he acted out the speeches. It was like being in a
pulpit again. Somewhat shaky, but a pulpit all the same.

"Billis tells me we are going to see a truly sacred pig
today," he continued. "One whose tusks have made two complete circles! They have burrowed twice through the pig's
face and once through the jawbone. I understand men from
other villages come from miles about just to see the holy
tusker. The chief is going to kill the pig soon. He must.
For if that pig were to die, or if it were to break one of its
tusks, he would be a scorned man. Everyone would say, 'He
was unwilling to give the holy pig away. Now see! It is
nothing. It did him no good! A man with only a little pig is
better than the chieftain. For the man with the little pig can
give it away!' That's exactly what they'd say."

The crash boat rolled and turned. Fry was making bets
with himself that the chaplain would heave before the lee of
Vanicoro was reached. But the game little fellow stuck it
out. "You're lookin' better, Chappy!" irreverent Billis called
down from the bridge.

"I feel better!" the chaplain said. The boat was heading
for the bay of Bali-ha'i, a tiny island with rocky cliffs facing
the sea. "Looks good to see land again," he said.

As soon as the boat was anchored off the white sands of
Bali-ha'i, Billis was fighting a rubber dory over the side,
giving the coxswain all sorts of help and trouble. Fry, Benoway, and the chaplain climbed in. Billis shoved off and rowed
energetically toward Vanicoro across the channel. As soon
as the bumpy little boat hit land, Billis took charge of the
expedition.

A group of small boys had gathered to greet the Americans. Billis talked with them briefly and selected a lad of ten
to lead him to the high country near the volcanoes. Billis
and the boy walked in front, followed by Fry. The chaplain
and Benoway brought up the rear.

The party traveled through dense jungle, across small
streams and up steep hillsides. At the end of the first mile

everyone was sweating freely. The little chaplain dripped perspiration from his thumbs. Fry grunted and swore as the stuff ran off his eyebrows. Billis, surprisingly enough, seemed never to tire. Once he passed a native and his Mary. "Hiya Joe! Whaddaya know?" he called out in breezy fashion.

The grinning native had been across the sea to Espiritu. He called back, "Good duty, boss!"

"So long, Joe!"

A little while later a chief and his three Maries came along the narrow trail. Billis stopped and talked with them briefly in Beche-le-Mer. Then he grinned at the others. "He say there's a pig killing, all right. Up in the hills."

The narrow trails now became mere threads through the immense jungle. It was difficult to believe that these frail communications had serevd men and women for more than five hundred years. And they were still the only trails between the hill villages and the sea.

At last the men came to a native village. It was a sight new and strange to Benoway. It was not at all what he had been led to expect. Only by grace of custom could it be called a village. It was more correctly a homestead. Only one family lived there, and they were absent on a visit. Off to a sing-song somewhere deeper in the jungle. Or maybe to the pig killing higher up the mountainside.

Benoway and the chaplain were tired, so the party rested. The little boy looked on in open disgust while the white men panted and sweated and took off their hot shirts. The kraal in which they had stopped was about forty yards in diameter. Within the fence, made of trees bound together by lianas, not a blade of grass grew. The earth was reddish and packed hard. A few scrawny trees struggled through the earth, at odd angles from having been bent in youth. Probably the kraal had been there for three hundred years, or more.

Within the circle a collection of huts had grown up. Billis explained their uses. "This one for sleepin'. That one for cookin'. That one for chiefs' sons. That one for the wives. That one reserved for any special pigs. Over there the hut for Maries goin' to give birth. That far one for Maries men struatin'."

The total effect of the kraal was planned orderliness. It looked almost neat. Benoway commented on this fact to Billis. "Why not?" the latter asked. "They got nothin' else to do!"

The men were breathing more easily now. Throwing their completely wet shirts over their shoulders, they climbed upward toward the hill village where the ceremonial killings were to be held. As they neared that high place, weird screams penetrated the jungle.

"Them's the pigs!" Billis explained. His eyes were dancing with expectation. "Them pigs always seem to know." The absorbent jungle muffled the unearthly screams, and there were no echoes. Even though the ritual was holy, the doomed pigs screamed.

The kraal which the men entered was bigger than the earlier one. It was more pretentious, as befitted a chief who had lived in glory and who had a boar with double-circle tusks. The old man came forward to greet the Americans. He jabbered in some strange language with Billis. There was much solemn shaking of hands.

The chief's long beard hung in two points like a massive W. His face was heavily wrinkled. His teeth were good. Like most natives, he was very thin. He wore a string of shells about his neck. Around his middle he wore a thick belt of palm fronds. In front a woven lap-lap was suspended; behind, a tuft of leaves bobbed up and down. He looked like a rooster when he walked.

In spite of this, he maintained a solemn dignity. He motioned the Americans to a place in the circle of his guests. Seven chiefs were present. Each had brought his sons. In odd corners of the kraal the Maries of the chieftains were gathered, each group on a spot separated from the rest. There was no visiting among the Maries. But children and dogs raced about the huts. They knew a holiday when they saw one.

In the center of the kraal an altar had been built. It consisted simply of a circle of sanctified palm fronds with room for the old chieftain to stand in the center.

Now from a hut other chiefs brought a sacred frond from a tree growing near the edged of the ancient lake high up among the volcanoes. They blessed it as they gave it to their friend. They likewise blessed the heavy, brutal sacrificial club. It was made of ironwood, that unbelievable jungle wood that rusts in water. The old chief grasped the club, waved it in the air, and cried ritualistic phrases.

Blessed by his friends, possessed of the sacred palm frond and the ironwood club, the chief was ready. His six Maries

came forward from their recesses along the matted wall. Eac
led by a jungle rope the boars she had nurtured. If nee
arose, old men beat the reluctant sacrifices forward. Ther
was infinite screaming. The hot jungle was filled with soun
Relentlessly, with faces unmoved, the women staked the
pigs in a semicircle before the altar. Their chief touched eac
pig with the ceremonial frond.

The Maries then stood silent. They were naked except fc
a single strand of fiber about their waists and an even thinne
strand in front. "Old superstition!" Billis whispered. "If sh
moves that strand aside of her own will, it ain't rape."

From the altar the chief presented his oldest Mary with
long, ancient ironwood spear. As she held it aloft, he blesse
it. Then the old woman placed the spear upon the testicle
of the boar she had reared. As she did so, the other wive
in turn solemnly placed their hands upon the long spear. The
they moved to the next pig. They were seeking the blessin
of fertility.

Now from the huts came a terrible screaming. The chief
favorite Mary was bringing forth the pig whose tusks mad
two complete circles. It was a small pig, grown wizened i
misery. When it was tied, protesting, to its stake, the prou
woman who had coaxed it to maturity signified that all barre
women in the kraal were free to share the blessing of it
magic testicles. This they did, reverently, proud to participat
in their friend's good fortune.

The women retired. Within his circle of palm fronds th
old chief waited. "This is his wonderful moment!" the chap
lain whispered. "Watch."

Slowly the other chiefs moved forward. Their tail feather
bobbed in the hot sunlight. They chanted a song of praise i
honor of the man who was truly rich because he had s
much to give away. Half-doleful at first, they later burst int
violent shouting. At the height of their song, one suddenl
grabbed a pig that screamed horribly. Even Fry, who knev
what to expect, gasped.

Swiftly the old chief raised his massive ironwood club an
smashed it down upon the pig's snout. He then thundere
twenty blows upon the pig's skull. With great passion h
crushed every bone in the pig's head. Then, with delicat
precision, he gave two ceremonial blows that ended the sacri
fice. He completely caved in all the bones surrounding eac
eye. Yet in all his apparently wild smashing, he never touche

either of the tusks. Stained in deep blood, they fulfilled their function. They brought a fleeting immortality to the man who gave them away and to the woman who had reared them. Now they dug at the bloody earth into which they were tossed by excited chiefs who chanted new songs and hauled new pigs to the slaughter.

After the fifth pig was killed in this shuddery manner, Benoway found that he had to look away. In doing so he noticed that all other eyes were straining intently at the savage ceremonial. "It must have been like this when Aztecs killed their human sacrifices," he thought. But he, too, looked back when one pig in death throes broke loose and destroyed the circle of palm branches. Drenched in blood, the graceful branches trailed through the red dirt. "How different the significance we place on palm branches," Benoway thought.

"You'll notice," the chaplain was whispering to Fry, "that these people use palm branches, too. I understand the ancient druids did, also. Or something like palm branches."

Fry turned to relay this information to Benoway, but he saw that the doctor was sick at the stomach. "Sorry, old man," he said.

There was a new rain of crunching blows when the pig was recovered. The animal screamed madly, died horribly, and the ceremony drew to a close. Then a hush fell over the packed kraal. The pig of them all was finally hauled forward. For the last twenty minutes he had heard his fellows die protestingly, but he had made no sound. He remained quiet while the chiefs grabbed him. He allowed them to drag him before his ancient master. He cried out only slightly when the first terrible, face-smashing blow fell. By the time his eyes were beaten in there was no more than a dull murmur over the kraal. Benoway had to get up and leave. No one smiled.

The sacred ceremonial branch was broken by the chief. He threw it to the ground and made a short speech in which he divided the dead pigs among his friends. Then, with a rush, the chiefs and their sons fell upon the carcasses and began to dress the meat. They used long knives. With one slash they cut away the pig's head. Then they gutted him and threw the entrails to the Maries, who salvaged edible portions. Dogs dragged the remainders to the corners of the kraal. Finally the carcass was slashed into eight or ten pieces. Deftly, the jungle butchers passed tough loops of fiber through the tendons to make handles. These they handed to their wives.

The Americans were offered the four choice chunks. The chaplain started to decline for all, but Billis nudged him. "Hey, Chappy!" he whispered. "Take a couple. We can trade 'em down at the shore. They're mad for hog meat!" So the Americans took two large pieces. Billis breathed more easily. "Hell," he whispered to Fry. "You could get maybe a dozen pineapples for them!"

Young men and women now left the kraal to gather branches for the great fires that would be built. The chiefs talked among themselves for a moment and then deftly cut out the lower jaws from the heads of the dead pigs. From each jawbone two tusks, of varying quality, protruded. Some were mere circles. Others had grown back into the jawbones. All were dirty white against the dark red of the bloody bones.

The old men discussed long and ardently the attributes of each tusk. Never, they agreed, had any chief in their lifetime given away such fine boars. Lovingly the tusks were appraised, but when the double-circle ones were reached the men sat in silent admiration. Such tusks might never again be seen in their declining lifetimes.

Delicately the chief who had dispensed this largess picked up the jawbone with the sacred tusks. He deftly knocked at it with his knife. Then he grasped the tusks firmly and with a harsh, wrenching motion, tore them loose from their long tomb of misery. One he gave to Fry, one to the chaplain. He smiled at them and then nodded. They must go. Soon there would be dancing and feasting and love-making. That was a private affair.

Down the long trail to the ocean they went. The chaplain, after carrying his messy tusk for a short distance, said, "Benoway, do you want this?" The doctor leaped for it. Chappy smiled. "The appurtenances of the religion are slightly revolting."

"I feel that way myself, sometimes on Sunday in Connecticut," Fry laughed.

"You're right, lieutenant," the chaplain said. "But it takes strong ritual to affect some sinners."

Luther Billis swung along the jungle trails, pushing lianas from his face, shifting the heavy bundle of pork from time to time. He was singing snatches from an old South Seas song he had picked up from a Burns Philp trader:

Right above her kidney
Was tattooed the 'View of Sydney."

He was terribly pleased with the day's expedition. Close behind him followed the little native boy, dreaming his heart out as he watched the pork slapping Billis on the back.

Wine for the Mess at Segi

I think that Segi Point, at the southern end of New Georgia, is my favorite spot in the South Pacific. Opposite the brutal island of Vangunu and across Blanche Channel from Rendova, lies Segi promontory. Behind the point hills rise, laden with jungle. The bay is clear and blue. The sands of Segi are white. Fish abound in the near-by channel. To the north runs the deadly Slot.

I cannot tell you what the charm of Segi was. Partly it was the natives, who made lovely canes of ebony and pearl. Partly it was the mission boys, who, as you will see, sang in Latin. It was the limes, too, best in the Solomons, the fishing, the great air battles where your friends died, and the blue-green coral water. But mostly, I guess, it was Tony Fry.

On my trips up and down The Slot I made it a point to stop off at Segi whenever I could. Tony had a small hut on the hillside overlooking the tiny fighter strip. There I was sure of a welcome, a hot bath, some good food, and a native boy to do my laundry. I think the Roman emperors made war the way Tony Fry did. No man worked less than he, and few accomplished more.

An unkind critic would have called the indolent fellow a

cheap Tammany politician. A friendly admirer would have termed him an expediter, such as they have in big plants to see that older people work fast. I, who was Tony's stanchest admirer, call him a Yale man. Since I am from Harvard, you can tell what I mean.

Tony would never have died for Yale. Don't misunderstand me. I doubt if he even contributed much money to the college's incessant alumni drives. But when he pulled out the cork of a whiskey bottle, draped a long leg over a chair, pointed a long finger at you, and asked, "How about those planes?" you could tell at once that his combination of laziness, insolence, competence and good breeding could have been concocted only at Yale.

For example, it was Tony's job to run the Wine Mess at Segi Point. Officers who drank more than I never missed Segi, even if they had to wreck their planes to justify a landing. Admiral Kester might be low on whiskey; Tony Fry, no. Where he got the stuff I never knew until one Christmas. And that's quite a story.

Word seeped out that there would soon be a strike at Kuralei or Truk. There was pretty good authority for the belief that the crowd at Segi Point would be in on it! Therefore the skipper said, "This will be our last Christmas here. We'll make it the best there ever was!" He appointed the chaplain to look after the sacred aspects of the holiday. Tony Fry was given the profane.

It was the third week in December when Tony discovered that he could get no more whiskey from his regular sources. I was his guest at the time. He was a mighty glum man. "Damn it all!" he moaned. "How can a man celebrate Christmas with no Wine Mess?"

Now nothing prettier than the phrase "Wine Mess" has ever been devised in the armed forces. It is said that an ensign fresh out of divinity school once went into a Wine Mess and asked for wine. The man behind the bar dropped dead. A Wine Mess exists for the sole purpose of buying and selling beer, whiskey, rum, gin, brandy, bitters, cordials, and at rare intervals champagne. It is called a Wine Mess to fool somebody, and if the gag works, so much the better.

Well, Tony Fry's Wine Mess was in sad state! He decided to do something about it. With nebulous permission from his skipper he told Bus Adams to get old *Bouncing Belch* stripped for action. The *Belch* was a condemned TBF which Fry and

Adams had patched together for the purpose of carrying beer back from Guadalcanal. If you had your beer sent up by surface craft, you lost about half of it. Solicitous deck hands sampled it hourly to see if it was getting too hot.

The *Belch* had crashed twice and seemed to be held together by piano wire. Everything that could be jettisoned had been tossed overboard, so that about the only things you could definitely rely upon when you got up in the air were gas tanks, stick and wings.

Four pilots had taxied the *Belch* around the South Pacific. Each loved it as a child, but none had been able to finagle a deal whereby it got very far from Tony Fry. It was his plane. When ComAirSoPac objected, he just sat tight, and finally Admiral Kester said, "Well, a certain number of damned fools are killed in every war. You can't prevent it. But Fry has got to stop painting beer bottles on his fuselage!"

For every mission to Guadalcanal Tony had his crewmen paint a rosy beer bottle on the starboard fuselage. The painter took pride in his work, and until Admiral Kester saw the display one afternoon at Guadal, the *Bouncing Belch* was one trim sight as it taxied in after a rough landing. Tony always rode in the bombing compartment and was one of the first out. He would pat the beer bottles lovingly and congratulate the pilot on his smooth landing, no matter how rough it had been. His present pilot, Bus Adams, was just slap-happy enough for Tony. Fry was mighty pleased with *Bouncing Belch*. It was some ship, even if he did have to scrape the beer bottles off. "I suppose," he philosophized, "that when you got braid you have to sling it around. Sort of keep in practice so that if you ever meet a Jap . . ." His analogy, whatever it was, dribbled off into a yawn.

We started out from Segi one stinking hot December morning at 0900. We had with us $350 in mess funds, four dynamotors, a radio that would pick up Tokyo Rose, and an electric iron. We proposed to hop about and horsetrade until we got refreshments for Christmas.

Since we knew there was no whiskey in the warehouses at Guadal, we decided to try the Russells, the secondary liquor port in the Solomons. At Wimpy's, the jungle hot-dog stand where pilots came for a thousand miles to wink at the Red Cross girl, we learned that the Russells were dry. "But there's some up on Bougainville!" a Marine SCAT pilot assured us.

"Got two bottles there the other night. Off'n a chaplain. For a Jap uniform. He was sendin' it home to his two kids."

We revved old *Bouncing Belch* for about a minute and roared northward up The Slot. When we approached Segi I prayed that Bus wouldn't buzz the field. But of course he did. I pulled my shoulders together, tightened my stomach, and waited for the whining howl that told me we had reached the bottom of our dive. At such times I prayed that TBF's were better planes than the little blue book said.

Then we were off again, past Rendova, Munda, Kolombangara, Vella and up to the Treasuries, those minute islands lying in the mouth of Jap positions on Bougainville. Aloft we saw the tiny airfield on Stirling Island, the famous one at which the young pilot asked, "Do you tie her down in a heavy sea?" And ten miles away four thousand Japs studied every plane that landed. In this manner a few Americans, fighting and bombing by day, guarding the beaches in the tropic night, by-passed the Japs and left them not to wither but to whimper.

Now we were over Bougainville! A dark and brooding island, most difficult of all our conquests after Guadal. Its natives were the meanest; its rains the hardest, its Japs the most resourceful. We skimmed the southwestern coastline, searching for Empress Augusta Bay. Then, heading for the gaunt volcano's white clouds of steam, we put the *Belch* down at Piva North. It was growing dark. There was the sound of shell fire near the airstrip. It was raining. It was Bougainville.

We found a jeep whose driver took us to a transient camp. That night, amid the rain, we met a group of F4U pilots who were fighting daily over Rabaul. We talked till nearly morning, so next day it was useless to try to do any business. Tony and Bus arranged to go out on a bombing hop over Rabaul. They rode in a Liberator and were very silent when they got back. Rabaul was a flowery hell of flak in those days.

Early next morning at about 0930 Tony set out in a borrowed jeep. Later that day he returned with no whiskey but two ice-making machines. By some queer accident the two valuable articles had been sent to Bougainville in excess of need. Tony traded our radio for them.

"What will we do with them?" I asked. They filled the jeep.

"They tell me there's some whiskey at Ondonga!" he replied. "Fellow flew up here yesterday."

We decided at once to fly to Ondonga to see what trades we could make. Before we took off a long-faced lieutenant from the tower came out to see us. He carried a map.

"Got to brief all pilots. Stay clear of the Professor," he said.

"Who's the Professor?" Tony asked.

"Best Jap gunner in the islands. Hangs out on a point . . . Right here. Shortland Islands. Knocked down three of our planes so far."

"What's his game?"

"Has a radio beam like the one at Treasury. If the sky covers up, he goes on the air. Sucks the damn planes right over him and then lets go!"

"Any tricks in clear weather?" Bus asked. Our sky looked fine.

"If you get Treasury and Shortland mixed up, he lets you get close and then pops you down. Intelligence says he's phenomenal. Stay clear of the guy."

"Let me see that aerial view of Treasury again," Bus asked. "Yeah, I was right. Two small islands with cliffs. I got it OK."

"Brother," the sad lieutenant warned. "You keep 'er OK! We bomb the Professor once in a while, but he's death on bombers. Come back all shot up! Boy, if all Jap shooters had eyes like him, this war would be plenty tough."

"You bet!" Bus agreed. "It would be plenty tough!"

With some apprehension we stowed our ice machines and started south. We circled the volcano and watched plumes of smoke rise high into the air. Behind the jagged cone, among tall mountain ranges, lay an extinct crater filled with clear blue water. Billy Mitchell Lake it was named, a strange monument to a strange man.

Beyond the lake we saw smoke from Jap encampments. There was the jungle line on Bougainville, the roughest fighting in the Pacific. There the great Fiji Scouts, Americals, and our only Pacific Negro battalion slugged it out in swamps, jungle heat, and perpetual gloom. We dipped low over the Jap lines, a gesture Bus could never forswear. Then we sped southeast for Ondonga.

We found no whiskey there. Just enough for their own Christmas celebration. But they thought a shipment had come in at Munda. Try the Marines on top of the hill. It was a fifteen-minute hop from Ondonga to Munda, but it was the longest fifteen minutes of my trip to the South Pacific.

We took off without difficulty and flew over Kula Gulf,

where our Navy had smashed the last big Jap attempt to re-take Guadal. We could see ships beached and gutted, and one deep in the water. But as we turned to fly down the channel to Munda, we started to lose altitude. The engine gradually slowed down.

Bus elected not to tell us anything, but when he started crabbing down the channel both Tony and I knew something was seriously wrong. From time to time Bus would pull the nose up sharply and try to climb, but after he nearly stalled her out, he gave that up.

"Prepare for ditching!" he said quietly over the interphone. "She'll take water easy. But protect your faces! Tony, sit on the deck and brace yourself."

I took my parachute off and wedged it over the instruments facing me. If I crashed badly my face would crack into something soft. I was sweating profusely, but the words don't mean much in recollection. Even my lungs were sweating, and my feet.

We were about two hundred feet over the water. The engine was coughing a bit. We were near Munda. Then we heard Tony calling over the interphone: "Take her in and land on Munda. You can do it, Bus!" His voice was quiet and encouraging.

"It's the carburetor, Tony!" Bus called back. "She may cut out at any minute!"

"So might a wing drop off. Take her in, I tell you. You can make it easy, Bus. Call the airfield!"

Bus started talking with Munda again. "Permission to stagger in," he said. "Got to land any way I can get in. Even cross field. I'll crash her in. Permission to stagger in!"

"Munda to 21 Baker 73. Munda calling. Come in. Field cleared!"

"Will try to make it from channel approach. Is that one ball?"

"Channel approach one ball. Wind favorable."

"Well, guys!" Bus called. "Stop squinchin' your toes up. Here we go!"

He tried to maintain altitude with the heavy TBF and swing her down channel for a turn onto the field. Before he had gone far he realized that to bank the plane in either direction meant a sure stall. That was out. He then had to make an instant decision whether to try a down-wind, no-bank, full-run landing or to set her down in the ocean and lose the plane.

"Coming in down wind. Clear everything!"

From my perch in the radio seat I could see Bus' flashing approach. The airplane seemed to roar along the tops of the trees. I could not imagine its stopping in less than two miles. Then, straight ahead gleamed Munda airfield! It was a heavenly sight. Longest of the Pacific strips, it had been started by the Japs and finished by us. In twelve days we built as much as they did in almost twelve months. To port the mountain marking the airfield rose. At the far end of the field the ocean shone green above the coral. I breathed deeply. If any field could take a roaring TBF, this one could.

But at that moment a scraper, unwarned of our approach, started across the near end of the strip. I screamed. I don't know what Bus did, but he must have done the right thing, for the old *Belch* vaulted over the scraper and slammed heavily onto the coral. Two tires exploded in a loud report. The *Belch* limped and squealed and ground to a stop.

As usual, Tony was the first out. He looked at the burred wheel hubs and the slashed rubber. He looked back at the scraper, whose driver had passed out cold, grazed by a TBF tail wheel. Then he grinned at Bus. "Best landing you ever made," he said.

It would take two days to put new wheels, tires, and carburetor in the *Belch*. Meanwhile, Munda had no whiskey. That is, they had none to sell. But as hosts, well. They could help us out. We stayed in the camp formerly occupied by the Jap imperial staff. It was on a hilltop, magnificent in proportions. A bunch of Marines had it now, fliers and aviation experts. They were glorious hosts, and after telling us how wonderful they and the F4U's were, they showed us to a vacant hut. We were glad to get some sleep, for Marine entertainment is not child's play.

But there was no sleep for us! Around our tent metal stripping had been laid to drain away excess water. Two days before a pig had died somewhere in the bush. All that night huge land crabs crawled back and forth across the tin.

"What the hell is that noise?" Tony shouted when he first heard the unholy rasping of crab claws dragging across corrugations.

"Sounds like land crabs!" Bus said with a slight shiver in his voice.

"Oh, my God!" Tony cried and put his pillow over his ears. But the slow, grisly sound of land crabs cannot be erased in that manner. They are gruesome creatures, with ugly purple and red bodies as big as small dinner plates. Two bluish eyes protrude on sticks and pop in angular directions. Eight or nine feet carry the monstrous creatures sideways at either a slow crawl or a surprising gallop. A big, forbidding claw dangles in front below the eyes. This they sometimes drag, making a clacking noise. Upon tin their hollow, deathly clatter is unbearable.

Finally it became so for Tony. With loud curses he grabbed a flashlight and a broom. Thus armed he dashed out and started killing crabs wherever he could see them. A sound wallop from a broom crushed the ungainly creatures. Before long the tin was strewn with dead crabs.

"What the hell goes on?" a Marine pilot yelled from another hut.

"Killing these damned crabs!" Tony replied.

"You'll be sorry!" hte Marine cried mournfully.

But we weren't. We all went to sleep and had a good night's rest. It was not until nine o'clock next morning that we were sorry.

"My God!" Tony groaned. 'What's that smell?"

"Do you smell it, too?" I asked.

"Smell it?" Tony shouted. "I thought I was lying in it!"

"You'll be sorry!" Bus whined, mimicking the Marine.

"It's the crabs," Tony cried. "Holy cow! Smell those crabs!"

How could we help smelling them! All around us, on hot tin strips, they were toasting in the tropical sun. And as they toasted, they gained terrific revenge on their tormentor. We suffered as well as Tony. Our clothes would reek of dead crab for days. As soon as we could dress, we left the stinking hut. Outside, a group of Marines who had learned the hard way were waiting for us.

"You'll be sorry!" they chanted. The garbage detail, waiting with shovels, creosote, and quicklime, grinned and grinned at Tony as he tiptoed over the mess he had made.

Next morning we shoved off for home. We were disappointed. Christmas was only five days away, and we had no whiskey. In disgust Tony gave one of the ice machines to the Marines for a hot-water heater. "You can never tell what might be just the thing to get some whiskey," he explained. Dismally we flew our disappointing cargo south along the jagged shoreline of New Georgia. We were about to head into Segi Channel when Bus zoomed the *Belch* high into the air and lit out for Guadal.

"I'm ashamed to go back!" he shouted into the interphone.

"Where we going?" Tony asked languidly.

"Anywhere there's some whiskey."

"There's some in New Zealand," Tony drawled.

"If we have to go there, that's where we'll go!" Bus roared.

At the Hotel De Gink on Guadal we heard there were ample stores on Espiritu Santo. That was five hundred miles south. And we had no satisfactory compass on the *Belch*. "We'll trail a C-47 down," Bus said. "And we'll pray there's no clouds!"

I arranged a deal with a New Zealand pilot. He would wait aloft for us next morning and let us follow his navigation. It would be a clear day, he was sure.

Since we had to leave at 0430 there was not much reason to sleep, so we killed that night playing Baseball, a poker game invented by six idiots. You get three cards down. Then you bet on three cards, face up. Lucky sevens are wild. Fours are a base on balls, so you get an extra card. On threes, of course, you strike out and have to leave the game. Unless you want to stay in, whereupon you bribe the umpire by matching all the money in the kitty. You get your last card face down. Then one card is flipped in the middle. If it's a one-eyed jack, a blind umpire calls the game and you start over with a new deal and the old kitty! If a nine appears, it's a tie game, and you all get an extra card, face up. By this time it's pretty risky to bet on anything less than five nines. So the pot is split between the best hand and the poorest. Trouble is, you can't tell what the man next you is bidding on, the three queens that show or the complete bust that doesn't. It's a man's game.

At 0345 we trailed out into the tropic night. Orion was in the west. Far to the south Canopus and the Southern Cross appeared. It was a lonely and beautiful night.

Guadalcanal was silent as we left the De Gink. But as we approached Henderson Field the strip was alive with activity. Liberators were going out to photograph Kuralei at dawn. Medium bombers were getting ready for a strike. And two C-47's were warming up. The *Bouncing Belch* was out of place among those nobler craft. We wheeled the tired old lady into position and waited for the New Zealand C-47 to ake the air. We followed, and before the transport had cleared Guadal, we were on its tail. There we stayed, grimly, during the tedious overwater flight. It was daylight long before we reached Espiritu. Eventually we saw the long northwestern finger of that strange island.

As soon as Bus was satisfied that it was Espiritu we dipped twice to the C-47. Its pilot waved to us. We zoomed off through the bitter cold morning air. We were on our own. Bus gunned the engine, which had been idling to stay back with the C-47. Now the *Belch* tore along, and at the same time we lost altitude. The old girl became liveable once more. The intense cold was gone.

We hurried past the great bay at the northern end of Santo, down the eastern side of the island, well clear of its gaunt, still unexplored mountains. The morning sun was low when we passed the central part of Santo, and I can still recall the eerie effect of horizontal shadows upon the thickest jungle in the South Pacific. A hard, forbidding green mat hid every feature of the island, but from time to time solitary trees, burdened with parasites, thrust their tops high above the mat. It was these trees, catching the early sunlight, that made the island grotesque, crawling, and infinitely lonely. Planes had crashed into this green sea of Espiritu and had never been seen again. Ten minutes after the smoke cleared, a burnt plane was invisible.

As if in contrast, the southern part of the island was a bustling military concentration. The *Bouncing Belch* sidled along the channel and sought out Luganville strip. Bus eased his adventuresome plane down, and before we were fairly stopped, Tony had wangled a jeep. How he did it one never knew. He came back much excited. He had not found any whiskey, that was true. But he was certain that at Noumea the Army had more than a thousand cases. All we had to do was get there.

It was over six hundred miles, due south, and Bus had never flown the route before. He studied the map a minute and said, "We'll hop down to Efate. That's easy. Then we'll pick up some big plane flying the rest of the way. OK?" Who could object? At five that afternoon we were in Noumea!

This time Tony was right! There was whiskey in Noumea. Barrels of it. Using our official permit, we bought $350 worth and then tossed in all the spare cash we had. We traded our dynamotors, ice machine, electric iron, and hot-water heater for more. If we could have traded the rear end of the *Belch* we would have done so. We wound up with twenty-two cases of Christmas cheer. We locked it in a warehouse, gave the mechanics at Magenta two bottles for checking the engine, and set out to find some fun in Noumea.

Next morning Bus and Tony looked at one another, each waiting for the other to make the suggestion. Finally Bus gave in. "Tony," he drawled, "what do you say we fly up to Luana Pori and look around?" Fry, as if his heart were not thumping for such a trip, yawned and said casually, "Why don't we?" And I, who had never seen either Luana Pori or the Frenchman's daughter, made patterns with my toe and wondered, "Why don't they get started? They're both dying to go."

We flew north over the hundred islands of New Caledonia, down the valleys between massive mountains, and over to Luana Pori. Bus lowered the *Belch* for a wild buzzing of the plantation. The Frenchman's daughter ran out into the garden and waved. I could see her standing on tiptoe, a handsome, black-haired Javanese girl. She turned gracefully with her arms up and watched us.

"Hey?" Bus cried through the interphone. "Does that look like home?"

"You get the plane down," Tony replied. At the airfield he gave the mechanics a quart of whiskey for a jeep. As we drew near the plantation, I could see that he was excited. Then I saw why. At the white fence the Frenchman's daughter was waiting for us. She was like an ancient statuette, carved of gold.

"This is Madame Latouche De Becque Barzan," Bus began. But she ignored me. She rushed to Tony, caught him in her arms, and pulled his face down for a shower of kisses. Every gesture she made was like the exquisite posing of a jeweled statue.

"Tony!" she whispered. "I dream you coming back. I see you so plain." She led him to a small white house near the edge of her garden. Bus watched them go and shrugged his shoulders.

"To hell with it," he said. "Let's go into the bar. Hey, Noé!" he shouted. "Get some ice!"

Bus led me to the salon at Luana Pori. I had heard much of this place, of the way in which American officers used it as a kind of club. But I was unprepared for the shock I got that afternoon. On the edge of jungle Latouche had a grand

alon, soft lights, a long bar, pictures in bamboo frames,
nagazines from New York, and a piano. Bus laughed when
e saw the latter. He sat down and picked out "The last time
saw Paris" with two fingers. He tried a few chords.

"The ice, Monsieur Bus!" a tinkling voice behind me an-
ounced. I whirled around. A young Javanese girl more deli-
ate even than her sister, stood in the doorway. Bus leaped
rom the piano and caught her by the waist, kissing her across
he bowl of ice. "This is Laurencin De Becque," he cried
elightedly. "And your sisters?"

"They coming," Laurencin said softly. In a moment they,
oo, appeared.

"Marthe," Bus said gravely, "and Josephine." He kissed
ach one lightly.

"Not so many Americans here now," Laurencin said to me.
They all up north. I think they try to take Kuralei next."
gasped at the easy way she discussed what to me was a
op secret.

"Of course," Josephine said, fixing Bus a drink. "If there
re many wounded, we get a lot of them back here later on.
test cure."

"What goes on here?" I asked Bus in a whisper.

"Sssh! Don't ask questions," he replied. Before he had
nished his drink two Army majors drove up with a case of
rozen chicken.

"Noé!" they called.

"He not here today, major," Josephine cried.

"Show me where to put this frozen chicken. We'll have it
or dinner tomorrow." The major disappeared with Josephine.

"Boy," the other major said. "This Major Kenderdine is a
aution. He just went up to the commissary and said, 'Calling
or that case of frozen fowl.' He got it, too. I don't know
vhose name he signed."

When Kenderdine reappeared he smiled at Bus. "Goin' to
y in the big push?" he asked.

"You know how it is, Adams replied.

The major nodded toward the white house on the edge of
he garden. "Fry come along?" he asked.

"Yep," Bus said.

"You ever hear about Fry and Adams down here, com-
nander?" the major asked.

"Not exactly," I replied.

"Ask them to tell you sometime. Quite a tale." He poured

himself a drink and held his hands out to Marthe, the smallest of the three wonderful girls. She dropped her head sideways and smiled at him, making no move. I noticed that she wore a ring.

"Is that child married?" I whispered to Bus.

"Sssh!" Bus said, but Laurencin heard my question.

"Oui, commander," she said. "We all married." Josephine blushed. "All 'cept Josephine. She be married pretty soon. You watch!" Laurencin patted her sister on the arm. Marthe disappeared and soon returned with some sandwiches. As I ate mine I studied this fabulous place. Two more Army officers arrived at the entrance to the garden. "Hello, Bus!" they cried. "Tony here?" They nodded toward the house.

At that moment Tony and Latouche appeared. The lovely girl was sad. She walked toward us, leaning slightly on Fry. He was grinning at the Army officers. "Looks as if the Navy is goin' to make the next push, too," he said.

"Like Gaudal!" a captain joked. "You guys get a toehold. Then yell for us to take the island."

We looked up. A two-engined plane came in for a landing. It would be our pilot to Espiritu.

"We better be shoving!" Bus said. "It's a long hop to Santo. That C-47 won't wait for us."

Bus kissed the three younger girls but did not even shake hands with Latouche. She was lost in a world of her own, telling Tony to take care of himself, giving him a handkerchief she had lately bought from an Australian trader. She stayed behind in the salon when we went to the jeep escorted by the Army men and the three sisters. We buzzed the garden while waiting for the C-47 to take to the air. The younger girls ran out and threw kisses to us. But not Latouche. Goodbyes for her were terrible, whether one said them to human beings or to airplanes.

The C-47 landed right behind us at Luganville. "We'll be going north at 0400," the pilot said. "You can tag along if you want." We felt so good, what with our cargo of liquor, that we decided to hold a premature holiday. Tony had friends everywhere. That night we decided to visit on the other side of the island. In driving over to Pallikulo we came upon a weird phenomenon of the islands. The crabs of Espiritu were going to the sea! We met them by the coral pits, more than eight hundred in a slimy, crackling trek across the road. Nothing could stop them. At uncertain times land rabs are drawn to the sea. In endless waves they cross whatever comes between them and the water. We stopped the seep, aghast at their relentless, sideways heaving bodies.

"You mean we drive right through them?" Tony asked.

"That's right," I answered. Reluctantly, Tony put the car in second and forged ahead. As our tires struck the frantic rabs, we could hear crunching sounds in the night. It was ickening. Crabs increased in number as we bore through hem. From the opposite direction a large truck came upon hem. The driver, accustomed to the experience, ignored them, nd killed thirty or forty as he speeded through their grisly anks.

Tony swallowed, jammed the car into high, and hurried n. After about two hundred yards, the avalanche ended. We vere through the crabs! Those that lived pushed on toward he ocean.

At 0400 we were in the air again, climbing to 12,000 feet, vhere the temperature felt like Christmas. From the bomb ay Tony whistled "Jingle Bells" into the mike. Bus had told us he didn't like the performance of the *Belch* and hoped he would make it all right. I had broken out new life jackets t the time, and Tony, thinking of his cargo, had shuddered.

But we made it into Guadal! As we landed a groundcrewman hurried up and told us we were spitting oil. It was ydraulic fluid. So that was it! Bus laughed and said all the ld girl needed was another drink. But even as he spoke the ort wheel slowly folded up until the knuckle touched coral. Then even Bus' eyes grew big.

"Can you fix it by 1400?" he asked.

"Can't do it, sir!" the mechanic replied.

"If you knew what we had in there, you'd be able to," 3us said.

"What's in her?" the mech asked.

"Tomorrow's Christmas, ain't it?" Bus countered.

"You ain't foolin' there, sir!" the mech grinned.

"Well, maybe you fix that hydraulic system, maybe tonorrow really will be Christmas!"

The mech hunched his shoulders up and tried not to appear oo happy. "You can take her up at 1400. But I ain't sayin' ou can get her down later."

"You see to it that she gets up, pal," Bus said. "I'll get her lown!"

When Bus and I looked around, Tony was gone. We didn't

see him for several hours, and then at 1400 an ambulance clanged furiously across the field.

"Where's the *Bouncing Belch?*" the driver cried in some agitation.

"My God!" I shouted. "What's up! What's happened?"

"Nothin'," the ambulance driver replied. "I just want to get rid of this damned washing machine and get back to the hospital." He jumped out of the ambulance and threw the doors open. There was Tony Fry, riding in comfort, with the prettiest white washing machine you ever saw!

"Don't ask me where I got it!" he yelled. "Give the driver two cases of whiskey!" We broke out the whiskey and turned it over to the sweating driver. He shook Tony's hand warmly and drove off as we loaded the washing machine, priceless above opals, in the *Belch*.

"I better warn you fellows," Bus said, "that we may have some trouble getting back to Segi. OK by you?"

We nodded. Any thought that *Bouncing Belch* might conceivably give trouble was so difficult to accept that we would have flown her to Yokohama. Especially if Bus were pilot.

We knew that take-off time was critical. Would the wheels hold up? We held our breath as the old girl wheezed into position. The propeller whirred coral into the bushes. Slowly Bus released the brake. With terrifying momentum, for we must get up fast, we roared down the strip. We were airborne. "Oh boy!" I sighed.

"Are the wheels up?" Bus asked.

There was a long silence and then Tony's languid voice: "All but the starboard!" he said. "And the port is dragging, too!"

"Well, anyway, we're up!" Bus said. "Even if the wheels aren't."

"Now all we got to do is get down!" Tony replied.

We were over Iron Bottom Bay, off Guadal, where many Jap ships lay rotting, and where American ships, too, had found their grave. Along the shore several Jap cargo vessels, gutted and half-sunk, stuck their blunt snouts into the sandy beach. We were on our way. Home for Christmas!

Somewhere north of the Russells Bus said to us, "It's a tough decision, fellows. If we try to snap those damned wheels into position, we'll probably spring the bomb-bay doors and lose our whiskey. If we belly land, we'll break every damned bottle anyway."

There was a grim silence. I had no suggestions, but slowly, from the bottom of the plane, Tony's voice came over the interphone. "I thought of that," he said. "All the whiskey's out of the bomb bays. Moved inside. I'm sitting on it!"

"You wonderful man!" Bus shouted. "Shall we snap 'em down?"

He rose to 9,000 feet and went into a steep dive. I pressed my feet and hands against the bulkhead, but even so felt the blood rushing into my head. Suddenly, we snapped up violently. My head jerked back and the blood started down to my feet.

"Any luck?" Bus asked.

"Didn't do the wheels any good," Tony reported. "Damn near killed me. Whiskey cases everywhere."

"Get 'em squared away!" Bus ordered. "We'll belly land her!"

"Good old *Bouncing Belch!*" Tony said.

At the moment we were over the island south of Segi. Although I was considerably frightened at the prospect of a belly landing, I remember studying the unequaled loveliness of that view. Below us lay hundreds of coral islands, some large, some pinpoints with no more than a tree or two. From the air they formed a fairyland.

For the coral which pushed them above the water also grew sideways under the water, so that the area was one vast sheet of rock. From above it looked like a mammoth gray-green quilt, with tufts of islands sticking through. Here and there along the quilt deep patterns of darkest blue ran helter-skelter. They were the places where coral broke off, and the ocean dropped to five or six thousand feet! It was over this vast sea of islands south of Segi that we sweated and crossed our fingers and made preparations for landing.

We padded our heads, and braced ourselves. Tony wedged the dangerous whiskey cases against the washing machine. I wondered how he would sit? He was the one would take a fearful beating if we bounced.

Bus cleared with the tower. Word sped through the men of Segi. To heighten their apprehension and relieve his own, Bus announced, "I've got a washing machine, nineteen cases of whiskey, and Tony Fry in the bomb compartment." Then, with nerve and know-how, he brought *Bouncing Belch* in for her last landing.

Bus did his job well. He used neither a full stall, which

would crush the plane and Tony, too, nor a straight three-point landing which might nose the old girl over. Instead he skimmed the strip for perhaps a thousand feet, feeling for the coral with his tail wheel. Slowly, slowly, while we ate up the safe space on the runway, *Bouncing Belch* reached for the coral. Then, with a grinding crunch, she felt it.

We skidded along for two hundred feet on our tail assembly, and Bus let her go! The old *Belch* pancaked in and screamed ahead, cutting herself to death upon the coral!

This time Tony was the last man out. In fact, we had to cut him out, and then he handed us first the nineteen cases of whiskey, next the washing machine, and finally himself. He grinned at Bus and reached for his hand. "Best landing you ever made!" he said. He was sweating.

That night we celebrated on Segi Point! Many toasts were drunk to the *Bouncing Belch*. There would never be another like her! Our beer ship was gone! Tony, in honor of the occasion, set up his washing machine and ran through a preliminary laundry of six khaki shirts and some underwear. Already the washer was supplanting the *Belch* in his affections.

At 2300 the chaplain held Christmas Eve services. Even men already drunk attended. In simple manner the chaplain reminded us of Christmas. He read in slow voice the glorious passage from St. Luke: *"And it came to pass . . . to be taxed with Mary his espoused wife . . . And there were in the same country . . . I bring you good tidings of great joy . . . lying in a manger . . . and on earth peace, good will toward men."* Then a choir of mission boys, dressed only in khaki shorts, rose and sang five Christmas carols. They sang "Adeste Fideles" in Latin, and "Silent Night" in German. Their voices were majestic. Between numbers they grinned and grinned at the little sailor who had taught them the carols.

Finally the skipper took over. He said only a few words. "I see from the glassy stares of some of you men that you have already received certain presents." A roar went up! "I have a Christmas present of another kind for you!" He paused and unfolded a small piece of yellow paper. "The news is in, men! It came this afternoon!" The excitement was unbearable. "You have been selected to hit the next beachhead!"

There was a moment of islence, and then somebody started to cheer. The long waiting was over! Another voice took up the shout, and for more than two minutes Segi Point echoed with hoarse cheers. These men had their Christmas present, a grim and bloody one. Yet their shout of thanks could be heard half a mile away along the shore.

The Airstrip at Konora

W HEN Admiral Kester finally finished studying Alligator operations he said to himself: "They'll be wanting a bomber strip at Konora to do the dirty work." He looked at his maps. Konora was a pinpoint of an island, 320 miles from Kuralei. When you went into Konora, you tipped your hand. Japs would know you were headed somewhere important. But they wouldn't know whether your next step would be Kuralei, Truk, or Kavieng. Therefore, you would have some slight advantage.

But you'd have to move fast! From the first moment you set foot on Konora, you knew the weight of the entire Jap empire would rush to protect the next islands. You couldn't give the enemy much time. When you went into Konora, the chips were down. You batted out an airstrip in record time, or else . . .

At this point in his reasoning Admiral Kester asked me to get Commander Hoag, of the 144 SeaBees. Immediately. Soon Commander Hoag appeared. He was a big man, about six foot three, weighed well over 200 pounds, had broad shoulders, long legs, big hands, and bushy eyebrows. He wore his shirt with the top two buttons unfastened, so that he looked sloppy. But a mat of hair, showing on his chest, made you forget that. He was a Georgia man. Had been a contractor in Connecticut before the war. As a small-boat enthusiast, he knew many Navy men. One of them had prevailed upon him to enter the SeaBees. To do so cost him $22,000 a year, for he was a wealthy man in civilian life. Yet he loved the order and discipline of Navy ways. He was forty-seven and had two children.

"Commander Hoag to see you, sir!" I reported.

"So soon?" the admiral asked. "Bring him in."

Hoag loomed into the doorway and stepped briskly to the admiral's desk. "You wished to see me, sir?" I started to go.

"Don't leave," Kester said. "I'll want you to serve as liaison on this job." The admiral made no motion whereby we might be seated, so like schoolboys we stood before his rough desk.

"Hoag," he said briefly. "Can you build a bomber strip on Konora?"

"Yessir!" Hoag replied, his eyes betraying his excitement.

"How do you know?" Kester inquired.

"I've studied every island in this area that could possibly have a bomber strip. Konora would handle one. There are some tough problems, though. We'd have to round up all the Australians and missionaries who'd ever been there. Some tough questions about that island. Maps don't show much."

"Could the strip be completed for action within fifteen days of the minute you get your first trucks ashore?"

Without a moment's hesitation Hoag replied, "Yessir."

"Lay all preparation to do the job, Hoag. D-day will be in five weeks. You'll be the second echelon. You'll probably not need combat units, since the Marines should reduce the island in two days. But you'd better be prepared. Logistics and Intelligence will give you all the assistance you demand. You can write your own ticket, Hoag. But remember. Tremendous importance accrues to the time table in this operation. Bombers must be ready to land on the sixteenth day."

"They will be," Hoag replied in a grim voice that came deep from his chest. "You can schedule them now."

"Very well!" the admiral said. "I will."

I worked with Commander Hoag for the next five weeks. I was his errand boy, and scurried around to steal shipping space, essential tools, and key men. It was decided to throw the 144th and five maintenance units of SeaBees onto Konora. Some would build roads; others would knock down the jungle;

others would haul coral; some would run electrical plants; important units would do nothing but keep gigantic machinery in operation; one batch of men would build living quarters.

"Coral worries me," Hoag said many times as he studied his maps. "I can't find records anywhere of coral pits on that island. Yet there must be. Damn it all, it would be the only island in that general region that didn't have some. Of course. Somewhere in our push north we're going to hit the island without coral. Then hell pops. But I just can't believe this island is it. One of those hills has got to have some coral. God!" he sighed. "It would be awful if we had to dig it all from sea water. Get those experts in here again!"

When the experts on coral returned, Hoag was standing before a large map of Konora. The island was like a man's leg bent slightly at the knee. It looked something like a boomerang, but the joining knee was not so pronounced. Neither leg was long enough for a bomber strip, which had to be at least 6,000 feet long. But by throwing the strip directly across the bend, the operation was possible. In this way it would cut across both legs. Since the enclosed angle pointed south, the strip would thus face due east and west. That was good for the winds in the region.

"Now men," Hoag said wearily. "Let's go over this damned thing again. "The only place we can possibly build this strip is across the angle. The two legs are out. We'll agree on that?" The men assented.

"That gives us two problems. First might be called the problem of the ravine. Lieut. Pearlstein, have you clarified your reasoning on that?"

Pearlstein, a very big Jewish boy, whom his men loved because of his willingness to raise hell in their behalf, moved to the map. His father had been a builder in New York. "Commander," he said. "I'm morally certain there must be a big ravine running north and south through that elbow. I'm sure of it, but the photographs don't show it. We can't find anyone who has been there. They always landed on the ends of the island. But look at the watershed! It's got to be that way!"

"I don't think so," a young ensign retorted. It was De Vito, from Columbus, Ohio. He graduated from Michigan and had worked in Detroit. There was a poll of the men. The general opinion was that there was no severe ravine on Konora.

"But commander," Pearlstein argued. "Why not run the strip as far to the north as possible? Cut the length to 5,000 feet. If you keep it where you have it now, you'll get the extra length, that's right. But you're going to hit a ravine. I'm certain you will."

Commander Hoag spoke to me. "See if a strip 5,000 feet long would be acceptable," he ordered. I made proper inquiries among the air experts and was told that if no longer strip was humanly possible, 5,000 would have to do. But an extra thousand feet would save the lives of at least fifteen pilots. I reported this fact.

Everyone looked at Pearlstein. He countered with another proposal. "Then why not drop one end of the strip as far as possible down this east leg? You could still run the other end across the elbow. And you'd be so far north on the elbow that you'd miss the ravine."

"See if they could use a strip like that?" I was told. "Let's see. Wind on takeoff and landing would come from about 325 degrees."

I soon returned with information that our airmen considered 325 cross wind much less acceptable than earlier plans they had approved. "It's all right for an empty, normal plane," I reported. "But these bombers are going to be loaded to the last stretching ounce."

Hoag stood up. "Plans go ahead as organized. Now as to the coral!" The commander and his officers gathered about the map. With red chalk he marked two hills, one at the northern tip of the elbow and one about halfway up the western leg. He then made many marks along the shoreline that lay within the bend of the knee.

"We can be pretty certain there will be coral here," he reasoned, indicating the shoreline. "But what do you think about these two hills?" His men argued the pros and cons of the hills. In some South Pacific islands SeaBees' work was made relatively easy by the discovery of some small mountain of solid coral. Then all they had to do was bulldoze the wonderful sea rock loose, pile it onto trucks, haul it to where it was needed, and smash it flat with a roller. The result was a road, or a path, or a dock, or an airstrip that almost matched cement. But on other islands, like Guadalcanal and Bougainville, for example, there was no coral, either in mountains or along the bays. Then the SeaBees swore and sweated, and for as long as Americans lived on those islands, they would eat lava dust, have it in their beds at night, and watch it disappear from their roads with every rain. If, as some Navy men have suggested, the country ought to build a monument to the SeaBees, the SeaBees should, in turn, build a monument to Coral. It was their stanchest ally.

"The Australians are here, sir," a messenger announced.

Two long, thin men and one woman, old and un-pretty, stepped into the room. Commander Hoag gave the tired woman his chair. The men remained standing. They introduced themselves as Mr. and Mrs. Wilkins and Mr. Heskwith. Eighteen years ago they had lived on Konora for three months. They were the only people we could find who knew the island.

It was quiet in the hot room as these three outposts of empire endeavored to recall the scene of one of their many defeats in the islands. They had made no money there. The mosquitoes were unbearable. Trading boats refused to put into the lagoon. The natives were unfriendly. Mr. Heskwith lost his wife on Konora. He had never remarried. Even though we were rushed, no one interrupted the dismal narrative.

The Wilkinses and Mr. Heskwith had then gone to Guadalcanal. We wondered what had been the subtle arrangements between Mr. Heskwith and Mrs. Wilkins. Faded, in an ill-fitting dress, she seemed scarcely the magnet that would hold two men to her thatched hut for eighteen years. "At Guadalcanal we were doing nicely," Mr. Wilkins concluded, "when the Japanese came. We saw them burn our place to the ground. We were up in the hills. My wife and I were some of the first to greet the American troops. Mr. Heskwith, you see, was scouting with the native boys. He met your men later. Mr. Heskwith has been recommended for a medal of some kind by your naval forces. He was of great service to your cause."

Gaunt Mr. Heskwith smiled in a sickly manner. We wondered what he could have done to help the United States Navy.

"Very well," Commander Hoag said. "We are proud to have you people and Mr. Heskwith here to help us again. You understand that you will be virtual prisoners for the next four or five weeks. We are going to invade Konora shortly and are going to build a bomber strip across the bend. Just as you see it on this map. We dare not risk any idle conversation about it. You'll be under guard till we land."

"Of course," Mr. Wilkins said. "We were the other time, too."

The three Australians then studied the map in silence. We were abashed when Mrs. Wilkins dryly observed, "I didn't know the island looked like that." We looked at one another.

"Now point out where you lived," Commander Hoag suggested.

"It was here," Mr. Wilkins said, making an X on the map.

"No," his wife corrected. "I'm sorry, David, but it was over here." They could not even agree as to which leg of the island they had settled on.

"Could you take the map down from the wall?" Mr. Wilkins asked. "It might be easier to recall." Commander Hoag and one of his officers untacked the large map and placed it on the floor. "That's better!" Mr. Wilkins said brightly. He and his wife walked around the map, squinted at it, held their heads on one side. They could not agree. Mr. Wilkins even found it difficult to believe that north was north.

"See!" Commander Hoag said quietly. "It's the same on other maps. That's north." Still the Wilkinses could not determine where they had lived. "But try to think!" Hoag suggested. "Which way did the sun rise?"

"They asked us that in the other room, sir," Mrs. Wilkins explained. "But we can't remember. It's been so long ago. And we wouldn't want to tell you anything that wasn't true."

"Mr. Heskwith!" Hoag said suddenly. "Perhaps you could tell us something." The thin fellow was studying the western leg of the island. "Do you recall something now?" Hoag asked.

"I'm trying to find where it was we buried Marie," the man replied. "It was not far from a bay."

Hoag stepped aside as the three middle-aged people tried to recall even the slightest certainty about the far and unhappy chapter of their lives. No agreement was reached. No agreement could be reached. Time had dimmed the events. It was all right for people to say, "I can see it as plain as if it was yesterday." But some things, fortunately, do not remain as clear as they were yesterday. The mind obliterates them, as Konora had been obliterated.

"May I ask a question, sir?" Lieut. Pearlstein suggested.

When the commander assented, he took the three Australians to the head of the map. "Now it would be very helpful if you could tell us something definite about this bend here. You see the airstrip has to pass right over it. Were any of you ever in that region?"

All three volunteered to speak, but by consent granted eighteen years before, Mr. Wilkins acted as chairman. "Yes," he said. "That's the logical place to settle. We went there first, didn't we? But we didn't like it."

"But why didn't you?" Pearlstein asked triumphantly.

"No breeze," Wilkins said briefly. Pearlstein's smile vanished.

"Did you ever go inland at this point?" he continued.

"Come to the question, Pearlstein," Hoag interrupted impatiently. "What we need to know," he said in a kindly manner, "is whether or not there is a deep ravine across the bend?"

The Australians looked at one another blankly. Mutually, they began to shake their heads. "We wouldn't know that, sir," Mr. Wilkins said.

"The only person likely to know that," Mrs. Wilkins added, "is Mr. Davenport."

"Who's Davenport?" Hoag demanded with some excitement.

"He's the New Zealander who lived on the island for about a dozen years," Mrs. Wilkins explained.

"Why didn't we get Davenport up here?" Hoag demanded.

"Oh!" Mrs. Wilkins explained. "The Japs caught him. And all his family."

Hoag was stumped. He spoke with Pearlstein a few minutes while the Australians studied the large map of the tiny island. Pearlstein returned to the map. "Can you think of anyone who might know about that bend?" he asked. "You can see how urgent it is that we satisfy our minds as to that ravine." The Australians wrinkled their brows.

"No," Mr. Wilkins said aloud. "The skipper of the *Alceste* wouldn't be likely to know that."

"Not likely," Mrs. Wilkins agreed.

It was Mr. Heskwith who had the bright idea! He stepped forward hesitatingly. "Why don't you send one of us back to the island?" he suggested.

"Yes!" the Wilkinses agreed. They all stepped a few paces

forward, toward Commander Hoag. He was taken aback by the proposal.

"There are Japs on the island. Hundreds of them," he said roughly.

"We know!" Mrs. Wilkins replied.

"You think you could make it?" Pearlstein asked.

"We could try," Mr. Wilkins said. It was as if he had volunteered to go to the corner for groceries.

"You have submarines to do things like that, don't you?" Mrs. Wilkins asked.

"Do you mean that you three would go up there?" Commander Hoag asked, incredulously.

"Yes," Mr. Wilkins replied, establishing himself as the authority.

"I think I should go," Mr. Heskwith reasoned.

"He has been in the woods more," Mrs. Wilkins agreed. "Maybe three of us should go by different routes."

Commander Hoag thought a minute. He stepped to the map. "Is either of these mountains coral?" he asked.

"We don't know," Mr. Wilkins answered.

"Pearlstein! Could a man tell if a mountain was coral? How far would he have to dig?"

"I should say . . . Well, five feet, sir. In three different places. That's a minimum sample."

Commander Hoag turned to Mr. Heskwith. "Would you be willing to risk it?" he asked.

"Of course," Heskwith replied. It was agreed upon.

I was given the job of selecting from volunteers ten enlisted men to make the trip. All one hot afternoon I sat in a little office and watched the faces of brave men who were willing to risk the landing on Konora. There was no clue to their coming, no pattern which directed these particular men to apply. I saw forty odd men that day and would have been glad to lead any of them on a landing party.

They had but one thing in common. Each man, as he came in to see me fingered his hat and looked foolish. Almost all of them said something like: "I hear you got a job," or "What's this about a job?" I have since learned that when the Japs want volunteers for something unduly risky, their officers rise and shout at the men about ancestors, emperors, and glory. In the SeaBees, at least, you sort of pass the word around, and pretty soon forty guys come ambling in with their hats in their hands, nervous like.

Married men I rejected, although I did not doubt that some of them had ample reason to want to try their luck on Konora. Very young boys I turned down, too. The first man I accepted was Luther Billis, who knew native tongues and who was born to die on some island like Konora. The gold ring in his left ear danced as he mumbled something about liking to have a kid named Hyman go along. I told him to go get Hyman. A thin Jewish boy, scared to death, appeared. I accepted him, too. The other eight were average unimpressive American young men. It would be fashionable, I suppose, to say that I had selected ten of America's "little people" for an adventure against the Japs. But when a fellow crawls ashore on Konora at night to dig three holes five feet deep, he's not "little people." He's damned big, brother!

As soon as the group was dispatched, Commander Hoag and his staff seemingly forgot all about them. Mr. and Mrs. Wilkins were sent back to Intelligence. In their place Admiral Kester's leading aviation assistants were called in. Commander Hoag was tough with them.

"I want plenty of air cover on this job," he said briskly as I took notes. "And I want it to be air cover. No stunting around. I don't want the men distracted by a lot of wild men up in the air. And under no circumstances are your men to attempt landings on the airstrip until I give the word." The aviators smiled at one another.

"An aviator's no good if he's not tough," one of them observed.

"Right! Same goes for SeaBees. But tell them to save their stuff for the Nips. Now what do you think of this? You men are the doctors. Tell me if it's possible. Let's have a constant patrol of New Zealanders in P-40's for low cover. They like those heavy planes and do a good clean-up job with them. Give us some F6F's or F4U's for high cover. And send some TBF's out every morning, noon, and night at least two hundred miles."

"You'll tip your hand, commander," an aviator observed.

"You're right. But the Nips will know we're on the move the minute we hit Konora. Can't help it. So here's what we'll do! We'll send the TBF's in three directions, Kuralei, Truk, Rabaul."

Problems of air cover were settled. Then logistics men appeared and said what ships we could have and when. Oil tankers were dispatched from San Diego to make rendezvous three weeks later. Commissary men discussed problems of food, and gradually the armada formed. On the day we finished preparations, eighteen bombers plastered Konora. The island was under fire from then on. It knew no respite. And from all parts of the Pacific Japan rushed what aid it could. Those Jap officers who had smugly advised against building a fighter strip at Konora—since it would never be attacked—kept their mouths shut and wondered.

Finally Commander Hoag's staff moved its equipment and maps on board a liberty ship. That night, as we mulled over our plans, Mr. Heskwith and Luther Billis returned from their expedition. Billis was resplendent in tattoos and bracelets. He looked fine in the ship's swaying light. Mr. Heskwith was thin, rumpled, reticent.

"We had no trouble," the Australian said quietly. "It was most uneventful."

"Was there a ravine?" Lieut. Pearlstein asked eagerly.

"A deep one," Mr. Heskwith replied. "Runs due north and south. Two small streams filter into it."

"How deep? At this point?" Hoag demanded.

Mr. Heskwith deferred to Billis. The jangling SeaBee stepped forward and grinned. "Not more than twenty feet," he said.

"And how wide?"

"Thirty yards, maybe," Billis answered. He looked at the Australian.

"Not more," Mr. Heskwith agreed.

"And the two mountains?" Hoag inquired.

"The hills?" Heskwith repeated. "We could not get to that one. We don't know. We were able to dig only one hole on this one. It was late."

"But was it coral?"

"Yes."

Billis interrupted. "We got coral, but it was deeper down than any hills around here. Lots."

"But it was coral?"

"Yes, sir!"

Commander Hoag thanked the men and dismissed them. He smiled when he saw Billis clap a huge hand over Mr. Heskwith's frail shoulder. He heard Billis whispering: "Guess we told them what they wanted to know, eh, buddy?"

Hoag turned and faced his officers. "There is a considerable gully there. Don't call it a ravine. We assume this hill is coral.

Probably three feet of loam over it. All right. We're taking chances. We lost on one and gained on the other. Got a gully and the coral to fill it with. Pearlstein. We'll give you all of 1416, and the heavy trucks. You'll beat a road directly to that hill. Don't stop for anything. Food, huts, gasoline. Nothing. Rip the loam off and move the hill over to here!" He indicated the gully. Before anyone could speak, he barked out eight or ten additional orders. Then he dismissed the men. When they were gone he slumped down in a chair.

"I don't know what we'd have done if there had been a ravine and no coral!" he said. "I guess God takes care of Americans and SeaBees."

On the way north I got to know Commander Hoag fairly well. He was an engaging man. The finest officer I ever knew. The fact that he was not a regular Navy man kept him from certain supercilious traits of caution that one expects in Annapolis graduates. Hoag was an enterprising man and a hard worker. On the other hand, his social position in civilian life was such that he had acquired those graces of behavior which mark the true naval officer and distinguish him from men of the other services.

Hoag's men idolized him and told all sorts of silly stories about things he had done. Even his officers, who lived with him daily, revered him and accepted his judgment as almost infallible. I got a sample of that judgment when he confided to me why he had given Pearlstein the job of filling the gully.

"You see," he said thoughtfully, as he watched the Coral Sea, "Pearlstein was right. By shrewd deductions that were available to all of us, he concluded that there must be a gully there. Then he stuck his neck way out and argued with me about it. He was argued down. Or, if you wish, I threw my rank at him. Then it turns out that there really is a gully there. So the logical thing to do is to give it to him to take care of. You watch how he goes about it! He'll steam and swear and curse, but all the time he'll love that gully. Proved he was right and the old man was a damned fool! I'll bet that Pearlstein will fill that hole in a new world's record. But how he'll bitch!"

From time to time on the trip I would hear Pearlstein muttering to himself. "Of all the silly places to build an air-strip! I *told* them there was a gully there!" When he got his special group together to lay plans for their assault on the coral hill, he confided to them, "We've got a mammoth job to do. Biggest job the SeaBees have tackled in the South Pacific. We've got to move a mountain in less than fifteen days. I kept telling them there was a big hole there. Any guy could see there'd have to be. But I think we're the team that can fill it up!"

It seemed to me, as I listened to the various officers talking to their detachments, that each man in that battalion had generated a personal hatred for Konora and everything related to the airstrip. Men in charge of heavy equipment kicked it and cursed it while they lovingly worked upon it in the ship's holds. Luther Billis, who was in charge of the trucks and bulldozers, was sure they were the worst in the Navy. "Look at them damn things!" he would moan. "They expect me to move a mountain with them things. They ain't a good differential in the bunch. But I guess we'll do it, all right!"

At Guadalcanal two experts came aboard our liberty ship. They carried papers and conferred with Commander Hoag in hush-hush sessions. Finally he called us in. One of the men was a commander and the other a civilian in military uniform. Hoag introduced them and spoke briefly. "Gentlemen," he began. "I have good news and bad news for you. Bad news first. We are going to have to replan our entire layout. We've got to dredge our coral from the inner shoreline of the knee, right here. Got to get enough live coral to cover the airstrip, exclusive of the revetments. You gentlemen will be expected to lay plans accordingly. The good news is that if we use live coral for our runways, they will be better than any in the area. Because, we can keep that coral living with plenty of salt water every day. And live coral binds better, is more resilient, and won't throw dust!"

A storm of chatter greeted this announcement. Was the old man nuts? Hoag let his energetic men damn the project and then called upon the civilian to explain. "It's preposterous I know," the expert said briefly. "But we have more than proved that coral will stay alive for some days if watered daily with fresh sea water. If the organisms remain living, they grow ever so slightly and fill the interstices that otherwise would develop. Your airplane then lands upon a living, resilient mat. All you have to do is to keep feeding it sea water."

The visiting commander then took over. "We decided to make the experiment . . . No, it's not an experiment! It's a fact! But we decided to do it for the first time in a big way on Konora. We have a ship off Lunga Point with special dredging equipment. And we have four massive, glass-lined milk trucks with rustproof spigots for watering. We've put it up to Commander Hoag. We're not forcing this upon him. Meeting his schedule is still of paramount importance. But you'll have a much better job if you use this new method."

There was a long silence. Then an ensign spoke up. "You dig the coral from under the water?"

"Yes, sir."

"Special equipment?"

"Yes, sir."

"Gasoline or Diesel?"

"Diesel." There were no more questions. Commander Hoag thought a moment, studied the map. He was going to make some comment but thought better of it.

"That's all, gentlemen," he said dryly. "You know what this means. Run your roads down here. Oh, yes! That's what I was trying to remember. You'll have to run trucking lines to each end of the airstrip. Pearlstein tells me it will take at least twelve days to make his fill. We'll work both ends and meet in the middle."

The visitors left, and that night our ship started north. Behind us trailed the new ship, with its strange equipment. I noticed particularly that the officers no longer ridiculed the idea of live coral. "That guy may have something," one of the wiriest of the young men said. They did, however, complain bitterly about the extra work. To hear them talk you would have thought it absolutely impossible to build an extra road on Konora.

All arguments ceased, completely, when five troop transports of Marines met us one morning. It was a solemn moment when they hove into sight. We knew what the ships were, and that our lives and fortunes depended upon those Leathernecks. At such moments a bond is established that no subsequent hardships can ever break. From that moment on, the Marines in those ships were our friends. We would see none of them until we hit the beaches they had won for us, and some of them would never speak to us, lying upon the shores . . . Those Marines were our friends.

Two days later heavy warships swung into line, and next morning we were at Konora. All day our forces alternated between aerial bombardment and naval shellfire. It was awe-inspiring to witness the split-second timing. It was wonderful to contemplate the brains that went into the operation. It was sickening to imagine one's self upon that shore. I recall my thoughts distinctly: "A long time ago the Japs came down like this and shelled us on Guadal. Strange, but they'll never do that again!"

In the night great shells whined through the air, and at 0400 we saw the first Marines go ashore. The landing was neither tragic nor easy. It was a routine Marine landing, with some casualties but with planned success. At four-thirty in the afternoon the first SeaBee detachments went ashore. They were to throw up huts and a camp area. That night they were attacked by Japs and four SeaBees were killed.

At daybreak our first heavy lighters headed for shore. They carried Luther Billis, a dozen bulldozers, and Lieut. Pearlstein's men. I saw them as they hit the shore. In three minutes a bulldozer edged onto the sand and started for the brush. In four minutes more a tree was toppling. All that day Pearlstein and his men drove madly for the coral hill. It took two companies of Marines to protect them. At sunset that day Pearlstein was halfway to the hill. His men worked all night, with ghostly flares, and two of them were wounded.

One of the wounded men was Luther Billis, who insisted upon being in the front lines. He suffered a superficial flesh wound, but a corpsman who treated him was a bit of a wag. He had with him a homemade purple heart, which he pinned on Billis' pants, since the "big dealer" could not be made to wear a shirt. Next morning Billis barged into the head of the line where they were serving coffee. "I'm a bloody hero!" he bellowed. "Special privileges." He then proceeded to revile the Marine Corps in frightful language. "They didn't protect me!" he roared. "Ran away when the going got tough!" The Marines, who had taken a liking to the fat nomad, countered with an improvised sign painted with mercurochrome: Billis Boulevard. The name still stands on Konora.

There were more Japs on the island than we had anticipated. It would be incorrect to say that the SeaBees had to stop operations in order to fight the yellow devils, but each working party had to have infantry protection. If Marines were not available, SeaBees had to provide their own snipers. Artisans forty years old who had expected to work in Pearl Harbor and sleep between sheets, swore, bitched, and grabbed rifles. I doubt if the SeaBees altogether killed two Japs. But they sure used up a pile of ammunition!

By the third day the Marines had a perimeter safely estab lished. That night at seven o'clock Pearlstein reached his fir objective: the coral hill. Billis and some rowdies set up terrific small-arms barrage in honor of the event. The Ma rine commandant sent a special runner to see what ha happened. He was furious when he heard the explanatio and called for Hoag.

"I won't have your men firing that way!" he snapped.

"Yes, sir!" Hoag replied briskly. But he said nothing t anybody about the rebuke.

On the fifth day, with tractors and bulldozers making shambles of Konora, I went to see how the live-coral proje was developing. In the lagoon, within the protecting angle c the bend, an energetic crew had established a dredgin process. They had half a dozen massive steel maws whic they sank onto the coral bottom. The maws were then slowl dragged onto the beach, where a tripping device threw th collected coral into piles. As I watched, a giant steam shov came slowly out of the jungle behind me, like a pterodacty It moved with horrible slowness, crunchingness, and grindin It took up a position on the beach from which it could scoo up the live coral. Trucks were already waiting for their fir loads.

"Would you like to see what we're getting?" an office asked me. I went with him to the farthest dredge. We waite until a fresh batch was hauled in and tripped. Then w stepped forward to examine the catch.

In the crushed pile at our feet we saw a wonderland. Cor grows like an underwater bush. It is of many colors, rangin from exquisite pastel greens to violent, bleeding reds. Ther is blue coral, orange, purple, gray, amethyst, and even no and then a bush of stark, black coral. Like human beings, grows white as it approaches death.

The officer broke off a branch of living coral and hande it to me. It was purple, and was composed of a stony bas already calcified. Next that was a pulpy, mineral segmen pale white in color. The extreme tip was almost purely veg etable. It exuded a sticky milk which smelled noxiously. Ove all were suction caps like those on the tentacles of an octopu They were potential tips which had not matured.

It was impossible to believe that this tiny organism and i stony shell had raised the island on which we stood and wa at that moment raising thousands of new islands throughou the Pacific, most of which would never break the waves but would remain subterranean palaces of rare wonder. It was equally difficult to believe that the evil smelling whitish milk would shortly go to work for the SeaBees!

The days dragged on. I say little of Pearlstein, but I heard that he had run into all sorts of trouble. On the seventh day he got more than his share. A Jap bomber came over, one of nine that tried, and laid an egg right on Pearlstein's steam shovel. Killied two men and wounded one. The shovel was wrecked. I was sent up to see what I could do to get him another.

Pearlstein had tears in his eyes. "Goddam it all," he said. "You try and try! Then something like this happens!" He surveyed the ruined shovel. I knew little about machinery, but it seemed to me that the shovel was not too badly wrecked. After the dead bodies were removed, we studied what was left of the machinery.

"Billis?" I asked. "Couldn't you run that without the controls? I mean, couldn't you counterweight it with a tractor? The boom still works."

Billis and his men looked at the complex job I had set them. "It could be done, sir," the dirty fat man said. "But it would take . . ."

"Let's start right away!" Pearlstein cried when he perceived what might be done. "Look, fellows. All we'll have to do is bulldoze the coral over here. We won't move the shovel again. Let's see what we can do!" I left Pearlstein, bare to the waist, high up the boom of the shovel, loosening some bolts.

At night we could hear shots in the jungle. Some men swore that Japs had infiltrated the lines and stolen food. Others were afraid to sleep. But gradually the lines were pushed back and back. There were now apparently no Japs within the knee. And Marines had landed at each tip, so that two tightly compressing pockets were all that remained for the yellow men.

On the eighth day New Zealanders put on a terrific air show for us. Two squadrons of Jap fighters came over and shot us up fairly badly. Eight men were wounded and three killed. But the New Zealanders, in their crushing style, drove the Japs into the sea. Everybody stopped work, of course, and we counted seven Jap planes crash either in the sea or on Konora. One wild Jap tried to crash on the airstrip but instead crashed into the coral hill, where he completely demolished Pearlstein's improvised shovel and injured four men.

That night we had a hurried meeting. It was decided that the steam shovel at the live coral pits should be moved to the hillside. For if the gully was not filled, it mattered little whether live coral were available or not. Therefore, at 2100 a strange procession set out across Konora. Billis rode in front on his favorite bulldozer. Any tree that might hinder passage of the steam shovel was knocked over. It was astonishing to me how easily a huge tree could be uprooted and shoved aside. Billis later told me it was because the roots had nowhere to go. They could not penetrate the coral.

Slowly, with horrible noises, we inched our way along the jungle trails. At one place water had collected and the bulldozer bogged down. We waited an hour till another came to haul it free. Then together, like monsters, they shoved tree after tree into that depression. Slowly, the giant shovel edged its way onto the bridge, into the middle and across. By that time Billis was on ahead, knocking down a banyan.

At the foot of the hill six tractors threw down cables and inched the shovel up the incline. At dawn it was in place. At dawn a smart young ensign at the live coral pits had completed a platform arrangement whereby dredge loads could be emptied directly into trucks. At dawn work went on.

All this time Commander Hoag was a great, restless reservoir of energy. He worked with all hands, helped to build the platform at the live coral pits. He was constantly with the wounded and had to bite his lip when he watched a fine young friend lose a leg. But mostly he was on the airstrip. It progressed so slowly. God, it crawled along!

Starting from either end two companies with tractors had knocked down all the trees and pushed them into the southern extremities of the ravine. Hoag would not permit trees to be used as filler for the airstrip itself. That must be coral. Next the foot or so of topsoil was bulldozed away to block the highest section of the ravine. In this way the normal flow of rain water was diverted into the ocean without crossing the strip. That left a long, fine stretch of native coral rock, broken in the middle by the ravine.

Again starting from either end, bulldozers slowly pushed the top layer of coral toward the ravine. By that time Pearlstein's trucks were beginning to roll. Coral from the hillside rumbled to the airstrip twenty-four hours a day. At the same time, live coral from the sea was hauled to the two ends. Six steam rollers worked back and forth constantly. At the north side of the strip, a company of carpenters built a control tower. Electricians had already completed two identical power plants and were installing flood lights. From then on day and night were the same on Konora.

As yet no one but Hoag was sure the airstrip would be completed on time. With his permission I sent Admiral Kester a message telling him to schedule bombers for the field at the appointed time. On the sixteenth day the bombers would be there! We wondered if there would be a field for them to land on?

At this point a wonderful thing happened. Luther Billis disappeared for two days! We thought he was dead, lying somewhere in the bush, but on the evening of the second day he appeared in camp with two Japanese Samurai swords. He gave one to Commander Hoag just before he was thrown into the brig. After dinner the Marine commandant came over and asked if Commander Hoag wouldn't please drop charges against Billis. It seems some Marines had been saying how tough they were, and Billis listened for a while and then bet them that he could go down the west leg and get himself a sword, which they wouldn't be able to do down the east leg. It seems that Billis had won, and it wasn't quite right, the Marines thought, that he should be punished. Besides, he told them where the Jap camp was.

Commander Hoag thought for a while and released the "big dealer." Billis told us all about it. Seems his old lady ran a newsstand in Pittsburgh. He sent her a Jap ear from Guadal and she hung it up in the store. People came from all over to see it. He'd promised her a Jap sword, too, so he thought he'd better be getting one. He was going to send it to Pittsburgh. What Commander Hoag did with his was the old man's worry.

That night we had torrential rains. Floodlights on the field silhouetted men working in water up to their ankles. The gully, thank heavens, held. The dirt and trees had really diverted the rains. In the morning there was hardly any sign of water. Men who had slept through the deluge refused to believe there had been one.

By this time the milk trucks were running. The drivers were subjected to merciless ridicule, especially one who forgot to turn the spigots off and arrived with an empty truck. That day one of Pearlstein's drivers coming down the hill at a great clip, overturned and was killed. The truck was ruined beyond repair. A SeaBee was then stationed at the dangerous spot to warn drivers to keep their speed down, but next day another truck went right on over. The driver merely broke both legs, but the truck was wrecked.

"I can't make them slow down!" Lieut. Pearlstein objected. "They know the schedule!"

The Japs knew the schedule, too, apparently, for they started sending large numbers of bombers over at night plus four or five solitary nuisance raiders. "We'll have to turn off the lights," Commander Hoag reluctantly decided. But when work lagged way behind schedule, he announced that the twenty-four hour shift would be resumed.

American night fighters were sent to help us. They knocked down two Jap fighters the first night we kept the lights on, and from then on not one SeaBee was killed by bombing. Men working on the strip could not praise our aviators enough. It was a good feeling, having Yank fighters upstairs.

On the morning of the fifteenth day Lieut. Pearlstein, gaunt, unshaven, and nervous, reported to Commander Hoag. "You can finish the airstrip, sir. The gully won't take any more coral." Hoag said nothing. Held out his hand and shook Pearlstein's warmly. As the lieutenant was about to leave, Hoag made a suggestion.

"Why don't you sleep on one of the ships tonight? You could use some rest."

That afternoon a strange insident occurred, one which I have thought about time and again. An SBD flying medium high cover tangled with a Jap intruder and shot it down. The Nip went flaming into the sea. They always tried to hit the runway, but this one failed. Before he took his last long fling, however, he did manage to pepper the SBD, and the pilot had a difficult choice to make. He could try a water landing, or he could head for the uncompleted field.

"Clear the middle of the strip!" he called to the tower. "I'm coming in."

When his intention was apparent, Commander Hoag became almost insane with fury. "Stop that plane!" he shouted to the operations officer, but the officer ignored him. Hoag had no right to give such an order. Trembling, he watched the SBD approach, swerve badly when the unfilled portion loomed ahead, and slide past on a thin strip that had been filled.

The enlisted men cheered wildly at the superb landing. They stormed around the plane. Brandishing his revolver, Commander Hoag shouted that everyone was to go back to work immediately. He was like a wild man.

From the cockpit of the SBD climbed Bus Adams. He grinned at me and reached for the commander's hand. "You had no right to land here!" Hoag stormed. "I expressly forbade it. Look at the mess you've made!"

Adams looked at me and tapped his forehead. "No, no!" I wigwagged.

"Get that plane off the strip at once. Shove it off if you have to!" Hoag shouted. He refused to speak further to Bus. When the plane had been pulled into a revetment by men who wondered how Bus had ever brought her in, Commander Hoag stormed from the field.

That night he came to see Bus and me. He was worn and haggard. He looked like an old man. He would not sit with us, nor would he permit us to interrupt his apology: "For six weeks I've done nothing but plan and fight to have this strip ready for bombers on the sixteenth day. We've had to fight rains, accidents, changes, and every damned thing else. Then this afternoon you land. I guess my nerves must have snapped. You see, sir," he said, addressing Bus, "we've lost a lot of men on this strip. Every foot has been paid for. It's not to be misused lightly."

He left us. I don't know whether he got any sleep that night for next morning, still haggard, he was up and waiting at 0700. It was the sixteenth day, and bombers were due from Guadalcanal and Munda. The gully was filled. On the seashore trucks were idle, and upon the hill the great shovel rested. On the legs of the island desperate Japs connived at ways to outwit Marines. And all over the Pacific tremendous preparations for taking Kuralei were in motion. It was a solemn day.

Then, from the east, specks appeared. They were! They were the bombers! In the radio tower orders were issued. The specks increased in size geometrically, fabulously. In grandeur they buzzed the field, finest in the Pacific. Then they formed a traffic circle and the first bomber to land on Konora roared in. The strip was springy, fine, borne up by living coral, and the determination of free men. At this precise moment three

Japanese soldiers who had been lurking near the field in starving silence dashed from their cover and tried to charge the bomber.

Two were shot by Marines, but the third man plunged madly on. Screaming, wild, disheveled, his eyes popping from his horrible head, this primitive indecent thing surged on like his inscrutable ancestors. Clutching a grenade to his belly and shouting *Banzai,* he threw himself forward and knocked Commander Hoag to the ground.

The grenade exploded! It took the mad Jap to a heaven reserved for the hara-kiri boys. It took Commander Hoag, a free man, a man of thought and dignity, a man for whom other men would die . . . This horrible, indecent, meaningless act of madness took Hoag to his death. But above, the bombers wheeled and came in for their landings, whence they would proceed to Kuralei, to Manila, and to Tokyo.

Those Who Fraternize

"THE loneliness! The longing!" An aviator was throwing words into the cool night at Konora. We knew the landing on Kuralei was not far off. We were thinking of hungry things.

One of the words hit Bus Adams. "Damn!" he cried. "I tell you! Sometimes out here I've had a longing that almost broke my guts in two." Stars blazed over the silent lagoon. "To bomb a Jap ship! To see a football game in the snow. To kiss the Frenchman's daughter."

The last bottle of beer had been drained. It was time to go to bed, but we stayed on beneath the coconut trees. Bus watched Orion upside down in the topsy-turvy sky. "Have I ever told you about the Frenchman's daughter?" he asked. We leaned forward. A Frenchman! And his daughter! It sounded like a fine, sexy story. In many ways it was.

There were two houses at Luana Pori—Bus began. There was the Red House for enlisted men. In there the charge was five dollars, and you had to wait in line. At the Green House the charge was ten dollars, but business was conducted more or less on a higher tone. The Green House was for officers, of course.

From what I hear the Red House was a sordid affair. The girls were mostly Javanese or half-caste Melanesians. True, a couple of pretty French girls were kept as bait, but at the Red House you didn't bother much about looks. After all, it wasn't an art gallery.

The girls at the Green House were of a different sort. They could talk with you in English, play the tinny piano, and even serve tea in the society manner. With them it was a matter of professional pride to include in their operations some of the social refinements. Might be a dance, a bridge party, or a tea. Even a formal dinner. At the Green House you didn't just go up and knock on the door and ask for the girls. If you had done that a surprised elderly French lady would have appeared and shown real confusion. There were various ways of getting to visit the Green House. In time you discovered what they were. If you were interested.

Right here I want to make one point perfectly clear. The Frenchman's daughter had nothing to do with the two houses at Luana Pori. Of that I am convinced. I know that Lt. Col. Haricot thought he had proof that she owned them. I don't believe it. And as for her father-in-law's wild charge that his son met her in the Pink House, down in Noumea . . . well, he was a crazy old coot who would have said anything. You know that he finally beat his brains out against the wall of his prison cell. Actually.

The girl was part Javanese. She was about twenty-three, weighed less than a hundred pounds, and was five feet three. She was slim, wiry, and self-confident. She had wide shoulders and thin hips. Her fingers were very strong. A Marine said that when she stroked an old man's cheek "it was like she was playing the violin."

She had a small head, but not a pinhead, you understand. She made it seem smaller by wearing her hair parted in the middle and drawn tightly over her ears. She had many variations of this hair-do. The one I liked best was when she tucked a frangipani behind her left ear. You know the frangipani? A white, waxy flower. Very sweet. Looks like the dogwood. But darker. The same way she looked like all the beautiful girls you've ever known. But darker.

Her old man was the planter I told you about. Quite a character. Lived up north. Her mother was a Javanese servant girl. It was hard to tell which of her parents she was like. She was an Oriental, that's true. She had the slant eyes. But she had French traits, too. Like her old man she was clever, witty, pensive, industrious, hot-tempered, and—well—pretty damned sexy. In a nice way, you understand. Nothing rough! At other times she was mystical and brooding, silent as a cat. She got these things from her Buddhist mother.

I met her, said Bus, in the damnedest way. Put into the airstrip at Luana Pori and borrowed a jeep. I drove up past the two houses to her plantation. You know, white picket fence and big flower garden. "Madame Barzan," I said. "Up north. A pilot was shot down. He died. Not in my arms exactly. But he told me . . ."

She smiled at me with her little head on one side. "I hear all about you, Mister Bus Adams. At the airport they say, 'He one good guy.' Knock off that stuff, Bus. You like to have dinner here tonight?"

I think, said Bus, everyone who dined with Latouche Barzan will agree that dinner with her was a memorable affair. On her plantation were many small houses. What they were all for I never knew. One was a marvelous salon. It was made of woven bamboo, floor, roofing and side panels. In it were twelve or fifteen chairs, four small tables, three long benches and a bar. Before dinner we gathered there for drinks.

You could find most of the officers on Luana Pori at Latouche's. Everyone was welcome. We all loved to watch her placid Oriental mask break into naughty French lights and shadows when she was teasing some elderly colonel for some tires for her Australian car or a truckload of oil for her generator. She would pout and suck in her high cheeks. And then, if you were a man standing near her, you had to fight hard to keep from kissing her. She knew this, for I've often seen her rub very close to some older officer and laugh at his dumb jokes until I'm sure the old fool's head was in a whirl. That was how she got so much of the equipment she needed.

"Ah, major!" she would pout. "I like to build one small house for butcher. How I gonna get some cement? You got some Portland Cement?"

Not that she was stingy with her money. As you'll see, she fed half the American Army on Luana Pori. But there wasn't anything to spend money on. If the Army had cement . . . Well, it was only sensible to invite the Army to dinner.

"Bus?" she asked me one night. "Where I get some Remington .22 shells?"

"What in the world do you want with .22 shells?" I asked.

"For shoot wild chickens! How you think we catch wild chicken we serve here all time? Salt on his tail?" She laughed softly at her joke.

No matter what you paid for her dinners, they were worth it. A door lock, an ice machine, new copper wiring, an aviation clock set in mahogany from a propeller. They were well spent.

About seven in the evening Noé, the Javanese servant, would announce dinner in a high voice. We would then pass from the salon to the dining house. This was severely plain, with one very long table made of jungle planks rubbed brown. Latouche sat the head of table. I sat beside her, at first. While we waited for the soup to be served there was a moment of great anticipation. Then Latouche's three sisters entered.

First was Josephine. She was nineteen. More Javanese than Latouche. Slim and with breasts you could sleep on forever. She was engaged to a Marine sergeant. He pulled the engagement gag so he could live with her while he was on Luana Pori. But when he almost got killed on Konora, he became like a wild man. His C.O. let him hitch-hike back more than two thousand miles to marry her. She was like that.

Laurencin was seventeen. Beautiful like Latouche. Marthe was only fifteen when I first saw her. She was the queen of the group. Having lived among older men from the beginning of the war, she had acquired some damned cute little ways. She knew this and kept her soft almond eye directed down toward her plate. Then once or twice each meal she would raise them at some young officer and knock him silly with her charm. There was a good deal of food spilt at Luana Pori, mostly by young men looking at Marthe.

Latouche served excellent meals. She butchered a beef at least twice a week, had her natives scour the woods for wild chicken and the shore for sea food. Occasionally, when American hunters bagged a deer up in the hills she would cook it for them. And whenever a food ship arrived from the States, someone would always manage to steal a truckload of steaks and turkeys and corned beef and succotash and sneak it into Latouche's shed at night and whisper, "Our steward is a louse! He can't cook water. Uses no spices at all!"

"Ah, well!" Latouche would sympathize. "In the jungle!

What you expect? I give this to Noé! We see what he can do with it."

When dinner was over Latouche led her guests back to the salon, where six or seven attractive French women of the islands were waiting. I never clearly understood who these girls were, where they ate their meals, or how they got to the plantation. They always went home in jeeps.

The introductions over, Latouche would slip back to the dining house, where I waited for her. "Who are those girls?" I asked one night as she curled up in a chair with me.

She smiled, a Javanese sort of smile. "I like men," she said. "American men I like very much. Is no good men by themselves all the time." I understand not less than six marriages resulted from Latouche's dinners.

But for me the best part came when Noé finished removing the dishes and took the pressure lamp back to the kitchen. Then Latouche and I sat in the shadowy darkness of the dining house and played records on the old Victrola her father had brought her from Australia. She loved American music. I had to laugh. I used to sit there in the dark and think of wives of colonels and majors back home telling their bridge clubs, "John gets so lonesome on the islands. The children and I sent him some records last week." And there they were, in Latouche's white dining house.

There were also some Javanese records. I loved those crazy melodies, especially when Latouche accompanied the wailing music in a sing-song voice. When she grew tired, she would kiss me softly in the ear and whisper, "This next one for Mister Bus Adams, special." Then she would play Yvonne Printemps' French recording of "Au clair de la lune." She said it was an old record. The machine was not good, and the needle scratched. But the music sounded fine there at the edge of the jungle. You know how it goes. *Dum-dum-dum-dum-dum-dum.* The girl's name is spelled Printemps, but you say it Pran-tom. You don't sound the final *ps*, and she can really sing.

The last record was for Latouche. Then I kissed her, and she closed her eyes, and I could feel her shivering, but not from love. By the way, have you ever heard Hildegarde sing "The last time I saw Paris"? Not much of a song, but brother, when you hear it in a bamboo room, with Latouche Barzan twisting nervously in your arms . . .

"Bus?" she whispered. "Paris? What it like?"

I would try to tell her. I made up a lot, for she was mad to know about Paris. All I remembered was wide beautiful streets and narrow crooked ones. I recalled something about the opera there, the Louvre, and Notre Dame. Mostly I had to think of movies I had seen. Once I got started on the Rue Claude Bernard, where I used to live near a cheese market. I embroidered that street until even the cheese merchant wouldn't have known it. But it was worth it, for when the music stopped and my voice with it, Latouche would kiss me wildly and cry, "Oh, Bus! I wish you not married. I wish my husban' he dead. You and I we get married . . ."

"Latouche!" I whispered. "For God's sake, don't talk like that."

"Why not? I wish my husban' he dead up there in the hills. Then everything all right. I marry some nice American."

"Stop it!"

"Whatsamatter, Bus? You no wish your wife she dead sometime?"

"It's not funny, Latouche!" I protested. My forehead was wet.

"I not say it funny," she mused, quietly buttoning her dress. "I talk very serious. When you kissing me? When you taking my dress off? I s'pose you never wish your wife dead?"

I felt funny inside. You know how it is. You're out in the islands. You have a wife, but you don't have a wife. Sometimes the idea flashes through your head . . . Without your thinking it, understand. And you draw back in horror. "What in hell am I saying? What kind of a man am I, anyway?" And all the time a girl like Latouche is in your arms, her black hair about your face, the smell of frangipani everywhere. And when she hammers that question at you, as if she were the horrible little voice . . . Man, you take a deep breath and you don't answer.

I didn't blame Latouche for wanting her husband dead. Achille Barzan was a pretty poor sort, the son of French peasants who had been deported to Noumea years before for some crime, no one remembered what. They had chopped their plantation from the jungle. Alone they planted coconut trees and nursed cacao bushes into trees. They lived like less than pigs for eight years, getting no returns, going deeper into debt. Then, just as the plantation started to make money, their son married Latouche De Becque, bastard daughter of a renegade Frenchman who lived with one colored girl after another. Their only comfort was that Latouche had brought a dowry. Her father stole it from some planter up north. And the girl was good-looking.

"Too good-looking!" old Madame Barzan observed. "She'll bring sorrow to our son. Mark my words."

The old woman had early detected Latouche's willfulness. It was no surprise to her, therefore, when Achille had to knock her down and forbid her to visit Noumea. Nor could the family do anything to make her stop ridiculing old Pétain. The Barzans, mother, father, son, saw clearly that only the grim marshal's plan of work and discipline could save France.

"Why, look!" Achille said. "Every De Gaullist in the islands is what Pétain said in his speech. Undisciplined!" In Noumea, where people understood such things, most substantial men were Pétainists. Only the rabble were De Gaullists. Latouche herself was proof of that. A half-caste! A bastard half-caste, too! You might as well call her a De Gaullist. The words meant about the same.

The Barzans were pleasantly surprised, therefore, when Latouche suddenly became disciplined, accepted her husband's judgment, and became a respectable Pétainist. They were even more surprised when two boats put into the bay and a group of fiery men, led by Latouche's own father, stormed ashore and placed everyone under arrest. Everyone, that is, except Achille, who fled to the jungle.

"There they are!" Latouche reported icily. Standing before the two miserable Barzans she denounced them. "They want to give up," she said with disdain.

"Take them away," Latouche's father ordered.

At this old Madame Barzan's peasant mind snapped. "Thief! Whore!" she screamed, beating at Latouche with her bare hands. An undersized De Gaullist from Efate tried to stop her outcries, but old man Barzan thought his wife was being attacked. Grabbing a stick of wood, he lunged at the little man and beat him over the head.

"Throw them in jail!" Latouche's father commanded.

Madame Barzan, gabbling of "thieves and murderers and whores," died in the boat. The old man remained in jail. The little fellow he had beaten was still affected after two years. His head jerked and he couldn't pronounce the letter *s*.

Latouche rarely spoke of the wretched family. She brought her three sisters to the plantation before the Americans came. She reasoned that the Yanks would occupy Luana Pori. She

wanted her sisters ready. Even during the agonizing days of
the Coral Sea battles she refused to move inland. "I think
Americans, they win. If they lose, I finished anyway. Japs
probably make that dirty bastard Achille Barzan commissioner
of Luana Pori, I s'pose."

Shortly after she told me about her husband I left the Navy
camp and moved up to the plantation. Latouche and I had
one of the little white houses among the flower gardens. It
was made of bamboo, immaculately clean. Six or eight of
Latouche's dresses hung along one wall. On the other was a
colored print showing a street in Paris. Six books were on
the wicker table. *Gone with the Wind* and five Tauchnitz
editions of German novels. There were two chairs, one covered with flowered chintz.

Latouche and I were very happy in that little house. Mostly
she wore a halter made of some cheap print from Australia
and a pair of expensive twill shorts a colonel had got her
from Lord and Taylor's, in New York. She went barefooted.
We slept through the hot afternoons, waiting for the crowd
to come out for dinner. Noé would bring us cold limeades,
slipping into the little house whether we were dressed or not.

I often try to recall what I wrote my wife during those
days. "Darling: The deep sores on my wrists are better now.
It is cooler on this island." But the sores that ate at my
heart, I didn't tell her about them.

It was about this time that Lt. Col. Haricot led his raid on
the plantation. He stormed into the salon one night about
seven and stood at attention like a gauleiter. "Everything on
this plantation stolen from the United States government will
be hauled away tomorrow morning," he announced. He even
clapped his hands, and a very young lieutenant made a note
of the order. Then he nodded to a French woman much
older than Latouche and started to go.

"But I own everything," Latouche said, interrupting his
passage.

"Are you the madame's daughter?" he asked, pompously.

"I am the madame!" Latouche replied, nodding. "Madame
Barzan!"

Haricot, who had been given his job of civil affairs officer
because of a year's French he'd had in Terre Haute high
school, bowed low and said, "Eh, bien, Madame Barzan . . ."

"I know!" Latouche cried. "I know very well, Colonel

aricot. You think I some mean old woman steal govern-
ent property from U.S.A." She pouted at him.

"No," he replied cajolingly. "Not steal. But you have it all
e same, and I've got to get it back."

"What you think you take?" Latouche asked, her chin
uck out.

"That electric generator," Haricot replied.

"Colonel Hensley gave me that." The colonel was taken
oack by the name.

"He had no right to do that," he blustered.

"And I have it rebuilt," Latouche insisted. "No damn good
hen I get it. Salvaged! See, I got bills right here. I no s'pose
ou take that away, Colonel Haricot!"

"Everything goes tomorrow morning. We start at nine
'clock. This stealing of government property has got to stop."
le clicked his heels again and left. He'd teach these French-
en a thing or two.

Of course, we worked half the night hiding G.I. gear all
rough the jungle. In the morning Haricot appeared with
is men and hauled away the odds and ends we had over-
ooked. But they didn't take the generator! Latouche calmly
aded a Marine revolver with American ball cartridges, and
ood guard over the power plant. Haricot studied her wryly
or a moment and ordered his men elsewhere.

When the work was completed the colonel appeared in the
alon. "Gentlemen," he said dramatically. "This place is now
ff limits. A guard has been posted! You will all leave!"

Sure enough, at the white picket fence two soldiers stood
uard with automatic rifles. "The heat's on!" an officer whis-
ered to me, but that night we all sneaked back along the
ore for dinner in the bare room. Latouche was pleasant and
ven happy.

"I jus' find out the colonel is not married! I think we have
ome very good fun with him!"

The fun started when the sergeant in charge of the guard
pplied to the colonel for permission to marry Mlle. Marthe
e Becque. "Who's she?" the colonel asked. "Some little tart?"

'She's Madame Barzan's sister, sir."

"You mean up at the plantation?"

"Yes, sir!"

"Damn it all! I told you to guard the place, not invade it.
ow long has this been going on?"

"I fell in love with her."

"What were you doing inside the gates?"

"I wasn't inside the gates, sir! She came outside. That i after I went inside."

"What in the world goes on here?" the confused colone shouted. "You jump in that jeep!"

Latouche greeted Haricot with demure attention. "Some thing missing at the camp?" she asked.

"Sir?" the colonel bellowed at me. "What are you doin here?"

"Problem at the PT base, sir," I explained. "Importa business."

"Oh!" the colonel replied. After all, it was customary fc the Navy to have a lieutenant doing what a colonel did i the Army. He studied me and then turned toward Latouche

"Army in trouble, Colonel Haricot?" she asked.

"This man says he wants to marry your sister."

"My sister? Laurencin? Noé!" she called. "Send Laurencin.

"It's Marthe," the sergeant protested, but Latouche ig nored him.

"You shut up!" the colonel ordered.

Soon Laurencin, blushing prettily, entered the room. She like her sister, had a sprig of frangipani in her hair.

"What's this I hear, Laurencin?" Latouche demande abruptly. "You fall in love with this boy?"

"It's Marthe!" the sergeant protested.

"You be still!" Haricot thundered. He was rather enjoyin the scene. By heavens, he could understand how the youn fellow . . .

Laurencin held up her frail hands. "I never seen him be fore," she said.

"What's that?" Haricot demanded.

"It's her sister!" the sergeant said again.

"I know it's her sister," the colonel shouted.

"Oh!" Latouche cried in mock embarrassment. "Oh, Colo nel Haricot!" She gently pushed the colonel in the chest. "O course! My other sister! Noé! Ask Marthe to come in!" Sh took the colonel by the arm and pressed quite closely to hin "Come over to this chair," she suggested. "It's warm today.

When Marthe came in there was no acting. She went t the sergeant and held his hand. Colonel Haricot, buttered u by now, smiled at the young girl. "And what is your name?

"Marthe," the girl replied.

"And you want to marry my sergeant?"

"Yes."

"Well, you can't do it!" Haricot blustered. "Too many marriages out here. Bad for morale."

This turn of events pleased Latouche highly. She did not want Marthe marrying the first boy she met. As a matter of fact, Latouche had her eye on Haricot as a very proper husband for either Laurencin or Marthe. He had money, was not ugly, and looked as if his wife could manage him pretty easily.

"You hear what the good American officer says, Marthe?" Latouche asked, shrugging her shoulders. "You cannot get married!" Latouche patted the sergeant on the arm. "It's maybe better." Then she returned to Colonel Haricot and brushed against him several times. "I s'pose maybe it's best if the sergeant doesn't stand guard any more. My sisters are so pretty. Always the men fall in love with them."

"Ah, no! The guard remains!" The colonel bowed stiffly as he had seen Prussians do when delivering unpleasant ultimatums to French girls in the movies.

Before we went to sleep that afternoon I whispered, "That's a mean trick."

"Marthe's all right," Latouche replied, fluffing her hair across the pillow. "Do her good. Girls got to learn about men. Got to learn fast these days!" She laughed and started to hum "The last time I saw Paris . . ."

"You better keep your eye on Marthe," I said. "The girl's in love."

"Skipper?" she asked. "What's Paris like in winter? Snow?"

I tried to recall. So far as I knew, it was just like any other city in the cold. I was about to say this when I remembered an opera I had seen in New York. *La Bohème.* A Spanish girl sang it. In the third act, I think, this Spanish girl is trying to meet a soldier in a snowstorm. I told Latouche about it, and the little guard house. She rose on one elbow. Her eyes flashed as if she actually saw Paris in the snow. When I stopped speaking she cried, "Oh, Bus!" and the wildness of her emotion made the little house creak until I was sure it could be heard in the salon.

That night Lt. Col. Haricot returned to the plantation. I could guess what turmoil had brought him back. He said to himself, "I'll go back there and look the place over. See that the guards are on duty. See that everything's on the up and up." I'm sure that's why he thought he was coming back.

But when he entered the dining house and found a dinner party in progress, he was taken off guard. "I . . ." He sputtered a bit. Then he became ashamed of himself and his motives. He snapped to attention and said in low, harsh tones, "Madame Barzan! If you don't quit this, I'll close this joint up forever. And," he threatened darkly, "I'll close your two houses up there on the hill, too!"

Like an angry cat Latouche sprang at the man and slapped his face four times. Then she kicked him in the legs. I was the first at her side and pulled her away. "Never say that, Colonel Haricot!" she hissed, trembling in my arms. "They not my houses! Next time I kill you!"

The colonel was astounded. He absolutely did not know what to think. He had never associated with women who slapped and kicked. He never met such women in Terre Haute. In his world when a house was put off bounds, it was off bounds. No right-thinking officer would trespass. But here on Luana Pori everything was different. Even officers ignored the rules of common decency.

He turned sharply and left the dining room. At the wicket gate he stopped and gave the sentries strict orders to shoot if any officers tried to leave the plantation. Then he drove hurriedly down the road.

"He can raise plenty of trouble," a captain said.

"He not gonna do nothin'," Latouche replied.

"Why are you so sure?"

"The colonel all messed up inside," Latouche said simply. She reached over and patted Laurencin's hand. "He get himself fixed up pretty soon. He's all right."

At that moment Colonel Haricot was pacing up and down his bare office at the base. He was trying to dictate an order arresting all military personnel at the plantation. The words wouldn't come. "Oh, go to bed!" he told his typist. "What was it, after all?" he asked himself. "I insulted a young woman and she slapped my face. I never insulted a woman before in my life. My Mother taught me better than that. That girl had a right to slap me." He began to build up a pretty impressive case for Latouche. But he knew that his authority was being flouted. And he loved authority.

"Corporal!" he shouted. That sleepy fellow came back to the bare office. "Oh, go on back to bed!" the colonel said.

"Wish he'd make up his mind," the corporal muttered.

"I'm sorry," the colonel shouted. Deep within him a voice

ept saying over and over, *"They were having a good time. And I'm not having a good time. I've never had any fun since I left high school in Terre Haute. Maybe they sing after 'inner! Or maybe they just sit around and talk. There was othing wrong there tonight. And they were having a good ime."*

"I'll go back and apologize," he said firmly. "That's what Mother would tell me to do. I was terribly rude up there. 'll go back and apologize. Corporal! Corporal!"

At the gate the sentry challenged him. "It's me! Colonel Haricot. Anybody leave yet?"

"Oh, no sir!"

"Pretty scared in there, I guess?"

"Oh, yes, sir!"

When Haricot arrived we were all in the salon. The officers ose and bowed. Haricot was in his early forties and fat. His ump was quite round and bobbed grotesquely when he licked his heels before Latouche. "I have come to apologize," e said simply. "I acted like a fool."

Latouche rose, extended her lovely hand, and forgave him. She managed to brush against him hesitatingly as she did so. Col. Haricot made a motion as if he wished to sit down and apologize further. But Latouche had foreseen this. Gently wining her arm in his she said, "I am so sorry, Colonel Haricot. After you so nice to come back this way. I have engagement with the pilot here." Whereupon, with no further comment, she grabbed my arm and led me from the salon.

Outside she sprang into activity. "Noé!" she called in a ow voice. "Hurry! Find Laurencin!" When that frail girl, hen only seventeen, came up, Latouche hurriedly adjusted er sister's dress, straightened the flowers in her hair, and issed her. "Look pretty," she whispered. She patted Laurencin's hips, fluffed up the frills of her dress. "Now you' big hance!" She half slapped, half pushed the hesitating Laurencin toward the salon door where Colonel Haricot was preparing to leave. "Good luck, Laurencin," she whispered. "This ou' big chance!"

A few days later the guard was removed. This was a mistake, because one night the plantation was aroused by shooting. Latouche and I had already gone to bed. Colonel Haricot was in the garden with Laurencin. I hastily dressed and went out toward the sound of the shooting. To my surprise I found a naval officer in the salon. An enlisted man was arguing with him, trying to get a revolver away from him.

"Where's the girls?" the officer bellowed.

"Come on, Lieut. Harbison!" the enlisted driver begged.

"Don't pull me, son!" the drunken officer cried. He waved his gun at the serious enlisted man. Then, seeing me, he lurched across the salon to greet me. "Where's the girls?" he demanded.

"There are no girls here," I said.

"Don't give me that. I know you fliers! Keep everything for yourself! I know you. Girls used to be here. Plenty of them!" He banged into a post as I sidestepped him. The bamboo walls shook. Latouche appeared at this moment.

"There she is!" Harbison cried. "You remember me, baby! That time the PBY went down. You remember me!"

"Throw him out, Bus," Latouche said quietly.

"You try to throw me out!" Harbison bellowed. "Nothin' but a goddam whore-house. I know you, sister! I know you!"

I leaped at the intruder. But he saw me coming. With a quick football manner he sidestepped me, tripped me, and smashed me in the face as I went down. The revolver butt knocked my jaw loose, and I fainted.

About three o'clock in the morning I came to. I was in Latouche's little house. On the bed. And I had the strangest feeling. My jaw was numb. The Army doctor had shot it full of cocaine. And I thought I heard my old friend Tony Fry talking, from a great distance.

"I should never have brought that foul ball down here," Tony was saying. "But don't worry! Latouche and the enlisted man beat him up. Swell job."

My eyes closed with pain and Tony patted me on the head. "You tried, Bus," he said. "But you should see what the enlisted man did to Harbison. Latouche helped, too."

Later that night, when the room was empty, I heard Tony's voice again. He was talking to Latouche in that quiet, earnest way he had. He was saying, in French, "Paris is the city most lovely. I went there with my Mother as a little boy." And I knew by the silence that I would never sleep with Latouche again. The pain in my heart grew greater than the hurt in my face. I tried to bury myself beneath the covers, but the Army doctor had them pinned to the sheets.

When I awoke next morning a French woman about

twenty-five was fixing up the room. "Who are you?" I asked, through clenched teeth.

"Lisette," she replied.

"What are you doing here?"

"Latouche, she bring me up early this morning."

"What for?"

"For take care of you, Mister Bus." She motioned to an Army cot.

"Where'd you get that?"

"Colonel Haricot. He bring it up las' night." Lisette was pretty, plump, and kind. Her husband was in Africa. Hadn't been heard from since Bir Hacheim. She knew what a man down from the islands needed. They moved us out of Latouche's bedroom in about a week. When I could get around again I looked up two old parachutes for Lisette, one red, one white.

I didn't see either Tony or Latouche for three days after the brawl. They went to live in a little house near the edge of the jungle. Noé took them food. Finally, they came to see me. They motioned Lisette out of the room. Fry looked at me and said nothing. Latouche stood far from the bed and said in a hurried sing-song voice, "I sorry, Bus. You one good man. I wish I had a man like you. A good fighter. Tony tell me about you at Munda. What you do. I wish we meeting for the first time, Bus. No other husban'. No other wife. I sorry, Bus."

At night I would hear Tony at the small piano, picking out French tunes and themes from the operas. When the salon was empty, when Colonel Haricot's jeep had left, I would see Latouche dancing by herself among the chairs while Tony worked the small Army radio Colonel Haricot had given Laurencin.

"Come back to bed," Lisette would snap in French. "Leave them alone! Now Latouche has herself a man!"

I could not drag myself from spying. God, I don't know how I felt. But I would hear Lisette's soft voice again, in English: "Coming back to bed, Bus. It's her affair."

I should have stopped Tony right then. I knew he was fascinated by Latouche. But I never guessed at what would happen. With the rest of us, well, you know how it was. The girls were there. They were lonely. We had lots of money and Navy gear. It was a nice life.

But with Tony it was different. He learned to speak a little

Javanese. He went everywhere with Latouche as she supervised the plantation. Didn't show up at camp for days in a row. They sat on a bench in the garden and he read to her. Latouche, I'd never seen her the way she was then. She told him the history of the islands, how her father had come there as a boy. They talked in French, in English, and in broken Javanese. At night a light would burn in her little house till almost morning.

Our drowsy routine was broken when we found that Marthe was going to have a baby. "That sergeant!" Latouche sniffled. "That goddam sergeant!"

"Well," I said. "I told you this would happen."

"Oh, you!" she shouted hoarsely. "What good that do now?" She pulled Marthe tenderly into a big chair made of teakwood. "How this thing happen?" she asked softly.

"I love him," Marthe replied in French.

"Sure you love him!" Latouche agreed. "We always do. But how you do it?" Marthe buried her head on her sister's shoulder. Latouche rocked her back and forth. "How you do this thing?" she whispered.

"We get a room in the Green House," Marthe said.

Latouche sprang to her feet and threw Marthe to the floor. She kicked the pregnant girl and jumped upon her, slapping her face. Then, in great fury, she dashed to her bedroom and returned with her revolver. I dived at her and caught her by the wrist. I wrenched the revolver from her.

She panted heavily for a moment and then said, "We go now, Bus." I followed her to the jeep Colonel Haricot had loaned her. She climbed in. We drove to the Green House. Eight or ten cars stood outside.

Latouche left the jeep and strode up to the door. Inside we could hear the cheap piano and sounds of dancing. Latouche pushed the door wide open. The girls inside gasped as they saw her flashing beauty. "It's Madame Barzan!" they whispered, and drew back along the wall.

Latouche surveyed the garish room. Then, seeing the madame in a plush chair, she walked up, grabbed the plump middle-aged woman by the shoulders and dragged her to her feet.

"Damned fool!" Latouche hissed. She slapped the woman's face eight or ten times and gave her a brutal shove in the stomach. The whimpering madame fell backward into the chair. Latouche scowled over her. "Good thing the officer take away my gun. I kill you for sure! My sister in here!" She turned slowly and studied the room and its occupants. "We go!" she said.

Back at the plantation Latouche sought Marthe and told her she was sorry. She placed her arm about the lovely little girl and began to cry a little. "Is no good," she mumbled. "All this love-making with soldiers. Somebody get hurt. This time maybe it's you! How long you gone, Marthe?"

"Three month," the fifteen-year-old girl replied.

"Oh, mon Dieu!" Latouche sighed. "Well, what we can do, Tony? What you think? We make her get married?"

"We usually do in America," Tony replied. "We call it compounding the error."

From the snorts and puffings outside we judged that Colonel Haricot had arrived with the offending sergeant, whom he was giving some sound abuse. He entered the salon in the grand manner, bowed low to Latouche, and tenderly approached Marthe as if the poor child were already encouched.

"Well!" he shouted at the embarrassed sergeant. "What are you going to do about it?"

"I want to marry her," the sergeant said, stepping beside his pale sweetheart.

"It's about time!" the colonel snorted. Then he magnanimously grasped the sergeant's hand, adding in a voice of great emotion, "It's good to see a decent fellow play the man." The sergeant was bewildered. He had wanted to marry Marthe from the first day he had seen her.

At this moment Laurencin entered the salon. The colonel looked at her briefly and dropped his head, blushing furiously. "We are going to be married, too," he said.

"Oh, Colonel Haricot!" Latouche cried, as if she alone in the salon were surprised at this astonishing news. As senior naval officer present I was very crisp, very proper. I extended the congratulations of my service.

"I don't know what they'll say in Terre Haute!" Haricot chuckled. "But to the devil with them, whatever they say. You know, gentlemen, I've had more fun in this house . . . More honest-to-John fun . . ."

"That's true of a lot of us, colonel," Fry said.

"It's awful to think of leaving this plantation," Haricot confided.

"Moving north?"

"Yep," he replied. "I wrote to my Mother about Laurencin.

Her being half Javanese, you know. Mom was very broad-minded. Been giving money to missions all her life. A Baptist, Mom is. She said if she'd given all that money to save souls, she guessed some of them must be saved by now!" He nudged me and grinned broadly. "Get it?" he asked.

But the colonel put his foot down when a double wedding was suggested. "After all," he observed righteously, "there is a difference. A considerable difference." What it was that constituted the difference, his rank as compared with the sergeant's or Laurencin's virginity as compared with Marthe's family status, I never knew.

Latouche took me aside after the colonel had left and begged me to get her three old parachutes, one red, one yellow, and one white.

"I can't just go out and steal parachutes," I protested.

"You got two for Lisette," she reminded me.

"But she was special."

"I not something special?" she asked, pirouetting. She twirled near me and I tried to pull her into the shadows. She pushed me away. "You Tony's friend, I think," she said.

"Then ask Tony to get the parachutes."

"I can't, Bus! I want to surprise Tony." She ran her fingers down my shirt sleeve. And I knew I was in the parachute business.

Lt. Col. Haricot and Laurencin were married in the salon. An island missionary, a Baptist, officiated. Tony Fry was best man. I gave the bride away. As always, I had tears in my eyes. I'm a sucker for a wedding. Latouche, in a simple white store dress, stood inconspicuously with her sister.

But at the reception Latouche appeared in the doorway dressed in shimmering parachute silk. We all gasped! Not even if I was drunk could I imagine a girl so beautiful. She had taken my three old 'chutes and cut them into many pointed strips. Do you know parachute silk? Soft as a baby's breath. Well, she had made herself a sweeping gown that measured more than twenty-five yards around the hem. Yet the silk was so delicate that it came to a thin band about her tiny waist. She wore a bodice that seemed nothing at all. Up here she was framed in silk, and we didn't look at much but Latouche that night. Strange, but the clashing red and yellow colors blended delicately against her golden skin.

"You were mine, once, baby," I whispered to myself.

As she passed me in the salon she pressed my hand and

d in a hushed voice, "Meet me by the shed. Please." My
art thumped as I hastened down a dark path which led to
e little huts in which the Javanese workmen lived. Latouche
s waiting for me in the shadows. To my dismay, Tony was
th her. "A surprise!" she said.

There, ahead of us, in a hollow square formed by two huts,
e shed, and a bamboo screen, the local Buddhists had set
a temple. They were holding sacred ceremonials to honor
e marriage of Marthe De Becque and her American
geant.

In the darkness two teak logs had been placed upright
out twenty feet apart. Between them were nailed three wide
k planks, one above the other, to form an altar. White
ths were placed over each plank. Candles flickered on the
most cloth. Four bronze objects, like plates, glistened on
e lower planks.

On a finely woven mat in front of the altar an old Buddhist
iest, in white pants and black silk coat, knelt and prayed.
a either side of him, sitting cross-legged, were two other
vanese, also in black. One hammered a small drum in irreg-
ar rhythms. The other tapped a tinkling bell at intervals.
time the drum and the bell filled our minds and seemed
echo all about us.

We sat upon the ground. In ghastly and uncertain light
m flickering candles Marthe and the sergeant stood before
e priest. Women from the plantation, Javanese prostitutes
m the two houses, and old men from the cacao bins
aned in the night. The drum and bell beat on.

The priest rose and blessed the couple before him. Upon
arthe he placed the special blessing of fertility, a kind of
iestly second-guessing. An old Javanese next to Tony ex-
ained the meaning of the rites. Fry, who was learning the
guage, replied sagely.

The drum beat on. The tinkling bell haunted my ears when
became aware of a disturbance behind me. Suddenly there
s shouting in Javanese and then bold words in French.

"Mon Dieu!" Latouche cried and became pale.

"This is it!" Fry whispered, licking his thin lips.

Into the holy place strode a gaunt Frenchman. Achille
rzan was down from the hills. "Idolaters!" he shouted.
hieves! Adulterers!" He rushed toward the altar and
ocked it over. Then seeing Latouche in her brilliant dress
lunged at her. I interceded. Barzan struck me with a heavy

club. I stumbled backward. I thought my arm was broke

Seeing this, Latouche screamed and rushed from the e
closure. Her flowing gown caught in the bamboo screen a
pulled it down. Her flying skirt flashing in the candlelig
she rushed up the hill toward the safety of her white hou
Although my arm was aching, I tried to stop Barzan. I ma
a football dive for him but bumped into Tony Fry instea
If I had been quicker on my feet, I might have stopped
tragedy.

For Latouche did not reach her room in time to lock t
door. In a wild burst of fury Achille Barzan pushed his w
into the white house. Swinging his club over his head,
lunged at his wife. There were four pistol shots. Barza
stumbling backward, clutched twice at the stars, and fell dea

In the long questioning that ensued Lt. Col. Haricot w
superb. The French interrogators liked him. He had a Fren
name and could speak their language badly enough to w
both their respect and pity. He was also a moral man, a m
of sentiment.

He insisted that Latouche had acted in self-defense. Th
she was a proper and well brought up girl. That Achi
Barzan was a bully and a tyrant. That Achille was a dir
dog and a Pétainist as well. "Nothing to do with the case
the commissioner said.

"It shows he was without honor!" Haricot insisted. Th
colonel spoke for both Tony and me. We were not allowe
to testify, for example, that we even knew where her roo
was. I was not asked if I had heard her threaten to kill tw
different persons. Nor did I speak about her wish that h
husband was dead. No, we were model witnesses.

"Had Tony Fry been a frequent visitor at the plantation'
He had. "Was he, what you might call . . ." Oh, no, he w
not! "Had he ever, what you might say . . ." Never! "The
colonel, what was he doing at the plantation?" The colon
blustered and asked Fry what he was doing there. "Learni
to speak Javanese." "Could the lieutenant speak a litt
Javanese?" He could and he would. "What did the lieutena
say, interpreter?" He said, "Copra will stay high if the Unite
States keeps on buying."

At this point Colonel Haricot pointed out four facts. "Ha
Achille Barzan threatened his wife?" He had. "Had he trie
to break the American pilot's arm?" He had. "Had he raise

club to strike his wife?" Nine witnesses saw that. "Had she
not him in self-defense?" Obviously.

Bien! What can one say? Especially when this fellow Hari-
ot keeps talking all the time? Well, commissioner? Well . . .
es . . . Of course, Madame Barzan must be arrested, yes.
mere formality. Colonel Haricot's testimony has already
ken care of that.

When news of the tragedy reached old Papa Barzan in
rison he went wild with sorrow and cursed Latouche far into
e night. He screamed that his son had met her in Pink
ouse in Noumea. That she was an evil devil. But the old
llow was deranged. That's clear from what happened a few
ays later when he heard that Latouche had been released.
he old man backed up and dashed himself against the wall
ur times until he broke his neck.

Of course, Colonel Haricot had to leave Luana Pori. He
ad, in a sense, disgraced the Army. Marrying a half-caste.
lixed up in a murder. He kissed Laurencin lovingly before
e left, and prayed to God that he left in her womb a
aughter as lovely as she.

Josephine's sailor came up here to Konora. He helped to
ake our beachhead against the Japs. One night he almost
ent mad, for he saw among the coconut trees torn and
lasted by the shell fire, one that bent toward him like the
im Javanese girl on Luana Pori. They gave him permission
ter to fly back and marry her.

Marthe's sergeant was not so lucky. He stopped a bullet
a the surf right out there where you're looking. A friend
ho had raised hell when the sergeant married Marthe saw
im bouncing face-down on the coral and thought, "Maybe he
asn't so dumb."

My own life was disrupted when the colonel left. That same
ay Lisette received a cablegram from Rome. Her husband
ad been rescued from a prison camp. He was with the
mericans in Rome. An old man brought the cable, and
isette started to cry. I paid the old man and sent him away.

"He'll get through all right, now. I know!" Lisette whim-
ered in French. "Dear God, I prayed so hard for him."
ears flooded her eyes and she could say nothing. She patted
y arm. She wiped her face. She took my handkerchief and
lew her nose. "I got to leave, Bus. I gonna be a good wife
ow," she said.

Of the lovers at the plantation only Latouche and Tony re-

mained. Like children lost in a dream of Christmas the
wandered about the gardens and the beaches. I came upo
them one day, far below on the white coral. Latouche wor
nothing, simply that golden body slim and twisting in th
shallow water. It was then that I, too, left the plantation an
started to pack. I knew we were moving north to Kuralei.

I had done little more than get the jeeps and bulldozer
ready for the ship when Tony came to see me. "You i
trouble?" I asked when I saw his grave face.

"Holy cow, no!" he replied, breaking into a fine smile
"Bus, I want you to be my best man."

I took a deep breath. Looked at the shadows under th
palm trees. Then at Tony. He was dressed in dirty slacks
sneakers, and a sun helmet. He looked like a beachcombe
a very special beachcomber. "Latouche?" I asked.

"Yes."

"But, Tony! They won't grant you permission. Not afte
what happened."

"I'm not asking for any permission."

"What are you going to do?"

"The Buddhist priest. Saturday night. Nobody needs
know a thing."

"But the Navy . . ."

"Nobody needs to know."

My head was a bit dizzy. God knows I knew what a ma
felt out there on that plantation. The long days, the ocear
the jungle creeping up on you. And that little white hous
The laughter of living girls. But marriage? An old fool lik
Haricot from Terre Haute, or a sailor from Boston, mayb
But Tony Fry . . .

"Listen, Tony," I pleaded. "You got hot pants. So have
So has everybody else. But you don't have to marry the girl!

"Bus," Tony said softly. "If you weren't my best frien
and you said that. Well, I'd bust you one in the mouth.
Smiling, he suddenly whipped his right fist up from his knee:
But remembering my tender jaw, he pulled his punch and h
me beside the head. We stumbled into a chair.

"You got it bad, Tony," I mumbled.

"I want you for my best man. I'm getting married."

"It won't stand up in court," I said, rubbing my hea
"You're just kidding yourself and the girl."

"Now look, Bus," Tony said very quietly. "I know what
want. I'm a big boy. See? All my life I've seen guys lookin

or the girl they wanted. Hungry guys, growing old. Empty
inside. Bus, this girl's for me. She fills me up. To overflowing.
This is it."

"If you try to take her back to the States, Tony! Everyone
will think she's a Jap."

"I won't," he replied. "And maybe I won't go back to the
States. I like this life. The hot afternoons and cool nights.
I like these islands. I've got some cash. Maybe life here is
what I've been looking for. This Pacific will be the center of
the new world. This is our future. Well, I'm part of it. This
is for me."

"Tony, you're forcing me," I said. "What do you know
about the Pink House in Noumea?"

"You tell me, Bus. What do you think? Honestly?"

"You asked for it, Tony. Here it is. You don't know Latouche. That Achille Barzan deal! Do you know she dreamed
of his death? That she prayed for it? The girl's little better
than a murderess! I'm sorry, Fry, but there it is."

Tony rubbed his nose to hide the fact that he was laughing.
"Bus," he chuckled. "You're a lovely guy. That Achille Barzan deal, as you call it. What would you say if I told you
that Latouche and I planned every step. For days and days.
Natives reported each morning where Barzan was hiding. We
paid them to let Barzan overhear that Marthe was getting
married. When and where. We knew he was coming. We
considered six different ways of doing him in. I wanted to
shoot him myself. Take a general court. Self-defense. Latouche could join me later. But she figured a better way. She
knew he hated her because she went on being a Buddhist.
Same time she was a Catholic. We knew Barzan would try
to break up the wedding."

"So it was all an act?"

"No, it was real. Your arm was almost broken, wasn't it?
He tried to kill her with a club, didn't he? Just as we planned
it."

I laughed at myself. "And I was running like a fool to try
to save her! From Achille! Boy, oh boy!"

Tony grinned at me, in that silly old way of his. "We
figured on that, too, Bus. We knew you were sentimental.
That you liked to protect women. We knew you would try to
catch Achille before he reached the door. Why do you suppose I bumped you when you started to chase him? Did you
think you stumbled?"

We looked at one another across the dusty jeeps and bul
dozers there along the shore. Tony dragged out some paper
"How about signing them for me, Bus?" I leafed throug
them. Statements to his bank that Latouche De Becque Ba
zan Fry was his lawful wife. A will. A letter to his insuranc
agent. The usual stuff. I witnessed them for him, sealed the
in an envelope, and censored it.

That Saturday night the moon was full. You know how
rises out of the jungle on such nights. First a glow, then th
trees burst into flame, and finally the tallest ones stand lik
charred stumps against the moon itself. In the moonligh
with the drum beating and the little bell ringing, Tony marrie
the girl.

I kissed the bride and hurried back to the fighter strip.
couldn't think. To hell with dinners and Luana Pori an
crazy men like Tony Fry and women like Latouche. I wa
sort of tied up inside. You fellows know what to do in a cas
like that. Even though it was against orders I revved up
plane and took off. Into the darkness. But when I was ove
the jungle and out across the ocean, the moon made every
thing bright and wonderful. I flew back very high. Below m
was the plantation. Just a sliver chopped out of the dar
jungle. I could see the salon, the little house Lisette and
had, Latouche's sleeping house, the white fence. I dived an
buzzed the place until my ears rang. I'd give them a weddin
present! You know what a plane does for you at a time lik
that. You can climb and twist. It's like playing God. An
when you come down, you can sleep.

On Sunday the ship came to take us north. I hurried ov
to the plantation to get Fry. I found him sitting on a benc
among the flowers. Latouche in a skimpy brassiere and short
lay with her head in his lap. He was reading Chinese Le
to her.

"This book says the future of America is with Asia,
Latouche said in French.

"You know, Bus?" Tony began. "This guy is right. Yo
wait. We'll all be out here again. We'll be fighting China o
India or Malaysia. Asia's never going to let Australia sta
white. Bus, if you're smart, you'll move out here somewher
This is the crossroads of the world from now on."

"Time's up!" I said. Tony closed the book and looke
at me.

"Bus!" Latouche said softly. "Get me one flower for m

hair." I picked her a flamboyant. It was too big. "I take one piece of that green and yellow grass," she said. She wore it at a cocky angle.

"The ship's in," I said.

"Well," she replied. "It got to come some time."

"I'll go pack," Tony said. Latouche shrugged her shoulders and followed him across the garden. In her evanescent clothes she was a dream, not a girl at all. She was the symbol of what men think about in lonely places. Her buttocks did not bounce like those of tramps in Scollay Square, nor heave like those of fat and virtuous dowagers. Her shoulders stayed in a straight line as she walked. Her black hair blew lightly over her shoulder. Her legs were slim and resolute, an anchorage in the ocean of any guy's despair. She disappeared into the tiny house.

Well, you know what happened. We moved up to Santo and waited there a while. It always makes me laugh when I see a war movie. The hero and his buddy get on a ship in Frisco and right away land on the beachhead, where the buddy gets killed and the hero wipes out four Jap emplacements. You get on the ship at Frisco, all right. But you get off at Luana Pori. You wait there a couple of months. You move up to Santo and wait some more. At Guadal you wait, and in the Russells. But the day finally comes when even a moron can see that the next move . . .

The Strike

IT was now midsummer. The sun blazed directly overhead, and at times it seemed as if we could stand the heat no longer. But we had to work, for a strike was in progress. Upon us depended the success of Alligator, the great Kuralei operation.

So all through the steaming hell of January and February we worked on. Each day a few men would find their prickly heat unbearable and would have to be hospitalized. Or fungus would break out in their ears. Or athlete's foot would incapacitate them. Incessant glare of sun on coral sent some to the hospital until their eyes recovered, and once or twice men keeled over for no reason. We sluiced them off with cold water and sent them to bed for the day. But mostly we worked on.

I was in a strange Navy. I saw two major strikes, and yet I never set foot upon what you would call a real warship. I was as true a naval officer as circumstances would permit, and yet I never saw a battleship except from a considerable distance. I never even visited a carrier, or a cruiser, or a destroyer. I never saw a submarine. I was a new type of naval officer. I was the man who messed around with aircraft, PT boats, landing barges, and the vast shore establishment.

For a long period prior to the actual landing on Kuralei and before the attack on Konora, I served as Admiral Kester's representative at the Naval Supply Depot which was to provision the fleet serving in those operations. I left Noumea with trepidation, for I had never before worked with the men who labor in silence behind the front, hauling, shoving, and bickering among themselves. It now became my duty to help the housekeepers of the Navy.

The Depot to which I was thus attached was located along the southern edge of an extensive channel. Much of the fleet could have been stationed there, but we got only the supply boats and small craft that provision larger units. At times we would have as many as one hundred and twenty ships in our channel, ships from all over the world. They brought our Depot a massive supply of goods of war. Some of the cargoes they carried were strange, and illustrated better than words the nature of modern war. Three ships came in one week loaded mostly with paper. We built a special warehouse for it, two hundred feet long and sixty-five feet wide! In it we had a wilderness of paper. One man did nothing but take care of brown manila envelopes! That was all he did for twenty-one months! Yet into those envelopes went the plans, the records, the résumés of the world's greatest fleet. We had another man whose sole responsibility was pens, ink, paper clips, and colored pencils. This man came to his tropical job from Minnesota. He had sores in his armpits for almost eighteen months. Then he went back to Minnesota.

SeaBees had constructed the Depot. It consisted of an area two miles long, a mile deep. Two hundred odd quonset huts were laid out in neat rows along the shoreline of the channel. Three thousand men worked at the Depot. One entire company of SeaBees did nothing but oil the coral to keep dust down. Ten men had no responsibility but to mend watches as they arrived from ship and aircraft navigators. Sixteen men were bakers, and all night long, every night, for two years, they made bread, and sometimes cake.

We had two docks at the Depot, and a special road paralleling the shoreline up and down which rolled trucks day and night, seven days a week, month upon month. The drivers were all colored men, and their commanding officer permitted them to paint their trucks with fanciful names: *The Dixie Flyer, The Mississippi Cannonball, Harlem Hot Spot,* and *Coconut Express.*

More gear lay on the hot coral than ever we got into the buildings. Twelve men walked among this gear day after day, endlessly, from one pile to another. They checked it to see that rain water was not seeping through the tarpaulins. They also guarded against mosquitoes that might breed in stagnant pools behind the stacks.

There were no days at the Depot. Sunday was not observed. Nor was there day itself. As many men worked at night as did during daylight hours. In this work strange things happened. Two truckloads of jewelers' gear would be lost! Completely lost! Trucks, invaluable watches, hair springs, all records. Gone! Then, three months later the gear would be found at some place like Noumea or San Diego. It was futile even to guess at what had happened. All you knew was that one night, about 0300, that jewelers' gear was in the Depot. You saw it there! Now it was in San Diego!

Constantly, in a stream that varied only in size, officers and men from the fleet came to the Depot. The came with chits, signed always by some nebulous authority whom they considered sound but whom the men at the Depot had never heard of. "We got to have two thousand feet of Grade A wire," a seaman would plead urgently. "Give him 1200 feet!" There was no appeal. "We need four more gas stoves." "Give him three." "Skipper says we got to have two more Aldis lamps." "Where you headed?" "North." O.K. Give him two."

In two weeks you heard every possible excuse for getting equipment. You became calloused and looked at everyone as if he were a crook. At church, if you went, you wondered, "What's he saying that for? What is it he wants?" Suspicious, charged with heavy responsibility, eager to see the fleet go forth well armed but knowing the men of the fleet were a gang of robbers, you worked yourself dizzy and knocked off twenty-five percent from each request.

If to the above characteristics you added a capacity to do twice as much work as other naval officers, a willingness to connive and battle endlessly for what you wanted, and an absolute love of red tape, you were a real Supply Officer!

Captain Samuel Kelley, 54 years old, five feet four, 149 pounds, native of Madison, Wisconsin, graduate of Annapolis, was a Supply Officer. He was a small man of tireless energy and brilliant mind. He would have succeeded in anything he tried. Had he stayed in the regular line of the Navy, he would surely have become an admiral in command of a task force. Slightly defective hearing made such a career impossible. It was a good bet, however, that he would one day be admiral in charge of the Supply Corps.

It was Captain Kelley that I came north to work with. I was taller than he, so that when I reported, I tended to stoop a bit in his presence. His first words to me were, "Stand at attention. Put your hat under your left arm. And never wear an aviator's cap in this Depot."

Captain Kelley had a mania against aviators' baseball caps. Men in the air arm of the Navy loved the tight-fitting, comfortable little caps. And when Marc Mitscher started wearing one, it was difficult to keep the entire Navy from following suit. But no men serving under Captain Kelly wore baseball caps. He issued the order on the day he arrived to take charge of the Depot. Next day he put two enlisted men in the brig. The day following he confined an officer to quarters for four days. After that, we learned our lesson.

Captain Kelley instituted other innovations, as well. The Depot was a supply activity. Quickly officers of the regular line found themselves ousted from good jobs and relegated to minor posts. Several of the line officers demoted were civilians at heart and had no concern with their naval future. They protested the captain's decision. Within three days they received orders elsewhere and took with them unsatisfactory recommendations that would forever prevent them from being promoted in the Navy.

The captain's principal innovations, however, concerned free time, entertainment, and recreation. Each morning we would see him outside his quarters doing ten pushups, twenty stomach bends. He was in much better physical condition than his junior officers, a fact which gave point to his subsequent actions. First he lengthened the working day. Daytime hands reported to work at 0700. They worked till 1200. After one hour off, they worked until 1700. One night in eight they worked all night and had the next day to sleep. This meant a sixty-three hour week; with the thermometer at 95 or more. Two officers made formal protests. Unfortunately, they were line officers and were transferred.

Shortly after this protest the captain made another announcement. All games were canceled. "The men can rise an hour earlier, if they wish. They can do setting-up exercises. All this time off for games is unnecessary. The devil finds work for idle hands." So all games, except crap and poker, were abandoned.

On the night of the day athletic schedules were discarded, some toughies cheered the captain as he entered the moving-picture area. He promptly turned, ordered the lights extinguished and the movie operators to their quarters. We had no shows for a week, and in that time all seats in the movie area were torn out. Coconut logs were strung along the ground for men to sit upon. When the movies were reopened, the same toughies cheered again. The entire Depot was restricted to quarters, and for a month we had no shows. By that time sager counsels prevailed among the men, and when movies were resumed, there were no cheers. From then on, officers and men alike met the captain with stony silence. If he came into the club, all present stood at attention until he was seated. No one spoke above a whisper until he left.

"The Navy ashore is too lenient," the captain told us one day at dinner. "A great movement is on. I have been sent here to bring some kind of discipline into this organization. I propose to do so. We will shortly be faced with responsibilities almost beyond our capacity to perform. At that time there will be no place for weaklings."

That was the first news his subordinates had that a strike was scheduled. It was tremendous news. From then on speculation never ceased as to where the strike would be directed. Men argued until late at night the relative merits of Truk, Rabaul, Kavieng, and Kuralei. Strong spirits advocated Kuralei; weaker men shuddered at all four.

In the course of this discussion I discovered two interesting facts. The first was that most of the Supply Corps officers didn't give a damn about the strike. They never argued about when it would hit or where. Their concern was in how many bolts would be needed, how much gasoline. Yet when the final score was tallied, I repeatedly found that it was these indifferent officers who had made the strike possible. Details entrusted to the agitators and debaters might go awry, but not the fine-spun responsibilities of the dry, uninterested supply men.

My second discovery was much more challenging. I found that I was the only man at the Depot who was sure where the strike was headed! Not even Captain Kelley knew!

I used my discovery as only a mean man would. I sat next to the captain at mess and frequently felt the steel of his impartial goad. He disliked me, but not particularly. I was merely another undisciplined line officer, and what was worse, a reserve. "A mountebank, a huckster, a dry goods salesman!" I once heard Captain Kelley describe a reserve officer who joined the Navy from a large Cleveland store. I had no illusions as to what he thought of me. When he called me to his office and told me that as long as I was attached to his staff I would report to work at 0700 not 0702, he added icily, "Perhaps the training will stand you in good stead when you return to business life."

Therefore, when I found myself with a weapon in my hands, I used it like a bludgeon rather than as a rapier. At least once each day I would refer to some admiral. I'm not sure that Admiral Kester even remembers my name. I was merely his messenger. But at the Depot one would have thought that Admiral Kester and I were . . . well, that he consulted me before making any decision. Whenever I mentioned him or Admiral Nimitz, whom I saw once, at a distance, or Admiral This or Admiral That, I looked right at Captain Kelley. He knew the game I was playing, but he couldn't tell whether or not I was bluffing. If I really did know some admirals, then later on I might be able to hinder his progress in the Navy. He had to be careful how he handled me! On this battleground Captain Kelley and I arranged a truce. He left me to myself. I did not undermine him with his own affairs. It was this armistice that made life bearable for me. And the structure of the armistice was my snide, mean, contemptible insinuation week after week that I knew where the strike was directed and he didn't. I never said as much, but I certainly devised a hundred means of imparting that suggestion to Captain Kelley!

My plan of battle did not endear me with my fellow officers who groaned and sweated under the Captain's saddle. They called me, "Old Me'n'e Admiral!" They were a bit envious. I tried to be a good sport about it and affected never to know what they meant.

I was therefore most pleased when an old friend of mine was assigned to the Depot for additional duty in connection with the strike. Lieut. Bus Adams was older than I and a world roustabout. He was a pilot, and in the recent fighting over Konora had been banged up a bit. As relief from further flying duties, he was sent to the Depot to advise on aviation details. He reported to the captain with a dirty aviation cap under his left arm.

"Those caps are not permitted in the Depot," Captain Kelley said sharply.

"I have wings, sir," Bus replied.

"Mr. Adams! I determine the uniform here!" Bus did not acknowledge the rebuff. Nor did he stop wearing the baseball cap. Slouched over his left ear, it became a badge of freedom around the Depot. For some hidden reason, perhaps like the reasons which protected my special privileges, Captain Kelley refrained from forcing the issue with Adams.

He used subtler methods. At meals, which I remember as a horrible experience, the captain would relate one story after another of naval aviators who had been disciplined, broken, returned to civilian life. He spoke of courts-martial, inefficiencies, thefts, and other discrepancies until one would have judged all aviation personnel to be subnormal and a menace. Day after day we heard these sallies directed at Bus.

Adams refused to let the captain get under his skin. Instead, he would make ultra-polite conversation in which some aviator always won the war single-handed. He was especially fond of an offhand reference to Billy Mitchell or the *Prince of Wales* and the *Repulse*. His choicest barbs were usually unpremeditated. Once he said, "I suppose Seversky will replace Mahan in the next generation at Annapolis!" Captain Kelley actually slobbered his coffee at that remark. A much more telling blow was also offhand. Adams observed one day that disposition of one's forces was of paramount importance. "For example: A squadron of twenty good fighters aloft at Pearl Harbor would probably have kept ten American warships from being sunk."

A few other officers were also strong enough to ignore Captain Kelley. Most of them were reserve line officers. They were as far in the Navy as they would ever get. They loved the service, but had no allusions as to their worth. They were classified A-(V)S, which meant "Aviation Volunteer Specialist," but which everyone knew meant "After Victory Scram!" One very wealthy ensign in Communications merely waited for peace and a return to Long Island. He viewed Captain Kelley as one might have viewed any other temporary plague.

The other officers had to bear the captain's cold furies. They would sit at their desks and pray for 0900 to pass. Generally speaking, if Captain Kelley did not upset the Depot and publicly excoriate his assistants by 0900 in the morning, they were safe for the day. Usually they were not so lucky. Some minor defect in their work would be discovered by the captain, and before everyone in earshot, the culprit would be humiliated. Day after day Captain Kelley raged and stormed at his officers. Frequently, the cause, if ignored, would have been forgotten by noon. As it was, however, there grew up in the Depot a clique of eight or ten officers who daily sought to divert the captain's wrath from themselves by pointing out someone else's mistakes. In this way officer was set against officer, and there developed an atmosphere of hatred deeper than any in which I had previously lived. No defection, however small, escaped attention. Like boys before a whipping post, the officers would breathe easily because it was someone else that morning, not they.

Bus Adams refused to play any part in that dirty game. Several times he took the blame for petty discrepancies which it would have been beneath the dignity of a naval aviator to dispute. "Hell," he used to say to me. "Why should I dirty my hands in that foul stew? What can that bunch of sisters do to me? Next month I'll be tangling with Zeros. I can't waste my energy on the Supply Corps!"

But next month never came. Instead, one dismal incident after another occurred, until I wondered whether I was working with men or children. One especially petty affair will explain what I mean. Captain Kelley's incipient deafness made it necessary for him to ask that certain conversation be repeated. "What's that, Mr. Adams?" he would say, leaning forward slightly. Bus, accordingly, made it a point to drop his voice at the last sentence of any interesting comment he was making. "What's that, Mr. Adams?" the captain would ask in his birdlike manner. Then Bus would shout something proving that aviators alone were saving the Navy. I remember once when his bellowed reply was, "He flunked out of flight training, so they found him a job in the Supply Corps!" Another time he echoed, "We would have sunk two more Jap ships, but we ran out of supplies!"

Bus could speak like Charles Laughton, the actor who portrayed Captain Bligh in *Mutiny on the Bounty*. Frequently when he had two or three whiskeys safely stowed he would thrust his lower jaw out, walk like a martinet on the bridge, and stick his face into mine. "What's that, Mr. Christian?" he would sneer in the manner of the great slave-driver. Bus repeated this performance often enough so that enlisted men finally got wind of it. Then, for several weeks, two hundred warehouses rang with the battle cry: "What's that, Mr. Christian?" Then for Christian, the luckless mutineer, was substituted the name of any officer who might at that moment be under Captain Kelley's heel. "What's that, Mr. Adams?" would come bursting forth from some dark building. In mock terror a clown on the outside would chatter in reply, "Yes, Captain Bligh!"

It became my unpleasant task to visit each of the two-hundred-odd buildings and tell the men in charge that no further catcalls would be tolerated. I pride myself on the fact that not once did I wink or show by any outward manifestation what I thought; although at times I must admit that I found it difficult to keep a straight face when some able mimic would sham mock horror at the thought of my suspecting him. I remember one gaunt lad in particular called Polikopf, whose strange name later became famous at the Depot. He was a gifted mimic, and one of the first to adopt the cry, "What's that, Mr. Christian?" He feigned ignorance of what I was talking about.

"Very well, Polikopf," I said, "but in the future save your gibes for the enlisted men. It's dangerous to go about mocking naval captains."

"Aye, aye, sir!" he replied in military fashion. I could detect no mimicry in his voice, although there must have been much in his mind. "I'll follow your advice, sir! Save my efforts for the enlisted men."

The result of my extensive tour was that any bitterness the enlisted men felt for Captain Kelley was thereafter hidden. I took no sides in the arguments that were rife among the officers and men alike concerning the captain's ability. As a matter of fact, I now think he was one of the ablest men I knew in the Navy. The incident of the hurricane doors will show what I mean.

One day the Depot received orders from Noumea to take proper precautions against hurricanes. Our entire island received the order. Other activities made up a routine hurricane bill whereby personnel would be evacuated to safe land and gear lashed down as well as possible.

Such cavalier precautions would not do for Captain Kelley. He appointed a committee to study what should be done in event of sustained and gusty winds up to 150 miles an hour.

e established one building as a testing ground, and ran mall handcars loaded with concrete down inclines to determine at what point quonset huts buckled. He studied all e could find on hurricanes, and then asked me to converse ith planters and natives in the region to discover what they new of hurricanes.

I visited each available plantation and learned from the wners that hurricanes occurred about once in nine years. he season lasted from January through March. They started ith heavy rains which lasted two days. On the beginning f the second day winds began to rise, and on the night of e second day they came in short bursts, followed by calm pells in which the rain was intensified. If that stage was eached, a proper hurricane was in progress, and it must blow self out.

From natives I learned much about the big winds. In their orrible Beche-le-Mer they told me much that was fanciful nd more that was instructive. One old man who had lived ear the channel for half a century told me, "Wind he come, e come, he come. Takem, takem, takem! Trees he go, ocean llay, allay! Bimeby wind he go Vanicoro, he go Banks, he go, e go. Bimeby stop." The old man told me this with much aving of arms and many words I did not understand. It was nough, however, to lead my inquiries in the right direction. I etermined that whereas floods and lightning might come when the wind was east and north, trees were usually blown lown only in the first stages of the hurricane when wind blew rom the southeast. By the time it had worked around to he west, danger was gone.

I relayed this information to Captain Kelley. Characteristically he decided instantly that any quonsets whose ends opened to the southeast must be completely repacked so that gear inside would strengthen the relatively frail tin walls. This was a prodigious job, and when the captain informed is officers that work on the project would start immediately, hey showed astonishment.

"We must take no risks that can be avoided," he insisted.

"Can we do this before the task force arrives?" an officer sked.

"If not, we must do it while the force is here," said Captain Kelley. "We shall stow gear at one end of the building and ssue it at the other end. By tomorrow noon see that all issue

desks are placed at the north or northwest ends of the build
ings."

Two nights later the Depot was in the swing of a full nine
hour day followed by special four-hour emergency duty a
night, ending with another nine-hour day till dawn. Each ma
worked thirteen hours a day, seven days in a row. On th
seventh night they worked an additional six hours and wer
then given a day to sleep. Lights blazed all night. Men shove
and sweated. Even middle-aged men who normally worke
as guards were called to duty. A company of Marines wa
brought in to take over their guard duty.

Navy chow ashore is rarely as good as it is afloat, and fo
enlisted men it is usually much worse. As work increased
quality of chow decreased, and lamentations were loud
Nevertheless, men worked on. With no beer, no movies, poo
food, frightened officers, and relentless Captain Kelley i
charge, the men worked on, ninety hours a week. Tension, a
such times, mounts.

Half the buildings were secured against hurricane whe
two unfortunate things happened. The rain started and th
fleet came in. The rain alone could have been tolerated. Th
skies opened torrentially every morning, afternoon, evenin
and night. "Like a cow on a flat rock," old Navy hands said
In between the sun shone and generated steam wherever
water lay. Men's shirts were never dry save for one fleetin
instant when the sun had finished evaporating rain water an
sweat had not yet started to pour. Mold grew everywhere
and men afflicted with fungus found it spreading rapidly. Th
rains were started.

But to have rain and the fleet at one time was too much
For most ships' crews the Depot was a place to loaf and a
place from which the most wonderful things could be pro
cured, if . . . If you knew somebody, you might get a radio
If you could wangle a chit, you might get two new knives
If you pestered a hot, ill-tempered storekeeper long enough
he might give you a wrist-watch band in desperation. And i
you could manage to finagle a boiled ham, or a tinned turkey
or a coconut cake . . . well, you could probably get an entir
quonset hut! And the storekeeper thrown in!

All day men of the Depot would work and quarrel wit
men of the fleet. Then at night they would wrestle with boxe
to protect their buildings against a hurricane which migh
never come. And invariably the fleet wanted what had two

days before been packed at the bottom of the pile against the doors. It was my job to keep the enlisted men happy, and I think I succeeded. At any rate, the Depot never before had handled so much gear in so short a time. But I could not have succeeded in keeping spirits up had I not received help from a most unusual quarter: a man in a long black coat! Said he was from Naval Intelligence!

He appeared one night at about 0200. It was a dark, rainy night, and work had been knocked off. The floodlights were dark, and in the channel rode a hundred ships. Mysteriously, at the east end of the Depot a man in a long black trench coat appeared. "Naval Intelligence," he whispered to the guard. "What's up?" the guard whispered in return. "Horrible," Longcoat replied. "Jap saboteurs have landed at the other end of the island!" "Oh, my God!" the guard whispered. "Stand your post! "We're getting reinforcements. They're going to try to blow this place up. Stop the strike! We've got to outwit them. I'll be in charge. When I flash my light once, you will fire twice. Up in the air. That'll keep us together. Then the troops can take over!" "Yes, sir!" the guard replied grimly.

Up and down the buildings the man in the long coat went. Few of the men standing guard had ever expected to be addressed by a man from Naval Intelligence! They were stunned at the audacity of the Japs. But they were ready!

At about 0235, the man in the long coat suddenly appeared where three guards could see him. Flash . . . The guards fired twice each into the dark night. Longcoat hastened to another vantage point. Flash . . . Four more guards fired. Down the long row of buildings hurried Longcoat, flashing his light and drawing a fusillade. When he reached the last guards he flashed his light four times. A true volley of shots responded. Then Longcoat disappeared.

By the time the second batch of guards had fired, half the officers were out of bed. By the time the last watchman had followed instructions, many officers aboard ships were awake. Lights flashed in earnest now. Bells jangled, and before long Captain Kelley himself appeared, quiet, incisive, and determined.

"It's a hoax, sir!" a lieutenant reported.

"What's that, sir?" Kelley asked.

"A hoax, sir. Somebody fooled the guards!"

Captain Kelley said nothing. He grew pale with anger and personally interrogated each guard. He did not raise his voice nor display his rage in any way. Relentlessly, he pursued his questioning, and by the time he had reached the last guard descriptions and hints had mounted so rapidly that we knew for certain who the culprit was.

We went directly to his bunk, and there we found him, shoes wet, and a long coat at the foot of his bunk. It was Polikopf! He had followed my instructions to the letter!

Captain Kelley did the speaking. "Polikopf?" he asked.

"Yes, sir!" the boy in the bunk replied.

"Stand up!" Naked, Polikopf obeyed.

"Put your clothes on!"

"Yes, sir!"

"Did you give the guards orders to fire?" Captain Kelley asked.

"Yes, sir!"

Captain Kelley turned his back on Polikopf. "Arrest that man!" he ordered. The Master-at-Arms led Polikopf away.

By that time sleep was impossible! I and another officer inspected all guards, checked their revolvers, and issued new ammunition. When we reached the office, base police were there. While we talked the Island Commander called on the phone. Blinker was going out to all the ships. One replied, in the slow code of a learner, a message which all could read: "God help Polikopf!"

God and Bus Adams did help Polikopf! God helped by having created in man a sense of humor. Nobody could listen to the story of what happened without smiling. If you had enough rank, you laughed. And if you were an admiral, you roared, but only behind doors.

Polikopf's adventure, had it occurred in peacetime, would have been disastrous. He would have been jailed, at the least. But in the South Pacific, with a great strike in the offing, with Japs trying to infiltrate positions, and with nerves on edge, his actions were a hilarious burlesque of naval life! Men laughed more at Polikopf and his long coat than at any movie the area ever had! For myself, I think it was the long coat that saved him. The idea of anybody in a long coat, all wool, when the thermometer was at 90, was so hilarious that one simply had to laugh. And the burlesque of Naval Intelligence, which is the most secret and circumspect of all military organizations, was too much. Everyone had to roar at the long, woolen coat.

That is, everybody but Captain Kelley. He was coldly furious, and ordered a court-martial first thing next morning. But when the problem arose as to what Polikopf was to be charged with, Captain Kelley was stumped! He started to speak three times. Each time he stopped. "Damn it!" he said, sending Polikopf back to his cell. "This needs some looking into!" He went in to breakfast.

Bus Adams was the officer who threw the gall into Captain Kelley's wound. He laughed about Polikopf at breakfast while the captain was thinking. "You know," the insolent pilot said, "I don't see what we can try the boy for."

"Don't call him a boy!" Captain Kelley snorted. "He's a grown man!"

"What are you going to charge him with on the specification?" Adams asked.

"Impersonating an officer, for one thing," Captain Kelley replied.

"But he didn't, sir," Adams contended. "He never said he was an officer!"

"He wore an officer's uniform!"

"Excuse me, sir," Adams replied. "There were no insignia on that coat."

"How do you know?" Captain Kelley asked.

"I looked," Adams answered.

Captain Kelley put down his coffee. "Why did you look, Mr. Adams?"

"Because," Bus replied, "I've done a lot of work with Polikopf. I wouldn't be surprised if he requested me for counsel!"

Captain Kelley was choleric. Although he could hide his feelings when talking with guards and Polikopf, such insolence from Adams was beyond his understanding. He rose and dismissed us. Adams followed us out of the mess hall. "I'll bet I get back to flying pretty damned soon now!" he said. "This case is foolproof! Polikopf hasn't *done* anything. Peace, it's marvelous!"

Bus was dead right. Polikopf hadn't done anything. At first Captain Kelley was going to get him for impersonating Naval Intelligence, but Polikopf had never said he was Naval Intelligence. All he did was mutter the words mysteriously. The

Captain tried to pin a charge of giving an unlawful order
but he knew that wouldn't stick. For Polikopf hadn't ordered
anybody to do anything! He had merely suggested it. He
and Adams went round and round in circles, Bus never
yielding a point. Captain Kelley finally thought of something.
In speaking to one of the guards Polikopf had stepped into
a restricted area. The man had broken a lawful order! This
was it!

They would try Polikopf for trespass! But again God intervened, and Bus Adams. Everywhere Navy men met, Bus
would merely drop the hint that "Boy, this time they really
got him! Trespass!" At that the assembly would break into
a roar. In time the laughter reached Captain Kelley. He called
Polikopf to his office. Then he dismissed the Master-at-Arms.

"Polikopf," he said. "We can't hold you. Much as I want
to. This is a Navy of laws. You can thank heaven it is.
intended to punish you drastically for what you did. You
endangered the war effort. You impeded our work. Fortunately for you, I would have to cook up some general
charge to punish you adequately. The Navy doesn't like that.
It's a Navy of laws, Polikopf. You have rights that even
can't trespass . . ." Inadvertently, he winced at the word.

"You may go, Polikopf. Your time in jail is your punishment." Captain Kelley wheeled around and looked out the
window. Then he whipped his chair around once more. "Man
to man, Polikopf, and what either of us says must never leave
this room? Agreed?"

"Yes, sir!"

"Did Lieut. Adams put you up to this?"

"Oh, no! Excuse me, sir. No, sir!" The sailor was so
obviously astonished by the question that he must be telling
the truth. Captain Kelley dismissed him.

From then on Bus Adams had rough sailing. A great carrier
came into the channel for supplies. Bus was forbidden to go
aboard. He was not permitted to fly with pilots he had known
in the States. They zoomed the volcanoes on Vanicoro and
flew low over jungle villages. He had to stay behind on desk
work that mysteriously piled up. He worked and swore and
worked. Like the rest of us, he did more work in a week
than he had ever before done in a month. He began to reconsider some of the snide jokes he had once pulled on the
Supply Corps. "Real officers with their brains beat out!" he
used to say. Now he began to wonder if maybe the Seashore

Navy wasn't the real Navy and the Big-Boat Boys merely a gang of vacationists!

Even the weather conspired against Bus. He finally arranged to borrow a plane from the carrier on his day off. To hell with sleep! He could sleep any time, but he couldn't fly into Vanicoro volcanoes again. But on the day he was to fly, definite word was received that a hurricane was moving north! All ships for the strike moved out into the ocean under forced draft and headed away from the great storm.

We had to stay and take it! We stayed at the Depot and watched other activities move onto higher ground. We tied down our sleeping quarters while other units abandoned theirs and fled to safe positions. We locked doors, moved trucks against weak walls, hustled delicate instruments and chronometers to a small hill, broke out helmets to wear in case trees should blow over, and waited.

The fleet was gone by the time night fell on the second day of rain. There was a strong wind from one point off south. Gradually it veered to sou'-sou'-east. There it stayed and increased in velocity. It was now forty miles an hour, but it was still constant.

I had the watch that night, and for a while I hoped that the wind was subsiding. It did, for half an hour. Then a huge gust came in eight or ten violent puffs. I judged the velocity of the puffs to be about ninety miles an hour. Then there was another calm. I saw the rain perpendicular against the tired lights. Slowly, slowly it began to slant toward the coconut palms, in from the empty channel. Then, with a burst of tremendous power, the slanting rain was cracked like a whip and lay out parallel to the ground. A light went out, and then another. Wires were whipped away like the rain. Coconut trees threw their palms toward the hills, as if eager to flee, and some went down.

"Building 97 is buckling!" a voice cried over the phone. Our plan was to rush fire trucks and dump wagons to any building that weakened, but before I could put the plan into operation, I could hear, above the storm, the sound of a quonset hut ripping to pieces.

"Building 185 is going! All men safe!" another voice reported, and then that phone went dead.

Runners came into the barricaded office breathless and afraid. "It's rough out there!" one advised. "We can't send trucks into it. We'll have to trust to luck!"

We did. All that night men kept running to and from my watch to tell me of incidents that occurred. At 2300 Captain Kelley left his post at the switchboard and came in with me. Two other officers reported from a foot tour of the buildings.

"They're holding, captain," the inspection party reported.

In furious gusts the wind howled and drove water through every opening in every building and shack. One generator burned out and half the Depot was in darkness. Cooks brought kettles of coffee at 0300. "Potato shack done for," they reported. A jeep must have been left in neutral against strict orders. The wind caught it and dashed it through the night until it struck a building.

Then quiet followed, and from all parts of the Depot men rushed in with reports. Dripping from rain and sweat they blurted out their news and left. Mostly they cried, "They're still standing!"

Captain Kelley's buildings stood that night and the next day. I tried to sleep in the morning after I got off watch, but a falling tree capsized the hut next to mine and severely crushed two officers. I helped to drag them free of the ruins and spread ponchos over them until doctors arrived. After that all huts were cleared. In the afternoon two more were capsized by trees.

But still the buildings along the waterfront held. Only four blew apart, but in one of them a man was killed. The other two hundred buildings stood fast, and by eight o'clock, the hurricane was over.

It was followed by a mournful rain that lasted two days. Roads were washed away and life was miserable, but the hurricane was past. As several of us walked among the buildings, surveying what had happened, I tried to remember what a tropical hurricane was like. It was strange, but I could remember little. There were no massive waves, for we were in a protected channel. To me a hurricane will always be a jangle of bells, horizontal rain, and deathly silence. It will also be the sound of steel buildings tearing apart and coconut trees snapping off.

When the great storm subsided forty ships of the fleet hurried into harbor and demanded immediate supplies. So our enlisted men turned promptly from holding buildings up to emptying those same buildings. Again the Depot went on a thirteen-hour day for every man, and finally the laggard ships were filled.

When the last one pulled away, the strike was on! We had done everything that could be done. Like villagers who have watched a haggard army pass through in pursuit of the enemy, we put our hands to our foreheads. For us the battle was ended.

But that very night there limped into our channel a worn and beaten ship. It was the old ammunition carrier *Torpex*, loaded with explosives for the strike. Acting under orders, it had stayed at sea during the hurricane rather than venture into a harbor where it might explode. The *Torpex* had fled to a position away from the hurricane, but a tail of the storm caught the unhappy ship. For three horrible days the small, desperate *Torpex* had lashed through heavy seas. Decks were awash, stanchions were torn away, and even the permanent superstructure was scarred. Two men were washed overboard. Six others suffered injuries for which they were hospitalized at the Depot.

The *Torpex* lay in midchannel, lighted fore and aft and with guard boats to ward off chance stragglers. Accidents with ammunition ships were weird, because no one was ever able to determine what had caused the accidents. There were no witnesses. Therefore, all available precautions were taken. At its lonely berth the *Torpex* was no more lonely than its crew and officers. It was the backwash of the invading fleet. Its officers were ghosts who came after the heartier crew had left.

On the third night after its arrival, four officers of the *Torpex* happened to run into Bus Adams at the Officers' Club. Bus was having a whiskey when they passed his table. He knew one of them, and in the manner of all naval personnel, invited them to have some drinks with him, to eat dinner with him that night, and to spend the night with him, if possible. Not yet recovered from their recent severe experiences, the *Torpex* officers were delighted. Bus drove them to the dock so they could send necessary messages to their ships. Then he brought them to dinner.

Captain Kelley was not pleased. In the first place, he suspected any of Bus Adams' friends. In the second place, they were slightly drunk. And in the third place, one of the officers said something which caused the captain apparent concern.

"Did I understand you to say, sir," this officer asked at dinner, "that you lived in Madison?"

"Yes, sir," Captain Kelley replied. "I did."

"I used to attend the University there."

"You did?" the Captain inquired coldly.

"Yes, sir. I was a Phi Chi."

Captain Kelley stared at the man for a moment, and said no more during the rest of the meal. After he had left, Bus invited me to join the four officers and himself on a small veranda overlooking the channel. It was a peaceful scene. The *Torpex* rode at anchor, its two guard boats moored some distance away. Wrecks of four huge quonsets lay strewn about the Depot, but moonlight danced quietly upon the roofs of two hundred others. Negro truck drivers hurried endlessly up and down the water front. At one dock a barge was loading with gear for the *Torpex*. And along myriad paths through the Depot trucks, lifts, dollies, mules, finger lifts, cherry pickers, stone crushers, and paint machines moved in prim precision.

It was an orderly scene, a quiet scene after rush and hurricane. A low moon hung to the south, and coconut trees were everywhere. It was a tropic night in early March. Autumn would soon begin and there would be some respite from the heat. We felt at ease when suddenly from the bay came a great noise and rush of wind. The *Torpex* exploded!

Destruction was instantaneous and complete. The *Torpex* and the two guard boats were never seen again, no part of them. Our dock was blown down and all hands on the loading barge killed. Four quonsets nearest the channel were blown apart. And the blast did not last five seconds!

All that we saw was a flash of light. All that we heard was a great sigh of wind that knocked us to the deck. And the *Torpex* was gone.

Of the crew she carried, only our four guests and two enlisted men remaining in our hospital lived. The rest had vanished. It was later said that the two men in sickbay knew at once what had happened and that neither would speak to the other all night.

Our four guests reacted differently. One, a tall Kansan, said nothing, picked himself up from the deck, turned his back on the bay and started drinking. Another, from Massachusetts, kneeled on the deck and said a prayer. Then he, too, started drinking. A third, from Oregon, kept swallowing in heavy gulps and biting his lips, first his lower lip and then his upper lip. Later on he became very hungry, and we cut open a can of chicken. The fourth man, from Wisconsin, started talking. It was he who answered the telephone and reported his four friends alive. Then he told us all about the *Torpex*, who her captain was, a fine man, who her officers were, and how the enlisted men never gave them any trouble. He told us about his home in Madison, and how he was going back there to University and take a law degree when the war was over.

He talked in a low, rapid voice. From time to time he would ask one of the other officers to corroborate what he was saying. He would snatch a small piece of the canned chicken or take a quick drink of whiskey, and then he would be off again. Finally, when the terror had worked itself out, he sat on the veranda and looked at the magnificent channel, where the *Torpex* had been. Little boats were hurrying about. We knew, we knew too well, the grisly haul those fishing boats were taking that night.

The man from Madison turned his back to the scene. He could still hear the chugging engines, though, so he started to talk again. "You know," he said, "our skipper was the finest man. He was so considerate. We could go to him with anything and he would listen to us just as patiently. He had three kids, and at every port there would be eight or ten letters from each of them. He loved them very much. The only time he ever spoke about them to me was to show me his girl's picture. She was about fifteen and lovely. He said, 'It's really funny, you know. She'll probably have been on her first date and fallen in love by the time I get back. I haven't seen her for twenty-one months. And do you know what I was thinking?' he asked me. 'I was thinking something foolish. But I kind of wish that she would marry a naval officer. And not necessarily an officer, either. I don't mean it that way at all. Just some nice boy from the Navy.' He blushed and then put her picture away."

The man from Madison drew a deep breath and reached for some more chicken. "I'll break out another can," Bus volunteered.

"My skipper," the future lawyer continued, "doesn't seem at all like yours. He's a cantankerous man, isn't he?"

"He is that!" Bus agreed.

"If you won't tell anyone," the lawyer said in a low voice, "I think I can tell you why. Men aren't born mean," he said slowly. "Things make them that way. I think Captain Kelley is the same man I heard about in Madison. He had a daughter, too. Just like my skipper. Only his daughter fell in love with an Army man. A flier. He was a fraternity brother of mine. I only saw him once. He left the University to join the Air Corps. Well, he was killed, and then they found out Captain Kelley's daughter was going to have a baby. The Captain was furious, I understand. So she killed herself."

I was watching Bus Adams as the officer from the *Torpex* told his story. Adams had the fresh can of boneless chicken in his hand and was looking down at the lights in the channel. He squeezed the can until some of the liquid ran down his wrist. Then, politely, he offered some chicken to the hungry, deep-breathing young fellow from Oregon.

Bus stood looking at the dark shapes in the channel for a long time. He left the chattering lawyer, and I spent the rest of the night listening to the man talk himself out. Then I put him to bed. I also took the boy from Oregon in to his bunk. He sat on the side of the bed all night long. The other two officers had to be carried to their quarters. As Bus and I went to ours he said to me, "Perhaps you'd prefer to miss breakfast."

"I'll be there," I said.

It was a shaken, uncertain crew that ate breakfast next morning. The sun was bright, but death was in the air. Bus Adams looked as if he had not shaved. Captain Kelley was grim and precise. We ate our papayas and lime in silence.

Then Bus spoke. "I should like a transfer to a fighting squadron," he said. Captain Kelley stared at him. To discuss business at breakfast was an unforgivable breach of etiquette.

Bus continued. "I just heard that Screwball Snyder is up north. He's one hot pilot. I'd like to fly with him." He said this last directly to Captain Kelley, who ignored him.

"This Screwball Snyder was quite a boy," Bus went on. "And quite a lad with the ladies!" Again he spoke directly to Captain Kelley. Again he was bitterly ignored.

"Screwball and I flew across country once," Bus said in slow, clear, loud tones. "He bet me that he could sleep with a different dame in every city we stopped at."

The other officers were horrified. Such talk had never before passed current at our mess. They looked at one another. I looked at Captain Kelley. His face was ashen. He looked at his plate and crumbled a piece of toast in his left hand. There was a long silence, and then Bus spoke again. His voice was cold and gray.

"And do you know . . ."

Captain Kelley rose from the table. His junior officers rose, too, as a compliment to their skipper. Dropping his napkin unfolded, he left the mess hall. That afternoon Bus Adams, fighter, tough guy, roustabout, was on his way north to share in the bombing of Kuralei.

Frisco

I was on the LCS-108 when we hit Kuralei. I joined the small ship at Noumea and was on it nine days before we hit the beachhead. I got to know the crew pretty well.

LCS-108 was a landing craft, very small, loaded with guns. It was the smallest ship that went to the invasion under its own power. Its job was to carry an initial assault crew of twenty-five volunteers who were willing to do anything at the invasion and to do it first. This crew expected to wade ashore through three feet of water breaking on coral against an enemy-held beach. The other seventy-five men formed a heavily armed reserve unit to throw in where the fighting became thickest. The crew itself, about thirty men, were to man the antiaircraft guns and harass the enemy with rockets.

The skipper of the 108 was an Annapolis ensign. His men truly worshipped him. "God help us if we meet a Jap battleship!" his men told me. "Cap'n will head right for it." I am sure he would have.

The exec was a young school teacher from Nevada. He was an ensign, too, as were the other two officers. The exec spoke in a high voice. One of the seamen told me, "Only difference between the skipper and the exec is that if you d wrong the skipper could knock you down. The exec just makes you feel awful small."

I think the skipper was secretly miffed at having aboard an officer senior to himself. In case of trouble, you know. But I knew nothing about ships and was, I hope, no hindrance.

We made rendezvous at D-minus-two. It was a glorious feeling. You went to bed alone on the vast ocean. In the morning you were surrounded by big important ships of the line. I relaxed. If Jap planes did break through they would surely overlook a mere spot on the ocean like us. The skipper on the other hand, tried always to maneuver his craft so that in case of attack he could flank some big ship from a starboard torpedo. He doubled the antiaircraft watch. I don't know when he slept. He was all over the ship, his first command. I saw him in the most unlikely places.

D-minus-one brought frequent squalls. This scared us, because Jap torpedo planes like to dive through small clouds and pepper the ocean with fish. We had four alarms that day, but no Jap planes. Night fell and the storms went. We sailed under a magnificent sky, bright with stars. Then, in the distance, we saw other stars blazing in fury across the sky! The warships were at Kuralei! The bombardment was on!

We watched the fiery display for hours. Men who would work as never before when the sun came up, could not drive themselves to sleep. They clustered about the rails and guns to watch the American Navy in its first great Pacific bombardment. I tried to sleep, but could not. Once, when the noise had become familiar, I dozed off for a moment. But I was soon awakened by a tremendous dull thump. There were cries on deck, and I thought we must be hit. I hurried topside and saw an eerie sight. The Japs had hit one of our oilers. She blazed like a torch. As I watched, both fascinated and horrified by what I saw, one of our greatest battleships passed between us and the flame. For breathless moments the tremendous ship was silhouetted. Then it left the flame and so far as we could tell vanished.

The oiler burned itself out and was sunk. In hushed groups we watched new salvos strike Kuralei. But no longer were we sure that no shore fire would hit us.

Like the men on deck, I could not sleep. Yet the bombardment tired my eyes and dulled my brain. It was too massive to understand. I went below to my own bunk and found that I was simply incapable of staying there alone. Like the youngest seaman, I was assailed by thoughts that were not meant for lonely harvest.

I went forward to the crew's recreation room. I knew that I was intruding, yet I had to. The enlisted men of LCS-108 were not unpleasant to me, since I had no authority over them. In fact, I think they may even have been glad to see me. They thought I knew much more than I did.

"How many men on an oiler, sir?" they asked.

"I don't know," I replied.

"Do you think they all went down, sir?"

"There are always some survivors, aren't there?" I reasoned. "Seems to me out there would be a pretty good place, if you had to get it anyway. Look at all the ships!"

"That's right!" the men said. They nodded to one another. The thought cheered me, and I think it did the same for the men. Suddenly I felt that a strong portion of America was there to protect us during the next few days. And we, in turn, were protecting others. In the days that followed these reciprocal thoughts came back to me time and again. The sense of belonging is one of the great gifts men get in battle.

As the night wore on the exec came down. He, too, was unwilling to stay in his quarters. Men coming off watch drifted by for a drink of water and stayed. The air was heavy with smoke. As always in such Navy groups, somebody started singing. *Where the deer and the antelope play* . . . We joined in, trying to hit close harmonies and holding notes until they fairly groaned to be let loose.

A coxswain was, by nature and by talent, leader of the singing. He was a slight boy under twenty. He had a fine Irish tenor. Before the last notes of a song had died away, he would lead forth with another. Soon, as in every songfest I attended, he started the two old favorites of all males voices. In high falsetto he sang, "I'm coming, I'm coming! For my head is hanging low." I think we sang that song at least eight times. The real singers amongst us introduced variations and trills I had not heard before. The bellowers simply hit a few notes and held them deliciously long.

Then the coxswain started the other favorite. *Silent night, holy night! All is calm, all is bright.* He had a fine voice for the carol and was joined by a bass who rumbled the low notes. It may seem strange that men aboard a ship about to go into action would choose to sing a German carol, a carol in fact so German that it sounds rude in English. Yet they did elect hat song, and when they sang it, it was not German, even though more than half the men sang it in that language. Nor, n a sense, was it a religious song. It was merely a succession of glorious notes which men could hold onto with affection as if they were, indeed, memories.

Our singing was interrupted at 0230 by loud explosions. We hurried on deck in time to see a series of ammunition dumps on Kuralei go up. Spires of flame shot several hundred feet into the air, subsided, and then sprang higher. Again our ships, hundreds of them it seemed, were illuminated. Full in our path a cruiser loosed a salvo and passed into the darkness. Soon another took its place. New explosions rocked the beaches.

After some minutes we went below again. The mood for singing was gone. A heavy-set fireman who by choice was in the assault party sat next to me on the table, our feet on a bench. "I tell you, sir!" he said. "I haven't seen anything prettier than that since Market Street on a Saturday night!"

"You mean Market Street in Frisco?" a gunner's mate asked. Several men leaned forward.

"Yeah! Market Street in Frisco!" the fireman said.

"What a town!" another fireman murmured.

"You can say that again, buddy!" a seaman said approvingly.

Conversation ceased for a moment. All the men near me were thinking of Market Street in Frisco. Suddenly two men started speaking at the same time: "I remember . . ." one said. "It was on Market . . ." the second began. They laughed and each indicated that the other should speak first. The cook, whom nobody liked, broke the impasse.

"I was in Frisco four days," he said.

"So what?" a voice inquired.

"So it was the best leave I ever had," the cook replied.

"What the hell did you do in Frisco?" the voice taunted. "Pick up a soldier?"

"Nyah, to you!" the cook replied. "It was Friday. I was having a fish dinner. I looked across the aisle and there was this babe."

"What was wrong with her?" the stooge asked.

"Where that babe was wrong," the cook said, "you'd never notice it!" The stooge had no comment. Men in the recreation room leaned forward. They were interested in what happened

when the cook, whom they otherwise detested, met a g
in Frisco.

"What happened, cookie?" someone asked.

"Well, this babe—and I ain't kiddin', fellows. She was ju
about through her dessert and there I was on me soup.
looked to me like she was givin' me the eye, but you kno
how it is. A smart girl. Maybe she is. Maybe she ain't. S
sort of puts it up to you."

"Thass the kind I like," a drooly voice interrupted. "T
kind that puts it up to you."

"Knock it off! So what happened, cookie?"

"So quick as a wink I ditches my soup and steps besi
her. 'You ain't finished your dinner!' she said. 'To hell wi
it!' I answered right quick. I give the waiter a couple
bucks and said, 'Keep the change!' Then the waiter sai
'But the young lady's?' So I slung him another two buck
Well, the dame really give me the eye then. She seen I w
a spender."

"What you was anglin' for you could of had for tw
bucks," the heckler observed.

"All right!" the cook said. "But this dame was class."

"Then what happened, cookie?"

"We stepped out! And brother, this dame was just what
said, class. When we went into a club or restaurant, gu
like you looked up, but plenty!"

"What did she take you for, cookie?" the voice inquire
"But plenty?"

"As a matter of fact," the cook replied. "She did. I spe
one hundred and eighty bucks on that dame in four days."

"Whew!" a seaman whistled.

"The hell you did, brother!" the persistent voice cried.

"So help me, I did!" the cook answered. "One hundre
and eighty bucks in four days. And it was worth more to me

"I suppose some of that was a hotel bill?" the drooly voi
asked.

"Hell, no! We stayed at her place!"

"Oh, she ran a flop house!" the voice interrupted. "I to
you what you got you could of had for two bucks."

"So what if I could?" the cook asked. "To me it was wor
one hundred and eighty. We had taxis everywhere. Best sea
everywhere. Went to two shows. Bought her some present
Hell, I seen you guys lose a hundred and eighty bucks in on
night at crap. What you got for it? Me? For my dough I ha

me the best time in Frisco, for four days, with a dame that
was strictly class!"

The men looked at cookie. They thought of him differently
now. Even the heckler grudgingly granted him a point. "You
got to admit it ain't to be sneezed at," he said. That was the
limit he would go in approval, but his ambiguous surrender
pleased cookie. He grinned.

All this time I was aware of a rasping sound in a corner
to my right. As cookie stopped speaking, I turned to see what
caused the sound. "It's only Norval," a seaman said. I twisted
my head farther and saw a thin, sour-faced fireman, perhaps
twenty-three years old. He looked at me with that grim stare
which officers see so often and which always means: "What
the hell are you doing here?"

"Don't mind Norval," a chubby seaman advised.

What was supposed to be wrong with the man in the corner
I never discovered. During that long, fateful night he sat in
the shadows. First he sharpened his bayonet to razor edge.
Then he honed an eight-inch dagger which he took from his
belt. When this was done he took off his shoes, and I saw
they were studded with long steel spikes. He sharpened each
one of these, carefully, patiently, like a ball player who hears
the opposing second baseman is a tough hombré.

All night Norval sat there. From time to time he looked
up at the foolish gossips about the table. Twice he caught my
eye. He glared at me contemptuously, blew breath through
his nose, and returned to his scratching, raspy files. When I
last saw him he was filing down the sear on his revolver, to
make it fire at the slightest suggestion from his trigger finger.
The steel of the sear was hard, and Norval's files made a thin,
piercing sound.

"Lay off, killer!" a seaman cried.

Norval continued with his sear. He did not even look up,
but the contempt of his shoulders and the toss of his head
eloquently asked his old question: "What the hell are you
doing here?"

"I had a swell time in Frisco," a machinist's mate said. "My
wife came out with me. We had a hard time finding a room,
but we finally did. Gee, we went to the zoo, and the art
gallery, and the Cliff House, and just about everywhere, I
guess." The room was silent. The last place in America most
of these men had seen was Frisco. Their last fun was there,

their last liberties. Some thought of the zoo; some remem bered four movies in a row.

"A funny thing," the machinist's mate continued. "Thi may seem funny to some of you guys. But my wife and m decided we didn't want to have any kids till after the wai But being there in Frisco and knowing . . . Well, we got little girl now. Like to see her?" At the first sign of encourage ment he whipped out a picture of as undistinguished a bab as I have ever seen. Men with no children looked at th bundle, grunted, and passed it on. Fathers appraised th infant, said nothing, and handed it along.

"I spent four days in Frisco, too," a thick-voiced fireman said. "In that YMCA on the Embarcadero. I had dinne every day at Joe Di Maggio's, and got drunk every night Boy, that was some four days! I met an Australian, and di we have a time! He got pinched, but they discharged him an told him to sober up. That night we put on a toot that yo could hear in Seattle!"

"Any you boys spend much time on Grant Street?" a sea man asked. "Well, I was down there one night and picked m up a Chinese doll. What do you guys honestly think abou chop-suey lovin'? You think it's all right?"

There was a heated discussion as to whether any white ma should date a Chink, the question being solved when th seaman flashed the picture he had of this particular almond eye. The photograph, taken of the girl in her night clu costume, made the earlier argument purely academic.

"What did you do in Frisco?" a fireman asked me.

"I seem to have missed the fun," I said. "Got in there on night and left the next night on the Clipper."

"You flew out?" the men asked.

"Yes."

"Was it in the Mars?" they asked.

"No. Regular Clipper." The fact that I had flown out mad me an authority.

"How soon do you think the war will end?" they asked.

"About four years," I said. This was greeted with silence The men thought what four years would do to them.

"We can hope, can't we?" a wag said in sepulchral tones "You know what they say, sir? *Optimist:* 'In 'Forty-five, i I'm alive.' *Pessimist:* 'You and me in 'Fifty-three.' *Realist:* 'Golden Gate in 'Forty-eight.' *Damned fool:* 'A bit of heaver in 'Forty-seven.'"

"I don't get it," a seaman said. "Why the damned fool?"

"Cause they won't be any heaven left in 'Forty-seven! Guys back from Europe will use it all up!" The wag slapped the table.

"You think we'll be kept out here that long, sir?"

"Somebody will be," I said.

"You think you will be?"

"Could be."

"Ain't you mad about it, sir?"

"I was at first," I admitted.

"What happened?" the men asked. They were interested. This touched them, too.

"Oh, I sort of decided that it doesn't matter much when I get back," I said. Then the closeness of battle prompted me to honesty: "I don't think that I'm going to be stopped merely because somebody else got there first. I got a lot of work to do!"

A chief petty officer looked at me. "That's exactly how I feel, sir. Boy, I got a lot to do when I get home! The longer I stay away the more certain I am I'll do it, too."

"What you gonna do?" a voice asked.

"That's my business," the CPO said.

"I felt that same way in Frisco," a storekeeper added. 'Said to myself, 'This is the last look for a long while. Make the most of it.' But you know what I did?" There was a furious bombardment outside. We looked at our watches. "I just couldn't make up my mind what to do first! So I lay in my damned room till about noon each day, got up, ate some lunch, and went back to bed. I went out a couple of nights, but it was lousy. I was glad when the ship sailed."

"Me?" a yeoman asked. "Them days wasn't long enough for me. Them Frisco street cars! Boy, I bet I rode a hundred miles a day on them babies. I'd get on and ask every pretty girl I met what she was doing. Kept right on until I made contact. Different dame every day. I been to Boston, Panama, San Diego. None of them compares with Frisco for a liberty."

"Say?" a seaman interrupted. "Ain't we movin'?" We remained silent. Yes, we were moving. We were moving toward the beach. Again we looked at our watches. A head appeared in the hatchway.

"Assault party!" Norval dropped his files and leaped for the gangway. "Assault party! Prepare to land. Prepare to land!"

When the smoky room was emptied, I went on deck. I the gray twilight of D-Day the first wave was going in. Fi raked them as they hit the coral. Jap guns roared in the gra dawn. But some of them got in! They were in! And now th battleships lay silent. The airplanes withdrew. Men, huma beings on two feet, men, crawling on their bellies over cora with minds and doubtful thoughts and terrible longings . . Men took over.

The Landing on Kuralei

WE would have captured Kuralei according to plan if it had not been for Lt. Col. Kenjuro Hyaichi. An honor graduate from California Tech, he was a likely choice for the job the Japs gave him.

As soon as our bombers started to soften up Konora, where we built the airstrip, the Jap commander on Kuralei gave Hyaichi his instructions: "Imagine that you are an American admiral. You are going to invade this island. What would you do?"

Hyaichi climbed into a plane and had the pilot take him up 12,000 feet. Below him Kuralei was like a big cashew nut. The inside bend faced north, and in its arms were two fine sandy bays. They were the likely places to land. You could see that even from the air.

But there was a small promontory protruding due south from the outside bend. From the air Hyaichi studied that promontory with great care. "Maybe they know we have two bays fortified. Maybe they will try that promontory."

The colonel had his pilot drop to three thousand feet and then to five hundred. He flew far out to sea in the direction from which our search planes came. He roared in six times

359

to see if he could see what an American pilot, scared and
a hurry, would think he saw.

Then he studied the island from a small boat. Had
photographed from all altitudes and angles. He studied t
photographs for many days. He had two Jap spies shipped
one night from Truk. They crept ashore at various poin
"What did you see?" he asked them. "Did you think the b
was defended? What about that promontory?"

He had two trained observers flown over from Palau. Th
had never seen Kuralei before. When their plane started
descend, they were blindfolded. "The bays?" Hyaichi aske
"And that promontory? Did you think there was sand in t
two small beaches there? Did you see the cliffs?"

Jap intelligence officers brought the colonel sixty-page a
seventy-page reports of interrogations of American prisone
They showed him detailed studies of every American landi
from Guadalcanal to Konora. They had a complete book
Admiral Kester, an analysis of each action the admiral h
ever commanded. At the end of his study Lt. Col. Hyaic
ruled out the possibility of our landing at the promonto
"It couldn't be done," he said. "That coral shelf sticking c
two hundred yards would stop anything they have."

But before the colonel submitted his recommendation th
all available Jap power be concentrated at the northern ba
a workman in Detroit had a beer. After his beer this workm
talked with a shoe salesman from St. Louis, who told
brother-in-law, who passed the word on to a man heading
Texas, where the news was relayed to Mexico and thence
Tokyo and Kuralei that "General Motors is building a bo
that can climb over the damnedest stuff you ever saw."

Lt. Col. Hyaichi tore up his notes. He told his superior
"The Americans will land on either side of the promontory
"How can they?" he was asked. "They have new weapons
he replied. "Amphibious tanks with treads for crossing cora
Almost a year before, Admiral Nimitz had decided that wh
we hit Kuralei we would not land at the two bays. "We w
hit the promontory. We will surprise them."

Fortunately for us, Lt. Col. Hyaichi's superiors were ab
to ignore his conclusions. It would be folly, they said, to mo
defenses from the natural northern landing spots. All th
would agree to was that Hyaichi might take whatever mater
he could find and set up secondary defenses at the promo
tory. How well he did his job you will see.

At 0527 our first amphibs hit the coral shelf which protruded underwater from the shore. It was high tide, and they half rode, half crawled toward land. They had reached a point twenty feet from the beach, when all hell ripped loose. Lt. Col. Hyaichi's fixed guns blasted our amphibs right out of the water. Our men died in the air before they fell back into the shallow water on the coral shelf. At low tide their bodies would be found, gently wallowing in still pools of water. A few men reached shore. They walked the last twenty feet through a haze of bullets.

At 0536 our second wave reached the imaginary line twenty feet from shore. The Jap five-inch guns ripped loose. Of nine craft going in, five were sunk. Of the three hundred men in those five amphibs, more than one hundred were killed outright. Another hundred died wading to shore. But some reached shore. They formed a company, the first on Kuralei.

It was now dawn. The LCS-108 had nosed in toward the coral reef to report the landings. We sent word to the flagship. Admiral Kester started to sweat at his wrists. "Call off all landing attempts for eighteen minutes," he said.

At 0544 our ships laid down a gigantic barrage. How had they missed those five-inch guns before? How had anything lived through our previous bombardment? Many Japs didn't. But those hiding in Lt. Col. Hyaichi's special pillboxes did. And they lived through this bombardment, too.

On the small beach to the west of the promontory 118 men huddled together as the shells ripped overhead. Our code for this beach was Green, for the one to the east, Red. The lone walkie-talkie on Green Beach got the orders: "Wait till the bombardment ends. Proceed to the first line of coconut trees." Before the signalman could answer, one of our short shells landed among the men. The survivors re-formed, but they had no walkie-talkie.

At 0602 the third wave of amphibs set out for the beach. The vast bombardment rode over their heads until they were onto the coral shelf. Then a shattering silence followed. It was full morning. The sun was rising. Our amphibs waddled over the coral. At the fatal twenty-foot line some Japs opened up on the amphibs. Three were destroyed. But eight got through and deposited their men ashore. Jap machine gunners and snipers tied into tall trees took a heavy toll. But our men formed and set out for the first line of coconut trees.

They were halfway to the jagged stumps when the Japs

opened fire from carefully dug trenches behind the tree
Our men tried to outfight the bullets but could not. The
retreated to the beach. The coconut grove was lined wit
fixed positions, a trench behind each row of trees.

As our men withdrew they watched a hapless amphi
broach to on the coral. It hung suspended, turning slowly
A Jap shell hit it full in the middle. It rose in the air. Bodie
danced violently against the rising sun and fell back dea
upon the coral. "Them poor guys," the Marines on the beac
said.

At 0631 American planes appeared. F6F's. They strafed th
first trench until no man but a Jap could live. They bombed
They ripped Green Beach for twelve minutes. Then the nex
wave of amphibs went in. The first two craft broached
and were blown to shreds of steaming metal. "How can thos
Japs live?" the man at my side said. In the next wave fou
more amphibs were sunk.

So at 0710 the big ships opened up again. They fired fo
twenty-eight minutes this time, concentrating their shells abou
sixty yards inland from the first row of coconut stumps. Whe
they stopped, our men tried again. This time they reache
the trees, but were again repulsed. Almost four hundred me
were ashore now. They formed in tight circles along the edg
of the beach.

At 0748 we heard the news from Red Beach, on the othe
side of the promontory. "Repulsed four times. First men no
safely ashore!" Four times! we said to ourselves. Why, that
worse than here! It couldn't be! Yet it was, and when th
tide started going out on Red Beach, the Japs pushed ou
men back onto the coral.

This was fantastic! When you looked at Alligator back i
Noumea you knew it was going to be tough. But not lik
this! There were nine rows of coconut trees. Then a caca
grove. The edge of that grove was Line Albany. We had
reach the cacaos by night. We knew that an immense block
house of sod and stone and concrete and coconut trees woul
have to be reduced there before night. We were expected
start storming the blockhouse by 1045. That was the schedul

At 1400 our men were still huddled on the beach. Keste
would not withdraw them. I don't think they would hav
come back had he ordered them to do so. They hung on
tried to cut westward but were stopped by the cliffs, tried

ut eastward but were stopped by fixed guns on the promontory.

At 1422 Admiral Kester put into operation his alternative plan. While slim beachheads were maintained at Red and Green all available shock troops were ordered to hit the rugged western side of the promontory. We did not know if landing craft could get ashore. All we knew was that if they could land, and if they could establish a beach, and if they could cut a path for men and tanks down through the promontory, we might flank each of the present beachheads and have a chance of reaching the cacaos by dark.

At 1425 we got our orders. "LCS-108. All hands to Objective 66." The men winked at one another. They climbed into the landing barges. The man whose wife had a baby girl. The young boy who slept through his leave in Frisco. They went into the barges. The sun was starting to sink westward as they set out for shore.

Lt. Col. Hyaichi's men waited. Then two fixed guns whose sole purpose was to wait for such a landing fired. Shells ripped through the barges. One with men from 108 turned in the air and crushed its men to death. They flung their arms outward and tried to fly free, but the barge caught them all. A few swam out from under. They could not touch bottom, so they swam for the shore, as they had been trained to do. Snipers shot at them. Of the few, a few reached shore. One man shook himself like a dog and started into the jungle. Another made it and cried out to a friend. "Red Beach! Green Beach! Sonova Beach!" You can see that in the official reports. "At 1430 elements from LCS-108 and the transport Julius Kennedy started operations at Sonova Beach."

The hidden guns on the promontory continued firing. Kester sent eight F6F's after them. They dived the emplacements and silenced one of the guns. I remember one F6F that seemed to hang for minutes over a Jap gun, pouring lead. It was uncanny. Then the plane exploded! It burst into a violent puff of red and black. Its pieces were strewn over a wide area, but they hurt no one. They were too small.

At 1448 a rear-admiral reported to Kester, "Men securely ashore at Objective 66." The admiral diverted all available barges there. Sonova Beach was invaded. We lost three hundred men there, but it was invaded. Barges and men turned in the air and died alike with hot steel in their guts, but the promontory was invaded. Not all our planes nor all our ships could silence those damned Jap gunners, but Sonova Beach, that strip of bleeding coral, it was invaded.

At 1502 Admiral Kester sent four tanks ashore at Sonova with orders to penetrate the promontory and to support whichever beach seemed most promising. Two hundred men went with axes and shovels. I watched the lumbering tanks crawl ashore and hit their first banyan trees. There was a crunching sound. I could hear it above the battle. The tanks disappeared among the trees.

At 1514 came the Jap's only airborne attack that day. About thirty bombers accompanied by forty fighters swept in from Truk. They tried for our heavy ships. The fleet threw up a wilderness of flak. Every ship in the task force opened up with its five-inchers, Bofors, Oerlikons, three-inchers an[d] .50 calibers. The air was heavy with lead. Some Jap plane[s] spun into the sea. I watched a bomber spouting flames alon[g] her port wing. She dived to put them out. But a second she[ll] hit her amidships. The plane exploded and fell into the ocea[n] in four pieces. The engine, badly afire, hit the water at a[n] angle and ricocheted five times before it sank in hissing rage.

One of our transports was destroyed by a Jap bomb. I[t] burst into lurid flame as it went down. Near by, a Jap plan[e] plunged into the sea. Then, far aloft an F6F came screamin[g] down in a mortal dive. "Jump!" a thousand voices urged. Bu[t] the pilot never did. The plane crashed into the sea righ[t] behind the Jap bomber and burned.

A Jap fighter, driven low, dived at the 108 and began t[o] strafe. I heard dull spats of lead, the firing of our own gun[s] and a cry. The Jap flashed past, unscathed. Men on the 10[8] cursed. The young skipper looked ashen with rage and hurrie[d] aft to see who had been hit.

The Japs were being driven off. As a last gesture a fighte[r] dived into the bridge of one of our destroyers. There wer[e] four explosions. The superstructure was blown away wit[h] three dozen men and four officers. Two other fighters trie[d] the same trick. One zoomed over the deck of a cruiser an[d] bounced three times into a boiling sea. The other came dow[n] in a screaming vertical spin and crashed deep into the water not far from where I stood. There were underwater explosions and a violent geyser spurting high in the air.

Our planes harried the remaining Japs to death, far out a[t] sea. Our pilots, their fuel exhausted, went into the sea them-

elves. Some died horribly of thirst, days later. Others were
icked up almost immediately and had chicken for dinner.

While the Jap suicide planes were crashing into the midst
f the fleet, a Jap shore battery opened up and hit an ammu-
ition ship. It disintegrated in a terrible, gasping sound.
Almost before the last fragments of that ship had fallen into
he water, our big guns found the shore battery and de-
troyed it.

Meanwhile power had been building up on Green Beach.
At 1544, with the sun dropping lower toward the ocean, they
ried the first row of coconut trees again. They were driven
ack. This time, however, not quite to the coral. They held
nto some good positions fifteen or twenty yards inland.

At 1557 Admiral Kester pulled them back onto the coral.
For the last time that day. He sent the planes in to rout out
hat first trench. This time, with noses almost in the coconut
tumps, our fliers roared up and down the trenches. They kept
heir powerful .50's aimed at the narrow slits like a woman
uiding a sewing machine along a predetermined line. But
he .50's stitched death.

At 1607 the planes withdrew. At a signal, every man on
hat beach, every one, rose and dashed for the first trench.
The Japs knew they were coming, and met them with an
nfilading fire. But the Green Beach boys piled on. Some fell
younded. Others died standing up and took a ghostly step
oward the trench. Some dropped from fright and lay like
ead men. But most went on, grunting as they met the Japs
vith bayonets. There was a muddled fight in the trench. Then
hings were quiet. Some Americans started crawling back to
ick up their wounded. That meant our side had won.

Japs from the second trench tried to lead a charge against
he exhausted Americans. But some foolhardy gunners from
cruiser laid down a pinpoint barrage of heavy shells. Just
eyond the first trench. It was dangerous, but it worked. The
aps were blown into small pieces. Our men had time to
eorganize. They were no longer on coral. They were inland.
On Kuralei's earth.

At 1618 Admiral Kester made his decision. Green Beach
vas our main chance. To hell with Red. Hang on, Red! But
verything we had was thrown at Green. It was our main
hance. "Any word from the tanks?" "Beating down the
eninsula, sir." It was no use banging the table. If the tanks
ould get through, they would.

At 1629 about a hundred amphibs sped for Green Beach. They were accompanied by a tremendous barrage that raked the western end of the beach toward the cliffs. Thirty planes strafed the Jap part of the promontory. A man beside me started yelling frantically. A Jap gun, hidden somewhere in that wreckage, was raking our amphibs. "Get that gun!" I shouted. "It's right over there!" He jumped up and down and had to urinate against the bulkhead. "Get that gun!" Two amphibs were destroyed by the gun. But more than nine made the beach. Now, no matter how many Japs counter attacked, we had a chance to hold the first trench.

"A tank!" our lookout shouted. I looked, but saw none. Then, yes! There was a tank! But it was a Jap tank. Three of them! The Jap general had finally conceded Lt. Col. Hyaichi's point. He was rushing all moveable gear to the promontory. And our own tanks were still bogged down in the jungle.

"LCS-108! Beach yourself and use rockets!" The order came from the flagship. With crisp command the young skipper got up as much speed as possible. He drove his small craft as near the battle lines as the sea would take it. We braced ourselves and soon felt a grinding shock as we hit coral. We were beached, and our bow was pointed at the Jap tanks.

Our first round of rockets went off with a low swish and headed for the tanks. "Too high!" the skipper groaned. The barrage shot into the cacao trees. The Jap tanks bore down on our men in the first ditch. Our next round of rockets gave a long hissss. The first tank exploded loudly and blocked the way of the second Jap.

At this moment a Jap five-incher hit the 108. We heeled over to port. The men at the rocket-launching ramps raised their sights and let go with another volley. The second tank exploded. Japs climbed out of the manhole. Two of them dived into the cacaos. Two others were hit by rifle fire and hung head downward across the burning tank.

The third Jap tank stopped firing at our men in the first trench and started lobbing shells at LCS-108. Two hit us and we lay far over on the coral. The same foolhardy gunner on the cruiser again ignored our men in the first trench. Accurately they plastered the third tank. We breathed deeply. The Japs probably had more tanks coming, but the first three were taken care of.

Our skipper surveyed his ship. It was lost. It would either be hauled off the reef and sunk or left there to rot. He felt strange. His first command! What kind of war was this? You bring a ship all the way from Norfolk to stop two tanks. On land. You purposely run your ship on a coral reef. It's crazy. He damned himself when he thought of that Jap plane dashing by. It had killed two of his men. Not one of our bullets hit that plane. It all happened so fast. "So fast!" he muttered. "This is a hell of a war!"

At 1655 the Marines in trench one, fortified by new strength from the amphibs, unpredictably dashed from the far western end of their trench and overwhelmed the Japs in the opposite part of trench two. Then ensued a terrible, hidden battle as the Marines stolidly swept down the Jap trench. We could see arms swinging above the trench, and bayonets. Finally, the men in the western end of trench one could stand the suspense no longer. Against the bitterest kind of enemy fire, they rushed past the second row of coconut stumps and joined their comrades. Not one Jap survived that brutal, silent, hidden struggle. Trench two was ours.

At 1659 more than a thousand Jap reinforcements arrived in the area. Not yet certain that we had committed all our strength to Green Beach, about half the Japs were sent to Red. Lt. Col. Hyaichi, tight-lipped and sweating, properly evaluated our plan. He begged his commanding officer to leave only a token force at Red Beach and to throw every ounce of man and steel against Green. This was done. But as the reserves moved through the coconut grove, the skipper of the LCS-108 poured five rounds of rockets right into their middle. Results passed belief. Our men in trench two stared in frank astonishment at what the rockets accomplished. Then, shouting, they swamped the third Jap trench before it could be reinforced.

At 1722, when the sun was beginning to eat into the tree-tops of Kuralei, our tanks broke loose along the shore of the promontory. Sixty sweating footslogging axmen dragged themselves after the tanks. But ahead lay an unsurmountable barrier of rock. The commanding officer of the tanks appraised the situation correctly. He led his ménage back into the jungle. The Japs also foresaw what would happen next. They moved tank destroyers up. Ship fire destroyed them. We heard firing in the jungle.

At 1740 our position looked very uncertain. We were still

six rows from Line Albany. And the Japs had their bloc
house right at the edge of the cacaos. Our chances of attai
ing a reasonably safe position seemed slight when a fine sho
went up. One of our tanks had broken through! Alone,
dashed right for the heart of the Jap position. Two enen
tanks, hidden up to now, swept out from coconut emplac
ments and engaged our tank. Bracketed by shells from ea
side, our tank exploded. Not one man escaped.

But we soon forgot the first tank. For slowly crawling o
of the jungle came the other three. Their treads were dar
aged. But they struggled on. When the gloating Jap tan
saw them coming, they hesitated. Then, perceiving the dar
age we had suffered, the Japs charged. Our tanks stood fa
and fired fast. The Japs were ripped up and down. One qu
the fight. Its occupants fled. The other came on to its doo
Converging fire from our three tanks caught it. Still it cam
Then, with a fiery gasp, it burned up. Its crew did not eve
try to escape.

At 1742 eleven more of our tanks landed on Sonova Beac
You would have thought their day was just beginning. B
the sun was on their tails as they grunted into the jungle li
wild pigs hunting food.

An endless stream of barges hit Green Beach. How change
things were! On one wave not a single shot from sho
molested them. Eight hundred Yanks on Kuralei without
casualty. How different that was! We got Admiral Kester
message: "Forty-eight minutes of daylight. A supreme effort

At 1749 the Japs launched their big counter-attack. The
swept from their blockhouse in wild assault. Our rockets spe
among them, but did not stop them. It was the men in trenc
three that stopped them.

How they did so, I don't know. Japs swarmed upon them
screaming madly. With grenades and bayonets the banzai bo
did devilish work. Eighty of our men died in that grim assau
Twelve had their heads completely severed.

But in the midst of the melee, two of our three tanks brok
away from the burning Jap tanks and rumbled down betwee
trench three and trench four. Up and down that tight are
way they growled. A Jap suicide squad stopped one by settin
it afire. Their torches were their own gasoline-soaked bodie
Our tankmen, caught in an inferno, tried to escape. Fro
trench three, fifty men leaped voluntarily to help them. O
men surrounded the flaming tank. The crewmen leaped

afety. In confusion, they ran not to our lines but into trench our. Our men, seeing them cut down, went mad. They raged nto trench four and killed every Jap. In a wild spontaneous sweep they swamped trench five as well!

Aboard the LCS-108 we could not believe what we had een. For in their rear were at least a hundred and twenty aps still fighting. At this moment reinforcements from the mphibs arrived. The Japs were caught between heavy fire. Not a man escaped. The banzai charge from the blockhouse ad ended in complete rout.

At 1803 Admiral Kester sent his message: "You can do it. Twenty-seven minutes to Line Albany!" We were then four ows from the blockhouse. But we were sure that beyond rench seven no trenches had been dug. But we also knew that renches six and seven were tougher than anything we had et tackled. So for the last time Admiral Kester sent his eloved planes in to soften up the trenches. In the glowering lusk they roared up and down between the charred trees, iccuping vitriol. The grim, terrible planes withdrew. There vas a moment of waiting. We waited for our next assault. We waited for new tanks to stumble out of the promontory. We waited in itching dismay for that tropic night. We were o far from the blockhouse! The sun was almost sunk into he sea.

What we waited for did not come. Something else did. From our left flank, toward the cliffs, a large concentration of Jap reinforcements broke from heavy cover and attacked he space between trenches one and two. It was seen in a lash that we had inadequate troops at that point. LCS-108 nd several other ships made an instantaneous decision. We hrew all our fire power at the point of invasion. Rockets, ive-inchers, eight-inchers and intermediate fire hit the Japs. They were stopped cold. Our lines held.

But I can still see one flight of rockets we launched that lay at dusk. When the men in trench two saw the surprise ttack coming on their flank, they turned sideways to face he new threat. Three Americans nearest the Japs never esitated. Without waiting for a command to duty they leaped ut of their trench to meet the enemy head on. Our rockets crashed into the advancing Japs. The three voluntary fighters vere killed. By their own friends.

There was no possible escape from this tragedy. To be aved, all those men needed was less courage. It was nobody's fault but their own. Like war, rockets once launched cannot be stopped.

It was 1807. The sun was gone. The giant clouds hanging over Kuralei turned gold and crimson. Night birds started coming into the cacao grove. New Japs reported to the block house for a last stand. Our own reinforcements shuddered as they stepped on dead Japs. Night hurried on.

At 1809, with guns spluttering, eight of our tanks from Sonova Beach burst out of the jungle. Four of them headed for the blockhouse. Four tore right down the alleyway between trenches five and six. These took a Jap reinforcement party head on. The fight was foul and unequal. Three Japs set fire to themselves and tried to immolate the tank crews. They were actually shot to pieces. The tanks rumbled on.

At the blockhouse it was a different story. Tank traps had been well built in that area. Our heavies could not get close to the walls. They stood off and hammered the resilient structure with shells.

"Move in the flame-throwers. Everything you have. Get the blockhouse." The orders were crisp. They reached the Marines in trench five just as the evening star became visible. Eight husky young men with nearly a hundred pounds of gear apiece climbed out of the trench. Making an exceptional target, they blazed their way across six and seven with hundreds of protectors. They drew a slanting hailstorm of enemy fire. But if one man was killed, somebody else grabbed the cumbersome machinery. In the gathering darkness they made a weird procession.

A sergeant threw up his hands and jumped. "No trenches after row seven!" A tank whirled on its right tread and rumbled over. Now, with tanks on their right and riflemen on their left, the flame-throwers advanced. From every position shells hit the blockhouse. It stood. But its defenders were driven momentarily away from the portholes. This was the moment!

With hoarse cries our flame-throwers rushed forward. Some died and fell into their own conflagration. But three flame-throwers reached the portholes. There they held their spuming fire. They burned away the oxygen of the blockhouse. They seared eyes, lips, and more than lungs. When they stepped back from the portholes, the blockhouse was ours.

Now it was night! From all sides Japs tried to infiltrate our lines. When they were successful, our men died. We would find them in the morning with their throats cut. When you found them so, all thought of sorrow for the Japs burned alive in the blockhouse was erased. They were the enemy, the cruel, remorseless, bitter enemy. And they would remain so, every man of them, until their own red sun sank like the tired sun of Kuralei.

Field headquarters were set up that night on Green Beach. I went ashore in the dark. It was strange to think that so many men had died there. In the wan moonlight the earth was white like the hair of an old woman who has seen much life. But in spots it was red, too. Even in the moonlight.

Unit leaders reported. "Colonel, that schedule for building the airstrip is busted wide open. Transport carrying LARU-8 hit. Heavy casualties." I grabbed the man's arm.

"Was that the transport that took a direct hit?" I asked.

"Yes," he said, still dazed. "Right in the belly."

"What happened?" I rattled off the names of my friends in that unit. Benoway, in the leg. The cook, dead. The old skipper, dead. "What happened to Harbison?" I asked.

The man looked up at me in the yellow light. "Are you kidding, sir?"

"No! I know the guy."

"*You* know him? Hmmm. I guess you don't! You haven't heard?" His eyes were excited.

"No."

"Harbison pulled out four days before we came north. All the time we were on Efate he couldn't talk about anything but war. 'Hold me back, fellows. I want to get at them!' But when our orders came through he got white in the face. Arranged it by airmail through his wife's father. Right now he's back in New Mexico. Rest and rehabilitation leave."

"That little Jewish photographic officer you had?" I asked, sick at the stomach.

"He's dead," the man shouted. He jumped up. "The old man's dead. The cook's dead. But Harbison is back in New Mexico." He shouted and started to cry.

"Knock it off!" a Marine colonel cried.

"The man's a shock case," I said. The colonel came over.

"Yeah. He's the guy from the transport. Fished him out of the drink. Give him some morphine. But for Christ's sake shut him up. Now where the hell *is* that extra .50 caliber ammo?"

The reports dragged in. We were exactly where Alligator

said we should be. Everything according to plan. That is all but one detail. Casualties were far above estimate. It wa that bastard Hyaichi. We hadn't figured on him. We hadn expected a Cal Tech honors graduate to be waiting for u on the very beach we wanted.

"We'll have to appoint a new beachmaster," a young office reported to the Colonel.

"Ours get it?" the colonel asked.

"Yessir. He went inland with the troops."

"Goddam it!" the colonel shouted. "I told Fry a hundre times . . ."

"It wasn't his fault, sir. Came when the Japs made tha surprise attack on the flank."

There was sound of furious firing to the west. The colone looked up.

"Well," he said. "We lost a damned good beachmaster. Yo take over tomorrow. And get that ammo in and up."

I grabbed the new beachmaster by the arm. "What did yo say?" I whispered.

"Fry got his."

"Tony Fry?"

"Yes. You know him?"

"Yes," I said weakly. "How?"

"If you know him, you can guess." The young office wiped his face. "His job on the beach was done. No mor craft coming in. We were attacking the blockhouse. Fr followed us in. Our captain said, 'Better stay back ther lieutenant. This is Marines' work.' Fry laughed and turne back. That was when the Japs hit from the cliffs. Our ow rockets wiped out some of our men. Fry grabbed a carbine But the Japs got him right away. Two slugs in the belly. H kept plugging along. Finally fell over. Didn't even fire th carbine once."

I felt sick. "Thanks," I said.

The colonel came over to look at the man from LARU-8 He grabbed my arm. "What's the matter, son? You bette take a shot of that sleeping stuff yourself," he said.

"I'm all right," I said. "I was thinking about a couple o guys."

"We all are," the colonel said. He had the sad, tired loo that old men wear when they have sent young men to die

Looking at him, I suddenly realized that I didn't give damn about Bill Harbison. I was mad for Tony Fry. Tha free, kind, independent man. In my bitterness I dimly perceived what battle means. In civilian life I was ashamed until I went into uniform. In the States I was uncomfortable while others were overseas. At Noumea I thought, "The guys on Guadal! They're the heroes!" But when I reached Guadal I found that all the heroes were somewhere farther up the line. And while I sat in safety aboard the LCS-108 I knew where the heroes were. They were on Kuralei. Yet, on the beach itself only a few men ever really fought the Japs. I suddenly realized that from the farms, and towns, and cities all over America an unbroken line ran straight to the few who storm the blockhouses. No matter where along that line you stood, if you were not the man at the end of it, the ultimate man with his sweating hands upon the blockhouse, you didn't know what war was. You had only an intimation, as of a bugle blown far in the distance. You might have flashing insights, but you did not know. By the grace of God you would never know.

Alone, a stranger from these men who had hit the beaches, I went out to dig a place to sleep. Two men in a foxhole were talking. Eager for some kind of companionship, I listened in the darkness.

"Don't give me that stuff," one was saying. "Europe is twice as tough as this!"

"You talk like nuts," a younger voice retaliated. "These yellows is the toughest fighters in the world."

"I tell you not to give me that crap!" the older man repeated. "My brother was in Africa. He hit Sicily. He says the Krauts is the best all round men in uniform!"

"Lend me your lighter." There was a pause as the younger man used the flameless lighter.

"Keep your damned head down," his friend warned.

"If the Japs is such poor stuff, why worry?"

"Like I said," the other reasoned. "Where did you see any artillery barrage today? Now if this was the Germans, that bay would of been filled with shells."

"I think I saw a lot of barges get hell," the young man argued.

"You ain't seen nothing! You mark my words. Wait till we try to hit France! I doubt we get a ship ashore. Them Krauts is plenty tough. They got mechanized, that's what they got!"

"You read too many papers!" the second Marine argued.

"You think when they write up this war they won't say the Jap was the toughest soldier we ever met?"

"Look! I tell you a thousand times. We ain't met the Jap yet. Mark my words. When we finally tangle with him in some place like the Philippines . . ."

"What were we doin' today? Who was them little yellow fellows? Snow White and the Seven Dwarfs? Well, where the hell was Snow White?"

"Now wait! Now wait just a minute! Answer me one question. Just one question! Will you answer me one question?"

"Shoot!"

"No *ifs* and *ands* and *buts?*"

"Shoot!"

"All right! Now answer me one question. Was it as tough as you thought it would be?"

There was a long moment of silence. These were the men who had landed in the first wave. The young man carefully considered the facts. "No," he said.

"See what I mean?" his heckler reasoned.

"But it wasn't no pushover, neither," the young man defended himself.

"No, I didn't say it was. But it's a fact that the Nips wasn't as tough as they said. We got ashore. We got to the blockhouse. Little while ago I hear we made just about where we was expected to make."

"But on the other hand," the young Marine said, "it wasn't no picnic. Maybe it *was* as tough as I thought last night!"

"Don't give me that stuff! Last night we told each other what we thought. And it wasn't half that bad. Was it? Just a good tough tussle. I don't think these Japs is such hot stuff. Honest to God I don't!"

"You think the way the Germans surrendered in Africa makes them tougher?"

"Listen, listen. I tell you a hundred times. They was pushed to the wall. But wait till we hit France. I doubt we get a boat ashore. That's one party I sure want to miss."

There was a moment of silence. Then the young man spoke again. "Burke?" he asked. "About last night. Do you really think he'll run for a fourth term?"

"Listen! I tell you a hundred times! The American public won't stand for it. Mark my words. They won't stand for it. I thought we settled that last night!"

"But I heard Colonel Hendricks saying . . ."

"Please, Eddie! You ain't quotin' that fathead as an authority, are you?"

"He didn't do so bad gettin' us on this beach, did he?"

"Yeah, but look how he done it. A slaughter!"

"You just said it was easier than you expected."

"I was thinkin' of over there," Burke said. "Them other guys at Red Beach. Poor bastards. We did all right. But this knuckle-brain Hendricks. You know, Eddie, honest to God, if I had a full bladder I wouldn't let that guy lead me to a bathroom!"

"Yeah, maybe you're right. He's so dumb he's a colonel. That's all. A full colonel."

"Please, Eddie! We been through all that before. I got a brother wet the bed till he was eleven. He's a captain in the Army. So what? He's so dumb I wouldn't let him make change in my store. Now he's a captain! So I'm supposed to be impressed with a guy that's a colonel! He's a butcher, that's what he is. Like I tell you a hundred times, the guy don't understand tactics."

This time there was a long silence. Then Eddie spoke, enthusiastically. "Oh, boy! When I get back to Bakersfield!" Burke made no comment. Then Eddie asked, "Tell me one thing, Burke."

"Shoot."

"Do you think they softened this beach up enough before we landed?"

Burke considered a long time. Then he gave his opinion: "It's like I tell you back in Noumea. They got to learn."

"But you don't think they softened it up enough, do you, Burke?"

"Well, we could of used a few more big ones in there where the Japs had their guns. We could of used a few more in there."

Silence again. Then: "Burke, I was scared when we hit the beach."

"Just a rough tussle!" the older man assured him. "You thank your lucky stars you ain't goin' up against the Krauts. That's big league stuff!"

Silence and then another question: "But if the Japs is such pushovers, why you want me to stand guard tonight while you sleep?"

Burke's patience and tolerance could stand no more. "Goddammit," he muttered. "It's war! If we was fighting the Eyetalians, we'd still stand guard! Plain common sense! Call me at midnight. I'll let you get some sleep."

A Cemetery at Hoga Point

I was flown down to Konora to recruit aviation replacements for LARU-8, which had been destroyed at Kuralei. As always, there were ten volunteers for each job up front. The skipper said, "Isn't LARU-8 the unit that waited almost a year for something to do?"

"Yes," I said. "Then it hurried to Kuralei just in time to catch a bomb in the belly."

"You're stealing my best men, but go ahead."

We flew the key men north. The rest of us waited for a transport. Tired and sweating, I leaned forward on the table. "Was Kuralei that tough?" the skipper asked.

"Not for me," I said. "Some of the fellows on the beaches, yes. But I did see a lot. You ever know Tony Fry?"

"Sure! He had that beer-bottle TBF didn't he? Used to see him in Guadal. He get it?"

"Yes," I said. I looked away. My right eye was twitching. I couldn't make it stop.

"Commander," the skipper said. "You're getting a case of nerves. What you need is a fishing party. I got some old togs. We'll go out and soak up some sun."

Konora was peaceful. As I gazed at it from the ammunition

scow on which we fished, the island seemed asleep. Its low hills were beautiful against the deep sky. In the bend of the island there was a white slash across the green hill. "That where Pearlstein ripped away the coral," I recalled. A gaunt steam shovel worked by the bay, lifting live coral for patching the airstrip. From time to time silvery bombers, white against the dark sky, settled down on the strip or rose from it in graceful circles.

Far out at sea slim birds of passage dived breathlessly at schools of fish. At the edge of the reef breakers shot silver spume into the air. Along the horizon the ultramarine sky joined the gray-blue sea. I closed my eyes from this enchanting beauty. It was so remote from the torn coconut trees of Kuralei.

"It's not bad from out here," the skipper said.

It was difficult to believe that on Konora nine hundred and seventeen Japs were buried in graves patiently dug by Marines and SeaBees. Nor did it seem possible that two hundred and eighty-one Americans lay on that island in timeless sleep. Only a few weeks before this peaceful land had been torn and twisted like Kuralei.

Our ammunition barge now lay opposite Hoga Point. I said to the skipper, "Would you think me crazy if I asked you to put me ashore here? I can't seem to get things under control. I'd like to walk back to camp through the trees."

"You're the visitor," he said indulgently. He had the coxswain row me ashore. In a few minutes I was standing at the head of a small promontory which climbed slightly from the sea until it reached a height of sixty or seventy feet above the waves. At that level it formed a plateau which overlooked the vast Pacific on one side and the soft lagoon on the other. Here, on the ruins of their enemy, the Americans had built their cemetery.

A white picket fence surrounded the burial ground. From one corner rose a slim steel flagpole. From it fluttered an American flag. Because the air was so clean, the white stripes and the stars shone more beautifully than any I had ever seen before.

Before me lay the dead, the heroic dead who took the island. Upon a strange plateau, on a strange island, in a strange sea, far from their farms and villages, they slept forever beside the lagoon which bore them to their day of battle. Over them the sea birds dipped in endless homage.

bove them the deep sky erected a cathedral. I cannot put
to words the emotions that captured me as I looked upon
e graves of my friends. Never once during the five weeks
helped to plan the operations that engulfed Konora, not
ace at Kuralei, did I believe that I would die. No more did
ny man who now lay still in death. The Marine in the prow
f the ship, he might die. The SeaBee who made noises when
e ate, he might topple from the crane. But not I!

Yet there before me lay almost three hundred Americans
ho thought as I had thought. They could not die. But there
ere the white crosses. I was appalled by the relentless man-
er in which one dead plus one dead plus one dead add up
o three white crosses. If you sit at home and read that two
undred and eighty-one men die in taking an island, the
umber is only a symbol for the mind to classify. But when
ou stand at the white crosses, the two hundred and eighty-
ne dead become men: the sons, the husbands, and the lovers.

Lonely and bitter, I leaned against the picket fence. It
as then that I noticed a tall, very thin Negro ambling
ward me. He walked like one of the mechanical ducks
hich dull-eyed men sell on the street corners of New York,
waddle-walk obtained by never lifting either foot completely
om the ground. But the Negro gave the shuffle a certain
ignity. He looked as if he owned Hoga Point, as if he had
ved there all his life.

"Aftanoon, suh," he drawled. He was dragging a rake
hich he pushed against the picket fence. Holding it with
oth hands before his chest, he leaned forward. "Yo'-all
ookin' fo' sumbuddy, suh? Or you jes' lookin'?"

"I'm just looking," I replied. "May I come in?"

"You certainly kin, suh!" the tall Negro replied. He pointed
o the gate in the white pickets. "Won't you please come in,
uh? It's a real pleasure to have officers visit the cemetery.
Me 'n' Denis, we doan' see much people up dis yere way.
lease to come in!"

I followed him to the gate, he on the inside of the pickets,
on the outside. Graciously he opened the gate and then
arefully closed it. "I finds sittin' under dem trees mos' bene-
cial," he said, indicating several tall trees whose shadows
ell within the fence. He slowly showed me to a rude hassock,
robably the stump of an old tree overgrown with moss. He
as correct. The seat in the shadows was beneficial.

"Me 'n' Denis, we sits here right often when de sun get

too hot. Sun in dese yere latitudes is pow'ful strong som
times." He spoke with a calm drawl which matched his ga
Gripping the rake handle firmly, he let himself down upo
the earth beside me.

"Who is Denis?" I inquired.

"Me 'n' Denis, we runs dis yere place," the Negro replie

"What do you mean?" I asked.

"Well, me 'n' Denis we is de only people dat works yere
he drawled. "Seem lak nobody else want to work in a pla
lak dis yere." With a languid sweep of his hand he indicat
the white crosses.

"Is Denis a colored man, too?" I asked.

"Yes," he answered. "Me 'n' Denis, we is bof' cullud. I
f'um Geo'gia. I f'um Mississippi."

"Isn't it strange," I asked, "for colored men to like wo
in a cemetery?"

My guide laughed, gently and easily. "Yes! Yes! I know
jes' what yo'-all means," he said. "All dem jokes about gho
and cullud men. But what yo'-all doan' see," he added quietl
"is dat dey ain' no ghos's up here!"

He waved his hand once more across the graves. I wait
for him to speak again.

"Up here," he continued, "dey is only heroes. Me 'n' Den
has often remarked dat never again will we be surround
only by heroes. I 'spect we likes our work better'n any oth
men on dis yere rock. Would you like to walk among
graves, suh?" he inquired. "We got some mighty in'resti
graves in here." Slowly, by means of the rake handle,
pulled himself to his feet. He led me to a small corner
the cemetery.

"Dese yere is de men dat took de las' Jap charge," he sa
softly, like the verger of the cathedral at Antwerp. "Wipe
out. Ever'one of dem." He dropped his voice still lowe
"Some of dem we couldn't even find. Dat is, not all of der
We jes' had to bury arms and legs and call 'em bodies."
raised his voice. "But here dey all lie. Sleepin'. It doan' mal
no difference to 'em now. Bodies or no bodies. Dey
heroes!"

"Over here," he said proudly, "we got de bes' man of 'e
all. Dat grave wid de flowers. Me 'n' Denis, we planted de
flowers." I looked at the garlanded grave. The plots arour
it were vacant, and the flowers grew in rich profusion, rig
up to the austere white cross: "Commander Hoag."

"As you kin see," the caretaker said solemnly, "dis here de commander. Commander Hoag hisse'f. Finer man never lived this side o' heaven. Ever'body says that. You know de commander?"

I replied that I had. The Negro droned on. "He about de bes' man I met in all de Navy. He kind to ever'body. Always greet you wid a smile. Wasn't afraid of bawlin' you out, neither. I remembers 'specially one time he give me 'n' Denis a bad time. Mighty bad time he give us. Had to do wid de officers' mess. We was mighty mad, at de time. But we got over it. 'N' here he lies. Daid lak de res'. Tell me, suh? What we gonna do if men lak de commander is killed all de time? Where we gonna git good men lak him? You 'spect there's men lak him ready to take his job?"

I slipped into Sunday school maxims. "Isn't is pretty true," I asked, "that good men always show up when they're needed? You don't think the SeaBees will fall apart just because Commander Hoag died?"

"Da's mah point!" the Negro cried. "Da's jes' mah point! Already we got a new skipper. Sure. But he ain' a good man! Not at all he ain'." The tall Negro looked about him slowly. "Lemme show you jes' what I mean." He placed his rake among the flowers on Commander Hoag's grave and leaned upon it. We talked across the grave of the fallen leader. Whenever the caretaker mentioned Hoag he would release one hand from the rake and point languidly downward.

" 'Bout two month ago we git an officer in de unit dat hated cullud folk. He give us a mighty bad time in de mess hall. One morning I tell him twice we doan' have no eggs. He git very mad. 'Won't have no goddam eight ball tellin' me what to do and what not to do!' He shouted. Later in de day Commander Hoag he hear about dis yere ruckus. He call us into his office. All us cullud boys. He stand up when we come in. 'Men,' he say, 'I'm mighty sorry to hear about what happen dis mornin'. Yo'-all know we doan' act lak dat in de 144th. You men got rights jes' lak ever'one else. I ain't gonna stand by and see 'em abused.' " The Negro pointed at the grave with his thumb. "He was a good man. Where we gonna git good men lak him?"

I repeated my former argument and the Negro disagreed violently. "No, suh!" he replied. "I cain' believe dat. Dey's only so many good men, and if you uses 'em up, where you gonna git de others? Take de 144th! When Commander Hoag died, who dey put in his place? De officer dat give us black boys all dat trouble. What he say de first day? 'Gonna be some changes here! Ain' gonna take no mo' nonsense f'um a lot of goddam niggers!' Da's why me 'n' Denis works up here. He punishin' us! Only he doan' know it, but we laks it up here. Ain' nobody to push us aroun'. Ain' nobody always tellin' us what to do. We is de boss!" He surveyed his lonely acres. "Up here ever'body is easy to get along wid. Doan' make no difference is you cullud or white. When yo' daid you fo'get all dat stuff." He lifted his rake from Commander Hoag's glave and ambled down the long lines.

"Dat one ova' dere," he said, pointing with his rake to a small white cross at the end of a row. "He git drunk. Run off'n de cliff one night and kill hisse'f. All his own fault. But now he daid. Back home I guess he a big hero. I kin jes' hear his folks sayin' kinda proud and heartbreakin' at de same time, 'Our boy, he died on Konora.' Da's one reason why I likes to work here. Up here dey all heroes. Ain' a mean man in de bunch." We walked among the fresh graves. Already their brutal outlines were softened by wisps of tender grass. Along the fence yellow flowers were in bloom.

"Dis boy over here what I mean," the caretaker continued, pointing with his rake to a grave undistinguishable from the others. "He quite a man!" I followed the rake past the graves of two Marine privates and a SeaBee carpenter's mate to an officer's grave. In the cemetery at Hoga Point distinctions end. There are no officers and men. There are only men. This was the grave of First Lt. Joe Cable, USMCR.

"He got hisse'f into some kind of trouble down south," the Negro droned on, pointing at the grave with a lazy thumb. "Had a fight on de boat wid some his own men. Ever'body called him Fo' Dolla'. Made him mighty mad. Well, dey kep' de fight sort of hushed up. But two nights before we land here, I und'stand dey was another fight. Dis time de lieutenant he slug another officer. De colonel hear about dis one. He furious. Say dey ain' got no right fightin' amon: deyselves when de Japs so near. De colonel he want to th'ov de lieutenant in de brig right den. But instead he give d: young fellow one mo' chance. Say if he pull hisse'f togethe on de beach, he goin' to forget all about it. What de colone doan' know is dat de boy, he pretty heartsick. Trouble h: got into down south. He pretty well fed up wid things i: general." The caretaker paused and reflected upon the grave

'Seem lak sometime it's de officers doan' know how to take
care of theyselves.

"Well, come de beachhead," he continued. "And dis yere
Marine, he about de bes' we got on our side. He go after
them Japs plenty tough. Lot of wise guys dat been plaguin'
him, dey keep dey big mouf' shut. Finally, he git his. Go
down all in a lump. Dey tell me de colonel see him go. Some
time de colonel come up here and look around. I figger he
pretty glad he let de lieutenant outen de brig. But maybe he
ain' so glad, neither. 'Cause if he keep de young man locked
up, he be alive now."

The caretaker wandered to the end of the cemetery and
shuffled over to the cool mound under the trees. Easing himself down by means of his rake handle, he waited for his
partner Denis to appear.

I did not join him but stayed among the graves.

Like the Negro I wondered where the men would come
from to take Commander Hoag's place. Throughout the
Pacific, in Russia, in Africa, and soon on fronts not yet
named, good men were dying. Who would take their place?
Who would marry the girls they would have married? Or
build the buildings they would built? Were there men at
home ready to do Hoag's job? And Cable's? And Tony Fry's?
Or did war itself help create replacements out of its bitterness?

I thought of Hoag as I knew him, a man who never
buttoned his shirt properly. He was from Atlanta, but he
championed the Negro. He was a rich man, but he befriended
his meanest enlisted man. He was a gentile, but he placed
Jews in positions of command. He was a man tired with
responsibility, but he saw to it that others got rest. Yet when
he died a loud-mouthed bully came along to take his place.
One night he called Pearlstein a kike. Threatened to have no
more trouble with a bunch of goddamned niggers. Called
hard-working young De Vito a "grease ball, and you know
how they stand up in war!" If he stayed in command much
longer, all the patient work Hoag had done would be dissi-
pated. The 144th SeaBees would be unfit to hit another
beachhead. Already they were beginning to fall apart at the
seams. The guiding spirit of their team was dead.

Each man who lay on Hoga Point bore with him to his
grave some promise for a free America. Now they were gone.
Who would take their places? Women? Old men? Or were

those who lived committed to a double burden? Theirs and the dead men's?

From the picket fence I heard a cheerful voice. It was Denis lugging a bucket of cold water. He laughed when he saw me by the graves. "You comin' up to see about movin' all dese yere bodies back to the States?" he asked.

"No," I replied. "Are they going to do that?"

"Da's what dey say," Denis laughed, wiping his jet forehead. "Seem lak nonsense to me. If'n I die out here, where I goin' to sleep happier dan wid de men I fought wif'? Where I goin' to get a more peaceful dreamin' place dan dis yere spot? Look at dem birds!" I followed the flight of four dazzling birds as they dipped toward the lagoon. "I s'pose you been talkin' to de preacher?" Denis inquired.

"Who's that?" I asked, and Denis pointed to his friend under the tree.

"Da's him. Da's de preacher! In Mississippi he call hisse'f a preacher!" He laughed and took the water to his friend. The caretaker took a long drink, and what was left in the cup he swished into the flowers.

"Doan' you mind what Denis say," he whispered to me. "Denis, he quite a cutup. Sometime he run off at de mouf'."